HEMLOCK

KIERSTEN MODGLIN

Cover Design by Kiersten Modglin
Copy Editing by Three Owls Editing
Proofreading by My Brother's Editor
Formatting by Kiersten Modglin
Copyright © 2023 by Kiersten Modglin.
All rights reserved.

First Print and Electronic Edition: 2023
kierstenmodglinauthor.com

To timeless love
And to the stories that let us live a thousand lives

"There are poisons that blind you, and poisons that open your eyes."

AUGUST STRINDBERG

PROLOGUE

I drive like a mad woman through the streets of Myers.

I can't get there fast enough. I've called his number seventeen times since I left the house, but I'm getting no answer. He either left his phone at home, or something terrible has happened. I can't allow myself to consider it. I'll never make it if I do.

I can see the smoke in the already dark sky long before I ever arrive on our street. The smell of it, even with my windows rolled up, permeates the air in my car. Each smoky breath I struggle to take bites at my throat.

My thoughts come in fragments: worry, fear, panic, anger. A blurry mosaic of terror.

I can't believe him. I grip the steering wheel tighter as I remember that. I'm so angry, but it's not my biggest concern. It can't be. I have to know he's okay.

When I pull into the driveway, all thought seems to dissipate. We're far enough out that no one seems to have noticed the fire yet. No one is here trying to help. I called for a fire truck on the way, but it will be another fifteen minutes at least before they arrive. Ten, if we're lucky.

I should've called sooner. I was too busy panicking to realize someone had to call, and that someone could only be me.

Once I've parked, I basically fall out of the Jeep, leaving the door open in a rush to get to the house. The entire top floor is engulfed in flames, which have begun to creep down the sides, burning the house from the back forward. Embers fly through the sky, and the heat reaches me where I am.

I shout, cupping my hands around my mouth to help the sound carry. It does no good. My voice is masked by the roar of the fire, by the creaks and groans of the old house as it burns before my eyes. Crying out again, I rush forward to the porch and unlock the front door as quickly as my suddenly uncooperative fingers will allow. I shove it open.

The air is so hot it feels like I've stepped into an oven. The heat sears my skin. Everywhere I look, flames lap at the things I love, melting and destroying everything in its wake.

I'm too late.

CHAPTER ONE

Maybe purchasing a house on a street named after a poisonous plant wasn't the best idea. It's certainly not at the top of the list of my smartest moves, but the more that I think about it, that list would be very short anyway.

It would not include wasting the last five years of my life on a man who told me over coffee in our shared townhome that he wasn't sure he'd ever want to marry me. It would not include spending those five years with him and choosing to split the holidays between his family in Boston and my mom here in Myers.

Now she's gone, and her last Christmas was spent alone. Thanks to me.

I push the thoughts out of my head as I round the curve on Hemlock Drive. What's done is done, and there's nothing I can do to change it.

After Nick and I broke up, I came home to spend Mom's final weeks with her. I didn't know how bad she'd gotten until I arrived, but being here with her when she needed me is something I'll never regret.

Add that to the top of the smart-moves list.

Not that she literally needed me. Dad left her enough life insurance after he passed that she was able to stay at the best nursing home in Myers. Her nurses were amazing. The food actually looked tasty, not just edible. I couldn't have asked for a better place for her, but still...I'll always wish I could've moved home before she passed.

It wasn't a wish I'd planned for before she died. I never thought I'd come back to Myers. Too many bad memories. Too many ghosts.

I pull to a stop at the end of the driveway of 40 Hemlock Drive, taking in the sight of my new home. The gravel drive is overgrown with weeds, and the grass is in need of a good mowing. None of that is comparable to the work the house itself needs.

Its wooden siding has been painted a burnt red for as long as I can remember, but the siding is chipping now, in desperate need of a new coat. Or ten. The inspection said the roof will need to be replaced soon and, even from where I sit, I can see a few spots where shingles are flapping in the wind.

An enclosed front porch spans the length of the house—concrete floored with just a single, metal door on one end. Once I get it painted, a pair of rocking chairs will look...

Er, well, maybe just *one* rocking chair.

Either way, it will look cozy. I can get a plant, too. Everything looks better with a plant, right? A pot of daisies, perhaps. Or dragon's breath, though that might be too much red.

Small, wooden lattices have been attached to both ends of the porch over the screen windows, though they're missing more boards than they have at this point, and the wooden railroad ties that frame the front walk are rotting and splitting in every direction.

I ease the car farther into the driveway, taking in the sight of the four-foot white fence that encloses the backyard. It might last this season, but sooner than later, I'm going to have to replace it, too.

Sighing, I shut off the car and rest both hands on the steering wheel.

This is it.

As of nine o'clock this morning, I'm officially a home-owner. Not only that, I'm officially the homeowner of the house I used to dream about living in. Granted, it was nicer then. When Mom and I used to drive past it, there were always flowers growing around the base of the porch. I remember the fence being so white it hurt your eyes to look at it. It always reminded me of a storybook.

Call it what you want, but I like to think it was fate that on the day I received my inheritance, the house was put up for sale. Granted, it wasn't in the condition I'd hoped it would be, but still. I'm not afraid of a little work. Elbow grease. That's all it'll take.

Its lousy condition meant I could pay for it in cash and still have a bit left over to do whatever repairs it needs.

I step out of the car and approach the porch, extra cautious in the ankle-deep grass. It's still early in the year for snakes to be out, but I'm not sure what else might be lurking here.

On the porch, I take careful steps. I've never been this close, and I can't explain the odd feeling I have as I draw nearer to the door. It's...colder, somehow, than I expected it to be.

Probably just nerves.

I'm the poster child for impulsive decisions at this point. One minute, I'm living with my longtime boyfriend in a town-home in Iowa City with no plans to leave. The next minute, I'm a homeowner in a town I haven't lived in since I was twenty-two years old, in a house I haven't seen since I was at least that age, if not younger.

So much has changed in the span of four months. I guess it's normal to feel a bit of nerves about this.

The keys are heavy in my hand, like the weight of a wedding ring you aren't quite used to wearing. I don't stop at the door. Instead, I walk to the window next to the door and peer inside, both hands cupped around my eyes.

The hair on the back of my neck stands at attention.

Suddenly, I'm no longer intrigued by this place. It's no longer the childhood home of my dreams. It's just a house that no one's taken care of in years. A house that is now my problem and mine alone.

I turn back to the door and stick the key in the dead bolt. I twist, but nothing happens. It takes a second to register that the door isn't opening as I continue to twist it. I pull the key out and study it. It's definitely the one I picked up at the office this morning.

And they only gave me one, stating I'd need to have the shed and back door rekeyed. The only key they had was for the front door. I pull it out and try the keyhole in the doorknob instead.

It turns and I push, but the door doesn't budge.

What the hell?

I try the dead bolt again, twisting the key with all my might.

Come on.

Come on.

Come on.

I groan, slamming my hand into the wood of the door. I'm lucky it doesn't fall in with the condition it's in.

What have I done? What did I do? Why did I think I could handle this?

I pull the key out, swipe it across my jeans, and try again, my eyes prickling with tears. I'm already picturing them having to remove the door. Having to bust through a window to get in. *Can someone sell a house without a working key? Why would they?*

I curse, slamming a hand into the door again.

"Need some help?"

A voice startles me from over my shoulder, and I spin around, my face flaming with embarrassment.

"Uh, yeah. If you can get it. I'm not sure what the—"

No.

Yes.

My conflicted emotions pull at me in every direction, my heart pounding loudly in my ears. My breathing catches as I take in his features. The features I once had memorized.

He hasn't changed all that much in the thirteen years since I've seen him. The same dark, curly hair, the same piercing blue eyes. He has a full beard now, where it was merely stubble back then. His thin, sage-green sweater is pulled tight over the muscles in his arms. I don't remember those being so prominent.

My gaze shoots back to meet his, realizing I've been staring for far too long without saying a word.

I'm both relieved and horrified to realize I'm not the only one. He's taking in my appearance, too. His face is pale, his jaw slack. I wonder what he must think of me now.

This is certainly not the way I hoped to meet him again, if I ever did. My jeans are worn and a size too big. The shirt I'm wearing has a mustard stain from a burger I ate on the way here. My blonde hair hasn't been washed in three days, and that's only minimally disguised by the bun at the top of my head. I haven't touched makeup since mom's funeral, and I desperately need to brush my teeth.

"Maggie?" he says—grunts, really, like it takes all the effort he has—in that gruff voice that sends a current of something strange and familiar through my body.

"Tuck?" My voice cracks.

"What are you..." we ask at the same time, both trailing off to let the other finish the question.

I blush, tucking a loose strand of hair behind my ear. "I just bought this place." Somehow, it's more embarrassing now how proud I felt this morning. Like I was really doing something. Now, standing in front of him on this rundown porch with a front door that won't open as if the house is physically rejecting me, I simply feel shame.

When he thinks of me—if he ever has—I want him to think I'm somewhere happy and successful. Living the life of my dreams.

Not here, back home, parentless, single, unemployed, and spending my every last dime to make my new house habitable.

Not here like this.

"You're... You moved back?" His Adam's apple bobs, and he takes a step forward. I swear I don't think he realizes he's done it. It's as if his feet are moving without informing the rest of his body.

"After my mom died," I say softly, dropping my head.

"I heard." He looks away, scraping a hand over the back of his neck. "It's... Wow. It's really good to see you again."

My cheeks burn again. I'm sure he's just saying the words, not thinking about what they mean or if he means them, but they're nice to hear nonetheless.

I bounce on my toes. "You, too. What are you doing here, anyway?"

"I..." He licks his lips, casting a glance over his shoulder. "I live next door."

"No you don't." The words shoot out of my mouth as I feel my heart plummet. He can*not* live next door to me. No wonder the door wouldn't let me in. It was trying to warn me.

He gives me that crooked, lopsided grin I remember so well. "Sorry."

"Sorry?"

"To...be the bearer of bad news, I guess." He points to the small white house behind him. "That's me."

"Oh." I'm not sure why he's apologizing. Not sure if he should. "Maybe I should apologize. I didn't realize you'd moved."

"It's been thirteen years," he says without missing a beat. Like he's kept count. Like he's just as pitiful as I am. "You thought I was still in the campus apartment?"

"I...I guess I wasn't thinking. Anyway, I won't be a bother," I say quickly. Always quick to minimize myself. Make myself scarce. I'm really trying to get better about that. "I mean, I'm going to do some work to the place and have it fixed up, which will really only help you with resale and stuff and..."

He nods slowly. As he does that, his eyes quickly rake over my body once more, as if trying to decide if he can handle this. Then, he gestures toward the key in my hand. "Do you...need help with that?"

"Maybe." My voice is soft. Whimsical. I didn't hear him, not really. I'm too busy thinking about how terribly awkward it's going to be living next door to Tucker. Sharing a space with him again. Waving hello in the driveway each morning.

Very domestic.

Very much *not* normal.

I clear my throat, shaking the fog my head. "I mean yes. Yes, please."

He chuckles under his breath and steps forward. "Here." His palm stretches out toward me, and when I place the key in it, my skin brushes his. I ignore the bolt of lightning I feel, the heat that blooms in my chest.

He's just a man.

I have no idea who he is now.

Whatever happened between us all those years ago doesn't matter anymore.

He approaches the door, sticking the key inside the dead bolt. "See, the trick is"—he jerks up on the doorknob as he twists the key, and I instantly hear a click—"you have to pull up a bit." He releases and pushes the door forward, and my house welcomes him quicker than it did me. As if he belongs here. Maybe he does.

This is his town, after all.

Not mine anymore.

"Have you had to open this door a lot or something?"

"No. These old doors just stick a bit. I deal with them daily at work." He passes the key back to me, careful not to touch my skin. His smile is soft. Sad.

Or maybe I'm just imagining it.

"Thanks." I push the key into my pocket.

"Is there anything else you need help with? Boxes?" He looks out at the rust-red car in the driveway.

"Oh. No. The movers won't be here for a few days. I just have a few things with me. But thank you," I add at the last minute.

"Sure." His blue eyes dart between mine. "You may want to

leave the windows open. Let it air out. It's been closed up for a while." He says it as the stale scent hits my nose.

"Right."

"And listen...I should've said it earlier, but I was sorry to hear about your mom."

A lump forms in my throat, so thick I can't swallow it down.

"I wanted to call. I just didn't..."

"Know what to say?" I finish for him. "I felt the same way when I heard about your grandpa."

"You sent flowers," he says.

"Yeah, but—"

We're interrupted by the sound of tires on gravel, and when I look over, I recognize the matte black Jeep pulling into my driveway.

"Expecting someone?" he asks, taking half a step away from me to get a better look.

The Jeep shuts off, and Clayton steps out. I spot his caramel hair, his sharp jaw. His eyes find me, green and searching. He smiles but then quickly notices the person standing next to me.

In his faded T-shirt, his shoulders go tense. Next to me, Tucker releases a low breath.

Just like that, it's all those years ago, the past written on each of our faces.

Just like that, everything I've tried to forget comes roaring back, demanding to be felt again.

CHAPTER TWO

FOURTEEN YEARS AGO

I'm finally going to do it.

Finally.

After years of putting my fears first and allowing them to run my life, I have my chance, and I'm not going to let it pass me by.

The bar is crowded, but he's all I see. I pinball my way through the dancing people, all too drunk and too loud to notice me, and point myself in his direction.

He hasn't seen me yet, his focus entirely on the phone in his hand, but then, as if he felt me—as if we're connected across the room by nothing more than molecules—he looks up.

His eyes scan the room slowly, cheeks pink from the heat and the alcohol and the excitement.

Does he know?

I can't help wondering.

When his eyes land on me, something inside my stomach flips.

Spins.

Screams out.

His face brightens, and he places his phone down, standing from the seat at the booth he's occupying. He holds out his arms as I draw nearer, and I launch into them.

"Hey." He kisses my cheek, the spot marked by a familiar burning sensation, and when his hands leave my waist, I feel it there, too.

"*Sorry I'm late,*" I shout over the music.

"No worries." As we sit down, he's looking at his phone again, but his focus finds me quickly. "Jesus, Maggie, you look hot. What's the occasion?"

I blush, pretending I didn't spend hours getting ready in hopes of getting such a compliment. "Aw, thanks. I just felt like getting dressed up. You look great, too."

His eyes linger on me a second longer. I could lose myself in his eyes—the most perfect green you've ever seen, with flecks of gray. When he runs his hand through his caramel hair, I squeeze my eyes shut, inhaling deeply to steel myself.

It's time.

I suck in another deep breath, gathering my hands in front of me.

"So, I wanted to talk to you about something."

He chuckles and pops a peanut from the bowl on the table into his mouth. "Okay. This sounds very formal."

My smile is small, and it doesn't reach my eyes. I feel like I'm going to be sick. I've never been so cold in all my life.

"Is..." He reaches across the table and pats my hand. "Is everything okay? You're scaring me."

"Clayton, you've been my best friend forever..."

"Duh, dork." When I don't smile, his expression grows serious, and he pulls back. "Why are you saying that?"

"Well, I've...I mean, I'm not sure how to say this other than to just come out and say it, and I've been freaking out about it because I'd never want to lose you or do anything to make you feel uncomfortable or—"

His hands shoot across the table again, this time to grip mine, his eyes almost as anxious and excited as I feel. "Hey. It's me. Whatever it is, you can tell me." His thumbs stroke the tops of my knuckles. "It's impossible for you to make me uncomfortable. You're the person I can be the most real with in the world. You know that."

"I do know." I suck in a deep breath, puffing my cheeks out. "Okay, do you remember the night of Allen's party?"

Recognition floods his eyes, followed by a darkness I recognize: *desire*. On his features, the emotion is both foreign and intoxicating.

The night when we nearly kissed two months ago is replaying in his memory the same way it's replayed in mine every night since.

He gives a hard swallow, glancing down, and when his eyes come back up, they take their time finding mine. "Yeah. How could I forget?"

I press my lips together. My heart is pounding so fast I feel as if I might pass out. I just need to say it. Just say the words. It can't be as hard as it feels in my mind. Nothing is ever as bad as the anticipation. "Ever since that night, something has changed for me. I've tried so hard to pretend it hasn't or to shut it down, but I can't ignore the way I feel. And if you don't feel the same, I understand, but if you do... If you do, I have to know." I stare at my hands, twisting them together, pretending to examine my fingernails. Then, ever so slowly, I look up.

His eyes lock with mine, his face pale. "H-how do you feel?"

"I—um—" I'm interrupted by his phone screen lighting up, the vibrations scooting it around the table.

"*Shit.* Sorry." He picks it up, holding out a finger to tell me to pause. "I'm sorry. I'm expecting this. Give me just...just two seconds." His eyes linger on me as he slides from the booth again.

"Sure."

When he steps away, I take the time to regain my composure. It's hard to tell how it's going. He seems receptive, at least. He's been holding my hand. It would be hard not to guess what I'm trying to say, and he hasn't bolted or tried to pull away.

I inhale slowly and release it just the same, smoothing a hand over my hair.

All too soon, he's back, but something's changed.

He doesn't sit.

His eyes are the size of basketballs, and he's not exactly looking at me, more like looking through me.

"Clayton?" Chills line my skin. "What is it? What's wrong?" Something's happened. A sort of knowing falls over me that makes me ill.

He glances at the phone, his lips breaking into a smile. "That was an agent from the Noel DeMarcum Agency in Nashville."

The phrase passes over me in an instant.

"They...Maggie, they want to sign me." At his words, the room seems to spin, taking me with it.

"*What?*"

He scoops me into a hug, my mind and stomach somersaulting as he does it. "It's happening. I can't believe it. It's actually happening."

Snapping back to reality, I hug him tighter. Everything he's worked so hard for. Everything he deserves. Everything he's ever wanted.

"How?" I ask as he sets me down. When he does, he has tears in his eyes.

"Um." He shakes his head, obviously still lost in thought. "They saw one of my videos on YouTube, I guess, and earlier today, I got an email that asked if someone from their office could call me this evening."

I smack my hands into his chest. "What? Why didn't you say anything?"

"I didn't even know if it was legit, to be honest. And, even if it was, I had no idea what they were going to say. I mean, I *hoped*, but I...didn't want to hope if I was just going to be let down. I didn't want to get your expectations up either." His gaze slides down my face, landing on my mouth. When he speaks again, his voice is barely above a whisper. His lips hardly move. "Maggie, this is everything I've ever wanted."

For a split second, I imagine he's saying this about me. *Us.* About what I've told him. I imagine our evening ending in a whole new way. *Could we both get everything we've ever dreamed of tonight?*

Tears blur my vision so the bar is a watercolor painting of red and blue neons. "I'm so proud of you. You've worked so hard. I always knew it was just a matter of time." He smiles, but it's sad. "What is it?" I ask, trying to understand that unreadable expression.

"I..." His eyes are locked with mine as he leans in. I'm not even sure he realizes he's done it. That he realizes how reminiscent it is of the party that night. He tucks a piece of hair behind my ear. "Maggie, listen..."

I close the space between us, my chest pressing against his, and warmth spreads throughout my core.

16

Maybe I've misread the sadness.

Maybe we *are* both going to get what we want most tonight.

I want you. I love you. The words are on the tip of my tongue just as my lips part—lips he's lowering his own to meet without me saying a word.

"They want me to come to Nashville. To... To move to Nashville." He pulls back, blinking, heartbreak conflicting with sheer joy on his face. My heart plummets. Ice slides down my spine. Sinking. Sinking.

"They...what? When? *Now?*" Cool tears fill my eyes again.

I was wrong.

That's not what's happening.

It's so far from what's happening, it hurts.

"*Now.* This weekend. They want to meet me. They're talking about me getting to open for one of their other clients. Writing, too. And putting out an EP." His chest swells with excitement, bumping into mine, and when he looks down, his smile falls. "I'm..."

"Don't say it."

"I'm sorry."

"I don't want you to be." I step back, lowering my head so he won't see my tears. Fresh tears for a brand-new reason. "This is everything you've worked for. It's a day to celebrate."

"I want you to know...if things were different—"

I put a hand on his chest, shaking my head. "Please, don't. Really. I'm so happy for you. So happy."

He lifts a thumb to brush a tear from my cheek. "You know I love you, right?"

But it's not the same. Not enough.

Not enough to make him stay.

And I just happen to love him enough to make him go.

"Always have, always will." I smile through my tears.

"Please don't cry." His expression breaks, his chin quivering. He uses his thumb to brush another tear from my cheek.

"These are happy tears." I swat his chest. "Now, go. Call your mom. Tell her the good news." I fan my eyes, pretending they're actually happy tears, even if he can see right through the lie.

"Are you sure? We're supposed to get dinner." He juts a thumb toward the table. "I can call her later."

I dry my eyes, drawing in a long inhale through my nose. "No. Don't be silly. I'll catch up with you tomorrow. This is more important. You should call your family and tell them the good news. We can grab something tomorrow or... When will you leave?"

He runs a hand over his face, staring at nothing at all as he thinks. "Friday night, probably. I have to figure out what I'll do with the apartment and—"

"It'll all be okay." When his eyes meet mine, finally, I'm giving him the best acting I ever have. Maybe I'm the one who deserves an agent. My smile is convincing, eyes dry and clear. "Go get 'em, rockstar."

He gives me a bright, perfect grin that makes my chest ache. He's so devastatingly handsome it hurts. "Yeah?"

"Yeah."

He kisses my cheek like he did when I first arrived, though this time it's hesitant, and then pulls his phone out. "I'll catch you later, though. Before I go?"

"Of course."

With a final look, he passes me, making his way out through the crowd, and I know—somewhere deep inside my bones *I know*—I've lost him.

Silent tears stream down my cheeks, and I make my way to the bar. This is not how tonight was supposed to go.

"What can I get you?"

"Gin and tonic," I say without glancing up. I'm still not looking, still trying to dry my eyes, when the bartender slides me my drink.

"Thanks." I move the lime to the side and take a sip, not bothering to notice if it's any good.

"Rough night?"

I grimace. "How can you tell?" My eyes come to focus on the man in front of me as I swipe away new tears.

He's tall, with thick shoulders and ropy arms. His dark-brown hair peeks out from under the sides of his baseball cap, which he wears backward. His hands rest on the bar, bright blue eyes glaring at me. "Tears are usually a dead giveaway. You want to talk about it?"

I sniffle. "Not really."

Someone farther down the bar draws his attention, and he disappears, leaving me alone. I drop my face into my palms.

I'd been so close to everything I'd ever wanted, but Clayton had gotten everything he wanted instead. Was it selfish to wish he hadn't? That his miracle had come later? Or that I'd worked up the courage sooner?

I could go with him to Nashville, perhaps. I could see about switching to online classes for the time being, but...

He didn't ask me.

That one truth stings more than any of the others.

He didn't ask me to go, and he didn't offer to stay.

He knew what I was going to say, and he walked away regardless.

"You sure you don't wanna talk? I'm a good listener." The

bartender is back, leaning down closer to me, his head propped up on his elbow.

"Could you just leave me alone?" I snap, not in the mood for whatever he wants.

He pulls back, still smiling. "Look, I'm just trying to help—"

"I'm obviously going through something, so the last thing I need is for you to be hitting on me right now—"

"Hitting on you?" He scoffs, the smile disappearing. It's replaced with a deep scowl. "Jesus, lady, you're snotting all over my bar. The last thing I need is to take home some girl who just got dumped, okay? I was trying to be polite—"

"I am *not* snotting all over your bar." I jab a finger at him. "And I didn't just get dumped. And I *certainly* wouldn't be going home with you, so nice try."

He rolls his eyes, patting the bar once as he steps back. "Unbelievable. You know what? Whatever. That's what I get for trying to be a nice guy, I guess. Let me know if you need anything else." With hands up in surrender, he walks away from me, his jaw tense.

Finally.

I release another sob and down the rest of my drink.

CHAPTER THREE

NOW

As Clayton approaches the porch, Tucker takes another step away from me. He puts up a hand without looking in my direction. "I should get to work."

"You don't have to go," I call after him. I'm not very convincing, even to my own ears.

"It's okay. Good to see you. I'll, uh, I'll be around." He says the last bit as he passes Clayton, which feels like it's more for Clayton's benefit than mine. He waves at me over his shoulder, then jogs down the steps.

Clayton hardly looks at him, moving straight to me. He's in front of me in an instant and leans forward, scooping me up into a bear hug. He squeezes me, grunting, and plops me down. "It's so good to have you home."

"It's good to be home." I fold my arms across my chest. "Feels weird, though, I admit."

It's not the first time I've seen him since I left. We've kept in touch, though only a few times a year. If we both happened to be in town for the same holiday, we'd grab dinner together, or he'd stop by the house until Dad died and Mom went to the nursing home. Then, it was always me going to his house. However, I can count on both hands the number of times I saw him before the funeral.

Since I made the plan to move home, we've been talking more than ever.

Still, it's odd to be standing here in this town. Both of us as former, and now current, residents.

"Yeah, I'll bet. What was Tucker doing here?" His upper lip curls as he says it. "I didn't realize the two of you were still in touch."

"We aren't. *Weren't.* I, uh, he...lives next door, apparently."

"*What?* You've gotta be kidding me." He looks toward the house next door. "You didn't know?"

"I had no idea."

He purses his lips with his brows drawn in, disappointment evident on his face. *Join the club.* Then, moving on, he glances up at the open doorway. "Well, enough about him. Let's see it, then, hmm?"

"Sure." I turn, then spin back to face him, a finger in the air. "Just don't be too shocked, okay? It's, like, *really* fancy. I just want to remind you I'm still the same old Maggie."

His eyes dance over me, like a thought has caught on his tongue. Then he laughs. "Fine. I'll try to remember that."

I push the door open, and we step inside. The living room is decently sized, with a brick fireplace in the center of the far wall. The walls are white and dingy, with dark-cherry wainscoting. The cream-colored carpet has stains in it and two giant wrinkles that run nearly the length of the room.

On the wall in front of us, there are two small, built-in nooks, which I plan to use as bookcases. Clayton crosses the room and runs a hand along one of the shelves. He blows a puff of air, sending dust flying in every direction.

"Well, it could use some TLC, but this place isn't terrible," he says with a grin.

"Not all of us are famous country singers," I tease him, wagging a finger. The fireplace is bookended by matching hanging lights that look like they haven't been updated since the sixties, big and bulbous, with opaque glass and gold pieces at the top and bottom. There are two identical windows with wooden bi-fold shutters that match the wood of the lower paneling. Near the door, there's a window seat and a large window blocked with more bi-fold shutters. I move toward it, pulling the shutters open to let in more light. It only makes the place look worse somehow.

"I'm just saying. This place could be really nice. Although, I can't say the same for the neighbors." He says the last part under his breath but clearly intends for me to hear it, which I do.

I give him a look, and he changes the subject.

"Did Garrett help you get some cleaners scheduled?"

The realtor.

Also, his brother.

"No. I'm going to do it myself."

"*All* of this?" He balks.

I shove my fists into my hips. "What? You don't think I can do it?"

"No. I know you can. I just don't know why you'd want to. If it's about the money, I'm happy to help."

It's awkward to talk about money with your best friend. With anyone, really. Especially when one of you is loaded, and the other is decidedly not. "It's not, but thank you. I've got it."

He shrugs. "Okay. Suit yourself." He gestures for me to go forward. "Lead the way."

I do, taking him through the small kitchen. The tile is old, seventies linoleum. Yellow and white gradients. But the cream-colored laminate countertops are in excellent shape—no cracks or stains from what I can see. And the wooden cabinets appear clean and kept up as well. The stove and dishwasher are newer, and the light fixture has been updated. I look up, examining it and taking in the wood-paneled ceiling.

Clayton is moving on, passing through this room and onto the next. He steps on a place in the floorboard that creaks and something about it gives me chills.

I freeze.

Something's wrong.

Something in the air shifts, and I suddenly feel as if I'm a solid block of ice. My stomach clenches like I might get sick. I squeeze my hands into fists, my skin clammy.

"Everything okay?" He glances over at me, noticing I've stopped.

"Yeah...I just..." I can't put into words what I'm feeling right now. Something strange. Something *wrong*. My whole body is rigid, and again, the hairs at the nape of my neck are standing up. I'm like a cat, sensing a dog just behind me, ready to attack. My knees feel weak.

"What's wrong?" He moves back toward me.

"I just got a strange feeling," I say softly. If I move, I feel as if I might fall down. *Why the hell is it so cold in this house?*

He puts a hand on my shoulder. "You need to sit down? It's probably all the dust in here."

"No, I'm okay." The feeling is already going away. Slowly being choked out and suffocated by my need to look and act normal. "I think I just need to eat something."

"Now, *that* I can help with. What do you say we go grab something to eat and come back and finish this later?"

"Do you have time?" I ask, wincing.

He cracks his knuckles. "I've got nothing but time. I'm at your service today, Maggs."

I hate when he calls me that. Sounds like the name of a Labradoodle, not a thirty-five-year-old woman. Still, the thought of food is too tempting. "Thanks. I had a burger on the way, but that was hours ago."

"What do you think? Lenny's?"

"Sounds perfect."

I don't care that I need a shower or that I should really be exploring the home I've only seen via video call up until this point. All I know is that I desperately want to get out of this house.

CHAPTER FOUR

THIRTEEN YEARS AGO

There is still an hour before we're supposed to meet, but I've been ready for the last half hour.

Well, technically, I've been ready for much longer than that. Like, for the last year.

When I got Clayton's text that he was back in town and wanted to see me, I won't deny the way my heart flipped in my chest. In a lot of ways, this past year has felt like a dream. The walking nightmare kind.

I've gone through the motions, attended—and aced—my classes, and even found time to go to a party or four. But I'm not sure I was actually there. In fact, I'm pretty sure I wasn't. Most of it feels like some distant memory from a night too drunk to really remember.

Only, I haven't been drunk. I've hardly drank anything without the person who keeps me safe at parties here to do his job.

But...now, I guess he has a new job.

An album getting ready to release. A social media account filled with images of him with famous musicians. We've stayed in touch some, but nothing like I'm used to. At first, when he was missing home, the calls and texts were more frequent. Weekly, at least.

Now, I'm lucky to hear from him once a month. I get my updates from Facebook like everyone else.

So when he arrived back in Chicago, and I was one of his first calls—at least, according to him—it was hard not to get my hopes up. We haven't mentioned what happened between us the night he got his big news. Or what *didn't* happen, more like. We've both moved on, having entire conversations as if it never happened.

But now he's back. At least for a few days. He didn't really give me a timeline. All I know is he got into town this morning and said he wanted to see me. Apparently, there's something he wants to talk about.

Again, I'm trying to limit expectations, but...I'll admit, I'm struggling.

Studying my reflection, I scrutinize every inch of my face. Have I aged since he saw me last? Will he notice the pimple on my chin I've tried desperately to hide with concealer like Jessica in my communications class taught me? Is my skin dull? Why does it never seem to glow like the women in the commercials?

None of this matters, really. It's Clayton. He's seen me without makeup more often than with. He was there when I was caked in mud as a kid and during the awkward haircuts that always seemed to fall just before school picture day. He's the one who sat in the front row—rolling his eyes the entire time—when I was the lead in the school's production of *Romeo and Juliet*. And when I nearly fell on my face at graduation.

He's always been here. For as long as I can remember.

But back then, he was just Clayton.

Now, he's *Clayton Beckett.*

The up-and-coming artist who just performed with P!nk at a show in Houston. Who wrote a song with Kenny Chesney and had coffee with Taylor Swift.

The Clayton he is now has seen and done things the old Clayton would've never dreamed of. I can't help feeling like I don't fit into his world anymore. That I might be under-whelming now that he has fans falling at his feet and other artists in his orbit.

I force the thoughts away. No matter what he's seen or been through over the past year, no matter what bright, shiny, beautiful people he's spent time with or... I don't want to think about what else... He's still just Clayton. And I'm still his best friend. The person who knows him best in the whole world. I still get access to him in a way no one else does.

This is just a phase of his life. Maybe that's what he's here to tell me. That it's not as amazing as he'd thought it would be without me. That he wants me to join him in Nashville.

I tuck a strand of my bright-blonde hair behind my ear, twisting the barrel curl around my finger.

This is it.

The night everything changes.

I can feel it in my gut.

Sure, it came a year late, but Clayton will always be worth the wait.

With that, I walk out of the bathroom. Kassara, my room-mate, waves at me as I go, blowing a kiss my way to wish me luck. "I want all the dirty details," she calls as I close the door on my way out.

It's a thirty-minute walk from campus to our favorite bar—the one I haven't set foot in since he left—and ordinarily, I'd take a campus cab, but I could use the time to clear my head. Plus, I really don't want to be pitifully early.

So, I walk. I pop an earbud in my ear and listen to one of his songs. It's all I listen to lately, and it's the way I feel closest to him when he's seven hours away.

At the bar, I make my way through the crowds, trying to tamp down my fear. My heart is racing the same way it did last time I was here, and my brain is reminding me—loudly—that time didn't work out so well.

I approach the bar first, needing a healthy dose of liquid courage.

When the bartender passes my gin and tonic across the bar, I realize I recognize him. He's the asshole who tried to hit on me when my life was imploding last year.

"What?" he asks, brows drawn down. "Why are you looking at me like I just kicked your dog? This is what you ordered, isn't it?" He lifts the drink into my eyeline.

"Sorry." I look down, neutralizing my expression. "I was just remembering the last time I was here." I pass him my card and take the drink.

He stares at me, slowly turning to process the payment. "What happened last time you were here?"

I chuckle under my breath. "Nothing."

"Okay…" He draws the word out, passing a receipt to me to sign. "If you say so."

Of course he doesn't remember. I was probably just one of the many girls he hit on that night. One of the many girls he served drinks to with a side of smirk.

"Your face is doing that thing again," he points out, giving me a suspicious look.

"Sorry." I stand, backing away from the bar with the drink in my hand. "Thank you."

29

When I turn, I spot a familiar head peeking over the top of a booth at the far end of the bar. A mix of brown and blond, toffee and caramel that makes you want to run your hands through it. His hair is slightly longer than when I saw him last. I steel myself, taking quick steps toward him.

When I'm nearly there, I puff out a long breath and say, albeit shakily, "Well, hey there, stranger."

He turns to me, almost in slow motion, his sea-green eyes finding mine. The room seems to freeze, everyone around us moving in slow motion. A smile creeps onto the corner of his lips, and he slides from the booth. He holds his arms out, and I fall into them, the pieces of my heart feeling whole for the first time in so long.

He smells different. I don't recognize the cologne, and there are definitely new, more-defined muscles against my chest and arms as I squeeze myself tighter into him.

He rubs my back, nuzzling his head against my shoulder. "I've missed you, kiddo."

My body tenses. *Kiddo?*

He hasn't called me that since we were literal kids, and he was always trying to rub his extra *year* of life in my face.

I ignore it. Maybe he's just as nervous as I am. "I've missed you, too. I want to hear all about..."

I can't finish what I'm trying to say because, as I'm talking, Clayton has eased back toward the booth and is holding out his hand. Someone else had been sitting next to him. Someone I couldn't see.

A manager?

A bandmate?

A woman.

Her pin-straight black hair is cut just below her shoulders and I can't help noticing her dazzling brown eyes that sparkle when she looks at him. She smiles at me with perfectly straight teeth. Her olive skin is smooth and flawless.

In a word, she's beautiful. Shiny, bright. "Hi. You're Maggie," she tells me, like I might not know. "I've heard so much about you."

My brain has short-circuited. I'm not sure when I took my last breath.

She loops an arm around his back, and his arm envelops her. "Maggie, there's someone I want you to meet," he says. "This is Raven. My..."

Archenemy who I was just getting ready to kick out of the booth.

Backup singer.

Housekeeper.

Lesbian friend.

"My fiancée."

Time of death: 7:15 p.m.

I'm dead. I've died.

My knees are wobbly. I suck in a shallow breath, plastering a smile on my face. "Your...*fiancée?*" I must've heard him wrong. The music is so loud in here.

"I know it must be a shock," she says with a wide grin, patting his chest as she beams up at him. "I told Clayton he should've told you, but you know how he is." She wrinkles her nose, looking back at me. "He wanted to tell you in person. Always one for the dramatics." She laughs, and I want to crush her windpipe. Smash in those perfect teeth.

I hate her.

I hate her.

I hate her.

I force something from my throat that I hope sounds like a laugh, my eyes falling on him finally. There's an apology there, somewhere deep, but mostly, he looks happy. He wants me to understand. To be happy for him.

How can I when my heart was just ripped out on the operating table? Plopped down in a metal bowl to be discarded as medical waste. Unsalvageable.

I can't tell him that, though. I'd be the worst best friend ever.

Still, how can he be engaged to someone I've never even heard him mention? How can two lives be so separated after just a year apart?

"I know you're probably thinking it's sudden," he says as if he can read my mind. "But Raven and I have been writing songs together all year and...well, it just happened."

"The engagement is new," she says, holding her hand out and wiggling her fingers in my direction. I look down, spotting the flashy diamond on her finger. "His parents knew he'd been planning it for a few months, but I had no idea." She grins again. "We both wish you could've been there. I know how special you are to him." She slips a hand down, clasping his in a way that can only be taken as possessive.

"His parents?"

His parents knowing only makes this worse. Only makes it more real.

"Yeah. Well, Carol said she knew this would happen after we met the first time, but to be honest, I wasn't even sure myself. I was cautious with him, but he was so sure. You know how he gets." Her smile is so wide her cheeks must be burning.

"You've met his parents?" I ask, trying to keep my voice steady. "Did they visit you all down in Nashville?"

I'm asking Clayton the question, but it's Raven who answers, still looking at him. "They visited once, but mostly we've come here. Well, we came to Myers, not Chicago, but close enough. It must've been...what, babe? Five or...maybe six times?" He nods, and she looks back at me, beaming. "Aren't they the sweetest?"

My eyes haven't left Clayton's. Him returning to Myers even *once* since he left is news to me. Why wouldn't he have told me? Why wouldn't he have wanted to see me?

The answer is clear: Because I was part of his old life. The life he left behind the day he walked away. He's only telling me any of this now because he knows I'll find out eventually.

I smile to avoid the sob I feel clawing at the back of my throat.

"The visits were never long," he says gently, reading my mind again.

"Oh, gosh, no," Raven agrees. "A day or two, tops. Just enough for him to show me where he's from. And, of course, we spent a few days at that gorgeous little lake house his parents own when we were writing part of his new album. Have you been there?"

"Yes," I croak. That lake house was ours. I once imagined us growing old there, raising our babies on its shore. That's all gone now. All the plans I had for my life have evaporated in the blink of an eye.

"Maggs and I spent most of our summers there growing up," he tells her, while pulling her closer to him.

"It's so beautiful," she coos. Her hand finds his chest, the light above our booth reflecting in the stone shimmering on her stupid, perfect finger.

"Yeah, it is." I clear my throat. I need to get away from here before I break down. "I'm so happy for you. Both of you. I know your parents must be thrilled, too."

He nods slowly. "Yeah, they are."

"Well, come on, then. Let's sit down and get some food.

I'm starving," Raven says, pulling him toward the booth seat. "I can't wait to learn more about you, Maggie."

They take a seat, looking at me expectantly, and I realize I still haven't budged. I grip the fabric of the dress I'm wearing, regretting tearing the tags off of it this morning. It's too fancy for this place anyway. Too fancy for the moment your life falls apart.

"I, um, actually, I need a drink. I'll be right back. Do you guys want anything?"

"No," Clayton says.

"Oh, that sounds—" Raven starts to answer, but I've already turned away. I make a hurried dash for the bar, realizing only when I get there that I still have a full glass in my hand. I tilt my head back, downing the drink.

The burn in my throat is nothing compared to the ache I feel a bit farther down.

"What'd he do this time?" comes the familiar, gruff voice.

I look up, setting my glass on the bar. "What?"

He drops down to place his elbows on the counter. "That's two times in a row he's made you cry, isn't it? You know what they say..."

"What do they say?" I ask with a scowl.

"Fool me once, shame on you. Fool me twice, shame on me." He pats his lip with one finger. "Or...in this case"—his finger points toward me—"you."

I curl my upper lip. "So you *do* remember me."

"Hard to forget." He backs up, hands in the air as if to say *I'm totally innocent here.* "And just so we're clear, I am *not* hitting on you."

"Not this time."

"Not ever. You are *not* my type, trust me." He adjusts the backward ball cap atop his head.

"Great. You're not mine either."

His eyes bounce up toward Clayton. "Clearly." He nods, holding out a hand for the glass. "Can I get you another?"

"Um..." I glance over my shoulder, where Clayton has slid toward the end of the booth. He catches me watching him and offers a small smile. I turn my attention back to the bartender.

"Yeah. I guess so."

He sets to work and returns a few minutes later, but when I hold out my card, he shakes his head. "On the house."

I narrow my eyes at him. "Why?"

He leans forward. "I'm helping you out. For the record, he hasn't taken his eyes off you since you walked away."

Heat blooms in my lower stomach. "Yeah, right."

"Let him think the hot bartender bought you a drink." He shrugs one shoulder. "It's not the worst thing."

"Hot?" I raise a brow. "Might as well add in humble, too."

"Where's the fun in humble?" His smile is lopsided but endearing. Dark curls peek out from underneath his cap. "What's your name, anyway?"

"I'm Maggie."

"Short for Margaret?"

"Maggie," I reiterate. "No one but my grandmother has ever called me Margaret."

"Fine. Hi, Maggie. I'm Tucker."

I tip my drink toward him before taking another sip.

"So, what's the story there?"

I feign ignorance. "Story?"

"Well, every time I've seen you in here, it's been with him. And you guys seem close, but I've never seen anything that would suggest a relationship, though he does make you cry a lot."

"What are you? A stalker?" I ask, bristling.

KIERSTEN MODGLIN

"I prefer the term 'observant.'"

I sigh, dropping my cheek into my palm. "If you must know—"

"Oh, I must," he jokes, flashing that smile again. It's starting to grow on me, I have to admit.

"He's my best friend."

"Your best friend who wants to fuck you?"

I scowl.

"Your best friend who you want to fuck?" he guesses again.

"My best friend who just introduced me to his fiancée."

He sucks in a breath through his teeth. "Damn. So, it *is* the second one." He checks over my shoulder.

"It's complicated. And anyway, last time we were in here, he was telling me he was leaving to move to Nashville."

"Ah. You scared him away?" he teases.

"He got a record deal."

His eyes widen. "No shit?"

"Yeah."

Looking over my shoulder again, he squints his eyes. "Who is he? I don't recognize him."

"He's still starting out. His album releases in a few months. He's just had a few singles."

"Hmm. So he moved to Nashville to chase his dream, and I'm guessing he didn't ask you to go with him when he left?"

"No," I say simply. "And now, he's engaged. So, that's that."

He clicks his tongue. "Maybe."

"Maybe?"

He smirks. "Did I mention he hasn't stopped looking over here? And, if I was an angrier man"—his hand goes to his chest—"I might have to say something about the glare he's giving me."

36

I blush, looking down. "Oh, that. No. He's just protective of me. Always has been."

"If you say so."

A woman calls his attention farther down the bar, and he turns from me to refill her drink. I finish the last of mine, thankful my nerves earlier today mean I snacked all day long, otherwise I'd definitely be feeling it by now.

I set the glass down and turn around, noticing the song has changed to something slow. "You and Me" by Lifehouse. My chest goes tight as Raven practically pushes him out of the booth, and they make their way to the dance floor.

I should look away, spare myself the heartache, but I can't take my eyes off of them. The irony of the song choice isn't lost on me. It's like no one else in the bar exists. No one else in the world. He slips his arms around her waist and lowers his mouth to her ear, making her blush evident even from where I stand.

He's forgotten about me.

He loves her. I can see it plain and clear. This isn't something that can be fixed, and I'm not sure I'd want to even if I could.

He deserves to be happy, and if she makes him happy...who am I to stand in the way of that?

Fresh tears burn my eyes as I force myself to say a silent goodbye to my best friend, the future I'd always envisioned, and the man I thought I'd grow old with.

I don't even realize I've moved away from the bar until a hand touches my back, and I feel a warm breath on my neck. I glance over my shoulder, surprised to see Tucker standing there. "What are you doing?"

"Dancing with you." He nudges me forward from the base of my spine. An inch lower, and his grip would be totally inappropriate. "Come on." On the dance floor, he spins me around, pulling my body against his.

He's warm. Firm beneath his loose T-shirt. My hands go to his arms, and he nudges them upward to his neck, his hands resting on my hips. His blue eyes sear into me, and for a moment, I forget where we are.

"Aren't you supposed to ask?" I whisper.

"Is this you turning me down?"

Behind us, Clayton and Raven are suddenly in my line of vision. He lowers his lips to hers briefly, and everything inside me goes cold.

"Don't look at them," Tucker whispers, moving closer to me, though I don't know how it's possible. He smells of mint and cedar, a combination that spreads warmth to my limbs. "Touch my hair," he orders, his mouth against my ear.

"What?"

"Do it," he says. "At the nape of my neck. Run your fingers through my hair and keep looking at me."

"What are you talking about?"

"Just...trust me, okay?" He pulls back, staring at me with a look I don't recognize. His grip tightens on my hips, and he drags me closer so we're touching at every point up to our chests, swaying in place.

When I catch Clayton's eye over Tucker's shoulder, it clicks for me. Suddenly, I understand what we're doing here. It seems silly. Clayton doesn't care who I'm dancing with for any reason other than to make sure I'm safe. He's not going to be jealous.

"Quit looking at him. Look at me." He pulls my eyes back to him, and I scrutinize him.

"Whatever this is, it won't work."

"Trust me, it will." He dips his mouth down to my neck,

pressing a kiss to the exposed skin. It's brief—lasts only seconds —but I feel the tingle of it for much longer.

"What was that?"

His finger touches my cheek like a breath, and I wish he'd keep it there longer than he does. "He needs to see you blush for another man."

Every muscle between my legs clenches at his words. At the way he's looking at me as he says them. "Why are you doing this?"

He smirks. "Maybe I'm just hoping for a big tip."

I narrow my eyes at him, and he laughs.

"Or maybe I'm just a nice guy."

That makes *me* laugh.

"What? You don't think so?"

"Last time I was here, you accused me of, if I remember right, *snotting* all over your bar during the worst night of my life."

"Your memory is fine. It's your self-awareness that needs some work. You *were* snotting all over my bar."

"I was not."

He gives me that annoying, snarky smile, but he chooses not to argue further. "Why was it the worst night of your life? Because he left?"

I look down. "Yeah."

"But he came back."

"With a fiancée."

"To quote the one and only Michael Scott, 'Engaged ain't married.'"

I roll my eyes. "I don't know who that is, but regardless, I lost. Fair and square."

He blinks, shaking his head. "Hold on. One, you don't watch *The Office*? I'm not sure we can be friends anymore."

"Are we?"

"Are we friends?" he asks. I nod. "Yeah. Yeah, we're friends." He pushes out his lips. "And friends don't let friends give up so easily. If you want him, you can still have him. You just have to put in some effort."

"And what would your advice be? Make him jealous?" I tease, running my fingers through the hair at the base of his skull. My fingers bump the baseball cap, and he removes his hand from my waist to adjust it. When he lowers his hand back to my hip, he presses his thumb into my hip bone. His Adam's apple bobs.

"Mm-hmm," he mutters, almost as an afterthought.

"Somehow, I don't think dancing with a stranger is going to make him jealous."

"And what do you think would?" His eyes are trained on my lips, waiting for an answer. I cut a glance at Clayton again. Despite talking to Raven, he looks my way the second I look his. Like he can feel me. Like we're drawn together. I know he has to still feel it, so how can he be with her?

How can he be going to marry her?

I look away, leaning my head forward on Tucker's chest without thought. I don't allow myself to second-guess it or wonder if it's appropriate or what he's thinking. I just close my eyes and relax; I sink into him. To my relief, his hands pull me in closer, and his chin comes to rest on the top of my head.

Silent tears fall down my cheeks. If he knows I'm crying, he doesn't mention it. When the song ends, I step back, and he uses his finger to lift my chin toward him.

"Thank you," I say softly. "For...whatever this was."

Without a word, he leans forward and presses a kiss to the side of my mouth so his lips brush mine only slightly—the kind of kiss you'd give your grandmother at a funeral. So, why, as he walks away and back to the bar, do I feel it on every inch of my skin?

I make my way back to the booth in a bit of a haze, where I find Clayton and Raven sliding in on their side.

"Hey." Raven beams. "We thought you got lost."

"Yeah, sorry. I was—"

"Who was that?" Clayton asks, cutting me off with a bit too much enthusiasm.

I play dumb. "Who?"

"The guy you were dancing with."

"Oh, Tuck?" I have no idea if he goes by a nickname, but it feels nice rolling off my tongue. "He's, uh, he's...I don't really know what he is. It's still new."

I don't know why I'm lying, although, maybe I do. When I glance back over my shoulder, he winks at me from behind the bar, and something tells me he wouldn't mind the fib.

"He's a bartender?"

I don't like the way he says it, but the Clayton I know isn't actually judging his job. He's...what, exactly? *Is this him being jealous? Did Tucker's ridiculous plan actually work?*

My cheeks burn from the smile that fills my face. I force it down. "Yes. He is."

"Doesn't really seem like your type," he says.

"I think he's cute," Raven offers encouragingly.

Clayton tucks an arm around her tighter but doesn't agree.

"Anyway, I actually need to go. I forgot I have a paper due, and—"

"Wait, really? You're leaving already?" Clayton turns toward me. "I was looking forward to hanging out again."

But not looking forward to it enough to try to see me any of the times you've been home in the last year...

I take a step back without saying that. Instead, I force a

smile that practically kills me. "Yeah, I was, too. I'm sorry. Hopefully we can all hang out again before you leave town. Congratulations on, well, everything. It was nice to meet you, Raven."

"You too." She waves her fingers at me. "So nice."

I lean down and give Clayton an awkward, one-armed hug, and when I turn around, Tucker is heading our way.

"Ready to go?"

"Yeah," I say loudly so they can hear me. When we're far enough from them and close enough to the door, I ask, "How'd you know I needed you?"

"It looked like you were leaving. Figured it would look better if it wasn't alone."

"Can you just leave the bar like that? Aren't you supposed to be working?"

He waves a hand. "The guys can cover me for the rest of the night."

"The rest of the night?" I eye him, my jaw dropping open as we step outside. "That's presumptuous."

He laughs, emphasizing his next words, "*While I walk you home.* Jeez, get your mind out of the gutter."

"Well, thank you. But I'm good now. You don't have to walk me home."

"I don't mind," he says with a shrug. "Unless you're opposed to great company and killer conversation."

"Maybe don't use the word 'killer' when you're trying to convince a girl to show you where she lives," I say, fake wincing.

"Noted." He laughs, pretending to unsheath an imaginary knife from his belt and drop it on the ground. He kicks it away for good measure. "See? I'm unarmed and come in peace."

I shake my head, rolling my eyes. "I'm this way," I say, pointing toward the sidewalk that leads back to my apartment.

He glances over at me, his hands shoved into his pockets. "So, did our plan work?"

"I'm not sure," I admit. "He asked who you were, but that was it, really. I just had to get out of there. But...thank you for doing this. And for the dance. I owe you one."

"No problem. The guy got what he deserved."

"He's not a bad guy," I tell him. "Really. It's not his fault I have feelings for him."

He nods, pulling a hand from his pocket long enough to nudge me out of the way when a couple passes us. "Still, if he's so good, he could've given you a heads up about his fiancée, don't you think?"

"I'm sure he just didn't think about it."

"*Or*," he offers, "he did, and he knew you might not come if he told you."

"He wouldn't have been wrong," I admit.

"But that should've been your choice to make."

"He's my best friend. It would've been selfish of me not to come. I would've regretted it later."

He looks like he wants to say more, but he refrains. The walk back to my apartment is an easy one, completely paved and relatively quiet, but the weather has turned colder—or maybe I'm just no longer warmed by adrenaline pulsing through my veins.

"So, how long have you been working at the bar?" I ask to fill the silence.

"A few years."

"Do you like it?"

"I don't *hate* it. It can get interesting."

"Where are you from?"

"A little town called Myers. It's a few hours south of here," he says, kicking a rock on the sidewalk as we pass it.

The answer shocks me so much I stop in my tracks. *Is this a joke?* "Wait, really?"

Noticing I've stopped, he does, too, turning back to look at me. "Yeah, why? You've heard of it?"

"Uh, yeah. It's... It's where I'm from, too." I move to catch up with him, and he waits for me before he starts walking again.

"Seriously?"

"Mm-hmm. Born and raised."

"I guess I shouldn't be surprised. Seems like everyone from home ends up in Chicago in some capacity eventually. Is that where, uh, *lover boy* is from, too?"

I laugh. "Yeah. We both grew up there. Lived a few houses down from each other all our lives. Our moms were best friends."

He spins his hat around, so it's forward on his head. As he does, I stop, realizing we've made it to my apartment. It doesn't feel like we've been walking long enough. "This is me." I point toward the building up ahead.

"Cool. Well, look, if you need me, you know where to find me. If you need another fake dance or...whatever."

"Thanks." I don't know whether to hug him or shake his hand or just walk away.

"Um, should I give you my number just in case?"

"Do you want to?" Now, it's my turn to smirk as I press up on my toes.

"I wouldn't want you to think I'm hitting on you," he says, hands up with a cocky grin.

"Right. I'm not your type."

He nods. "Exactly. But, you know, if you needed to get a hold of me for some sort of fake-dating emergency, a phone number would be ideal."

"True." I purse my lips. "Okay, fine." I pull out my phone and take down his number. "I'll text you if I need anything, but don't hold your breath. Clayton won't be in town for long."

"Fair enough," he says simply. "But just in case." He points toward my apartment building. "Um, get home safe, yeah?"

"Thanks, Tucker."

He walks backward away from me for several steps, then when he's far enough away, he turns, adjusting his cap again.

Why do I feel sad to see him go?

CHAPTER FIVE

NOW

I'm back in the house because I can't think of a single excuse not to be. I'm a grown woman. I have no reason to be afraid of a house. *My* house.

My mom worked hard to be able to leave me with something, and this is what I have to show for that hard work. Her life savings and insurance policy went into buying this house and moving me from Iowa City back to Myers. I can't waste that. I have to make her proud.

I roll over on the air mattress I've set up on the living room floor, staring up at the water stain on the ceiling. It looks old, nothing to be concerned about probably, but then again, it could be harboring black mold.

Shouldn't the inspector have caught it?

I'll have to look at the report tomorrow.

I fold both arms under my head, taking a breath. This is what being a homeowner feels like, I guess. A load of pressure, a load of work, and a small amount of pride.

I was brought home from the hospital into the home I grew up in, so maybe I took homeownership for granted as a kid. My parents were never private-jet-flying, caviar-eating rich, but we were always comfortable. Vacations every year, cheerleading camp in the summer, new clothes before school. I was fortunate not to want for anything.

Still, that did little to prepare me for the real world. When I graduated and started fresh on my own, I realized how hard it was to make ends meet on a small salary. Starving artist and all that. Now, my paintings sell occasionally—mainly reprints I sell online for a fourth of the cost of my originals—but it's enough to get by. Most of my art is in the moving van, which is still somewhere in Iowa, but I brought one of my paintings with me. Mom's favorite. I glance over at where it hangs on the wall, on a nail left by the previous owners.

It's an oil painting of cerulean warblers in trees near a lake a few miles from here. As a kid, I spent nearly every weekend there with Clayton. The lake holds some of my favorite memories.

A noise interrupts my thoughts, and I sit up in bed, clutching the fleece blanket to my chest. I listen, trying to determine where the sound came from.

Several long, painful seconds pass with me waiting before I hear it again.

Scraaaaatch.

Scraaaaatch.

It sounds like something dragging the ground. Or someone crawling.

Stop it, Maggie.

I'm being ridiculous.

I can't tell if it's coming from outside or in, nor do I know which would be worse. I'm being paranoid, and I know it. Everything about this house just has me on edge. Every sound is a murderer lurking. Every shadow is a ghost.

I stand from the bed as quietly and gracefully as I can—which is not much. My phone is charging a few feet from the bed, the cord stretched from the far wall, so I pick it up and check the screen.

I weigh my options, however limited.

I could go outside, which sounds terrible. Search the house, which sounds worse. Call the police, who will probably laugh me off the line. Call Tucker, who is probably sleeping and wants nothing to do with me. Call Clayton, who would definitely come but is at least thirty minutes away, and that's if I can wake him up.

I tap the phone screen again.

It's just after midnight.

No. I can't wake anyone. I don't need anyone's help.

I'm a grown woman, and I can search my own house. Besides, I'm sure it's nothing. A mouse, maybe. Or...or a tree branch scraping the siding outside.

I quickly search for something to use as a weapon. My ball bat is outside in the trunk, but I keep a stun gun in my purse. I ease across the room, the floorboards creaking under my weight, and pull it out.

I listen for the sound again, but it doesn't come. Could it be that I've already given an intruder a heads-up that I'm awake and coming for them? Could it be that I was just imagining things in the first place?

I step toward the kitchen, moving through it and ignoring the chill that runs over me as I do. The kitchen leads to a small hallway with three bedrooms. There is no main bedroom and en suite here. Just three tiny bedrooms and a small hallway bathroom. From the pictures I saw, I know the upper floor is a converted attic space, though, with carpet on half the room and mostly unfinished sheetrock on the walls.

The ceilings slant from the roof, but with enough work, I think I could make it into an owner's suite with its own bathroom.

At least, that's the hope.

The first bedroom smells of stale urine, and I assume it was either a child's bedroom or they kept animals inside it. A cat, perhaps. I make a mental note to tear up the carpets, hoping to find salvageable hardwoods underneath.

There are no curtains on the windows, which means I'm staring out into the dark night.

It also means someone could be outside staring in, and I'd never know it.

I clutch the stun gun tighter and step forward.

Another step.

Another.

I ease down onto the floor and stare out.

From where I am, I can see the house that belongs to Tucker. To my surprise, a light is on in a room at the back of the house. I wonder what he might still be doing up...

Again, I consider calling him now that I know he's awake, but I force the option away. I can't. I won't.

I'm not sure what Tucker living next door will mean for me, but I let him ruin enough of my past to know I can't go through that again. I will be friendly. Neighborly. But that has to be the extent of it.

I will never let Tucker Ford into my life again.

I stand, moving away from the window. The room has a small closet, and my heart seems to stall as I check it, but I find nothing. The next room still has the indentations of the bedframe from the last owners in its dingy, gray carpet.

This bedroom is colder than the first room, but there's no urine smell, which is nice. The room has wood-paneled walls which someone somewhere down the line has painted white, though it's chipping in places.

This room gives me the creeps, but I can't explain it.

Like I'm being watched.

It's that feeling... The knowing. The indefinable sense that someone is staring at you from a place you can't see. I spin around, searching the darkness beyond each of the windows and trying not to look as terrified as I feel—for the sake of my potential audience, I suppose.

I pause at the door to the last room at the end of the hall, something about it giving me pause. I place my hand on the doorknob, feeling the metal cool my palm.

Something isn't right.

I can't explain it.

Something is crawling up my spine, growing roots in my stomach, screaming at me, and begging me to understand that *something* isn't right here.

Something about this house is wrong.

But, no.

It can't be wrong because it's mine.

It feels wrong because I'm alone. No longer with Nick. No longer with my parents. Or Kassara. No longer with anyone. For the first time in my life, I'm living completely and utterly alone, and that's what terrifies me.

That somehow, I might fail at this, too.

With that acceptance, I push the door open and step into the room. My blood runs cold, though there's no reason for it to. The room looks the same as the first. Small and in desperate need of a paint job, with uncovered windows. The closet is standing open. I peer around the room, refusing to give in to my gut instinct that tells me to run.

I can't.

I won't.

This is not a scary movie or a thriller novel.

I'm just a girl spending her first night alone in a new place. That's it.

I shut off the light and step out of the room, slamming the door shut. When I do, the hallway light flickers. I take a step.

It flickers again.

With another step, I'm plunged into darkness. I grab my phone, tapping the screen and turning on the flashlight for light as I rush down the hall and flip the light switch off from that end. I turn it back on, and this time, it sticks.

I puff out a breath, trying to laugh at my own fear, though it doesn't feel funny at all.

Probably just a faulty wire. I'll hire an electrician to check into it.

I haven't heard the noise again, so I make my way back to the living room and lie down once more. This time, I pull out my noise-canceling headphones and put them on.

I place the stun gun and my phone next to me and decide at the last minute that I'll sleep better with the light on.

The next morning, it takes several seconds for me to remember where I am and why. Nothing is familiar, and I know this place will take a few days to get used to.

I pull my headphones off my head, stretching. The light from outside makes this place less threatening, and I immediately laugh at myself internally for how ridiculous I was last night.

I probably imagined the noise and everything. How embarrassing.

I'm reveling in how ridiculous I was and how sane I am now when I hear a noise again. This time, it's footsteps.

I stand up and dart for the door. Pulling it open, it takes me half a second to realize what I'm looking at.

"What's this for?" I shout toward the man walking away from my porch after leaving a paper cup and a brown paper bag to the right of my door. I step out as Tucker turns to look at me over his shoulder, still walking away.

"Sorry, didn't mean to wake you. I figured you might be hungry. Not in the city anymore, Maggie. No Starbucks."

I scowl, displeased with the reminder, and bend down to pick up the items before taking a sip of the coffee. It's the perfect temperature and just sweet enough. He remembered my order.

"Well, thanks," I say softly, peering into the bag as I fully process how I must look. Still dressed in my ratty pajamas, hair sticking up in every direction. "And a bagel?"

He stops. "Yeah. Hopefully it's not cold. I knocked, but you didn't answer, so I thought I'd leave it in case you were just ignoring me."

"Sorry, I was sleeping." I glance into the bag again. "You didn't have to do this."

"It's no big deal. You said you didn't bring much with you. I assumed food wasn't the biggest priority. I've got soap and towels and stuff over at the house if you need anything." He chuckles as I take a bite of the bagel, surprised to see he added just the right amount of cream cheese on top. "And more food. I leave the back door unlocked, so just help yourself if I'm not around."

"Thanks," I say again, annoying myself with my lack of conversation skills. "Do you...want to come in?"

His eyes cut to the door behind me. "I shouldn't. I need to get to work."

"Right. I didn't ask what you do."

He points toward the white truck in his driveway, parked next to the old, familiar blue one. "I own a contracting company."

"You *own* it?" I ask, not bothering to hide my shock.

"Well, don't look so surprised."

"Sorry. That's just really impressive. Congratulations, Tuck."

He runs a hand over the ball cap on his head, looking away.

"Actually, you might be able to help me. I'd pay you, of course," I add quickly. "There are a few things I need done around the house. I'll have to prioritize, but I think there's some faulty wiring I need someone to look at. Is that something I could hire you for?"

"Faulty wiring?" He steps toward me with a look of concern. "What makes you think that?"

"I just have a few lights that keep flickering. One shut off completely last night and freaked me out." I laugh under my breath.

"I'll take a look at it now," he says, jogging up the porch stairs.

"What? No. I don't want to interrupt your day or cut in line. I can totally hire someone else if—"

He's already moving past me and into the house. "Show me which light."

CHAPTER SIX

THEN

The ringing of my phone wakes me up, and I roll over groggily, checking the screen with one eye open. His name is the last one I thought I'd see.

I answer quickly, wiping drool from the corner of my mouth.

"Clayton? Hey."

"Are you busy?"

"Sleeping," I say, sitting up. "What's wrong?"

"Nothing. I was going for coffee. Thought we could talk."

I check the time on my phone screen. "Yeah. Sure. Give me like fifteen minutes."

"Sounds good. I'll swing by your apartment. You're still in the same one, right?"

The question is a painful reminder of how far apart we've drifted. "Yep."

"Okay. See you soon."

I slide off the bed, rubbing the heel of my hand over my eyes, and make my way down the hall and into the bathroom. Kassara's door is still shut, so I assume she's sleeping and try to keep quiet as I pull my hair up, brush my teeth, and wash my face.

I don't have time for a shower, so this will have to do. Back in my room, I pull on a pair of yoga pants and a T-shirt. It's a far cry from the dress Clayton saw me in last night, but that didn't work either, so what's the use?

Twenty minutes later, he knocks at my door.

At one time, he would've just walked in.

He swings an arm around my shoulders as we make our way down the stairs. "Sorry you had to run out last night."

"Yeah, me too," I admit, fidgeting with my phone in my pocket. "Did you guys have a nice time?"

"Yeah, I guess. It's not really Raven's scene, you know? She prefers...*fancier* places. Not like us."

I nod, but I don't comment.

He pulls his arm off my shoulders with a sigh. "Anyway, I wanted to say I'm sorry if I sort of ambushed you last night with her. I was just so excited for you to meet her, and she was dying to meet you, and well, I figured I'd just rip the bandage off. But now I'm wondering if that was the wrong call. I mean, I know we left things in a weird place, and everything with Raven is sudden, but Mom convinced me you'd be happy for me and—"

"Hey." I turn to smile at him, briefly placing a hand on his arm. When he looks at me, it's as if I'm the only one who can ease his worries. So, I do. "It's fine. You're fine. Everything's fine. I was glad to meet her. And glad to see you again."

"Yeah?"

"Of course."

"And, look, what she said about us coming home, it was literally always last minute, and I never get to see my parents anymore, so I just lost track of time hanging out with them. I didn't plan *not* to see you. I hope you know that. I've...I've really missed you."

"I get it. It's not a big deal. But I've missed you, too."

He ruffles my hair and I brush it back down with my fingers.

"So, she's also a songwriter?" The reality of how perfect they are for each other is bitter in the back of my throat.

"Yeah, they originally brought her in to write a song for the album, but we ended up working so well together that we partnered up for most of the songs, and well, I don't know." He sighs, running a hand through his hair. "She's really great, Maggs."

"Seems like it."

"It wasn't anything I planned," he says, not looking at me. I think it's what he's been trying to say all along. An apology in the form of an explanation. He didn't mean to fall in love with her. To forget about me.

He just...did.

"I know," I say softly, my voice catching in my throat.

"So... What's new with you? Besides your new guy, I mean."

"Nothing really. Just school and work. Work and school. I've been painting a little bit."

"You haven't done that since, what, junior high?"

"Yeah, I know. It's been a big stress reliever for me."

He elbows me playfully, reminiscent of older times and simpler days. An ache builds in my chest. "What's got you so stressed?"

I glance down, nervously tucking a piece of hair behind my ear. "I don't know. I guess it's just weird to think I'll be graduating this year."

"Tell me about it. What will you do?"

"I haven't really decided." *Because up until yesterday, my plans were to move to Nashville. With you.*

God, how pathetic am I? Here I was planning a life with him while he was proposing to someone else.

I want to melt into a puddle and never show my face again.

"Nothing wrong with that. I mean, if everything hadn't worked out for me the way it has, who knows what would've happened?" He stops, staring at me, and for a moment I imagine exactly what might've happened if he hadn't gotten the call. Exactly where our life might've gone. His eyes flick down to my lips, then back up, and the air between us grows thick with anticipation. "Maggie, I..."

"I might try to find a job around here for a while and work on my painting," I say, interrupting him as I turn to keep walking. "You know, Mom says I could get a job at her old office. They're always looking for receptionists, and I know everyone up there anyway. Plus, you get to wear scrubs, so I'd always be comfortable. Win-win."

He keeps pace with me, ignoring whatever *almost* just happened. "And what about the guy?"

"Tucker?"

"Is he in school?"

"Oh, um..." In truth, I have no idea. "He graduates this year, too."

"Really?" His voice goes flat.

"Yeah. And, actually, he's from Myers, so maybe we'll both go back. Or, maybe we'll stay here."

"Cool. *Cool*," he says, drawing out the word the second time.

"Yeah, so make sure I have a plus one for the wedding." I elbow him, but when I look over, he's so pale he looks ready to faint. We're mostly quiet the rest of the way to the coffee shop.

Once we're inside and have ordered our drinks, we pick a table against the wall. It could be any of the many other mornings we've spent together, but this feels different. Heavier somehow.

It feels like goodbye. The real thing.

"So, when do you leave?"

"Hmm?" he asks, sipping his coffee. He took it black this time, though I've only ever known him to prefer cream and sugar. Probably a new superstar diet.

"For Nashville. Are you just here for the weekend, or..."

"Oh." He places the cup down, spinning it in place. "Actually, no. We're...Raven and I are moving back to Myers. We just picked out some land, and I'm having a house built."

"What?"

"Yeah. Well, it turns out I don't like Nashville all that much. I mean, it's fun and all, don't get me wrong, but it doesn't feel like home." His eyes search mine.

"And she agrees."

"Mm-hmm. She's always wanted to live outside of the city and she says she loves Myers, so we're going to see how it goes."

"That sounds...promising." My coffee is still too hot to be enjoyed, but I put the cup to my lips anyway for something to do.

"Yeah, I'll still go back when I need to, and I'm opening for a few tours this summer, but most of the writing can be done from here anyway. Especially since I'll live with my co-writer. The label said we'll make it work, so...yeah. I guess maybe I'll be seeing you around a lot more."

"I guess so." I finally take a drink, welcoming the burn.

CHAPTER SEVEN

NOW

Tucker dragged a ladder and tools over from his house and is currently checking every breaker, light fixture, and outlet in my house. While he's there, I'm trying to stay busy and away from him by bringing in the rest of my things from the car—the coffee pot, a suitcase of clothes, and boxes of dishes, curtains, toiletries, and cleaning supplies.

When I hear his voice behind me, I jolt, nearly knocking over the cleaning supplies I've been neatly organizing on the kitchen counter.

"What?"

"I said," he repeats himself, "doesn't look like there's anything wrong with your wiring, but it does look like some of the insulation has been torn up. You may have had a mouse or something up there messing with things." The *or something* of his sentence gives me pause. "If I were you, I'd put out some traps as soon as you can just to be sure."

"Great. Well, thanks for checking anyway. Sorry you're going to be late for work now."

"Eh"—he leans against the doorframe—"perks of being

the boss. Who's going to yell at me?" He looks up at the wall, rapping his knuckles against the wood. "Listen, you weren't kidding. There's quite a bit of work that needs done around here."

"Gee, thanks."

"I'm serious. The carpet in the living room needs to be torn up. It's a hazard, and you've got some weak floorboards in one of the bedrooms. There's no heat or air running to the top floor and not enough insulation between the levels. Plus, you've got a few major water spots that really need to be addressed. How are you going to handle all of this?"

I bristle at the comments, as if he's scolding me. As if I'm a child who doesn't know what she's gotten herself into. Granted, I don't, but I made a decision, and I'm still too stubborn to admit it might've been a bad one. "I'll manage. I have some money put back. I'll hire out, like I told you, to take care of the major stuff. I can do the painting myself, and the rest will come with time."

"The rest is still pretty major stuff. Your hot water heater looks as old as the house. The roof hasn't been touched or maintained in years. The windows are all—"

"*I get it,*" I shriek. "I bought a crap house, okay? Would you like to continue to lecture me, or can we move on?"

He pats the doorframe. "I didn't realize I was lecturing you. I'm trying to offer to help you out."

"No thank you," I say quickly, my tone too sharp.

"You said earlier you wanted to hire me."

"I changed my mind. I don't need your help."

"Fine." His hands go up. "Well, you never did, did you?"

"What's that supposed to mean?"

He turns around, stalking back down the hall for his ladder.

"Tucker!" I shout. "What is that supposed to mean?"

"You know exactly what it means." He grabs the ladder, holding it over his shoulder and squeezing past me in the narrow hall.

"Do I? Because the way I remember it, I took your help when you offered it, and you threw it back in my face."

He sighs, rolling his eyes and stopping in his tracks. His head rolls toward me. "Oh, I threw it back in your face, hmm? Pretty sure I did everything you asked, and in the end, you're the one who walked away."

"And you know exactly why I did that," I say, my jaw so tense it aches.

His nostrils flare as he stares at me, and suddenly, the hallway is too small. Too narrow. He's too close to me. He's all I can smell. All I can see. "I know you *think* you know."

I break, stepping away and storming past him. "What do you want from me, Tucker? We both know with our history, there's no way you can help me. We're already at each other's throats, and it's only been two hours."

"Well..." He huffs, trying to catch up. "Well, we're neighbors now. I guess we're going to have to learn how to get along." Though his words offer a sort of olive branch, his tone is gruff, still full of fight.

"Says who?" I stomp my foot. The floorboard underneath me groans, as if to prove his point that I need help.

"Says me." He takes another step forward, and now he's so close I can feel his breath on my lips, feel the heat from his body on mine. I shiver, which doesn't go unnoticed. His heavy gaze trails the length of my body.

"Fine. Whatever. I'll hire you, if that's what you want."

"You can't afford me," he replies dryly.

"Oh, please." I groan, rolling my eyes. "I'll figure something out. I'm not the same helpless girl you saved in the bar all those years ago."

He balks, opens his mouth, and closes it again. When he speaks, it's with a distance in his stare. "You were never helpless, Maggie."

"Maybe not, but I felt like it then. I don't need you to save me now. I need you to do a job. I need *someone* to do a job."

"Fine. I'll do it."

"Fine." I cross my arms.

"I'll come over at night and do what I can. I'm not charging you, so deal with it." I open my mouth to argue, but he goes on, "I only have one condition."

"What's that?"

"He can't be here when I'm here."

"You can't be serious."

"Oh, I am."

I groan. "Well, I can't control what he does."

"No. You could never do that either, could you?"

I roll my eyes again. "Clayton has no reason to be here, but I'm not going to tell him he can't stop by. So, if you can't handle that, then I guess this isn't going to work."

He presses his lips together, a muscle in his jaw twitching. Glancing away, he groans. "Fine, whatever." He grabs his ladder and heads for the door again. "See you tonight."

Before he reaches the front door, with me at his heels, he stops. Turns around. His eyes meet mine. "Can I ask you something?"

"When have you ever asked permission before?"

He doesn't respond to my snark, which tells me this will be more serious than I'm ready for. "Why didn't you tell anyone about that night?"

"Should I have?"

"After you left, I kept waiting for the police to arrive, to question me about what happened, but they never did. After the news broke, after you left, I just assumed..."

"I don't know," I admit. It's both an answer and a regret. A fatal flaw within myself. I should've told. I've said as much to myself every day. But then it was too late. "I'm not sure I ever could've."

CHAPTER EIGHT

THEN

When I step into the bar on the opposite side of town, the last person I expect to see is Clayton. I specifically chose this bar because it wasn't ours. Maybe he had the same idea.

To my relief, he's with a group of his old friends and not Raven, but it doesn't make it any less awkward.

Not only did he *not* invite me, but now it feels like I could be stalking him. I turn to walk out, but I stop when I realize he's seen me. His eyes meet mine from across the room where he's standing near the pool table, and he smiles sort of half-heartedly, more confused than anything, and offers a half wave over his head.

I wave back as casually as I can muster and make a beeline for a booth. To my dismay, within seconds, he's standing at the edge of my table.

"What's up, Maggs? What are you doing here?"

"Oh." I scramble to come up with an answer. I was just planning to come and grab a drink alone, which feels extra pathetic now. Why would he ever believe that? He's totally going to think I'm stalking him.

I need a plan. Someone. Something. Kassara is out with her boyfriend tonight, so I can't ask her to bail me out. The name planted firmly in my mind is screaming at me, but it's terrible. Pathetic. As if the top item on his to-do list on a Saturday night is to come hang out with me. Still, I hear myself saying, "I'm on a date. He's just running behind."

"Yeah? With the bartender dude?"

"Tucker, yes," I confirm. "We go here so he can avoid the one he works at."

"Makes sense." He licks his lower lip, casting a glance at the door. "Sucks he's late."

"Er, well, actually, I'm early," I say. "You know me."

He eyes me but doesn't argue. We both know I'm rarely early for anything.

"Well, um, I would invite you to come get a few beers and play pool with us, but I guess you're busy."

"Yeah…" I instantly regret my decision. I could've had a Raven-free evening with him, but instead, I'll be sitting alone with a date who will never show up.

As soon as the thought crosses my mind, I spy Raven emerging from the restroom. Somehow, she's even more beautiful than the last time I saw her. Her dark hair is pulled back in a tiny, sleek ponytail, and she's dressed casually in a tank top and jeans.

I look away. "Yeah, busy. It was good to see you, though."

He pats my shoulder and walks away, making a path back to his group. I pull out my phone, my cheeks hot with embarrassment as I send the single most mortifying text message of my life.

> I know it's last minute, but if you're free, I'm at Busy's and Clayton is here with a bunch of his friends. Trying not to look like I have no life. Could really use some help with that.

I press *send* and instantly realize I never gave him my number.

> This is Maggie, by the way. The girl from the bar.

> That you walked home.

> Oh. This message is for Tucker. Hope that's you.

> Just let me know.

> Or don't. You know. If you're busy.

> Okay. Bye.

It takes ten long minutes for me to get a response, but when I do, relief floods my body.

> On my way.

Twenty minutes go by before the door to the bar opens again, and Tucker appears. My heart flutters at the sight of him, but I'm sure it's only because he's literally saving my life.

He scans the bar and finds me quickly, heading my way.

He's dressed how he always is—jeans, T-shirt, backward

ball cap. Completely unflappable despite how quickly he must've gotten ready and headed here.

Unless he was already out.

Oh god, don't let me have interrupted him on a date.

Then again, why would he leave a date and come here?

"Sorry I'm late, honey," he says, kissing my cheek. He smirks and waves a hand my way, wanting me to slide over in the booth. "Scooch."

I stare at him. "Scooch? What? No. Sit over there." I point across from me.

"No." He sits down next to me anyway, nudging me over with his hip. "We're on a date. *On a date*, I sit here."

"What are you? Twelve? We can eat across from each other."

"If I was twelve, this would be highly inappropriate."

I snort and scoot the rest of the way over as he scans the room. "So, you stalked lover boy here, and he caught ya, hmm?" He doesn't bother looking at me when he asks.

"No," I say firmly. "I did *not* stalk him."

"Then you came here hoping to avoid me?"

"No. I was hoping to avoid *him*. Seems like he had the same idea. Probably Raven's idea, actually." Her name is a curse word on my lips, which I've painted red tonight and am only just realizing it probably looks like I'm trying too hard.

"Yeah. I noticed you never sent me your phone number. Would've been useful when I wanted to tell you he hadn't been back to my bar since that night."

"Oh." My heart sinks. Maybe Clayton really was trying to avoid me. Great, now I look even more desperate. Like I've been there looking for him, and now I've had enough time to search out the other places around campus.

"Don't worry. We're on a date tonight. Perfectly reasonable excuse."

"Who says I'm worried?"

He chuckles, looking away. "Your face literally screams your every thought. And right now, it's bellowing that it's worried he thinks you've followed him here."

I bury my face in my hands. "God, this is so embarrassing."

His hands cover mine, pulling them down. "Don't be embarrassed. Just be convincing that that isn't what's going on." After a pause, he adds, "As long as it isn't."

"It isn't." I quirk a brow. "And what do you mean by *be convincing*?"

"Same as we did when we danced together. If you make him think you're here to see me, that I'm the only one on your mind tonight, you'll have no reason to be embarrassed."

My eyes dart back and forth between his, not sure if he's completely insane or a genius.

"That is why you texted me, isn't it? To make him jealous again?"

"I... Yeah, I guess. I just didn't want to be here alone."

He nods. "Well, now you're not."

"What were you doing that you could just drop everything and show up tonight anyway?"

"Are you complaining?"

"Obviously not."

"Then don't worry about it. I'm here. And now I'm going to go and get us drinks. While I'm gone, I want you to watch me. Don't look over at him. Got it? Like we're the only two in here."

I nod. "Fine. Okay."

He slides from the bench, but he seems to think better of it and turns around, eyeing me with a grin. "Kiss me."

"*What?*"

"Kiss me."

My brows draw together. "I can't. That's ridiculous."

"He's watching."

"Oh." I meet his eyes, leaning forward ever so slightly. He matches me inch for inch, each of us moving forward a little at a time. And then, suddenly, there's nowhere else to move.

My lips brush his lightly. Then again. It's tentative at first, awkward and new. Like I've never kissed anyone in my life, and this is an entirely foreign concept. My cheeks heat with embarrassment, but he's calm. Patient. His tongue touches my lips as his fingers smooth over my cheek, pulling me deeper into him.

Suddenly, it's not new at all. It's as if we've been doing this for ages. In other lives. In dark rooms. Under covers. The room spins—too hot. I'm losing my mind. My heart threatens to beat out of my chest.

His other hand moves to cradle my opposite cheek, bringing me back to reality, and he guides my head to the side. His tongue tangles with mine, and I feel his kiss somewhere deep in my core.

I feel him everywhere.

And then, as quickly as it started, it ends.

He pulls away and stands from the seat, pressing one last kiss to my swollen lips.

What the hell just happened?

As if he can read the thoughts running through my head on my *apparently very-emotive* face, he gives me a smug grin and turns away. I'm at a loss, my body tingling, fingers icy yet somehow on fire, as I watch him approach the bar.

It feels like no time has passed at all when he returns with a beer and gin and tonic.

"For you." He slides the drink to me.

Maybe I shouldn't drink this. I know all the rules. I've heard all the warnings, and yet all I can think is…

"You remembered my drink?"

"Well, you have it *a lot.*"

I scowl. "Do not."

He takes a sip of his beer without arguing, and I lift my drink to my lips as well. It's not as good as the one he makes, but I refuse to tell him that. I could never give him the satisfaction.

He leans forward on the table, resting an arm in front of him. "So, confession time." He takes a deep breath. "Which of your siblings are you closest to? Do you have siblings?" His brows draw down.

"Oh, *I'm* the one confessing here?"

"That *is* how confession time works."

"I really don't think it is." I laugh. "But, um, yeah, okay. No, I don't have any siblings. My parents had me somewhat late in life, so it's just us. You?"

"Same. I was raised by my grandpa, actually. My parents were around, but they were never all that interested in being parents, you know? So, it was just me and him." He chuckles. "That man never misses a beat."

"So you two are really close?"

"Yeah. I was close with my grandma, too, but she died when I was twelve. So, since then, it's always been just us."

"I'm so sorry." The response is instinctual.

"Why?" he challenges.

"Why?"

"Yeah, why are you sorry? You didn't know her."

I feel like he's being confrontational, but there seems to be nothing malicious in his tone. "I…I don't know. It's just what you say. It's polite. I'm sorry you went through that."

He nods, peeling at the paper on his beer bottle. "Thanks. It's nice of you to say. I guess it just always feels a little empty. Have you ever lost anyone?"

"This is a deep conversation for Saturday night drinks." I laugh nervously. What is it about him that makes me so on edge? His directness is something I've never experienced.

"If I'm going to be your fake boyfriend, I should know these things about you."

"Is that what you are?" Now it's my turn to fidget with my glass.

"I'm whatever you need me to be."

"Why?"

"It's polite." He throws my answer from earlier back at me. "It's just what you do."

I narrow my eyes at him. "Very funny."

"I don't know. Call it my good deed of the year and stop stalling. Answer the question."

"When do I get to ask one?"

"You already asked me if I was close to my grandpa. Now it's back to me." He clicks his tongue, shaking his head. "See, being an only child did a number on your people skills. This is called 'taking turns.'"

I groan, resting my head in my hand. "No. I haven't lost anyone." My eyes find Clayton in the crowd, bent over the pool table. He shoots, and everyone around him cheers, though I can't see what's happened.

"*Now*, it's your turn." He tips his bottle toward me.

"And I can ask you anything?"

"Anything you want an honest answer to."

I swallow, trying to think. "What happened with your last relationship?"

"Ah, I married her," he says. "Four years next month."

My stomach drops. "What?"

"Kidding, obviously." He leans forward in his seat, eyes narrowing as he taps a finger on the bottle in his hands. "My last relationship was...probably high school, I guess. Just didn't work out. I moved away. She didn't. Same old story."

"How old are you?"

"That's two questions, cheater. It's my turn. What are you majoring in?"

"Business."

"That's a generic degree. What do you actually want to—" He stops himself, wagging a finger in the air. "Wait, two questions. I know. Uh, to answer your last one, I'm twenty-three. Now, answer mine. What do you actually want to do?"

"I like to paint," I say softly. "So, I chose business because I'd like to open a gallery someday."

He takes another drink. "Okay, fair enough."

I purse my lips. He doesn't think I can do it. Not that it's surprising. No one does. "So, did you graduate last year?"

"No. I'll graduate this year. I took a year off to decide what I wanted to do. Neither of my parents went to college, and my grandparents didn't either, so I wasn't sure it was for me."

"What changed your mind?"

We both know it's a second question I'm not allowed, but he answers anyway. "I don't know. I guess I just wanted to try something different. See a new place. Chicago was far enough away to feel like I got out without actually going far enough that I can't be around to help out when he needs me."

"And does he? Need you, I mean."

"You're a rule breaker," he teases, tapping the beer bottle on the table. "Yeah, here recently, he's started needing help more and more. We can't afford a full-time nurse or anything like that, you know. But I send money back to help pay for a part-time caregiver. Someone who can make sure he takes his meds and hasn't fallen or anything." He chuckles. "God, he hates her."

"I'm sure he really appreciates you doing that for him."

He looks over at me, catching my eyes in what feels like a double take. He sucks in a breath that feels like it's been pulled straight from my lungs, and he blinks away the glaze on his eyes, looking down. "He, uh, doesn't...know I do it. I arranged it with the company. He thinks he's covering it all, and I make up the difference." With a deep inhale, he changes the subject. "So, now I'm just waiting to graduate and move back home. I'll probably take over his shop. Move into the old house. Grow old on coffee and hash browns, like he has. Who knows? Maybe I'll come to the city once in a while. Visit your gallery."

I smile up at him, realizing maybe I misread him earlier. Perhaps he does actually believe I can do it.

Not that I care.

Not that his opinion does anything for me.

"I don't plan to stay here either," I say. "I'll move back home to Myers. Help out my parents."

"Oh, I didn't mean you'd be staying here. I assumed you'd end up in some city with lover boy."

"*Actually*"—I draw out the word—"apparently, he's planning to stay in Myers, too."

His jaw goes tight. "Well, what do you know? Small world."

"Small world indeed."

Something catches my eyes over his shoulder, and I glance toward the pool table, realizing Clayton is heading our way, with Raven in tow.

"You guys want to join us?" he asks when he arrives.

"We're good," I tell him quickly.

Tucker slides closer to me, turning to look at Clayton. "You know how it is. Gotta keep my girl to myself."

Clayton offers him a smile that's clearly forced. "I don't think we've met. I'm Clayton, Maggie's best friend."

"Tucker. Maggie's boyfriend." They shake hands, currently in a stare down with a small competition of who will release the other's hand first. "Funny, for a *best friend*, Maggie hardly mentions you."

"I'm Raven," she chirps, reaching for Clayton's arm to cut off whatever smart remark he had planned. "Good to see you again, Maggie. I love your hair today. Anyway, we should get back to the game, babe. The guys are waiting. If you change your mind, we'll save you a spot." She beams at me and pulls him away.

Tucker turns to me with a grimace. "What do you see in that guy?"

"What do you mean?"

"I mean, what is it about him that you like?"

"He's...I don't know. He's my best friend. He's smart. He's funny. He knows me better than anyone else in the world. I trust him."

"He hurts you," he says plainly.

"Not on purpose. He can't help it if he doesn't know how I feel. And, even if he did, I wouldn't want him to give up his dreams for me. I mean, who even knows if it would work out? I'm not worth that."

He seems to think over what I've said for a moment. "Okay, let me ask you this: would you have given up your art for him?"

Yes. The answer sits on the tip of my tongue, but I don't dare say it. It would be terrible. Pathetic. "No."

He purses his lips slightly. "For the right person, you don't have to give up anything. You'd find a way to make it work. Which is why he'd never have to give up his music thing to be with you, if it was what he wanted. And you can't convince me he doesn't know how you feel about him. That's what the little thing that just happened was about. He was letting me know he's around. Claiming ownership of you when he has no right to."

My cheeks heat. "He was not."

He inches closer to me. "He was, Maggie. He knows you want him, and maybe he wants you, too, but the problem is that right now he sees you as something he can keep around without having to actually do anything to keep you here. He thinks you're dispensable. A backup plan. He doesn't want to be with you, but he doesn't want anyone else to, either."

I can't help the way my chin droops at his words. Does Clayton really see me that way? Once, I might've argued no, but now, I'm not sure. It's hard to understand his actions lately. The push and pull. Hot and cold.

"I'm no one's backup plan," I say firmly. "That's not what this is. He chose her, and I'm moving on."

"Are you?" He raises a brow. "Because from where I sit, it looks like you're pining."

"I'm not. I came here to avoid him."

"And then when you saw him, you invited me."

"Because I didn't want to look pathetic."

"And yet, you're sitting as close to the wall as you can. You haven't touched me once, aside from the kiss."

"What should I do, then?" I ask with a gasp. "Hang all over you?"

"Yeah," he says with exasperation, like it should be obvious. "If I was out with a girl, and she was acting the way you are right now, I'd have already left."

"Well, aren't you just the sweetest?"

He drains the last of his beer. "Something tells me you didn't pick me for my sweetness, Maggie."

"I didn't *pick* you at all. *You* danced with *me* that night, if memory serves."

"And you texted me tonight. Now, do you want my help or don't you?"

"Yes," I squeak.

"Sorry, what was that?" He puts a finger behind his ear, teasing me. "I didn't hear you."

"Yes," I say, laughing in spite of myself. "Yes, I want your help."

He grins, though his expression turns unreadable, like he's restraining himself, second-guessing his plan. "Excellent. Then I need you to do exactly as I say."

A sharp tugging sensation swims through my core, heating me from the inside out over the look in his eyes. "Okay." I stare up at him with quiet uncertainty.

His eyes grow heavy, darkening. "Tell me to stop if you don't like something I do, okay?"

I nod. He scoots closer to me until my back brushes the wall. With one hand, he drags the hair away from my neck. I watch with wide eyes as he lowers himself toward me, his lips parting.

His mouth brushes the skin of my neck, tasting me, and then I feel his breath on the spot his lips were moments ago. He pulls back for half a second, like he can't breathe suddenly, and then he's back for more. This time, his mouth is possessive over my skin. His tongue traces a line from my collar bone to my ear.

I'm fighting to catch my breath, to calm my heart, but he seems to be working toward the opposite goal. His hand goes to my jaw, holding me in place as he traces the lines of my neck with passionate kisses.

I'm numb and on fire all at once, my body limp.

No one has ever kissed me the way he's kissing me. My entire body reacts to it in a way that has me confused. Without realizing I'm doing it, my hand goes to the back of his head, willing him to stay just where he is.

I feel his smile growing against my skin.

He uses his fingers to turn my face toward his, and our eyes lock. The blues are darker in the smoky, dimly lit bar. More dangerous somehow. He tilts his chin forward, daring me, begging me to give in, and I do.

I lean in, pressing my lips to his.

My heart pounds in my chest, my lungs compressing as I sink into his kiss. He presses in closer to me, and I pull my leg up onto the bench seat so he's in between my thighs, our chests pressed together. He holds both of my cheeks, kissing me like I'm the only oxygen available, and he's a suffocating man.

If this were anyone else, anywhere else, I would be mortified. This is so not like me.

And yet, I can't bring myself to want to stop.

As if he's heard my thoughts, he pulls back just slightly. "Nice work."

The words snap me out of my stupor, and I remember what's happening and why we're doing this. Because of Clayton. To make Clayton jealous.

He drags a thumb over my chin and down my neck, tracing the places his lips were moments ago. A wicked grin grows on his face as his finger goes lower, toward my chest, to the neckline of the v-neck T-shirt I'm wearing. My skin is burning, and I should tell him to stop, but I don't. I can't. He has me paralyzed. Frozen in place.

His eyes are challenging me, asking me where I'll draw the line as his hand goes lower, over my breasts. I tense slightly, but he shakes his head.

"No one can see you."

He's right, I realize, as I look around. No one's paying us any attention except for Clayton, and even he can't see what Tucker's doing to me. Not really. I meet his eyes across the bar, where he's gripping a pool stick so hard it looks as if he might snap it in half.

It's working.

Tucker's hand goes lower, until he's gripping the hem of my shirt. "Get on my lap," he says.

I hesitate.

"Unless you're going to call it quits already."

I scowl, pushing up on the bench and slipping one leg over top of him so I'm straddling his lap. I ease down, feeling the confirmation underneath me that he's as turned on as I am.

He smiles when he realizes I've felt him.

"I thought I wasn't your type," I say firmly.

"You aren't." He brushes hair away from my neck. "But that doesn't mean I'm not a guy."

I lean forward, deriving satisfaction from the feeling of him beneath me, the pained and somehow pleasure-filled expression on his face. I watch his eyes as I lean forward. He's holding his breath, waiting to see what I'll do.

I lower my mouth to his neck, kissing him the way he did me. His hands flex on my thighs as he releases a strangled breath. Underneath me, his length pulses.

"Fuck." That one word is enough to egg me on. I kiss him harder, swirling my tongue across his bare skin. My fingers go to his hair as I press my chest against his.

He's gripping my hips so tightly he might bruise me, but I

can't seem to care. I pull away, trailing my bottom lip up his neck, and bite his earlobe.

He jolts, lifting me off him in an instant. "Okay. That's enough for today."

"Sorry. Did I hurt you?" I ask. My skin is suddenly too hot. *What the hell was I thinking? What came over me?* I attempt to swallow down my humiliation.

"Did you hurt—" He releases an exasperated breath, running a hand over his face. "Jesus Christ, Maggie. You couldn't have hurt me less if you tried. I just...I think we're good. That was enough. Mission accomplished." Scarlet splotches cover his neck and cheeks as he stares at me like I'm some sort of angel or demon, but he can't tell which one. "We should go, yeah? I'll walk you home."

"Oh. Okay. Sure." I drop my head, not sure what is happening or what I did wrong.

"Just"—he breathes, adjusting in his seat and staring intently at his beer bottle like it's about to tell him the meaning of life—"give me a minute."

I nod, waiting several minutes before he finally gets up, then slide from the booth after him. He holds out a hand and laces his fingers with mine as we walk from the bar.

"Sorry about that," he says when it's just us. "I shouldn't have let it go so far. I got carried away."

"It's fine," I say. "Honestly. We were just goofing off."

"Yeah, I just...I didn't mean for it to happen. You don't deserve that shit, Maggie. Making out in some random bar."

"Oh, please." I groan. "I'm not a candlelight-and-roses girl, and something tells me you aren't that guy either. It was fine, and it served its purpose as long as he noticed."

He squeezes my hand, and I realize he's still holding it. I'd nearly forgotten. "Trust me, he did."

I release his hand when my phone vibrates in my pocket, and I pull it out to check. I grin broadly at the name on the screen.

> Be careful going home. I have a new song I want you to listen to. Can I come by your apartment tomorrow morning? Unless you'll be at his place.

"I guess you're right," I say, holding up the phone so Tucker can read the message before I reply to it. "He definitely noticed."

Tucker nods, but he doesn't say much else for the rest of the walk home.

CHAPTER NINE

NOW

This house stinks.

And I don't mean in a *what the hell did I get myself into* sort of way. I mean, it literally stinks. I was in the kitchen earlier, putting a few odds and ends I picked up at the store in the pantry, when I noticed it.

The pantry is old, obviously. It's been closed up, with its pretty floral wallpaper hidden behind two wooden doors. But there's nothing inside that should account for the smell. In fact, the kitchen is probably the cleanest room in the house.

I've sprayed everything down, mopped the floors and scrubbed the countertops, dumped mouse poop out of drawers, but there's nothing. Nothing to explain the scent of decay permeating the house.

It's like nothing I've ever smelled—a strange mixture of wood rot and rotting flesh. An animal must be dead here somewhere, but I'm scared to find it.

A knock at the door interrupts my cleaning, and I drop the sponge into the sink and rinse my hands before hurrying toward the sound. I'm expecting to see Tucker there, arms full of tools, but to my surprise, it's Clayton I find waiting for me.

He smiles sheepishly, holding up the two paper sacks in his hands. "I thought you could use some dinner?"

"Oh." My stomach grumbles at the thought. I've been surviving on snack food and the bagel from Tucker all day. "That sounds perfect, actually." I step back so he can come inside. "I don't have my furniture here, though. So, no table."

"That's okay. We can have dinner on the living room floor like old times." He sets the bags down and grabs the blanket from my air mattress. "Can I use this?"

"Mm-hmm. Sure."

He spreads it out and plops down on top of it, sorting through the food. "I'm sure you're in a bit of a culture shock right now with the lack of options," he teases. "But I brought your favorite. At least, I hope it's still your favorite." He holds up a styrofoam container, flipping open the lid to reveal a delicious-looking lasagna.

"Nonna's?" I gape.

"Where else?" He places it down and pats the space next to him. "Come. Eat. Enjoy."

"Ah, you're the best." I sink down next to him, wafting the scent toward my nose.

"I know." He grins proudly.

"I haven't had Nonna's Kitchen in years. I almost forgot how good it is."

"I assumed you hadn't. I figured it made a good welcome-home meal. I would've taken you there last night, but you were exhausted."

"And filthy," I chime in, reaching for a fork from my bag. "What'd you get?"

He flips his container open, showing me a plate of chicken

parmesan. I always get the same thing wherever I go. I have my favorites, and I stick with them. With Clayton, I'm not sure I've seen him eat the same thing twice.

He grabs a piece of bread from the open container between us and dips it in his sauce, tearing off a bite.

"Sorry about the smell, by the way," I say as it hits my nose again. "I'm trying to figure out what it is."

He lifts his nose, sniffing. "What smell?"

I lower my fork. "You don't smell that?"

"I don't smell anything. Er, well,"—he sniffs again—"cleaner. Lemon, maybe? Is that what you mean?"

"No. I'm talking about the dead-animal smell. You don't have to be nice. There's no way you don't smell it."

He shakes his head, expression serious. "I don't smell anything, Maggs. Honest. Do you think something died in here?"

"I don't know. I didn't smell it until today. I'm thinking it's because I turned the heat on earlier when it got cold in here. It's the worst in the kitchen, but I can't figure out where it's coming from."

"Want me to check it out?"

"It's fine," I assure him. "Really. I'll be okay. Let's just eat. This is delicious."

He takes another bite, looking around. "What color are you going to paint this room?"

I hesitate. "You'll think it's silly."

"Try me."

Glancing up at the wall, I think over the plans I've been concocting. "Well, I'd love to do a white background with a blue floral pattern all over the place. Or maybe some metallic gold with blue-and-pink trees right here." I point to the wall to our right. "Or maybe just a sage green with a really detailed accent wall around the fireplace. I don't know. I've thought about a few different options."

He stares at me as if waiting for the rest of the joke.

"I told you it was silly." I glance down, tucking a piece of hair behind my ear.

Running a hand over his mouth, he sighs. "It's your house. Why should it matter what I think? Or anyone else, for that matter?"

"I know, but I don't want it to feel kiddish."

His lips pull up into a wry grin. "So you're saying you've gone and grown up on me?"

I draw in one corner of my mouth playfully. "I'm afraid I have."

He takes another bite of bread, dripping sauce down his chin, and uses a napkin to wipe it up. "Good to know. And, for the record, gray or tan are always safe bets. And totally not *kiddish*." He winks. "I can show you some of the colors I had them use on my house if you want. Did I tell you I just had it repainted?"

"You did." I stand, dusting my hands on the back of my shorts. "I'm going to get a drink. Do you want anything?"

"Whatcha got?"

"Dr Pepper or gin," I say, walking to the kitchen and pulling open the fridge. Perhaps it's just the Italian food permeating my lungs, but for some reason, I can no longer smell the stench.

"Uh, gin is good."

I pull out two plastic cups, fill them with ice, and pour our drinks. "Sorry, I don't have any fancy way to serve them," I tell him when I return. "Or a mixer."

He taps his cup against mine as I sit down. "Wouldn't have it any other way."

I take a sip, the familiar burn cascading down my throat. "So, what's new with you? What have you been up to lately? Any new songs?"

He shakes his head and takes a drink. "Not really. I went to Nashville a few weeks ago to co-write some songs for other artists. I'm headed back there in a few days. But I'm still not making a ton of progress on my own stuff."

"That's okay, though, right? You told me you prefer writing for other people anyway."

He takes another drink, sighing. "I guess so. It's still my favorite thing. I'd just hoped to have made more progress on my third album by now. I feel like no one's expecting it to happen."

"So make it happen yourself. Shock them all."

He smiles, but it's sad.

"Do you regret leaving?" I ask, surprising even myself with the question. It's not one I've been brave enough to ask up until this point. "Not going back?"

"Sometimes," he admits, scooting back to lean against the wall as he rubs his belly. "I mean, it was the right thing to do at the time. I didn't love Nashville. I missed home. But I know it hurt my career. As much as they promised me it wouldn't, it did. And now, I'm basically a one-hit wonder."

"That's not true," I insist. "You had a great debut album, and you got to tour for your second."

"As an opener. I wasn't the headliner."

"Well, you will be with your third album. I know it." I beam at him.

"I doubt it. I'm getting too old for any of that now," he whispers, looking down.

"Too old? No." I blow a raspberry. "If you're too old, I'm too old, and that's just not even fair."

"I'm a whole year older than you. Make the most of the last of your prime." He winks.

"Shut up." I toss a napkin at him. "You are not too old to tour, if you still want to. Thirty-six is the new twenty."

"Yeah, maybe. To be honest, I'd be happy with at least one more album, even if it means no more touring. I like my quiet life, but I still have songs in me. Songs *I* want to sing." When he looks back up, the sadness that was present before is hidden well. "Anyway, what about you? Why did you decide to move back? You never really said."

"Well, first, because of Mom. I guess I wanted to feel closer to her, in a way. She always wanted me to move home." I pause, collecting myself so I don't cry. He waits patiently, watching me. "And I'd just lost my job."

"I'm sorry." He sits up straighter.

"It's fine. I didn't like it all that much anyway, and it wasn't personal. They downsized the entire HR department. We knew it was coming." I suck in a breath, trying to decide if I want any more to eat. "I got a nice severance package, and it gives me time to work on my paintings some, which have actually been selling, so that's cool. And then, Nick and I broke up. Well, we broke up before she passed." I take one last bite for good measure, then close the lid.

"I assumed." He nods. "When he didn't come with you to the funeral. Or here. But I didn't want to ask."

"Yeah. So, there was all of that, and then, when I got my inheritance—I mean, it wasn't much, but it was enough to buy something here. And I'd always loved this house. It just reminds me of a storybook. I mean, I know it's going to take a lot of work, but I had enough to buy it outright and still have a bit left over to do some work on it." I look up and around. "It just felt like the right thing to do. And, it didn't hurt that this was the only house I could afford to buy outright that had a roof, floor, and all four walls."

He chuckles. "Yeah, I mean, it does need a lot of work, but even Garrett said they were offering it for a steal."

"Yeah. I thought so. And we talked them down quite a bit, too. He was a lifesaver throughout the process."

"I'm glad. He's good at what he does." He pauses, moving his fork around his food a little more, though he's no longer eating either. "So, should I ask what happened with you and Nick?"

"Nothing happened, really. We just grew apart. I mean, we'd been together for five years, and whenever I wanted to talk about the next steps, like getting married or buying a place, not just renting...he was just never ready. Eventually, I got tired of waiting."

"Would you have married him?"

The weight of the question sits firmly on my shoulders. I can't bear to look at him when I answer, the ghosts of our past circling the room. "I think so. I mean, you don't spend five years with someone without at least considering it."

He nods, lying down on his side, his head propped up on his palm. "Well, I'm sorry it didn't work out."

"Thanks. What about you?"

"Me?"

"Are you dating anyone right now?"

"Nah." He runs a finger across the rim of his cup. "I've dated here and there, but never anything serious." He shrugs. "Maybe I'm just meant to stay single."

I study him, my chest tight.

He opens his mouth, inhaling. "Hey, do you ever think about what might've happened if...you know, if I hadn't left back then?"

"Sometimes," I admit. "Not so much anymore."

"Yeah." He nods. "I should've apologized to you for leaving the way I did, though. It wasn't cool."

"You didn't have a choice," I tell him. "It was your dream. I wanted you to go."

"Yeah, but was it worth it?"

I'm not sure if he's asking me or himself.

"I mean," he goes on, "it amounted to nothing, really."

"Don't be so hard on yourself. Even if everything you've already done is all that ever happens for you—*and it won't be*—you were still able to do what you love. To make money doing what you love. Your parents got to see you live that dream." Again, my voice chokes. My parents will never get to see me live mine, and that stings. It will never *not* sting because it will always be true. No matter what I succeed at in my future, my parents will only know the person I was before. "It was what you wanted at the time. Don't doubt it now. The past is the past. You can't change it, and you shouldn't want to."

Now, maybe I'm talking to myself. About all my regrets and second guesses. He picks at a loose thread on the blanket, rolling it around under his fingers. "What do you think about him living next door?"

I almost don't understand what he's asking, it's so off topic. "Tucker?"

"Yeah." He looks up to meet my eyes.

I shrug one shoulder. "I don't know. Like I said, the past is in the past."

"I guess I always assumed when you left, it was because of him."

"It doesn't matter anymore."

He nods. "Right. Whatever happened to the two of you, anyway?"

"We just fell apart," I say simply, my belly as hollow as if I hadn't just eaten an entire meal. I stand, clearing the dinner and taking the bags to the kitchen to avoid the subject that still haunts me.

I can't talk about that night or what happened or anything else. I can't ever tell Clayton the full truth, and that kills me. I have no reason to want to protect Tucker, and yet, I do.

When I hear footsteps behind me, I spin around. Clayton is standing there, a haunted look on his face.

"What is it? What's wrong?"

His eyes dance between mine, and he opens his mouth like he's planning to say something.

I step forward. "Are you okay?"

"No," he says, his voice dry. "*Yes*. I don't know." He lifts his hand to cup my jaw. "I'm just so glad you're back." Without warning, he leans forward, pressing his lips to mine.

It takes me several seconds to understand what's happening. *This is it.* Everything I spent so many years waiting for. Hoping for. Dreaming of. Everything I wanted so badly all those years ago. He sets his cup on the counter so both of his hands can hold my face, deepening our kiss.

I close my eyes, exhaling. My heart pounds in my ears.

He pulls away, staring at me as if he just caught himself by surprise, too.

My fingers go to my lips. "What was that?"

He swallows, face pale. "Something I think I should've done a long time ago."

CHAPTER TEN

THEN

"Okay, okay, here it goes." Clayton picks up his guitar from where he's sitting on my bed and strums a few chords. The moment I hear the first sounds of it, I'm taken back to the summer when we were ten, and he'd just gotten his first guitar.

He was terrible, at first—and for many years after, if I'm being honest— but eventually it clicked. Eventually, the hesitant, clunky player became a musician. And the musician became an artist.

He was always playing me new songs he'd written or new riffs he'd come up with. His dream came to life when his parents bought him a professional video camera, so he could start uploading his music to YouTube. Of course, devastatingly handsome as he is and with a voice like butter, it wasn't long before he took off.

And, well, the rest led to this moment right here. Him playing me a song meant to be added to a future album. Him becoming a superstar before my very eyes.

His voice is smoother now, less breathy, less raw. He's practiced. The lessons he's been taking have paid off. I close my eyes and listen, drifting off to the smooth sound of the song about a girl who got away.

Most of his songs are about love, which sells albums, I guess, but I can't help wondering if he feels the things he's singing about Raven. I picture them together on a couch, writing words, looking into each other's eyes, singing beautiful melodies.

How could he not fall in love with her?

How could she not fall in love with him?

I never stood a chance.

When he stops playing, his eyes lift to meet mine, his hands still on the guitar as he waits for my reaction. "Well? What do you think?"

"It's beautiful," I say. "Really. One of your best."

"Yeah?" He beams.

"Mm-hmm."

"It's the first one I've written on my own in a while, so it feels...I don't know, more scary, I guess. I haven't played it for anyone at the label."

"Why not?"

"I don't know. I mean, usually when they pick stuff apart, it's a team effort. And in the beginning, all the songs that were just mine were new, and I was just starting, so I could use all the insults and just take them back and work on getting better. But now they expect me to be good already, so what if they hate this?" He slides the guitar over off his lap and places it down. "Sometimes I guess I just miss the old days. When it was still all for fun. When I could just write a song and play it for you and count on the fact that you'd never tell me I should just hire professional songwriters for everything or that this song won't fit my brand. Sometimes I just want to write a song for me, you know? Not because it's what people expect from me."

"I get that."

"I used to have fun with this before there was a brand involved. Before other people's jobs were on the line, too. Before one mess up might cost me everything."

"You're fine, Clayton. I promise. The fans who matter will still be around, bad song or not, and this is *not* a bad song."

"You're not just saying that?"

"I wouldn't lie to you. How does Raven feel about it?"

He looks out the window, squinting as if he's staring at something. "I haven't played it for her yet."

The admission shocks me. "Why not?"

"I, um, well, it's not about her." His eyes find mine again.

Something cold drips through me. I'm almost afraid to ask. "Who's it about?"

He's quiet for a moment, just staring at me. Then, he says, "I don't know. No one. I guess. It's just...a song."

I deflate. "Oh. Right."

"It feels personal, though," he says softly. "Like a song that means something to me."

"Yeah, it sounds that way."

He runs a hand over the back of his neck, his cheeks flushing pink. "Listen, Maggie, before I left..."

"Yeah?" I prompt when he doesn't say more.

"Before I left, was there something you wanted to talk to me about? That night at the bar?"

I press my lips together. We both know what he's trying to ask, what he's trying to say, but I won't be the one to do it. I tried that night, but now he has a girlfriend. A fiancée. I tried, and he chose someone else. If he wants to change that, it's on him.

"It doesn't matter anymore. It was a long time ago."

"Right." He picks up the guitar again, strumming it a few

more times. "I just...I guess I just, ever since I've been home, I can't stop thinking that maybe I'm making a mistake."

I freeze. My heartbeat is loud in the back of my head. "A mistake?"

"Yeah."

"With the song?" I feign ignorance.

Say it.

Say it, Clayton.

All you have to do is say it, and I'm yours.

"Um... No. With..." He sighs. "Look, what do you think of Raven?"

I brush imaginary dust from my leg, breaking eye contact. "I don't really know her."

He nods. Looks down.

"But you love her, right?"

He looks back up and gives a sleepy bob of his head. "She's great."

He's not going to say it. He wants me to, and I can't. I can't put myself out there again. I take a deep breath, slapping my thighs. "You should play her the song, then." I stand.

"What?"

"You should play her the song. You love her, and she's great, and you're marrying her, and you should play her the song."

"You think?" He's slow to stand.

"Yes."

"Are you okay?"

"Fine. Great. Perfect, actually. I'm supposed to be meeting Tucker in a few minutes, though, so you should go."

"Right." He walks past me, casting a look over his shoulder. He could stop at any time. Stop and say the words. Stop and grab me. Tell me he loves me. Kiss me. But he doesn't. "I guess I'll see you around, then."

"Guess so."

With that, he disappears from my bedroom, and a few moments later, I hear the door shut.

Tears burn my eyes, but I refuse to give in to them. I'm not going to cry. I'm going to go and have fun. When I think of fun, only one person's face pops into my brain.

I don't allow myself to overanalyze it.

Instead, I pull out my phone and send a text.

> Where are you?

> In bed like a normal person

> Do you want to hang out?

> In bed? Absolutely, I do.

I roll my eyes.

> Out of bed.

> Less fun, but sure. Where?

> I'll come to you. Send me the address.

As soon as I send the message, I realize that may have been too forward. Maybe he doesn't want me to know where he lives. Maybe that's too personal. I start to send a quick message to take back the request or offer another option, but his reply reaches me first.

> 24 Blake Court, Apartment 3G. Just let yourself in. Try not to be too impressed.

I scoff.

> I'll do what I can to contain myself.

I change into a pair of jeans and a better shirt, running a brush through my hair before hurrying out the door. Tucker's apartment is only fifteen minutes away from me according to my phone's GPS, but I walk slowly, trying not to seem too eager.

As I go, I think over everything that happened with Clayton. Why does he insist on treating me this way? Was Tucker right that he sees me as a backup plan? Sometimes, I don't believe it. I know he cares about me, and I can see in his eyes that he feels something more than he once did, but why can't he admit it? Why is it so hard for him to just tell me that he likes me but so easy to propose marriage to someone else?

I guess that's what stings the most. Knowing that she's someone he just met, and he found it easier to tell her how he feels than me, the person he's known his whole life.

When I reach the address Tucker gave me, I stare at the small, brick apartment building. It's on the third floor, so I have to take the stairs, which clang and groan with every step.

When I reach his door, I'm out of breath and sweating. Perfect.

I knock on the door, and for several minutes, I worry he's given me the wrong address. I step back, reading it again, then move to the railing to look out over the street. *This is building G, isn't it?*

I'm vacillating between knocking again or turning around

and walking back down the stairs when the door swings open, and he stands in front of me, hair wild, gray T-shirt clinging to his chest.

He narrows his eyes, brushing his hair out of his face—trying to, anyway. "Sorry, ma'am, I didn't order anything."

"Shut up," I groan.

He chuckles. "I told you to let yourself inside. I don't ever lock the door." Backing up, he waves a hand around as if giving me a grand tour of the open-concept living room and kitchen. The apartment is small but clean. It smells of air freshener, which makes me grin, picturing him running around cleaning up as I headed over.

"Well, that sounds super safe."

"Eh, small-town habit I still haven't broken."

"Nice place."

"Thanks. Uh, do you want something to drink or..."

"I'm okay." I shake my head, sitting down on the arm of his couch. "Sorry to burst in on you like this—"

"You're fine."

"I know I woke you up."

"I was awake. Just not out of bed yet."

"Right. Well, I just thought we could hang out."

"Like...another fake date?" he asks, staring at me from where he stands across the room near the kitchen peninsula.

"Um, yeah. I guess. But, well, Clayton won't be there, so not really."

"So, a real date?"

Well, now I feel pathetic. "Or just friends hanging out?" I offer, shrugging a shoulder.

He stares around. "Yeah, okay. I just need to change." He gestures toward the ball shorts he's wearing. "What did you have in mind?"

"Lunch, maybe? It's too early, really, but too late for breakfast."

"You know they have a word for that, don't you?"

I giggle. "I can hardly picture you at a brunch place."

"I like bottomless mimosas as much as the next guy." He leans back against the counter. "I figured you'd invite lover boy instead. Did, uh, he stop by this morning?"

I'm surprised he remembered Clayton was supposed to come over. He'd seemed distracted last night when he dropped me off. "Yeah." I look down, not wanting to get into it. "It wasn't a great visit."

"Meaning?"

"Meaning he sort of hinted that he has feelings for me but wouldn't actually come out with it."

"Explain." His eyes go serious.

"He played me this song he wrote about a girl who he loved but missed his chance with, and, well, it wasn't obviously about me or anything. But...he said it wasn't about Raven, so I thought maybe... But, you know, songs are just stories. They can be about anything. And, anyway, then he started talking about the night he left and how he thought I was trying to tell him something—"

Tucker scoffs. "Like he doesn't know what you were trying to tell him."

"Right. Anyway, he tried to get me to tell him now, but I wouldn't. Because, like, if he's going to do this while he has a fiancée, then it should be him who admits how he feels about me. Not the other way around. I'm not a homewrecker. I tried to tell him how I felt before he left. I put myself out there, and it didn't work. So, I had to let him go. Now it's his turn. If he wants something to happen between us, he has to make that move. Not me. But he wouldn't. He said some stuff about wondering if he got it wrong with Raven, but that was it, really. I don't know. We just ended the conversation in a weird place."

"And then what? He just left?"

I nod. "Am I wrong? Should I have said something to him? Admitted how I feel?"

He shakes his head. "No. Look, you didn't do anything wrong. The guy's clearly an idiot, and I stand by what I said before. He's stringing you along because he can. The best thing you can do right now is distance yourself. Let him know this isn't going to work. He's taking advantage of you, Maggie."

"I know. I didn't see it before, but I do now. I just don't know what to do about it." I look down, running the toe of my shoe across his carpet. Looking at it closely, I realize there are vacuum lines there. "Am I totally pathetic?"

"No," he says quickly. "Maybe." He laughs. "We all are, a little bit."

"Gee, thanks."

He runs a hand through his hair. "The point is, you're pining over him. We all do stupid things when we're in love. We just have to keep you distracted until you realize you don't actually want to be with someone like that."

"Someone like what?"

"Someone who treats you the way he does. Who leads you on when there's no future. Leaves you here instead of asking you to come with him. Someone who will make you believe he cares about you while not avoiding hurting you."

He's not wrong, as much as it stings. "Yeah, maybe."

"Anyway, let me go change, and then we'll find something to do." He disappears down the hall and returns a few minutes later wearing a loose flannel over a T-shirt and jeans. The backward ball cap has made another appearance.

"What about you?" I ask, when he rounds the corner. "Why aren't you dating anyone?"

"I told you, I'm not really into dating. I've never been very good at it."

"I beg to differ," I argue as he holds the door open for me. We start to walk away, but I stop. "Wait. Lock your door."

"Okay, *Mom*." He spins around with a shake of his head and a playful glance over his shoulder, turning the key in the lock. "Better?"

"Much."

The skin around his eyes wrinkles as he studies me. Then, he slides his hand into mine, lacing our fingers together and lifting them to his lips. He presses a kiss to my knuckles.

Warmth spreads to my cheeks and I try to hide it with a joke. "You've sure got some smooth moves for someone who's never been very good at dating."

"Well, maybe it's never been this easy." He lowers our hands and bumps my shoulder with his. I smile to myself. "Probably because it's not real."

I'm slammed back to Earth. "Right."

He smiles nonchalantly, leading me down the stairs, and I have to wonder... *If it's not real, why is it starting to not feel so fake?*

CHAPTER ELEVEN

NOW

"I should've kissed you when I had the chance at Allen's party. And then that night in the bar before I found out about the record deal..." Clayton sighs, running a hand through his hair. "I knew why you were there. I knew what you were planning to talk to me about."

I've figured as much over the years, but it feels good to hear him say it. "You never told me that."

"I was scared, Maggs. I was terrified of what would happen if any of this ever became real. You're my best friend. I love you, and not just in that way. I love you in a way that when you're mad at me, it feels like I can't breathe. I love you in a way that when you left, it felt like my world fell apart."

"And how do you think it felt when you left?" I cry, sounding angrier than I meant to.

"You... You told me to go." His face goes slack. "If you'd told me to stay—"

"What? What would you have done if I'd told you to stay, Clayton? Left anyway? Hated me for asking you to make that choice? Or if you actually had stayed, then what? You'd resent me for it after a year or two. Always wonder what if. And what kind of person would I be if I could be okay with that? If I could ask you to give up your dream?"

"It was just bad timing. That's it. Everything happened so fast, and I didn't have time to catch my breath. I never meant to hurt you."

"I know that," I tell him, patting his chest and stepping farther away. "I know. And I wanted you to get everything you ever wanted. I did. I *do*. But you could've asked me to go with you. Why didn't you?"

"Because…" He shakes his head. "You were still in school. I was getting ready to graduate, but you didn't graduate for another year. I couldn't ask you to walk away. Your parents would've killed me. *My* parents would've killed me."

"There were other options, though. I could've taken classes online. I could've transferred. You didn't even try." My voice breaks with pain as I say the words, not from tears, but from anger. I've been so furious with him all these years, but I was never able to let it out.

"I'm sorry. I didn't know you wanted me to."

I want to bring up Raven, but it's unfair. No need to punish him further, to make him go through that loss again.

"Of course I wanted you to," I admit. "God, I wanted you to, so badly. But you didn't. And we both had to live with what that meant."

"If I'd known…"

"But you did know, Clayton. You did. You just admitted it. You weren't willing to go out on a limb for us then. I was disposable to you. A backup plan if everything else didn't work out."

"That's not true."

"It was. I felt it when you came back. You used me. Strung me along."

"You were with him," he cries, waving a hand in the direction of Tucker's house, a reminder that all the lies from that time still haven't been exposed.

"I know." I wave a hand in the air. "I know. None of this matters anymore. What happened happened, and we can't change it. We can't go back and fix any of it." I glance at the clock on the stove. "Look, it's late. I don't want to fight with you."

"I don't either." He stands in place, waiting for me to say more. So much has changed, and yet, so much hasn't.

"You should go home for tonight. We can talk about all of this tomorrow. I'm exhausted."

"Do you want me to stay over? We don't have to...I mean, nothing has to happen. I could just...just stay."

Fourteen years ago, that offer would've made me melt. Today, it just makes me more tired. "It's okay. I only have the twin air mattress. And we really should have clear heads—both of us—before we decide to unpack everything that just happened." I step forward, hugging him carefully. "Thank you for dinner, though."

"Okay," he says, looking a bit lost. "Sure. Yeah. I'll just go."

As I walk him to the door, I start second-guessing myself, remembering the noises from last night. The flickering lights.

"You okay?" he asks when we reach the door, and I realize he thinks I'm having doubts about us. About asking him to leave.

"I'm fine. I just...I heard some weird noises last night. I was thinking about that for some reason. But I have to learn to stay here alone."

"Noises?" He searches the room with his eyes. "What do you mean? Was someone here?"

"I don't think so. It's an old house. It just sort of freaked me out."

"You sure you don't want me to stay?" he offers again. "I promise to keep my hands—and lips—to myself." He gives me a devilish grin that says he'll do anything but.

"I'll be okay."

"You know…" He stares around the room again. "I'll check with Garrett. He might know more, but I think there used to be rumors this place was haunted."

"Don't tell me that," I shriek, chills lining my skin.

"I'm not kidding." When he looks at me, I believe him. "I'd kind of forgotten until you said that, but I think something happened here a long time ago. I can't remember what. He didn't mention it to you when you bought it?"

"No."

"Hmm." He clicks his tongue. "I could be remembering the wrong house."

"Probably are." It feels as though a golf ball has lodged its way into my throat, refusing to be swallowed down.

"Well, the offer stands for me to stay if you change your mind. Or you can come stay at my place, until your stuff is here."

"Thanks, but no. I should stay. It's my house. I'll have to learn to love it, ghosts and all." I laugh but feel the pure terror still radiating in my veins.

"Call if you need anything then. Any time."

"Will do."

He looks as if he may kiss me again. Like now that he's done it once, it might become a regular thing, and I'm surprised that I don't know how to feel about that. I'll know more in the morning. Tonight, I really am exhausted.

"See you tomorrow." He settles on a weird sort of salute, then heads across the porch and down the stairs. I watch him go, moths and crane flies swarming the dim porch light.

From where I stand, I can see the light on in Tucker's house. He'd said he would come by tonight, but I guess something changed his mind.

Seeing Clayton's Jeep in the drive probably did it.

Back inside, my phone is vibrating on the kitchen counter. I check it, realizing I have four missed calls.

When I spot the name, I groan.

Nick has been calling me a few times a day over the last few weeks. I wonder when he'll start to get the hint that I'm not planning to answer. We haven't spoken since the breakup unless it involved splitting the last of the bills or coordinating schedules so I could get the remainder of my things from our townhome.

I carry the phone into the living room and place it on charge, telling myself I'll worry about it in the morning.

From there, I open my suitcase and dig out my pajamas, heading into the kitchen where there are no open windows so I can undress. I make a mental note to get the curtains hung on the windows tomorrow, so I have a bit of privacy.

After I've changed into my pajamas, I brush my teeth in the small bathroom, studying myself in the tiny mirror, as Clayton's words come back to me. Could something bad have really happened here?

Don't realtors have to disclose that sort of thing to you?

Maybe that's just a myth. The memory of the putrid smell from earlier makes my stomach churn.

No. No. We're not going to go there.

I'm fine. Everything's fine.

I rinse my mouth and return to the kitchen, spotting the bags from dinner still sitting on the counter. The smell from earlier may be gone, but I have no desire to add to it, so I grab the bags, shove them into the trash can, and tie the garbage up, carrying it across the house and out the front door.

When I pull it open and spot the figure climbing my steps, I jolt, nearly dropping the bag of trash.

"Jesus Christ!"

"It's me," he says, hands up in the air. His blond hair hangs loose down to his chin, wild and charming all at once.

"What the hell are you doing here?"

"You weren't answering my calls."

"So you drove two hours to come find me, Nick? How did you even know where I was?"

"I spoke with Elle. She said you'd bought a house?" He says it as if it's the ultimate betrayal. "That you're moving back home? Why didn't you tell me?"

"Why would I have?" As soon as he leaves, I'm texting my best friend to end our so-called friendship. What the hell was she thinking? "Why are you here?"

"I mean, I know we took a break, but come on, five years doesn't just go away, Maggie." His olive-green eyes search mine. "You can't be serious about this."

"We didn't take a break. We broke up. I don't owe you any other explanation. It's done, Nick. Over. I'm here. I bought this place. I'm starting over."

"But...I love you."

I stare at him. I hardly recognize this man anymore. How could I have ever thought he was the one for me? Tears prick my eyes. "You didn't come to my mom's funeral," I sob, clutching a hand to my chest. "I told you about it, and you didn't show. That was enough for me to realize I don't want this anymore."

"I'm sorry about that, okay? Things were still weird between us, and you know how hard it is for me to get time off of work right now. I miss you. I want to fix this."

"It can't be fixed."

He licks his lips, shaking his head. "Is that really what you think?"

"It's what I know. Look, I don't have time for this. I'm exhausted. It's been a...weird day. You should go."

"Go where? There are no hotels within an hour of here. Come on." He reaches for me, giving a sly look. "I just drove all day."

"That's not my fault. What was your plan? You thought you'd just show up, and I'd fall back into your arms?"

He shrugs. "It's worked before."

All around us, the night is dark and silent. So different from the city. The light pollution can't reach me here. Aside from the lights at Tucker's house, it's as if the rest of the world has disappeared. Sometimes, that's what's so appealing about this town. About the space and distance it provides. "Would you move here, if I asked you?"

He narrows his eyes and looks up at the house. "What? *No.* I have a life in Iowa City." He grabs my hands. "*We* have a life in Iowa City."

It's the answer I was expecting and, to my surprise, it doesn't hurt all that bad. I think I've known I was done with Nick for a long time now. I chose safety and complacency over happiness.

"I have a life here now. I'm sorry."

"So that's it, then? Really?"

I just stare at him as if to say it's obvious.

"Well"—he looks behind him—"can I at least stay here for the night? I can't drive another hour to find a hotel. My knee is killing me. I'll sleep on the couch."

"I don't have a couch right now. I have a floor."

He sighs, scratching his head. "I guess I'll take that, then."

"Fine," I say. "If that's what you want."

"What I want is for you to get in the car with me right now and come back home."

"But your knee is killing you," I remind him, opening the door. "Come on."

Despite everything, I have no real ill will toward Nick. We just didn't work out. We weren't right for each other, but aside from his commitment issues, he treated me well. *Well enough.* He never cheated. Rarely fought with me. He was apathetic, sure, but never cruel. If he wants to sleep on the floor tonight, I won't stop him.

We settle into our sleeping spots—me on the air mattress and him on an extra blanket on the floor—and I lie on my back, staring at the water spot above my head again.

"So, why'd you move back? To get away from me?" he asks, his voice low. Sleepy. It's one I've heard many times.

"I just needed a change, I guess."

"That's what you told me when you moved there." I can hear the smile in his voice. The remembering. It would be so easy to get back with him. To slide into old habits.

Easy, but not happy.

Comfortable, but not right.

"It was true then, too."

"Wha—"

A knock on the door interrupts his sentence, and I roll over, staring at the window next to the door. It's covered with the bi-fold blinds, so I can't see whoever might be out there.

For once, I'm grateful Nick is here.

"Expecting someone?" he asks.

"Not really."

I step over him on the way to the door and pull it open. A tired-looking Tucker stands on the porch wearing a serious expression.

"Tucker?"

"You okay?"

"Um, yeah. Why wouldn't I be?"

"There's a weird car in your..." He trails off, his gaze landing somewhere behind me. I feel Nick's presence there. "Oh. Sorry. Didn't realize you had company."

"I'm Nick. The boyfriend," he says.

"*Ex*-boyfriend," I point out firmly, then step outside and shut the door behind me.

"I didn't mean to interrupt anything," Tucker says, already starting to walk away.

"You didn't," I tell him. "Nick showed up unexpectedly. He's staying because it's late, and there are no hotels in town." I don't know why I'm explaining this to him. I don't owe him anything.

"It's fine," he says, waving a hand at me. Clearly, it's not. "I just saw the car before I went to bed and wanted to make sure you were okay."

"Tucker, wait—"

"I don't..." He sighs, turning around with a bitter smile on his lips. He shakes his head slowly. "I don't want to do this with you again, Maggie. I can't. It's too much déjà vu for me." He throws his hands up. "Just...forget I stopped by. Have a good night."

With that, he jogs off the porch and disappears into the darkness.

CHAPTER TWELVE

THEN

Plans tonight?

When the text from Tucker comes in, my face heats.

"What's that?" Kassara asks, leaning across the table to be nosy. I pretend to pull the phone back but eventually give in and let her see.

"Oooh." She dips a fry into her ranch, then pops the whole thing in her mouth. "And what are you going to tell him?"

"That I'm out with you," I say, raising my brows. "Obviously."

"No way. You're going to turn down a night with your boy toy for me?" She clutches her hands at her chest, batting her eyelashes.

"Duh. I'm not blowing you off."

"Well, in that case"—she shoves two more fries in her mouth before dusting her hands—"I'm blowing *you* off. I need to finish the audiobook I've been listening to anyway." She waves a hand at me. "Text him, and tell him you're free."

"I thought we were going to see *Shutter Island*?"

"We can see it another time." She takes a sip of her soda and leans forward. "Listen, I love you. And I always want to spend time with you, but I haven't seen you smile the way he makes you smile in over a year. So, I say embrace it. Even if you have to *pretend* it's fake." She rolls her eyes, her to-die-for lashes brushing her brows.

Kassara's the only one I've told the truth to about Tucker and me. Not that anyone else cares enough to ask.

"We aren't pretending. It *is* fake."

She purses her lips, tapping a finger in the air. "The blush on those cheeks ain't fake."

I stick out my tongue. "Whatever."

"I'm just saying, it's good that he's here, you know? Whatever it is, he makes you happy. I'm happy for you." She winks. "And I have a murder mystery to solve, so if you'll excuse me." She stands, grabbing her purse and trash and blowing me a kiss before she saunters away.

I shake my head at her, relieved to be able to see Tucker—though that only makes me feel more confused.

> They just freed up, actually. What'd you have in mind?

> I'll tell you when I get there. You home?

> I'm at Little Lionel's.

> Be there in 10.

When he arrives, I've thrown away the last of my food and am sitting on a barstool near the door waiting for him.

"Where are we going?" I ask, staring at the bag slung over his shoulder. "And why are you being ominous about it?"

"I'm not being ominous, I'm being strategic."

"Strategic?" I stare at him as he wraps his free arm around my shoulders and ushers me out the door.

"Right, because I'm assuming if I told you where we were going before I got here, you'd say no."

"So, you're kidnapping me?" I ask with a laugh.

"Maybe. You into that?"

"Definitely not. And what's in there anyway?" I ask, gesturing toward the bag.

"Wouldn't you like to know?" It's his turn to laugh, and when he does, his chin tilts up to the sky, his whole body vibrating with deep, rumbling laughter. I love his laugh. Love the way it seems to fill me with warmth.

"I would, actually."

"Okay, fine. I'm not kidnapping you, you'll be relieved to know, but what we're going to do might not be your ideal version of a date night. I...I kind of need you to go with me to my study group."

"What?" I furrow my brow.

"Yeah." He uses a finger to smooth my forehead. "Don't look so shocked. I *do* study. A lot actually. I'm in a group for my ethics class, and the professor is...interesting."

"Who is it?" I wonder if I know them.

"Professor Eden. She actually leads the study group."

"Oh wow. Is it that tough?"

"Uh, she's a little *hands-on.*"

Something about the way he says it makes me side-eye him. His wry grin tells me all I need to know.

"She's hooking up with students?"

"Some." He shrugs. "Mostly the guys."

"And have you..." I swallow, my throat abrasively dry.

He pauses before answering, and I get the distinct feeling

he's enjoying my discomfort. "No," he says finally. "I'm not into that. I wouldn't even be in the group if I had a choice, but I actually need a good grade to graduate. It's the one course I'm struggling with. I mean, who knew ethics could be so hard? But, anyway, since I've turned her down, she's gotten kind of brazen."

"Meaning what?" The idea of a professor hitting on him, of anyone hitting on him, makes my skin itch.

"Meaning I think it'll be better if you're there with me." He glances at me out of the corner of his eye. "So you can protect me. If she sees I have a girlfriend, maybe she'll finally get the hint and back off."

Girlfriend. My stomach flips. The way that word feels in my chest isn't normal. He shouldn't be looking at me that way, shouldn't be saying these things. Especially when I know this is all pretend for him.

"So, you're using me?"

"I thought we could make the terms of our arrangement mutually beneficial." He smirks with one corner of his mouth. "If that's okay with you?"

"Fine," I say with a groan, but we both know I'm joking. He slides his hand down my arm, taking my hand in his palm, as we make our way across the quad and to the campus library.

Inside, we take our seats at the long, wooden table where a group of students have already gathered.

"Sup, Tuck," says one of the guys seated near the end of the table. He holds out a hand, and Tucker slaps it.

"Sneebly."

There are two girls closest to us who smile warmly at me. One gives a small wave, her elbow never leaving the table. "I'm Jess."

"Carrie."

"Hi. I'm Maggie."

Tucker grips my thigh gently, offering a reassuring smile. "This is Sneebly, Carter, and Ty." He gestures to the three remaining guys, and then to the one next to me. "And Aaron. You probably recognize him from the bar."

Now that he mentions it, I do recognize him as the other bartender usually working with Tucker.

"Hi," I say again, awkwardly.

"This is my girl," Tucker says, scooting his chair closer to me.

My stomach flips, my cheeks warming, but I have little time to dwell on the way the title makes me feel or the flames lapping at my belly over the look in his eyes as he says it, because at that exact moment, a woman walks into the room.

"Hello," she sings, crossing the space quickly. When she does, Tucker takes my hand, lacing his fingers with mine on the tabletop.

I study the woman. She's beautiful, with long, dark, wavy hair, a navy pencil skirt, and a red blouse to match her painted lips. She stops at the head of the table, taking a deep breath as she looks us over.

"Sorry I'm late, guys. Everyone here?" Her gaze rakes over the table, but stops when it lands on me. It shifts to Tucker's hand holding mine, then back. "Hello. I'm Eve. I don't think we've met."

"Your name is Eve Eden?" I ask, the question slipping out before I realize I've said it. Tucker's thumb smooths over my knuckles, and I hear him laugh under his breath.

To my relief, she giggles. It's obviously not the first time she's been asked. "My parents were very religious."

"Doesn't studying ethics tend to challenge religion?"

She nods again. "Precisely why I said *my parents* are religious." She looks around the room. "I'm sorry. Are you taking this class?"

"She's with me," Tucker says, his thumb tracing circles across my skin.

Eve's gaze falters. "Oh? I didn't realize this was what qualifies as a hot date."

I lean forward, touching his arm with my free hand. "We have plans after. It was just easier for me to come. I hope you don't mind."

"Not at all." She smiles, but it's venomous. She absolutely does mind, and I get a certain thrill out of knowing it. No wonder Tucker has been all too willing to help me out with Clayton. This is all but addictive.

She circles the table, leaning forward next to Carter to look at his book. "Okay, so who wants to talk about what we discussed in class this week?"

"Kohlberg's three levels of moral reasoning," Carrie says, staring at her notes.

"That's right. And what were they?" She glances over at Tucker, moving toward us. When she reaches us, her finger lands on his shoulder. He tenses, gripping my hand tighter. I turn around and drill my eyes into her, willing her to look at anyone but him. I'm not doing enough. There has to be something else. "Tucker? Do you remember?"

"Preconventional, conventional, and post," he utters.

"Good job." She trails a finger across his neck as she moves around the table, her eyes finally landing on me. Moving to stand next to Aaron, she leans forward, elbows and arms resting on the table, and I realize we now have a full view down her blouse.

An idea fills my mind, and I lean toward Tucker, turning

my head so I can whisper in his ear. "You were right. She really does have a way of *touching* her students, hmm?"

His cheeks flame, and he stifles a laugh, and when I look at Professor Eden, she's straightened her spine, glaring at us both. She couldn't have heard me, of course, but the whispered conversation was enough to draw on her insecurities.

She turns, her tone clipped. "What are the stages of preconventional, Aaron?"

He flips through his notes quickly. "Um..."

When I look at Tucker, he's watching me, something dark in his eyes. Like he's proud of me for my quick thinking. Or... maybe he's enjoying watching us compete for him way too much? I burn holes in the side of Professor Eden's face as we wait for Aaron to find the answer in his notes, which seem to be mostly doodles. She tucks a piece of hair behind her ear, clicking her tongue as she avoids looking at me. "Can anyone help him?"

"Avoiding punishment and self-interest," Carrie replies quickly.

Professor Eden turns, grinning. She walks to the end of the table and rubs Carrie's head like a dog. I suddenly feel like I'm in the first round of initiation to a cult. Tucker lifts my hand to his lips, kissing it gently. When I look at him, shocked by the move, he holds my eyes for several seconds, something unspoken passing between us. My insides are radiating heat I've never felt before, turning everything to liquid. If this is what faking it with Tucker Ford feels like, I can't put into words how lucky the woman who gets him for real will be.

I shouldn't be having thoughts like that.

Also, that woman will not be Eve Eden. Not if I have anything to say about it.

"Good girl," she purrs. "Now, who can talk to me more

about Kolhberg's experiment and his findings." She circles the table again, her words slow. I don't miss the way she keeps looking at Tucker or the way he leans in closer to me each time she moves near us. His fingers have likely left a permanent indention on my hand. I can't bring myself to care.

As the night moves on, with Tucker passing me appreciative yet somehow smug smiles every time Professor Eden calls on him or looks our way, I start to wonder if Tucker might've had other reasons to bring me here than just to get Professor Eden to back off. Perhaps he's getting a bit of pleasure out of watching me squirm with unwarranted jealousy. Perhaps he's trying to prove a point.

I have no right to be jealous of him. This is all fake. I'm not his type. And besides, it's Clayton I want. We're doing all of this for Clayton...*aren't we?*

When the study session ends, everyone clears their things and begins to head out.

"You off tonight, Tuck?" Aaron asks, slinging a bag over his shoulder.

"Yeah. You'll be good?" Tucker slips an arm around my waist.

"As ever. See you around." He pats his shoulder and heads for the door.

"See you," Tucker calls to a few other people as they move to leave, too.

Releasing me, he grabs his laptop bag, shoving his notebooks inside, and holds out a hand for mine. "Ready?"

"Tucker?" Eve asks from where she stands near the door. "Hang back, will you? I want to go over a few things with you."

"Uh, sure." He grips my hand, pulling me toward him. "We're in a hurry, though. Everything okay?"

Carter passes through the door last, giving Tucker a look I can't quite read, and then it's just the three of us.

"You can go, sweetie," she says to me, wrinkling her nose as if it's cute. "I just need to talk to Tucker for a minute."

"Well, she's my girlfriend, and that would be rude," Tucker says. "If it's about class, we can talk tomorrow morning."

She studies him for a minute, then looks at me, waiting.

I snuggle into Tucker's side, placing a hand on his chest. "I'm fine here. Actually, I'm glad I caught you while no one else is around." I lower my voice. "Earlier, when you were leaned down, we could all see straight down your top. I'm sure you didn't know, but...you know, girl code and all. I'd want someone to tell me." I grin at her broadly. "Maybe try a different top next time. I mean, unless you *want* your students to look down your shirt."

Tucker's hand squeezes my hip, and I can feel him physically refusing to laugh. My cheeks burn with pride. This shouldn't be so much fun.

Professor Eden presses her tongue to her top teeth. "Right. Thanks for looking out." She adjusts the neckline of her shirt.

"Of course. How embarrassing."

She flicks her eyes to Tucker. "I just wanted to remind you we have the final coming up. If you need any extra help, I'm always around." Without waiting for him to respond, she stalks past us, flicking a piece of my hair as she goes.

We wait until we're back outside before he says anything, but once we are, he bursts out laughing. "You were brilliant. Did you see the look on her face?"

As happy as I am about how tonight went, my repulsion outweighs my joy. "How is she just able to do that? Why would you even still go there? What is her problem? She was literally flirting with all of you."

"Yeah," he says, his laughter dying out. "That's why the group is as small as it is. When I first started, there were about twenty of us. Then, Professor Eden took over, and people started dropping like flies."

"So why are any of you still there? Why haven't you reported her?"

"It doesn't work like that. Who's going to take my word over hers? Besides, if I did tell, and then she wasn't fired, she could flunk me. It's not worth the risk."

"It wouldn't just be your word, though. Would it?"

He shrugs. "I don't know. Most of the group thrives on the attention. Ty couldn't care less about the class. He's just trying to hook up with her. Carter, Aaron, and Sneebly already have. Carrie's a teacher's pet who needs constant validation, and to be honest, I don't really know why Jess is there."

"And why are you? Why stay? If you can't turn her in, fine, but leave the group at least."

"I can't. I told you, I need to pass. If I don't, I can't graduate, and then all my grandpa has done to get me here, all the work I've put in, the time away from him, will have been for nothing. And besides, I can handle her if it means I get to graduate in a few months and get the hell out of here."

"I can't believe they let her get away with that. How has no one turned her in? And why does she want you to call her by her first name? None of the other professors do that."

He shakes his head. "If I didn't know any better, I'd say you were jealous."

I scowl, hating that he's proving my theory right. He brought me here to get Professor Eden off his back, but also to make me jealous, and it's working. "Hardly. I just think it's wrong. If she were a male professor hitting on female students, no one would let her get away with it."

"True." He nods. "But it doesn't matter."

"How can you say that? Someone should report her."

"She's friends with the dean and half the school board." The way he says *friends* makes me think there's more to it than that, but he doesn't elaborate. "People have tried in the past. It does no good."

My brows pinch together.

"Look, it doesn't matter. Thank you for helping me today."

"*Did* I help? She didn't exactly seem threatened by me. If anything, I just made her more competitive."

"Trust me, you helped. She was pissed you were there. Everything you did was brilliant."

"I mean, what was I supposed to do? *You could see right down her shirt*," I cry, frustrated by how happy he looks.

"I thought you weren't jealous," he says with a laugh.

"I'm not. I just...I had to do something. I improvised, trying to make her jealous, but it's not that easy. You're always so good at it with the, like, making out and dancing or whatever, but in a library, there was only so much I could do to help. Whispering and hand holding isn't exactly racy."

"You're saying you would've done more if we were somewhere more private?" he teases, wiggling his brows and pulling me toward him.

I give in with a sigh. "Well, you know, always willing to take one for the team."

He gives a laugh from somewhere deep in his throat, not opening his mouth. "Good to know." We've reached the point where we should turn right to take me home or left to go toward his place or the bar. "So, now that we've accomplished the mission, do you want me to drop you off at your apartment or..."

"Um, well, I don't have anything to do. But, if you're busy or something—"

"I'm not."

A smile plays on my lips. "Okay."

"Okay." He holds out his hand, and I place mine into it. "Where to?"

"I've got somewhere in mind."

Back at his apartment, he leads me to his truck—a '79 powder-blue Ford F-250 he proudly tells me about restoring with his grandpa as he drives us away from campus.

"Were you close with your grandparents?" he asks when there's a lull in the conversation.

"Yeah, kind of. My mom's parents are the best. They're still alive. Always around. They're the kind of people who make you feel welcome and like you're never a burden or bothering them. I spent a lot of time at their house after school while my mom worked. I was less close with my dad's parents, just because they live on the West Coast, so we only saw them on holidays, and they were more...standoffish, I guess. They both passed away a few years ago."

"That sucks," he whispers.

"Thanks."

"I still can't believe I never saw you around school when we were growing up. I mean, I don't know everyone, but I would think I'd have seen you."

"I went to a private school," I say gently.

"Ah." He's quiet. "So, you were a rich kid."

"My dad went there, so it was just a whole thing. We weren't really rich. He was on the board, so we got a discount."

"It's okay if you were a rich kid," he teases. "I won't judge you too much."

"I appreciate it." Out the window, I watch as we exit the interstate thirty minutes outside of the city. "So, are you taking me out here to kill me or…"

"Nah, your parents are rich enough to hire a good attorney. I'd go to prison for sure."

I roll my eyes. "Not letting it go, I see."

"I promised not to judge you, *not* to not tease you." He's silent for a little while. "You said Clayton lived next to you, right?"

"Mm-hmm. The next house over. We killed the grass tracking back and forth between each other's yards." I chuckle, remembering the warm summers after we'd learned to ride our bikes, the lemonade stands only our neighbors patronized, and the afternoons spent with popsicles melting down our hands on our front porches. So much of my life has been spent with him, it's hard to imagine a future where we're apart.

"Are you still in touch with your friends from back home?"

"Not really," he says. "I didn't really hang with the best people back then. When I left, I needed a clean break."

"I can totally picture you in high school."

"Yeah, right." He scoffs. "Try me."

"You can't tell me you weren't popular."

He shakes his head, but I'm not buying it.

I wiggle a finger at him. "With those eyes and that hair? Please. The girls were falling all over you."

"Did you just call me hot?" He gives me a side-eye, actually looking surprised.

"Oh, come on. You know you're hot. Don't make me say it."

"I think you just did."

I groan, throwing my face in my hands. "Regardless, you were popular but probably not into sports. Something with your hands—"

"Oh, I was *great* with my hands." He wiggles his brows.

"I meant like shop or something," I say with a sigh, swatting his chest. "God, you're such a perv."

"Yeah, I was that, too." He laughs.

"You're impossible." I stare out the window as he turns down a side road. "Seriously, where are we going?"

"Just a little bit farther," he promises. "It'll be worth it, I swear."

"I don't know that it will."

"Don't you trust me?"

"I'm in the truck, aren't I?"

"You are." He pulls the truck down a side street, slowing down as we round a curve. There's a huge oak tree that comes out of nowhere, but he knows to slow down before we smack into it. He's obviously driven this road before.

"Are you taking me to your secret lair?"

"Would I tell you if I was?" He points up ahead. "There. That's where I'm taking you."

I squint, trying to make out what's up in the distance. It's an old barn, I realize. In the middle of nowhere. Dilapidated and gray, it stands against the darkening sky and acres of an overgrown field.

"Is that where they filmed *The Texas Chainsaw Massacre*?"

"Funnily enough, yes it is," he teases. I toss my head back with a laugh as he pulls the truck to a stop. "No. Come on.

Aaron's family owns this land. We came out here to drink and have bonfires a lot our freshman and sophomore years."

"Why'd you stop?"

"Eh, just got busy. He started dating Kristin, and work got more hectic. School, too. We just don't get out here as much as we used to." He steps out of the truck, jogging around and meeting me as I open my door.

"Does he know we're here now?"

"Nah, but it's cool. Come on." He holds out a hand, leading me toward the barn doors, and pulls them open.

"It's not locked?"

"Some of the rooms are, but not where we're going." He points to a ladder that leads up to the hayloft. "Ladies first."

I step up onto the ladder, climbing carefully until I reach the top floor. Tucker is close behind me. The room is dark, like the sky outside, shadow-filled and dusty. There are hay bales in every direction, but not much else.

Tucker walks around me, his footsteps echoing in the quiet space, and pushes open the set of double doors at the end of the room, revealing a breathtaking view of the field surrounding us and the night sky.

"Oh, wow."

I take a step forward without even realizing it. The sky is lit up with more stars than I think I've ever seen in my life, a quiet blue fading into the horizon from the last bit of the setting sun.

"Nice, isn't it?" He sits down, dangling his legs over the edge. "Sometimes I forget nights like these exist in the city." He extends his hand, helping me to sit. "Careful."

I ease myself next to him, staring out into the horizon in awe.

"I thought you could use the reminder, too."

"A reminder of how much I miss home?" I ask.

"And that you can find home in the most random places, if you know where to look." He nudges my shoulder gently with his.

A smile tugs at the corners of my mouth, and we sit silently for what feels like an eternity, just breathing in the crisp, cool night air.

"What are you thinking about?" he asks, and I realize he's been watching me.

I lower my head to my chest, kicking my feet. Releasing a sigh, I look over at him. "Just picturing how romantic it must've been with you and Aaron out here watching the sunsets together."

It takes him a moment to process what I've said, then his face turns playful, and he shoves me sideways, keeping a tight grip on my arm to make sure I don't fall. "Oh, shut up."

I laugh. "I'll bet it was lovely."

"Ha-ha." His laugh is sarcastic. "You're really missing your calling as a comedian."

"Okay, fine. I was thinking about how much is going to change soon. When real life starts."

"Real life, hmm?"

"Yes."

"You don't think this is real life?"

I stare straight ahead, kicking my feet again. Soon, he joins me, our feet swinging in tandem over the grassy ground several feet below. "It's not really, is it? After graduation, we'll all have to get real jobs and places of our own. We'll stop planning and start actually doing."

"Well, when you put it like that, yeah. But, I don't know. It all feels pretty real to me."

I feel his stares burning into me again, and this time, when I turn my head, his eyes find mine. He opens his mouth slightly, a smile but also a look of fascination on his face. Like he can't quite figure me out.

His eyes fall to my lips, and suddenly I wonder... Is he talking about us? That *this* feels real? When it's the exact opposite of real...right?

I can't let myself start to think like that. It gets too complicated.

You aren't his type, Maggie.

Quickly, as if he can read my thoughts, he looks away, his attention returning to the fields. "Thanks again, for tonight."

"It wasn't a hard job," I remind him, echoing his words to me from before.

"Right." He closes his eyes, drops his head, and sighs.

And then, we just sit. For what can only be minutes as we watch the last of the sunset disappear into the horizon and the sky be consumed by a blanket of stars.

And, before I'm ready, before it feels possible, he's telling me we should go. So, we do.

CHAPTER THIRTEEN

NOW

When I wake the next morning, the house is icy. I shiver, pulling the blanket up over me when I hear a noise from the kitchen. I sit up, trying to remember where I am and what's happening.

"Nick?" I call, remembering my late-night visitor.

"In here," he replies.

I ease off the bed, shaking the blanket off of my legs. "What are you doing?"

"Well, I was trying to make you breakfast, but it seems like all you have are pizza rolls, chips, and candy, so I settled for instant coffee instead." He holds out a mug.

"Thanks. I haven't had a chance to go grocery shopping yet."

"Can I go for you?"

"No," I say firmly, placing the mug down on the counter. "No. Because you have to leave."

He gives me a patronizing grin. "But I just got here."

"No. You got here last night, and I let you stay, but I told you, you have to go now. I have no interest in rehashing the past. It's over."

"Come on, babe. You can't be serious. You can't just throw five years down the drain over a fight."

"It wasn't a fight," I tell him calmly. "It wasn't an argument. It was a complete difference of opinion about our future, and I'm no longer interested in being in the life of someone who isn't sure about me."

"I told you the truth. I don't know if I want to get married. To you or anyone else for that matter. That doesn't mean I don't care about you."

"It's not enough, Nick. Don't you get that? This is where it ends. I want to be married. I want a life with someone who doesn't cringe when I talk about spending our lives together. Or when I mention having kids someday."

His brows draw together, anger and confusion overtaking his usually unbothered face. "So, you're willing to give up everything we have, what we have *for certain*, for something imaginary? Potential? Really?"

"Yes. Because what we have *for certain* is not enough for me."

His upper lip curls. He's staring at me as if I'm being utterly ridiculous. I guess, in his eyes, I am. "You need, what? A piece of paper? What does that matter in the long run? I'm committed to you. I don't cheat, and *believe me*, I could. I—"

"Look, I get it. You're great. You are, Nick. And I have loved our time together. But it's not about the paper. It's about the actual commitment, which despite what you're saying, you aren't willing to show. I want someone I can build a life with, and you aren't ready for that."

"*Don't tell me what I'm ready for,*" he shouts. It's out of character for him. Usually, he's so calm.

I do my best to keep my voice steady. "I don't want to have this argument again. I can't. Please. I'd like you to leave."

His lips pinch together. "Who is he?" he cries, his face red. It's the closest to breaking down I've ever seen him.

"Excuse me?"

"There has to be someone else." He looks around, as if my secret boyfriend might pop out of a cabinet and say, "Oh, hey. You caught us."

"Don't be ridiculous. There is no one else. It's not about that."

"I don't believe you!" he shouts, slamming his fist on the counter. I flinch at the noise. The room is suddenly too small. I can't catch my breath. I take a step back, but I hit the doorframe.

"Please, Nick. Please just go." I rub my lips together, inhaling deeply through my nose. I have to keep myself calm, or this could all get so much worse.

"*Fuck that.* I'm not going anywhere until you tell me the truth," he bellows, taking another step in my direction. I side-step, hurrying to the living room. He wouldn't hurt me. I know that. He's never shown any signs of violence or aggression, but that doesn't stop the little knot of fear from forming just below my rib cage.

"Nick, you're being ridiculous. Please stop this."

"Oh, *I'm* being ridiculous? How about a woman who breaks up with you after five years for nothing? Without any explanation." He places a hand on his chest. "I've done nothing wrong."

"I gave you an explanation," I cry, losing my cool for the first time. "We had several conversations about—"

"*And I'm here trying to fix it!*" He stomps toward me. "So, sit. Let's talk."

"I don't want to talk." My voice quivers, and I hate it. I reach for the door, but he's faster. His hand grabs it. "Stop this. I want you to leave before I call the police and have them make you leave."

He laughs from somewhere deep in his chest. "Oh, *fuck you,* Maggie. If this is really how you're going to be—"

We're interrupted by incessant banging on the door. My eyes zip toward it.

"Maggie?"

Tucker. Relief swells in my chest. Nick releases the door, and I pull it open in an instant.

Tucker's eyes land on Nick. "What the hell is going on? I heard shouting."

"You again? Who are you?" Nick demands. He's a good foot taller than Tucker, and broader too, but Tuck doesn't back down.

"I'm the guy who's about to let your ass leave willingly before I kick it out."

"Maggie, who is this guy?" Nick demands.

"He's my neighbor," I say plainly. "Just please go, okay?"

"I just want to—"

"She said go," Tucker says through gritted teeth. "We won't ask nicely again."

Nick studies him, as if wondering if it's worth his time. In the end, like usual, I never really was. He scoffs. "Whatever, man. See you around, Maggie." He shuffles past us on his way out the door.

Tucker turns his attention to me. "Are you hurt?"

"I'm fine." I shrug him off. "He's harmless."

"Didn't sound that way."

"He's just defensive because he thought I'd come crawling back by now, and I haven't."

He's quiet for a moment, checking over his shoulder. "So, that's the ex?"

"Mm-hmm. The very one."

"You clearly have a type."

"Meaning?"

"He looks just like Clayton."

"Hardly."

"The blond hair. Green eyes. You can't tell me you don't see it."

"Maybe." I shrug, shivering. "Anyway, thanks. You didn't have to come over here. I wasn't expecting any help."

"I don't like him yelling at you," he says firmly, hands drawn into fists at his sides.

"Yeah, well, that makes two of us. Just so you know, that wasn't a regular thing. He never raises his voice." I'm not sure he believes me, but it's true. Whatever got into Nick, it's not the usual.

"That doesn't make it okay."

I shiver again, running my hands over my arms, and check over my shoulder. "Jesus, why's it so cold in here?"

Tucker looks as if he hadn't noticed. "What's your air set on?"

I go into the kitchen and check the thermostat, which is set to sixty degrees. "No wonder. Nick must've messed with it." I groan. He was always a hot sleeper, but this is ridiculous. I turn the heat up and return to the living room, where I find Tucker staring out the window.

"What are you looking at?"

"Is he coming back here?" he asks, not turning to face me.

"He shouldn't. I told him not to."

His jaw twitches. "I don't like him here with you."

"Excuse me?"

He spins around. "I don't trust him, Maggie."

I fold my arms across my chest. "Lucky for you, I'm a big girl."

"Well, you might want to inform him of that, since I just had to come over here and stop him from screaming at you like a toddler."

"I didn't ask you to come," I tell him indignantly.

"You know I couldn't just ignore that."

"That's not on me."

He groans and turns away. "You're just as stubborn as I remember, I see."

"Did you expect any different?"

"No. But I *did* expect you to still be just as smart."

I jerk back as if he's slapped me. "Excuse me?"

"You heard me. You were afraid of me, and you left. Disappeared without a trace. And now, you're here alone with some guy who's clearly unhinged—"

"Well, that's a stretch, and...I was never afraid of you." I stop, looking him over. "Is that what you thought?"

"You left town the day you heard she'd died, after you'd just seen me with her. I know it's why you left."

He's not wrong. Not entirely anyway.

"I was confused. And yes, I was scared, too. But not scared of you. I never thought you'd hurt me. Not physically anyway. There was just so much going on. With all of us. And after everything with Raven, I just...I couldn't be here anymore. There was too much baggage."

"So you didn't think I was guilty? You don't think I did it?"

I swallow and steel myself. "No."

He nods slowly. "Okay. Well, good to know, I guess. Are you going to ask me if I did?"

"No," I say again. "Is that what you've thought all these years? That I left because I thought you had something to do with what happened to her?"

He doesn't answer, but he doesn't have to.

"Tucker, that was never it. I left because I was mad at you. Hurt. I couldn't stand to be around you; I couldn't stand to be around Clayton. I just needed to leave and clear my head. And once I was gone, I couldn't bring myself to come back."

"Okay. Fair enough." He reaches for the door, but I stop him.

"I do want to ask you something else, though."

"Yeah?"

"What do you know about this house?"

His upper lip curls. "Huh?"

"I mean, I'm not sure how long you've lived next door, but..." *This is going to sound so stupid.* "Have you ever heard any rumors about it?"

"Um, no. I don't think so. Why?"

"Just something Clayton said that made me...uneasy, I guess. Like this place might have some sort of stigma around it."

"What do you mean?"

"It's probably nothing. Just...the thing with the lights, and I heard these weird noises the first night. Clayton mentioned he thought he'd heard rumors this place was haunted. I guess when we were kids."

"Seriously? Haunted? As in ghosts?" He studies me, brows drawn down. He looks amused, which infuriates me.

"Forget it."

"No." The smile is washed away. "No. I'm sorry. I mean, yeah, there might've been rumors, but your side of town also thinks everyone over here goes to jail by age twelve and feeds kittens to our pet snakes, so I never put too much thought into any rumors I heard." He adjusts his ball cap, pulling it off his head and tugging it back down.

His answer does little to calm my nerves. "Okay, bit of an exaggeration, but point taken. Did you know the old owners at all?"

"The ones who sold to you?"

"Yeah."

"No, not really. I mean, they were friendly, but they weren't around long."

I must appear terrified, because he shakes his head as if I'm losing my mind. Maybe I am. "Not because of a ghost problem, Maggie. They were younger. Outgrew it when they had a third kid. Anyway, it's an old house. Whatever Clayton's heard, it was a nonsense lie meant to drive up property values in your neighborhoods. I mean, I grew up next door. I never saw anything weird happening. No one ran out screaming in the middle of the night. And there were only one or two cult meetings I can think of."

My eyes widen, but not for the reason he thinks.

"I'm kidding," he says.

"You grew up in the house next door?"

He tips his chin forward slightly. "It was my grandpa's. The one I told you about...before. I moved back in to take care of him after college, and he left it to me when he passed. Anyway, if you're so worried, why don't you just look it up?"

I hesitate, glancing down. In truth, I know I could look into the house's history and probably find out anything I want to know, but if I do that, there's no going back. Maybe it's better not to know.

Regardless, I have to stay here. I own it and, in a town like Myers, it's not so easy to get out from under bad real estate. It's not as if people are scrambling to buy property here anyway, especially on this side of town.

The more I think about it, the more helpless I feel.

What did I get myself into?

"Do you want me to help you look?" he asks, stepping forward to draw my attention to him.

"I...I don't know that I want to know."

"It's probably nothing, Maggie. And, even if it's something, it's better to know. The reality can't be worse than whatever you're concocting in that head of yours."

"You're right."

"Where's your phone?"

I grab my phone from where it's still charging on the floor and type in the address. The first things that pull up are property listings. Records. I scroll through, not finding much that's helpful, until...

"This place has sold seven times in the last thirty years," I whisper, reading over the information. Each time but one, it seems the owner lost money on the sale.

He squints at the ceiling, thinking. "Yeah, sounds about right." Meeting my eyes again, he shrugs. "It's not that unusual."

"That's, like...every four years."

"Here." He points at my phone screen, drawing my attention to a period between 1991 and 2003. "This was a long time. They stayed here for..."

He trails off, and at first, I think he's doing mental math, but then I realize he's staring at something farther down the page.

A label.

Bank owned.

It was foreclosed on and bank owned from 1991 to 2003.

Since then, in just ten years, it's sold seven times. My blood runs cold.

"Don't panic," he says quickly. "I'm sure it's just because of all the problems I told you about. The house is kind of a money pit, and most people don't want to deal with that."

"Maybe." I'm not really listening. Instead, I start a new search. What happened before the house was foreclosed on?

40 Hemlock Drive Myers Illinois 1991

My muscles constrict as I spot the first result.

Four Dead in Apparent Murder-Suicide

Tucker places a hand on my arm as I click on the link. It's from a newspaper archive that's blocked by a paywall, but I can see a photo of the house—my house, this house— surrounded by police tape. An ambulance sits in the driveway.

I rush across the room and grab my purse, not caring how much it costs. I need to know.

I input my card information and click "confirm." Instantly, the page refreshes, and I have access to the full article.

I skim over it, picking up only the important details.

"Chris Collins, 25, is the prime suspect in what appears to be a murder-suicide. Victims include Collins's wife, Jolene Collins, 21, and their two children, Jason, 4, and Shelby, 6 months." I squeeze my eyes shut, looking away. "She was six months old, Tucker. A freaking baby."

He covers the phone with his palm, easing it out of my hands. When I open my eyes again, he's reading over the article himself.

When he's finished, he stares at me with a look I can't quite read. A mixture of worry and heartbreak. "What the hell? You didn't know? The realtor didn't tell you about any of this?" he asks.

I shake my head, fury radiating in my chest as I think of Garrett. Why would he have let me buy this place? Then again, I was adamant this was the one I wanted. The only one I was interested in seeing. Would I have let him talk me out of it?

Yes. The answer is certain.

If I had known what happened here, I wouldn't have bought this place.

I can't stay here. Panic climbs in my throat, clawing and scratching for a way out. My heart rattles in my chest like a hummingbird trapped in a cage.

I grab my neck, unable to breathe. Unable to think.

Images of bodies lying on the floor, lying right where I stand, fill my mind. Sounds of children crying. The smell. The smell of rot and decay I smelled yesterday. The cold. It all makes sense.

It all adds up.

Except it doesn't.

Nothing about this makes any sense at all.

"Maggie!" Tucker shouts, and I get the feeling he's said my name several times already.

My eyes find his, the edges of my vision blurring.

"Breathe," he instructs me. "Breathe now." He looks as panicked as I feel as I release a breath. My vision comes back to me slowly, starting to make sense in the periphery.

I check the windows, unsure if I want to be locked in or out.

"Whatever happened here," he says firmly. "No matter what happened... It doesn't matter. It was more than thirty years ago."

"Yeah, and no one has managed to live here for any length

of time since."

"Probably because they found out what happened, not because the place is haunted." He sighs, lifting a hand to his lips. He raises the phone, shaking it in the air. "This is terrible. And I'm sorry you didn't know, but you're safe, okay? I promise you. If you want to sell, sell. But don't go running away because you feel like you have to."

"I can't live here," I tell him, begging him to agree. I look away, suddenly remembering... "Clayton. Clayton knew about this. He wasn't lying. Why would he let me move here, into this house, if he knew?"

"Because he wanted you home," Tucker says, as if it's obvious.

"He's not evil. If he knew all of it, there's no way he would've let me buy this place."

Tucker purses his lips like he doesn't think I believe that. "He wants what he wants, Maggie. Always has. If buying this house was the only way you'd come home, you can't tell me you believe he wouldn't let you do it. I'm sure, if his brother knew, Clayton told him to keep his mouth shut. Why else would he wait until you're locked in to casually drop the news? Why else wouldn't his brother warn you?"

"M-maybe he didn't know. Maybe it was always just a rumor. We were all kids when it happened. Practically babies. I would've been..."—I do the mental math—"three, I guess. And you said you grew up next door. Do you remember any of this?"

"Not really, no," he says quickly, his eyes shifting. "I wasn't much older. Four or five, I guess. I do remember a boy who used to live next door. Vaguely. Very vaguely. It could've been Jason. We played together sometimes. My grandparents told me they moved away. I never really questioned it. And, even

137

with the rumors, by the time I was old enough to have looked into what happened, everything had died down enough I never thought about it again."

"So, Clayton would've had no reason to know anything either. Garrett would've been older, but still not old enough to really know. And, if the house has sold so much, it may not be something that gets brought up in its history anymore." I don't know why I'm trying to cover for Clayton now when I feel utterly furious with him. "Maybe he really didn't know. He wouldn't do that to me."

"If you say so."

"You just don't like him."

"Guilty as charged."

I study him with a huff. "Why?"

"You know why."

"Oh, don't give me that. You didn't care back then. We were using each other."

He rolls his eyes, his head following them as he looks away. "If that's what you need to tell yourself."

Great. Now, we're back to fighting. "That was the deal, Tucker. It was your idea."

"Yep." He hands the phone back to me. "It was the deal. Until it all changed, and you tried to pretend it didn't."

"It didn't." I sling my hands down at my sides.

"Keep telling yourself that," he says, shaking his head. "If you're okay, I need to get to work."

"And if I'm not?"

"I still need to get to work." He's not moving, even as he says it.

I drop my shoulders. "I'm fine."

"You always were." With that, he's out of the house, and I'm alone. Left with the ghosts.

CHAPTER FOURTEEN

THEN

The bar is especially crowded tonight, with celebrations all around after one of our football players just learned he's being drafted to the NFL. When Tucker texted me that he was going to be working late, I decided to stop by and wait for him, rather than making him pick me up.

Since the night at the barn, things have been different between us. Not bad or good different, just...different.

I'm trying to convince myself I'm imagining it, but more and more, he's inviting me around to do things. The movies last week, then a dinner-and-study session a few nights after. Lunch yesterday. And now, today, another of his mysterious dates.

When I arrive, I spot him behind the bar, hat backward. His hair is getting longer, and somehow, I like it more. When he spots me, he looks shocked, but the shock quickly transforms into a wide grin.

He lifts the hand holding a small towel and waves, motioning for me to come his way.

I plop down on a free barstool, and he leans forward over

the bar. I could swear his smile is visible to the satellites in space.

I watch him with amusement. "Are you having a stroke? Should I call 911?"

He scowls, swatting the towel at me. "I'm just cracking up that you couldn't stand to be away from me for another hour."

"Maybe because your inflated ego is starting to form its own center of gravity. I was pulled here by science."

"Chemistry, maybe." The corner of his mouth upturns.

"Yeah, one of those experiments that go wrong and stinks up the place."

"Only because we're so powerful. Dangerous." He nips at the air. "Magical."

"You, my friend, are one extraordinarily strange individual."

"You love me." His eyes shine at me in a manner that makes my face hot.

"The way fish love bicycles."

"Meaning they want to ride them?" He winks, tossing the towel over his shoulder as he pops the lid off a bottle of beer and passes it to the man waiting next to me.

"How many fish do you know that want to ride bicycles?"

He thinks it over, running his teeth over his bottom lip. The action does something strange deep inside my gut. "There are probably a few in a Dr. Seuss book, but other than that"— he pops my nose with his finger twice as he says each word— "just one."

"In your dreams."

"Oh yes," he replies, his voice suddenly low and very serious. I swallow. *Gulp* is more like it. "In most of them, actually."

He's never been so forward with me, and I check around to

make sure we're not putting on a show for Clayton, but he's nowhere to be found.

"He's not here," he says, reading my mind.

"Just checking."

"Did you come here for him?" His eyes are locked on mine, and the answer, I think, may determine how the rest of the night goes.

"No," I admit.

"Good." He steps away from me to take someone else's order, and I miss him. I physically miss him, and he's just feet away. What the hell is wrong with me?

I try to convince myself it's just because we're friends, because, besides Kassara, he's the best friend I have lately, but that only makes me feel more pathetic.

My phone chimes, and I pull it out of my jeans pocket.

Clayton.

I haven't heard from him in days. Somehow, he seems to know when I'm starting to forget about my sadness, even if just for a minute.

> What are you doing this weekend?

I look around, checking to see if he's here again, though I still don't see him.

> Not sure yet. Why?

> I'm going to the lake house. Thought you might want to come too?

When I don't reply right away, he adds,

> If you don't have other plans.

141

I think about it. On one hand, it would be nice to spend time together at the lake house like we used to, but on the other...

> Not sure I want to be the third wheel.

Unless he isn't bringing Raven. Unless he's going to use this opportunity to tell me they broke up, and he's realized—

> She's dying to get to know you better. I promise you won't be the third wheel.

"Tell him we'll come." The voice startles me, and I glance up to see Tucker reading the text from across the bar, which is impressive when you consider it's both small and upside down.

"We?"

"Come on. It's the perfect chance to show him how great we are together. If you want to make him jealous, there's no better way."

I chew my bottom lip, thinking. When I glance at him again, he's staring at the place where my teeth meet my lip the way a wild animal would stare at fresh meat.

I release my lip. "You know we'd have to share a room. To... make it convincing."

"I'd given it some thought, yeah," he admits. Patches of scarlet climb his neck, even in the dim bar light.

"And you think it'll be okay? I mean, not awkward?"

"I promise to be a perfect gentleman." He bats his eyelashes at me. "If you can manage to keep your hands off me."

"Ha. Won't be a problem."

He doesn't miss a beat. "Great."

"Good."

I pull up my phone and send the next text.

Tucker and I would love to come.

His response takes several minutes to come in.

He doesn't have to work?

Nope

K. Great.

I look up at Tucker, whose shit-eating grin makes me strangely exhilarated. *Man, I'm in trouble.*

CHAPTER FIFTEEN

NOW

I spend the day unpacking the remaining items. I have a Taylor Swift playlist going, and I am trying, but failing, to ignore the ever-present worry in my gut. Around every corner, it seems there's a ghost waiting for me.

In every room, an image I can't shake.

It goes beyond my imagination. In the bedroom that smells of urine, I could swear I hear a baby crying. It's so loud I have to leave the house to get it out of my head.

This is ridiculous.

I repeat the phrase so much it's become somewhat of a mantra. *There are no ghosts. It's just a house with a sad past.*

It's been years. The house has a whole history since then. Before then, too. It's one terrible thing that happened in a whole line of wonderful things, right?

For all I know, every moment before and after that could've been perfectly beautiful.

And besides, the painful reality is, if I don't stay here, I have nowhere to go. I could crash on Elle's couch for a while, sure. Or, god forbid, Tucker's. But where would that leave me?

Until the house sells, and I find a job here or sell several paintings, the cash I have to live on would be dwindling by the day.

Like it or not, I'm stuck.

When my phone rings in the afternoon and it's Clayton, I answer quickly.

"Hello?"

"Hey, did you call me this morning?" He sounds as if he just woke up.

"Yeah, I did, actually. Why didn't you tell me about this house before I bought it? I told you this was the one I was buying. You knew. You should've told me."

"Wait, hold on." His groggy voice goes serious. "What are you talking about?"

"What you told me last night. The rumors. You were right. People died here, Clayton. You knew."

"No," he says firmly, scrambling to calm me down. "No. I didn't know. I-I knew that I'd always heard rumors, but I had no idea if they were true."

"Why didn't you tell me about the rumors at all?" I demand. "You could've given me a heads-up."

"Maggie, I didn't know. I didn't want to talk you out of buying the house you seemed so set on. Besides, what does it matter?"

"People died here," I remind him, moving out to the porch. "*Children* died here."

He inhales a sharp breath. "I didn't know. I swear. People said it was haunted, but that was it. I don't believe in ghosts, and it's not like you do either..." He pauses. "Right?"

"No," I whisper, not sure if it's true. I'm not sure I've ever put much thought into it until now. Besides, two very real ghosts from my past haunt me every day, but I won't bring that up as I see Tucker's truck pulling down our street.

"Okay, then. Anyway, listen, can I come by later? I wanted to talk about last night, and it feels like it should be in person."

"I, um...I'm not sure."

"Come on, Maggie. You can't avoid me forever. I just want to talk."

"I'll call you, okay? I just need to get my head on straight."

"I can help with that." He chuckles. "You can talk to me, be honest with me, even if it's not the answer I want to hear."

"I know," I tell him. "Truly, I do. But I'm not sure what's going on in my head. Or my heart. And right now this house is the most pressing issue."

"Okay," he says softly. "Okay. Just...just promise you'll talk to me before you make any decisions."

I suspect he's talking about the man who's just made an appearance, walking up the drive with his phone to his ear. He doesn't seem to notice me standing there, so I take the time to appreciate him as he moves.

He's grown up well, developed muscles he didn't have when we were younger. His jaw is sharper, more defined. His hair is still as beautiful as I remember.

As if he can read my thoughts, he looks over, melting me with those blue eyes, even from so far away.

"Maggie? You there?" Clayton asks when I forget to answer for too long.

"Sorry. I'm here. I'll talk to you, I promise."

"Okay. See you soon, I hope."

With that, we end the call, but when I look back up, Tucker is gone.

Back inside, I shut the door and look around.

Okay, ghosts, if you are here, I'd just like to remind you this is my house now. I mean you no harm.

I sound ridiculous, even to my own mind. I cross the living

146

room and step into the kitchen, and when I do, the lights flicker. I look up, then away just as quickly.

No.

The light is still on. I imagined it.

You blinked. That's it.

It's cold again, I realize. Gooseflesh covers my arms. I rub them vigorously, trying to warm up. *Am I imagining this, too?*

At the thermostat, I see it's set to sixty degrees again.

So, maybe it wasn't Nick this morning who adjusted it after all. I turn it back up. I'll have to have Tucker look at it. There has to be something wrong with it, with the wiring perhaps, or a glitch in the hardware.

The last thing I need right now is to have to add a new HVAC system to my growing checklist, but it seems that might be the only way to fix this.

I send Tucker a text to ask him to come take a look when he gets a chance, and he's there less than fifteen minutes later, hair wet and smelling of soap and cotton-scented fabric softener.

"Where is it?" he asks, letting me lead him toward the thermostat in the kitchen. He fiddles with it, turning it down so it shuts off and then back up so it turns on. "How long has it been acting weird?"

"I just noticed it today, but it's the first cool day in a while, so I'm not sure. It just keeps going down and, like, defaulting to sixty."

He stares at it. "It's still on seventy now. When did you last adjust it?"

"Just before I called you."

"Hmm." He pulls out a screwdriver and pops the plate off the wall, inspecting the wires inside. "It's gotta be a glitch somewhere, but nothing's jumping out at me. Maybe it just got bumped or something. If it happens again, I can try cutting the breaker and running new wires, but I don't think that's it."

"Okay, well, thanks."

"I'll reset it for you, too, just in case. Let me just look up how to do that with this model."

He pulls out his phone, setting to work quickly, and once it's been reset, he puts his screwdriver away. "Do you want to stay at my house tonight just in case? I have a spare bedroom. It's supposed to get cold."

"I'm okay," I say. The absolute last thing I want to do right now is spend the night at Tucker's for any reason. "The movers are coming tomorrow morning, so I should be here."

"You know I live right next door, don't you?" he asks with a skeptical look. "You could just walk back over when they get here."

"It's okay. You're probably right. I may have just bumped it."

He nods, but I can tell he doesn't believe me. "Okay. Well, the offer's open. Door stays unlocked. Just come on in."

His words take me back to the last time I took him up on an offer like that. Thirteen years ago, I walked into his apartment unannounced and saw something I can never unsee.

Something that changed everything.

I blink the memory away, forcing my thoughts to something else. Anything else.

Before I can speak again, a woman screams from down the hall.

CHAPTER SIXTEEN

THEN

When we arrive at the lake house, Tucker is in an especially good mood. We step out of the truck, and he carries our bags inside—where we find Clayton and Raven gathered around the kitchen island drinking out of red Solo cups.

They grin at us from where they stand, though admittedly, neither looks entirely happy to see us.

"Any trouble getting in?" Clayton asks, looking directly at me as if we're in a staring contest and to look away would cause him to lose. "I know the roads down here can be tricky if you aren't used to them."

"No trouble at all," Tucker answers, slipping an arm around my waist. "Where should I put our stuff?"

"You can just set it anywhere," Clayton says dismissively.

"I meant, where's our room?" Tucker clarifies. "So we can get settled in."

Clayton glares at him. "Right. Um, it's your old room, Maggs. You remember where it is?"

I nod, not impressed by his obvious attempt to make Tucker feel like the outsider, and lead the way toward the stairs. On the top floor, I take him to the room we'll be sharing for the weekend and push open the door.

The entire lake house is rustic and cabin-like, and this room is no different. Its walls are made of cedar, the smell of which permeates the entire house. It reminds me of summer vacations and lazy evenings roasting marshmallows with water-logged hair and deepening tan lines.

It reminds me of Clayton and everything we used to be.

The room is large, with a bed against the wall to our left, a sliding glass door that leads to a private patio, and our own bathroom. It hasn't changed a bit since we were kids. Even the bedding is the same.

Being in this space, I can't help remembering the many nights I'd pass out on the bed, exhausted from a day spent on the water, or the time I made Clayton paint my toenails on the floor after I sprained my wrist during a particularly daring tree climb. If I move the rug under my feet, I know I'll find the blue stain we attempted to hide from his parents when he spilled the entire bottle. The room is laden with memories, and I find them at every turn. I used to hide my diary under this mattress, until the housekeeper discovered it. The bed still has one of my hair ties on its post.

And if these walls could talk, they'd tell stories about the hours spent watching movies here and the many private concerts Clayton put on for me back when he was learning to play guitar. If only we'd known then what the future would hold...

Tucker clears his throat, and I'm brought back to reality.

Inside the room, with the door shut, a wave of awkwardness passes over me. *Are we really doing this?*

Really sharing a room for a whole weekend like we're together?

Really going to pretend around the clock? Behind closed doors?

Tucker sets the bags down on the foot of the bed and looks around, releasing a whistle. "Well, you could've mentioned this place was such a shithole."

I laugh, the tension disappearing from my shoulders at once. "I know, right?"

He watches as I cross the room and stand in front of the patio door, staring out through the crystal-clear glass.

"We used to come here every summer. Spend the day out on the lake, then come back and crash and do it all over again the next one." When I look back at him, his expression is grim. "You okay?"

"Yeah," he says quickly, walking forward until he's next to me. "I was just thinking my summers were...well, not like that."

"I wish you could've been here." The admission slips out without thought.

"Trust me, you don't."

I turn to him. "Meaning?"

"I wasn't ready for you back then, Maggie. I would've said or done something stupid. Ruined it."

"So, you're ready for me now, hmm?" I tease, brushing his arm with mine.

"I guess we're going to find out, aren't we?" He juts his head toward the door. "Should we go back down, or would you rather let them keep imagining what we're doing up here?"

I roll my eyes. "You're impossible."

Clayton grills burgers for dinner, and we spend the evening around the fire pit. Everyone is a little buzzed from the wine in our glasses by the time the sun sets, and when the bugs start coming out, Raven swats at her arms for what seems like the hundredth time before she suggests a game.

"What sort of game?" Clayton asks.

"A drinking game," she says, as if it should've been obvious. "Never have I ever."

"Oh, I don't think that's a good idea," I say. "It's getting late anyway."

"What's the matter, Maggie? You chicken?" Clayton asks, staring at me from across the fire with an edge to his gaze.

"I'm in if you are," Tucker says, leaning forward to grab the bottle of wine on the table between us. "But I need a refill."

"Actually—" Clayton holds up a hand to stop him. "Hang on." He disappears inside the house and returns with a large paper bag. "I brought some stuff for you." He's looking at Tucker as he says this. "Since you're a bartender, I thought you could make us some drinks."

"Clayton..." I say, infuriated at the suggestion. "Tucker isn't the help."

"No, I know." His eyes pass from me to Tucker and back again. "I just thought, you know, maybe it would be fun." He looks back at Tucker. "I got a ton of stuff. Didn't know what you'd need. But...if you're not into it, it's not a big deal."

"Um, yeah. Actually, yeah. Why not?" Tucker sets his glass down and stands. "Did you get gin? There's a drink I tried out the other night I've been wanting to make for Maggie."

"Uh, no." Clayton stares into the bag. "I grabbed whisky and vodka. Will they work?"

It doesn't surprise me that Clayton didn't think to get my liquor of choice. Whenever we're together, we typically drink wine. He's never had much taste for gin and will only drink it when it's all I have. Still, Tucker's question is touching. He looks at me with a soft expression.

"Nah, it's gotta be gin. Have you got anything else inside?"

"Yeah, my parents have a full liquor cabinet. I'm sure we can find some."

"I'll come with you," I say, standing up, but Tucker shakes his head.

"I'm good. You relax. I'll be right back." His smile is meant to be reassuring, but it does little to make me feel better. He leans down and kisses my cheek as he passes by with Clayton just behind him.

When they're gone, Raven releases a little sigh. *Even her sighs are perfect.*

"This is so much fun," she says, looking out over the lake.

"Mm-hmm." I take a sip of my wine.

"So, you and Clayton came here a lot as kids?"

"Yeah. Every summer."

"It must've been a dream." She tucks one hand under her legs. "You and Tucker are precious, by the way. And the way he looks at you." She fans herself. "Don't tell Clayton I said anything, but those eyes are to die for." She smirks. "And the rest of him doesn't hurt."

I bristle at her comment but try to brush it off. "Thanks. Yeah, he's pretty great."

The door opens, and Clayton reappears. "What'd I miss?"

I watch behind him, but Tucker isn't there. "Where's Tucker?"

"Making our drinks," he says with a shrug, sitting down once again and squeezing Raven's thigh.

"You left him? Seriously?" I stand up.

"He's fine. I showed him where everything was and left him to work."

"Again, he's not the help, Clayton."

"I never said he was." He looks at Raven as if I'm being ridiculous. "Calm down. He was fine with it."

"You're being so condescending. Just because he's a bartender, he should make us drinks? No one here's asking you to perform a concert."

"Maybe you should. Wouldn't be the first time." He leans back in his chair, a smug look on his face.

I roll my eyes. "Seriously, this is not cool."

"I'm sure Clayton was just trying to be nice," Raven says, her voice soft. "To find something to connect with Tucker on. God knows the extent of Clayton's bartending skills is pouring beer into a glass." She gives him an adoring smile, and I want to vomit.

I head for the door.

"Where are you going?" Clayton calls.

"To be with my boyfriend," I say, my voice low. I desperately don't want to fight, but I'm so angry right now I'm practically buzzing with adrenaline. "So he isn't alone in a strange house while we all sit outside and—"

"Everything okay out here?" Tucker appears at the door, pushing it open as he balances four highball glasses in his hands. His eyes lock with mine, waiting for an answer.

"Yeah." I puff out a breath of relief. Seeing him again, all's right with the world. "I was just coming to find you."

"Missed me already, hmm? I was okay." His smile is soft as he hands me a glass. "Now, give that a few more seconds for the foam to separate." I spin around, eyeing the cocktail as he passes the other two out and sits down with his own. The liquid inside the glasses is yellow, with a foam covering the top few inches. He has garnished each glass with a slice of lemon.

"What is it?" Raven asks.

"It's called a Ramos Gin Fizz. I was looking up interesting gin drinks to try out for Maggie and came across this one. It's been my favorite so far." He takes a sip, tipping his glass toward Clayton. "So thanks for the suggestion. I'm glad I finally had a chance to make it for my girl."

Clayton practically glowers at him as Raven and I sample ours.

"Oh my gosh. It tastes like lemon meringue pie," Raven shrieks, dabbing foam off her lip. "This is the best drink I've ever had in my life. You have to give me the recipe."

Tucker tips his head toward her, then looks at me.

"She's right," I tell him. "It's delicious. Literally perfect." I lift it up, inspecting it as my throat goes a bit tight. "It was really sweet of you to do this. You didn't have to."

"Happy to," he says casually, leaning back in his chair. "Now, onto the game?"

"Yes. Right. Okay, I'll go first," Raven announces, bouncing up and down in her seat like a kindergartener who needs to use the restroom. She freezes. "Everyone knows how it works, right?"

We nod.

"Great. Okay, never have I ever gotten a speeding ticket." Clayton, Tucker, and I each take a drink, and Raven giggles. "You guys!" She's mock offended by our terrible driving. "Is it bad that I want to have done all these things so I can drink more of this?" She pretends to sneak another drink.

I kind of hate how much she's gushing over the drink, even if I want to do the same thing. It really is delicious.

"Okay." Clayton goes next. "Never have I ever lived in the same city all my life."

"Guilty," Raven chimes in, taking a sip of her drink. She looks at Tucker. "Your turn."

He eases forward in his seat, rubbing one hand over the side of his glass. "Okay. Never have I ever written a song."

Raven and Clayton drink quickly, but Clayton looks at me, his brows raised.

"What's that look?" Tucker asks.

"She should be drinking." Clayton's eyes don't leave mine.

"What?" Tucker turns in his seat to look at me.

"No." I fan away the attention, then wag a finger at Clayton. "No. That doesn't count."

"What doesn't count?" Raven asks, eyes wide.

"We used to write together when I started," Clayton informs them.

"We did not," I say, only partially faking my irritation. "I offered suggestions or told you when one line might work better. We were kids. Nothing I wrote qualifies as a song."

"Judges?" Clayton looks at Raven, who nods.

"I think you have to drink," she says, fake wincing.

"Half a sip at least," Tucker agrees.

"Fine." I groan, taking a small drink. "But, for the record, I heartily disagree with the decision."

"Fair enough," Clayton says with a laugh. "Your turn."

"Um, okay. Never have I ever...restored a truck," I say, eyeing Tucker. He grins, taps his glass in the air at me, and takes a drink.

"The one in the driveway?" Clayton asks. "I wondered. What year is it?"

"Seventy-nine," Tucker tells him.

"It's so pretty," Raven coos.

"Thanks."

The game continues on for another round of innocent questions before it veers off into dangerous territory.

"Never have I ever been in love with someone who doesn't

feel the same way about me," Raven says. The smile on her lips is sweet, though with the liquor in all our bellies, I know the question is anything but.

She watches me carefully as I consider my options.

I could lie, try to hide it, or I could act unbothered. From his seat, Tucker's eyes are locked on me as he takes a drink. I'm shocked by it—so stunned, I take a drink for something to do more than anything.

Clayton also drinks.

Then, it's his turn. "Never have I ever kissed someone who was in love with someone else."

Again, Tucker drinks without hesitation.

Something in my chest tightens. I look down. Suddenly, I'm not as interested in playing this game. "Maybe we should call it a night, guys. It's starting to get late."

"What? No," Clayton argues. "We're just getting started."

"Never have I ever broken the heart of someone I claim to care about," Tucker spits out.

Our eyes dance around, flitting from one person to the next. No one drinks.

I know whom that statement was intended for, but if Clayton does, he obviously doesn't think he's hurt me.

I stand up. "I'm going to bed."

"Maggie, wait," Clayton calls after me as Tucker stands.

"I'm tired," I tell him, not stopping as I make my way to the door. "Sorry. See you all in the morning."

Tucker's close behind, following me to the door and then upstairs. He waits until we're both inside our room before he speaks. When he does, my back is to him.

"I'm sorry if I upset you."

I turn around. "You didn't. It's fine."

"He just... He knew what he was doing. Trying to rile me

up. He's playing a game. That's what this entire weekend is meant to be. If you'd come alone, he wouldn't be acting this way. He'd pretend everything's fine while you sit around and have your heart dragged through the mud."

"It's fine, Tucker. I promise." I open my bag and pull out my pajamas. I've chosen one of the only matching sets I own, with navy-blue silk shorts and a button-down shirt. "I was just tired, and I could see things were going to get worse. I'm sorry he was being...well, whatever he was being."

"Himself," he says simply, putting his glass on the nightstand.

"Right. I'm going to go and change."

I disappear into the bathroom, and when I come back, Tucker is shirtless and wearing a pair of flannel pajama bottoms. He pulls a gray shirt over his head and then sinks down onto the bed.

"Are you glad we came?" he asks.

"Undecided," I admit.

"Are you glad I'm here?"

"Yes. If you weren't, I wouldn't have gotten to try this delicious cocktail." I pick up my glass, kissing the side of it.

A mischievous look overpowers his expression. "Good. Now that you mention it, I think we should finish said cocktails while playing the game."

"Never have I ever?"

He nods, reaching for his glass. He pats the comforter and turns to sit facing the spot I move toward. He's closer to the headboard while I'm at the foot of the bed, each of us with our legs crossed in front of us, drinks in hand.

The tension in the room is palpable.

"I'll go first," he says.

I give a hesitant nod.

158

"Never have I ever...had sex in this room."

Heat rushes to my cheeks. I shake my head. "I've only been in here alone or with Clayton."

"Your turn," he coaxes.

"Never have I ever...been in love with someone who loves me back."

He shakes his head slightly. "Not yet, anyway." His eyes flame with something dangerous, and his gaze flicks down to my bare legs. "Never have I ever touched myself in this room."

Heat swoops through my belly, my breathing hitching. He watches eagerly as I look away, taking a small sip of my drink and refusing to elaborate.

When I meet his eyes again, his cheeks are as red as mine feel. "Your turn."

"Never have I ever had sex somewhere public."

He smirks. Takes a drink.

Jealousy rattles at my ribcage. Unfounded jealousy. Jealousy that has no place here. "Where?" I demand, with a little too much anger in my tone.

"The bar," he admits.

I swallow.

"It was a long time ago."

"Okay."

"Never have I ever..." He pauses, sucks in a long breath, and his eyes dart back and forth between mine. "Never have I ever been jealous when I heard that answer."

I stare down at my drink, and he leans forward, lifting it from the bottom. "Let me help you there."

"Shut up." I scowl, bitterly taking a drink.

"So, you *are* jealous," he confirms.

"You're my fake boyfriend," I say in a whisper.

"Are you fake jealous? Or real jealous?"

I shake my head. "This game is dumb." Sliding off the bed, I make my way to the bathroom and dump the rest of my drink down the drain before brushing my teeth. I'm alone for a few minutes before he walks in. I stare at him in the mirror, at his confident stance, his smoldering gaze.

Entire cities are burning behind his eyes as he leans down, chin to my shoulder, lips next to my ear, and whispers, "I get jealous, too."

I feel his words on every inch of my skin. In every muscle in my body. On every surface. Within my pulse. Within my sweat. Between my legs.

I know it's just the alcohol in our systems and the close proximity we're sharing for the weekend, but still, everything about this situation has me exhilarated and terrified.

"Don't hurt yourself thinking too hard," he whispers, turning on his electric toothbrush. I rinse my mouth and leave the room, pulling back the covers and slipping into the side of the bed we've designated as mine.

A few minutes later, when he returns to the room, he flicks the light off.

Now, it's pitch black and silent except for the sounds of my ragged breathing. The covers next to me lift, and I feel the mattress sink with his weight.

For several moments, neither of us says anything.

At least, I think neither of us says anything. For all I know, his words are being drowned out by the racing of my own heartbeat in my ears.

He turns onto his side, and my face burns with the desire to turn and see if he's watching me or drifting off to sleep.

How could anyone sleep with the furnace currently going on between these sheets?

"Tucker?" I whisper, keeping my voice low.

"Yeah?" he replies, like he's been waiting for me to say something. Anything.

"Can I ask you something?"

"You can ask me anything."

"When you think of me...what do you think?"

Something like a growl comes from deep within his throat. "That depends on when I'm thinking of you."

"What do you mean?"

I hear rather than see him open his mouth, but he hesitates. "Are you sure you want to know the answer to this? Because I've had a little too much to drink to control what I say right now."

I turn to my side, too, so we're eye level with each other, inches apart. My eyes have begun to adjust to the darkness, so I can just make out his unreadable expression. "I want to know."

"Well, when I think about you with Clayton, I think he doesn't deserve you." He licks his lips. "When I think about you when I'm working, I think about how much fun we have together. How much I miss you."

My whole body is filled with waiting. Yearning. I need to know how this answer ends.

"When I think about you at night, or when I'm alone..." His gaze is soft as a caress in the dim moonlight as my eyes adjust further to the light, the grit in his voice stoking flames I didn't know existed in me. "I think about, if you were mine, all the things I'd like to do to you."

A delicious shudder heats my body. "Like what?"

A breath of air leaves his nose. His nearness is overwhelming. The scent of him. His body heat touching me, even though he doesn't. "Maggie..." My name on his breath sends waves of electricity through my core. "You're killing me."

I reach out without realizing it, touching his face, his sharp jaw covered in stubble. I run my fingers over his lips, and he kisses each one. I don't even know what I'm doing. My body seems to be acting of its own accord.

He doesn't move. Stays completely still as I'm free to explore him. I lower my hands to his neck, feeling him swallow as my fingers connect with his Adam's apple.

A knot forms in my throat as I move my hands to his chest. "Is this okay?"

"Yes." His voice is dry. Shaky.

I move my hands lower, assessing the muscles under his shirt, then skate my hands under the fabric to get a better feel. He makes no attempt to hide that he's watching me, though his face is stoic.

"Still okay?" I ask again.

His response comes as he takes my hand out of his shirt. For a brief moment, I assume I'm being rejected. Then he turns my hand, placing it firmly on the hardness between his legs.

He moves his hand away, but I'm not as quick to do so, though I eventually do. "Anything you do to me is okay," he whispers. "As long as it's what you want."

"I thought you weren't attracted to me," I mutter, the darkness and alcohol making me more daring than ever.

"Why would you think that?"

"You said I'm not your type."

"Ah." He chuckles under his breath again, reaching over and gripping my waist. "Right, *my type*." He drags me to him. "My type, Maggie, is hot."

I huff. "I'll try not to take offense to that."

"Shut up. You know you're hot." He brushes his erection against my leg. "I also need someone who makes me laugh. Someone I can talk to about anything and never get bored." His nose touches mine, sending a new wave of heat from my fingers to my toes. "Someone with a smart mouth." His lips touch mine ever so briefly. "And, most importantly"—he peppers my lips with kisses in between his next words—"some-one. Not. In. Love. With. Anyone. Else."

I pull back as if my body has been doused with cold water, but his hand remains on my waist.

"Tuck..."

"It's okay."

"Is that really what you meant? That's the reason I'm not your type?"

"It's okay, Maggie. I knew what I was getting into when I signed up for this."

"The fake dating?"

He nods.

"Is it still fake?" I ask.

I watch the shadows of his eyelashes against his cheeks, soak in the scent of him—his fresh smell mixed with the bonfire from earlier.

"You tell me."

I move my knee against him, against the very real evidence that tells me, at least for this moment, nothing feels fake to him. I don't want to hurt him. I don't know what—or who—I want. I could have him right now. I know I could.

But if I do, I'd be closing the door on Clayton forever.

Tucker's grip loosens on my waist. "It's okay," he whispers. Then, after a moment of hesitation, he leans in, pressing his lips to mine. My body responds to him, pulling him into me, parting my lips to deepen the kiss. One minute, the kiss is surprisingly gentle, then it's punishing and angry. We're back and forth like that for a while, his tongue sending shivers of desire racing through me, his hands on my body transforming the pit of my stomach into a hurricane of want.

All at once, he pulls back, panting to catch his breath. I'm confused by how much I want him. Suddenly, it doesn't feel like it's just the alcohol.

Suddenly, this all feels like something more.

"What was that for?" I whisper, still out of breath.

His response comes in a throaty grunt. "I don't know. Maybe... Maybe it was just for me."

Tantalizing. That's what he is. As he pulls back farther, I miss him. I miss his body on mine. His kiss on my lips.

He rolls away, but even as I lie here alone, his back to me, I feel his lips on mine. If I close my eyes, I can still feel him against me. His slow, drugging kisses and mesmerizing touches.

I should say something, but I don't. I can't.

Why can't I?

It takes me ages to fall asleep, but when I do, I dream of him.

CHAPTER SEVENTEEN

NOW

The scream lasts just a few seconds—long enough for me to register what it was—and when it ends, Tucker is standing in front of me with a strange look on his face.

"What was that?" I demand, looking in the direction the noise came from.

"What?" His brows dip. "You made a weird face."

"That scream." I point toward the hallway, my heart pounding in my chest.

He shakes his head, following my finger with his gaze. "Scream?"

"You didn't hear it?"

"What are you talking about?"

No. I know I didn't imagine this. I couldn't. I turn away from him, bolting toward the hall and into the first bedroom. I fling open the door and stare inside, but the room is empty. I only see my reflection in the mirrored closet doors.

"What is happening right now?" Tucker demands, following close behind me.

"I heard a woman screaming," I tell him, fully under-standing how ridiculous I sound.

"A woman?"

I push open the next door, but it's also empty, just like the third and final room. I turn around, trying to catch my breath. "You didn't hear a woman screaming?"

He stares at me as if he's seen a ghost. As if I'm the one who's haunting this place. "No, Maggie, I didn't hear anything."

I spin around. "I know what I heard. Earlier...there were babies, and...and then the thermostat."

"Okay." He puts a hand on mine. "I think you're just exhausted. You probably haven't been sleeping well if you're having bad dreams. Come to my house for the night. Please. You'll have your own room. You'll be safe."

A flash of a memory comes back to me—*two bodies in bed, naked. She's on her knees over him, taking him into her mouth. Her dark hair falls down over her face. Tucker looks up at me as I enter the room, an apology in his eyes. He calls my name, but I'm gone.*

The heartbreak is back, as real and painful as it was that night.

As much as I want to tell him no, I can't deny the terror I feel at the thought of sleeping here.

"Okay," I say finally.

"Okay. What do you need to bring? I'll help you carry it."

"Just my suitcase and phone charger." I open the bathroom door, checking behind it and in the shower for any sign of the woman. *Am I losing my mind? Has the grief over my mother's death caused some sort of mental breakdown?*

I grab my toothbrush and head back into the living room, where Tucker is gathering my things. "Come on," he says, in a way someone might when dealing with their elderly grand-mother. "Let's get you over there and sit down for a minute. You look exhausted."

He leads me to his house, and I feel like I'm in a dream. Everything is fuzzy, blurry. Like I've been drugged, though I've been given no drink.

His house is small and quaint but neat. Like his truck always was.

Taken care of.

He leads me through a small living room with a matching couch and recliner, past the galley kitchen, and down a hallway.

He pushes open the second door on the right, which looks like it was decorated by a grandmother in the seventies and never updated again. He pulls a quilt off the foot of the bed.

"It's a little dusty. I've never actually had anyone stay over."

At least not in this room, I think, but I don't say as much. He places my suitcase next to the bed on the floor, looking around. "There's a plug there for your phone and, um, the bathroom's right next door. I'm the last door at the end of the hall." He runs a hand through his hair. "Is there anything else? Are you hungry? I have...food. I could make something." He seems more nervous than usual. "Or a drink. Alcohol. Water. Anything?"

I shake my head, sinking down onto the bed. "No." I lick my lips, then look up at him. "Am I going crazy, Tucker?"

"You're just scared," he says, appearing relieved to have the conversation moving along. "Freaked out because of everything that happened there. It's normal. You just need time to process. You're going to be okay."

I nod, stifling a yawn. "I'm so tired."

"I'll let you get to sleep. Just... Like I said, come get me if you need anything. Or feel free to help yourself to whatever's in the kitchen." He opens the door, pointing next to it. "Bathroom's here," he reminds me, starting to walk away.

"Tucker?"

"Yeah?" He reappears, his expression eager. Nervous.

"Will you lock all the doors?"

He stares at me like he might've misheard.

"You said the doors are always unlocked. Could you...I mean—"

"Oh. Yeah. Sure. Consider it done."

"Thank you," I whisper.

With the door shut, I change into my pajamas and slip under the covers. In the quiet house, I can make out the sounds of him moving around. Water running in a sink. The refrigerator opening and closing. The television turning on, then ten minutes later turning off.

He paces down the hall and stops at my door. I listen, wondering if he'll come back. Wondering why he would. Wondering if I want him to.

All too soon, he's gone again, but this time, to his own room. I hear a door shut down the hall after the light under my door goes out. I wish desperately there was a TV in here or something I could use to distract myself from my frayed nerves.

I pull out my phone and scroll through it, but I'm not reading anything. I can't focus.

I can't do this. I slide out of bed and open the door, staring down the dark hallway. When I reach his bedroom door, I press my ear to the wood. After several silent moments, I knock lightly.

"Come in."

His words come quickly, like he's been expecting me. I grip the knob, turn it, and step inside his bedroom. It's double the size of the room I'm in, but still not huge, with a king-size bed against the wall. There's a TV on a dresser at the end of the room, and next to where I'm standing, a door to the en suite.

When he sits up, I realize he's shirtless. "Everything okay?"

I shake my head, but in the shadows of the dark room, I'm not sure if he can see me. "I can't sleep."

"Me either," he admits.

"Can I stay in here?" I hate how vulnerable I feel.

"Of course."

I approach the bed and pull back the covers, placing my phone on the nightstand before easing in next to him.

"I never thought we'd be in this scenario again," he whispers, trying to ease the tension.

"What? Neighbors hiding out from a potentially haunted house by sharing a bed?" I tease, rolling away from him and tucking my hands underneath my cheek.

"That's the one."

"I never thought I'd see you again," I admit.

"I was under the impression you didn't want to."

"Most days, I didn't."

He's quiet for a while. So long I worry I've made him mad.

"I'm sorry, Maggie."

"I know," I whisper, a tear cascading down my cheek and onto the pillow. "Me, too."

The next morning when I wake, Tucker is already gone, and there's a note lying on his pillow.

Had to get to work, but didn't want to wake you.
I'll call around nine to make sure you're awake for the

movers. Coffee's still warm and there's plenty to eat in the fridge. Help yourself. Call if you need anything. See you tonight.

I read over the note again, searching for any sign of the awkward conversation we had last night. The apology I've waited thirteen years to both give and receive.

I check my phone. It's just after eight, so I have time for a quick shower and a cup of coffee. As I stand, my eyes land on a painting hanging on his wall, and my breath catches.

How did I miss this last night?

I cross the room, running my fingers across the swirls of blue in the sky, the tiny white flecks of stars, remembering the tedious brush strokes it took to get it just right. I study the details of the old gray barn, the two silhouettes in the hayloft, my thoughts going fuzzy.

Tucker bought one of my paintings?

An original painting. Not a reprint.

How? *Why?*

Why didn't he tell me?

There's a tickle in my throat as I stare at the barn and the memory. It's one of the pieces of my art I'm most proud of, and seeing it again brings tears to my eyes. Or maybe that's not what's causing my tears at all.

Either way, if he wanted me to know about the painting, he would've brought it up. I dry my eyes and turn to leave the room, refusing to read more into this than what it is.

It's just a painting. I'm glad he likes it. It's just art. Don't make this a thing.

I head for the bathroom, forcing the thoughts of the painting and what it means out of my head. I have too much to do today to dwell on the past. I realize what a mistake I've made almost instantly. It's impossible to shower here and not think of him. The soaps and shampoo smell of him. The washcloth is still wet from his last shower.

I wash off at record pace and wrap up, heading for the spare bedroom to change into clean clothes. In there, I dress and brush my hair, taking an extra moment to peruse the room.

The dresser at the far side of the space is covered in knick-knacks and photos, some in black and white. An entire family line lives and dies on top of the dresser. I search for photos of Tucker but find none at first.

One photo does catch my eye, though.

I pick up the old, golden frame, staring down at the fuzzy photo there in front of me. The glass is dusty, and I swipe my fingers across it, forcing my eyes to focus. An older version of the man in most of the photos is sitting on a porch with two young boys on either side of him. The boys are grinning at each other while the man looks down proudly at them.

The picture looks like a candid shot. Like they didn't realize it was being taken. Upon a closer look, I find myself looking at the toddler with the dark curls and deep-blue eyes. Even back then, Tucker's crooked smile was unmistakable. It has to be him. I don't recognize the other boy in the photo, though.

Still, it's not the people in the photo I stay focused on for long.

It's the house.

And that's because...*yes, I'm certain of it,* I decide as I study it closer.

The house in the photo is the house next door. The one I now call home.

CHAPTER EIGHTEEN

THEN

We spend Saturday on the lake on Clayton's parents' boat. He brings beer, and we attempt to swim in the water, though in April, it's still much too cold, and we don't last long.

For the most part, everyone is civil, and the strangeness of last night seems to be forgotten.

When we get back to the house for the evening, we order dinner from a local barbecue place and stay in to watch *The Uninvited*. Clayton's choice.

I'm curled up against Tucker's chest, which rises and falls with every breath, when Clayton gets up suddenly and leaves the room.

I assume he's gone to the bathroom or to get another snack when I get a text.

Meet me in my room?

I hide my phone quickly, worried the light will disturb Tucker, but also that he might see, as I contemplate my next move. *Should I go find out what he needs, or is it smarter to pretend I never saw the text?*

I look over at Raven, who seems to be watching the movie intently. Finally, I stand. Tucker reaches for my hand.

"Everything okay?"

"Just going to get more drinks." The lie tastes bitter on my tongue, and I instantly regret it. I should tell him, but Raven would overhear, and I don't want to start any drama.

He squeezes my hand tenderly before releasing it, and I make my way into the kitchen, where I pull out two new beers for us and place them on the counter.

Then, I make my way down the hall, up the stairs, and to Clayton's room. Inside, I find him at the window.

"Hey." I push the door closed behind me. "Everything okay?"

"Yeah." He's not looking at me. "I just wanted to talk to you."

"Okay. What about?"

"Raven." He glances over his shoulder at me.

"What about her?"

He turns, sinking down onto the window seat with his hands in his lap. "I just don't know what I'm doing anymore, Maggie."

"What do you mean?"

"The more time I spend with her outside of Nashville, the more I wonder how well I really even know her."

"Well, it's been a short relationship," I tell him, choosing my words carefully. "You're still getting to know her. That's normal."

"Right. Not like how you and I know each other."

"No one will ever be like you and I." The unavoidable fact

that I fear will always haunt us. "You can't compare her to that."

He nods. "Yeah, I know, but I am anyway."

"What are you talking about?" I take a step forward.

He kneads his eye with the heel of his hand. "I think I'm making a mistake with her."

Instantly, my senses become heightened. "What? Why do you say that? Are you thinking of breaking up with her?"

"Maybe," he admits, looking up with a resigned expression.

"How long have you been considering that?"

"A few days, I guess. I've been wanting to talk to you, but, well, you're never alone."

"Neither are you," I remind him, placing my hands on my hips.

"Look, are you and Tucker serious?"

"Why are you asking that?"

He stands, stepping toward me. "Because I want to know."

"You can't ask me that, Clayton." I jab a finger in the air toward him. "*You* left, remember? You left, and when you came back, you were engaged."

"I'm not talking about me. I'm talking about you."

"Okay, fine. *Yes.* Is that what you want to hear? We're serious. I'm... I'm falling for him." My words catch in my throat, an odd sort of ache filling my chest at the thought. At the unexpected truth in my statement.

"And you think he's that serious about you, too?"

I nod. "I do, yeah."

He glares at me, frowning. "No."

"No?" I repeat.

"No, to answer your question, that's not what I wanted to hear."

"What exactly were you hoping I'd say?"

His hands are folded into fists at his sides, and he won't look at me. "That you didn't care about him. That you'd break up with him if...if I broke up with Raven."

"That's a horrible way to treat someone you're supposed to be marrying, Clayton," I say, a sourness settling in the pit of my stomach. "You need to make decisions for yourself. Not based on what I'm doing. And, once you have, then you can talk to me."

I pull open the door, so angry and confused and hurt, and when I do, I find Tucker standing at the bottom of the stairs looking up. The animation leaves his face when he sees me, replaced by worry.

"Maggie? You okay?"

I shake my head, opening my mouth to answer, but no words come out. I turn and make my way to the bedroom, defeated. I don't know what I expected from Clayton, but it was more than this. I thought he was someone different. Someone who treated people—me included—better.

I've seen a whole new side of him tonight, and I don't think I like it.

When Tucker reaches the door, his gaze is steely. He shuts it before speaking, his voice low. "What just happened?"

I drop onto the bed, staring into space. "He told me he's thinking of leaving Raven. He asked me if...if things between us are real." My eyes bounce up to meet his.

"And what did you tell him?" His voice is cold and lifeless. As if he expects the worst.

"I...I don't know. I mean, after what happened last night, everything is so confusing."

He steps forward, bending down to sit on the ground in front of me. "It doesn't have to be. I mean, this is what you've always wanted, isn't it? It's why we did this. So Clayton would realize he was making a mistake." His words are hollow, his voice worn and emotionless.

"I'm just as bad as he is," I whisper under my breath.

He takes my hands in his. "No, you're not. You're not bad, Maggie."

"I am. I'm indecisive and stringing both of you along, and... I mean, up until last night, I thought none of this was real for you, but now... *Is* any of this real, Tucker?" I wave my hand between his chest and mine. "Are we real?"

His stare gnaws at my confidence. "What do you want, Maggie? Because whatever you want is what I want. If you want to be with Clayton, I won't stand in your way. I'll survive it. But...if there's something else you want, I just need to hear you say the words."

I rigidly hold my tears in check. Clayton is the boy I've wanted most of my life. The one I've been in love with as long as I can remember. He knows me better than anyone. He's protected me. Taken care of me throughout childhood and our wild teenage years. He was like a brother to me, then a friend, and now... I've always dreamed we would build a future together.

But ever since Tucker came into the picture, things have made less sense. Now, the future is murky. I no longer see Clayton's face waiting for me at the end of the aisle or hear his voice as we bring our future children into the world.

Tucker has changed me. He's made me see the world in a way I hadn't before. Made me see myself as something new, too.

He's still staring, patiently waiting for me to make a choice that will destroy one of the men I love.

Love.

That familiar ache is back as I recall what I told Clayton earlier.

"I need a minute to think. A few days, maybe. We should call it a night. Is... Is that okay?"

The hurt is evident in his eyes, disappointment weighing heavy on his shoulders, but quickly, he recovers. "Of course. Do you want me to see if I can sleep in another room?"

I shake my head. "No. Don't be silly."

Taking turns in the bathroom, we undress and change for bed. Then we find ourselves back in the same position we were in last night—in the dark, listening to each other's breathing.

This decision feels impossible, but at the same time, it feels like the easiest one I've ever made. It's a decision I didn't even know I would have to make yesterday, when I thought I had no one who actually wanted to be with me. Now, I apparently have two people.

Still, when I think of Clayton, I can't look past the way he just spoke of Raven. Nor can I understand why, if he's feeling so conflicted, he hasn't just broken up with her and pursued me.

The whispered conversation in a bedroom while Tucker and Raven waited unsuspectedly downstairs felt wrong.

If I don't say yes to him, if I don't break things off with Tuck, will he still marry her? The truth is, I think he might, and that scares me a little bit. When I think of Clayton lately, it's all confusion. Anger. Fear. Hurt.

When I think of Tuck, on the other hand, I think of fun. Of the evening in the barn. Of the way he looks at me. Of the things he said to me last night.

Tucker chose me, he helped me, he protected me. Deep inside of me, I feel a pulse of electricity. Because, of course, I've known the answer all along.

I roll over to find him staring up at the ceiling with sharp concentration. He looks at me out of the corner of his eye. Waiting.

"Ask me again," I tell him.

His head turns to the side. "I don't—"

"Ask me what I told Clayton when he asked me if we were real."

He opens his mouth, his eyes locked on mine so hard it's as if he thinks he might shatter if he moves. "What did you tell him?"

"I told him... I think I'm falling in love with you."

The tenderness of his gaze is heart-rending. The prolonged anticipation is unbearable.

He stares at me as if I might not be real.

Maybe I'm not.

Maybe none of this is.

But if it isn't, I want to hold onto this dream for as long as I can.

"Say something," I whisper, begging him to end the torture.

He lifts a hand to my hair, brushing it back from my face. His mouth breaks into a warm, lopsided grin. "Thank god."

He leans into me, pulling my body against his. I bury my face into his throat. Both of his arms go around me, holding me snugly. He releases a choked breath, and I realize he truly thought I was going to end this.

Maybe he's been holding his breath all night, waiting for me to put him out of his misery.

My head fits perfectly in the hollow between his shoulder and his neck, and with it there, I'm reminded of the night in the bar. The night we danced together, and he held me through my tears.

I lean back without looking away from him. "Can I ask you something?"

"You can ask me anything," he promises. Same answer as always.

"How long has it been real for you?"

His soft breath fans my face as he sighs. "Truth?"

I nod.

"Since that first dance."

"The night we met?"

"No, no. The night we met, you were a jerk who snotted all over my bar, remember?" He chuckles. "But the next time, you were something that reminded me of myself. A little lost, a little broken. Someone who needed to be shown how beautiful she is."

I shake my head. "Where have you been hiding this sweet guy?"

His hand slides down my back, moving to grip my hip, and something like a growl releases from deep inside his chest. "I assure you, I'm not always sweet."

"Noted." I press a kiss to his lips.

"What was that for?" He repeats my question from last night.

I shrug one shoulder. "Just seeing what it will take to bring out your not-so-sweet side."

His eyes roll up toward the head of the bed. "Funny, I've been trying to keep him in all weekend."

"Yeah?"

He rolls his hips toward me, and I realize he's already hard. A spark of excitement is back, a swooping pull somewhere deep inside my stomach. "You have no idea."

"I'd like to meet him," I whisper, pressing a kiss to his chest, then his neck. "If you don't mind."

"You will," he says firmly, his grip keeping me from getting any closer. "But not here."

I freeze, pulling back a bit, but his thumbs smooth over my skin as if he senses my worries.

"You will," he repeats, "but when you do, I don't want to be sharing walls with...anyone."

The sound of his voice, the strained quality it has taken on, has my stomach in knots. I don't have to say anything else, and neither does he. A sort of understanding passes through us. He kisses me again, softly, then snuggles against me.

"Now, go to sleep," he instructs.

Suddenly, I can't wait to be home.

CHAPTER NINETEEN

NOW

I take the photo over to my house, comparing it to my porch. It's definitely the same one. But why does Tucker have it?

The movers arrive shortly after I get home, so I don't have much time to dwell on it. I show them to the rooms so they know where to unload the rest of my things and then sit back, overseeing and generally feeling awkward about the entire situation. Standing around doing nothing, I feel lazy, but when I try to help, I seem to be in the way.

Plus, my mind keeps drifting back to Tucker and the photograph.

Hours later, when the movers leave, I make my way through the maze of my furniture and belongings, somewhat relieved to smell the scent of home in this new space.

I study my surroundings, trying to decide where I should start. When I notice a box labeled **Bedroom** that's mistakenly been left on the kitchen floor, I cross the room toward it and haul it to its rightful place.

When I return to the kitchen, the light is turned off.

I freeze. It's still light outside, so it's not like I'm in the dark, but I could swear I just had the light on. I know I did.

No.

I refuse to play into the fear and paranoia.

I flip on the light, tear open a box, turn on one of my favorite motivational podcasts on my phone, and set to work.

I'm an hour in and four boxes down when I realize I'm sweating. I stop, wipe sweat from my brow, and go to get a bottle of water from the fridge. When I do, I glance at the thermostat, stopping in my tracks when I spot the temperature in red on the screen.

Eighty-two degrees?

Who would've ever turned it up so high?

I cover my face with my hands, then look again. Still eighty-two.

No wonder I'm sweating. I start for the thermostat when I sense a presence behind me. Every hair on my body stands on end.

No.

No.

No.

Please no.

I hear footsteps and squeeze my eyes shut. Then, I spin around quickly, a scream caught in my throat.

"Ah!"

"What the—"

"Clayton?" I cry. "What are you doing here?" I clutch my hand to my chest, so relieved to see him standing in my kitchen I could burst into tears.

"I knocked, but the door was open. You didn't hear me?"

I shake my head, reaching for my phone. "I guess I didn't hear it over my podcast." I pause it, noticing a missed call. It must've come through when I was in my bedroom unloading things.

"Oh. Well, I tried to call you. I was on my way to town and thought, since I hadn't heard from you after...the other night, I'd come and see if you wanted to get lunch."

"I'd love to," I say, "but the movers just dropped off all my stuff. Any chance you'd like to help me unpack instead?"

He grins. "Can I pick the music?"

"Only if it's not that Clayton Beckett guy," I tell him with a laugh.

"He's the worst," he agrees with a glimmer in his eyes. "Okay, where should I start?"

"Right now, I'm working in the kitchen, but I keep getting sidetracked in random rooms because several of the boxes ended up in the wrong place, so just grab a box and put things anywhere. I've already got my dresser set up for clothes, and the living room is coming together. If I can manage to clear a path so this place is semi-livable, that'd be great."

"Speaking of semi-livable, is there a reason your house is set to temperatures capable of cooking a meatloaf?" He fans himself with the collar of his shirt before tearing open a box.

"Yeah. There's something going on with the wiring, apparently. Tucker says it looks like everything's fine, but one minute it's freezing, the next it's..." I gesture toward the thermostat before leaning forward to turn it down.

"The wiring? That doesn't sound good." He tosses a handful of brown packing paper to the ground.

"Better than ghosts," I murmur.

He pauses with a plate lifted halfway out of the box. "Come again?" Then, before I can say anything to answer, he adds, "Because of the whole...murders thing? You actually think this place is haunted?"

"No," I say with a scowl. "Yes. I don't know. I don't believe in ghosts, okay? But there are these weird things that keep happening—"

"Weird how?"

"Like, the thermostat for one"—I wave a hand toward it— "and the patches of cold even when the thermostat's normal. And...this smell, the one I smelled the night you came over, but that hasn't been back. And... Last night I thought I heard babies crying and a woman screaming." I pause, fully aware that I sound as if I've lost my mind. "I don't know what's going on."

"Well, do you think it could be because you found out about the past? Maybe your mind is playing tricks on you? I'm sorry I told you anything, Maggie. Really. I never meant to freak you out."

"I know you didn't. And thank you. I want to think it's all in my head, but honestly, that scares me worse." I turn to continue unpacking the box I've been working on.

"Well," he says after a moment, "if it's bothering you so much, why don't you just leave? Sell the house and get something else?"

"I can't just sell the house. I bought it less than a week ago." *Has it really been less than a week?* I'm starting to lose track of my days.

"So? Garrett will help you. And I will, too. You can stay with me, or at the lake house if you want some privacy."

"No. That's okay." I dismiss the offer too quickly; it's clear by his face. "Thank you, I just...I want to figure this out on my own. I don't want to run away. I know perfectly reasonably that ghosts don't exist. There has to be an explanation. I've just let myself get scared."

"I'm sure that's it, I just...get the wiring checked out, okay?

I don't like you staying here if the wiring is messed up. It's not safe."

"I know. I will. Tucker has already said it all looks okay, but I'll have him look again, and if it keeps happening, I'll get a second opinion."

"Okay, good. Yeah, definitely get a second opinion."

We work in silence for several minutes, the music Clayton's playing on his phone turned down low before I speak again.

"So, are you writing anything new?"

"Not really," he admits. "Trying, but...you know. It's not the same."

"Why not?" I ask, a hand on my hip as I use the other to wipe sweat from my brow.

"I don't know. I mean, aren't I a little old to write love songs?" He waves a hand in the air as if love is some mythical idea.

"You are not too old. We've already talked about this. Everyone deserves love, you included. But if you feel that way, write about something else."

"Like what?"

"Well, you could go for what everyone else in country music writes about. Beer and trucks. Throw in a little bit about fishing if you really want to mix things up." I shrug one shoulder, which makes him laugh. "Or you could write about real things, like family, home, growing up."

"Yeah, maybe. I do have a few songs that I'm feeling pretty good about. I'm going to share them with the team when I go to Nashville this weekend."

"See! There you go. You have to keep believing in yourself. It's a waste of talent if not."

"Thanks, Mom," he teases.

I throw a wad of bubble wrap at him, but it misses by

several feet. "I mean it. Don't give up on yourself. You're too good to quit."

"Thanks." He gives a half smile, reaching for a mug in the box he's unpacking. "Maybe I'll bring my guitar by sometime and play some of the new stuff for you."

"Like my own personal concert?" I ask, batting my eyelashes at him.

"Like old times," he says seriously.

"Okay, but...you're getting old. Are you sure you can still do it?" I wrinkle my nose.

He scowls, and it's his turn to throw bubble wrap my way.

We work for the rest of the day, catching up like old times. He tells me about his latest attempts at new songs and how he's thought about opening up a music store in Chicago, and I tell him about my old job and the coworkers who made it interesting. For a while, it's easy to slip into old patterns with him. To forget everything we went through and all that happened between us.

When it's nearly dinnertime, and we've worked our way through what few snacks I had in the house, as well as the boxes to unpack in the kitchen and living room, he asks if I want to come with him to dinner.

I'm disgusting and need another shower, so I decline.

"But let me take you out soon, okay?" I add. "To thank you for helping me. I just want to do it on a day that I'm not covered in dust and sweat."

"Fair enough." He hugs me and heads for the door, but he stops long enough to say, "Today was fun."

"It was, wasn't it?" I smile to myself.

"And I meant what I said. The offer is open. If you don't feel safe here or if you want to sell, just say the word. We'll help however we can, and you know you always have a place with me."

"I know." I hug him again before saying goodbye. "Be careful going home." As he walks down the steps, I get the odd feeling someone is watching me again. Every hair on the back of my neck stands at attention.

I turn around quickly, bracing myself.

My eyes scan the room, but this time, I'm completely alone.

CHAPTER TWENTY

THEN

When we return home from the weekend at the lake house, Tucker has to work three nights in a row, and I need to study for my big finals coming up, which means I have to go three excruciating days without seeing him.

I hear from him occasionally, but it's not consistent, and his texts seem rushed.

By day four, I've started to question if both of us just let the weekend confuse us. Maybe he didn't mean everything he said and is regretting it now.

In an effort to not seem like a total loser, I make a promise to myself that I won't call or text him first. When he wants to see me, he'll make an effort.

That effort arrives when, on Friday, Tucker asks if I want to come with him to a baseball game. It's the last thing I expected, but I reluctantly agree.

He picks me up at my apartment, and we walk there together, a palpable tension between us.

"Sorry I've been so busy this week," he says. He's not

touching me. Not holding my hand. Something is definitely up.

"It's okay," I say gently. "Um, so...when were you going to tell me you are a baseball fan?"

He winces. "Is it a dealbreaker? Should I not show you my Chicago Cubs back tattoo?"

I laugh, relieved to see we at least still have the banter I've always appreciated. "Probably shouldn't ever show anyone that."

He laughs. "Nah, I'm not really into baseball. Aaron's brother is pitching in the tournament, and he had extra tickets, so I thought...I don't know. It could be fun to get out of our element a bit."

"Do we have an element?" I ask.

"The bar, mostly." He shrugs.

"And the barn," I point out.

"Not a long journey from *bar* to *barn*. Just one letter. And the lake house was...*bar*...ely tolerable." He struggles to make it fit, but I laugh anyway, reaching for his arm on instinct. He glances down at where I've grabbed him, his expression warming.

Our eyes meet for a second, and my whole body heats as if I've stepped in front of a fireplace.

"I missed you," I admit.

He pulls his arm away from me so he can wrap it around my shoulders, leading me through the gate and to the stands.

As we sit, we both seem to realize our mistake at the same time. A group of rowdy men are gathered near the dugouts, talking to the players. Among them is Clayton, whose red face and swaying stance tells me he's drunk.

I haven't heard from him since we left the lake house, and I barely said anything to him as we were leaving, but it hurts me to see him this way.

I don't want to think I could've hurt him. That's a guilt I'm not sure I could ever live with.

Tucker releases his arm from my shoulders, looking at me seriously. "Do you want to leave?"

"No," I say. "No. It's fine."

The game starts, and we settle in, sharing a carton of popcorn as we watch. I don't know much about baseball, but I know enough to understand that our team is good. Very good, in fact, and Aaron's brother is a complete star.

When he strikes out the other team, Tucker and I are among the loudest to cheer. I love being with him like this. Seeing him happy and fun and carefree.

I'm so caught up in enjoying it that I don't notice Clayton making his way up the stairs in the stadium toward us until he's sitting down in the empty seat next to me.

"Hey." He nods his head at me, his eyes red, lazy, and tired.

"How are you?" I ask. Tucker is making a concerted effort not to look over, but I can feel him growing tense beside me.

"Been better," he admits.

"Where's Raven?"

"Not here." His tone is sharp. Bitter.

I lean back in my seat. "You okay?"

"We had a fight." He turns his head, watching as the ball is hit and soars toward the outfield. When he does, I notice claw marks on his neck.

"Clayton, what happened?" I lunge forward, forgetting all else in an effort to pull his collar down and further inspect his injuries.

"I'm fine." He pushes my hands away.

Several people around us are looking at me, but I don't care.

"You are not fine," I cry, jabbing my finger toward his wounds. "That one looks infected." I pull my hand back, leaning forward so he'll meet my eyes. "What happened?"

"I told you," he says, his voice lower. "We had a fight."

A strange hardness knots in my throat. "She did that to you?"

He looks away, not answering. "I'm fine, Maggie. Don't mother me."

Next to me, Tucker moves his hand to touch my side. A gentle gesture that lets me know he's here.

"I'm not mothering you, but you need to get that taken care of. And, if she hurt you, you need to stay away from her. Report her. Something."

"Like you care," he snarls.

I suck in a breath, hurt emanating through me. "Of course I care."

His gaze flicks to Tucker. "Not enough."

"Do you have a problem, man?" Tucker asks, peering around me.

"Yeah, I do. You're with my girl."

"Seems like your girl's at home with an engagement ring on her finger"—he leans over, getting a better view of Clayton's neck—"and flesh under her fingernails, by the looks of it."

"You guys, stop!" I cry, putting a hand on each of their chests.

"Do you want to go?" Tucker asks, staring at me.

"Yeah, maybe you should," Clayton says, slurring his words.

"No," I say firmly to Tucker. "Stay. Just...let me go and get him into a campus cab."

"I'll go with you." Tucker starts to stand.

"No," I tell him. "Please. Please don't. Just stay here. Just... I've got this. I'll be back."

Clayton gives him a smug look and turns to walk away.

Tucker leans in, speaking softly, "You know he just wants attention, Maggie."

"He's drunk. He needs me right now."

"Oh, he needs you?" He reels back, his jaw tight. "Really? He didn't need you when he was breaking your heart."

"I can't do this right now," I tell him, shoving my hand in his direction. Clayton is busy stumbling down the aisle, bumping into people as he goes. "He's hurt and upset, and I just want to make sure he's okay."

He takes hold of my arm and lowers his voice, his eyes dancing between mine, begging me to understand and agree. "I don't trust him."

"But you trust me," I say, patting his chest. "Right?"

He swallows. "Yes."

"Then that has to be enough. If you trust me, you'll stay here and let me handle this."

He doesn't look happy, and I can't blame him, but eventually, he sits. I turn and hurry to catch up with Clayton, guilt pulling at me in every direction as I walk him outside of the stadium to wait for a cab.

While we wait, he turns toward me, bumping my arm with his. "Thanks for coming with me."

I don't look at him—can't. I'm too busy fuming with anger, though whether it's directed at Clayton or Raven, I'm not sure. "I'm just getting you in a cab." I look back up at him, pointing at his neck. "Do you want to talk about what happened?"

"Not really."

"Has she ever hurt you before?"

He looks away, hands shoved into his pockets. "She has a temper. She's never left a mark."

"That doesn't make it okay. I can't believe you never told me. Please tell me you're leaving her."

"Do you want me to?" When I look up, he's wearing a knowing smile I recognize and can read well.

"I want you to be safe. It's not okay for anyone to hurt you. What would you tell me if the situation were reversed?"

"I'd tell you I'm sorry I'm in prison now for beating someone's ass."

"This isn't funny." I turn to face him. "This is abuse. Domestic violence. You get that, right?"

He touches his neck. "I know. I do. It's just... I mean, does it even matter anymore? Her? Any of it?"

"What are you talking about? Of course it matters."

"Come on." He tilts his head to the side. "You're so good to me. You've always taken care of me. At the end of the day, that's what matters. It's you and me. Always has been. I don't know why I didn't see it before." He leans down, coming in for a kiss quickly.

I pull back, pressing both hands to his chest. "What are you doing?"

"It's me, Maggs. Come on."

I push harder on his chest to stop him. "No. I'm not... This is not happening."

The hurt in his eyes breaks my heart. "So, you're choosing him?"

"You should go home and sleep this off. Put some cream on your neck. I mean it, Clayton. It looks really bad."

His jaw is tight. He turns away from me. "You don't have to wait. I can get myself into a cab."

"I know you can, but I'm making sure you do."

We stand in silence, not speaking, both of us fuming for our own reasons. When I return to the stadium half an hour later, Tucker's demeanor has changed. He takes me home without asking to come inside, and I worry I've ruined everything.

CHAPTER TWENTY-ONE

NOW

I wake up in the middle of the night in the living room on the air mattress. I don't even remember falling asleep, just lying down to rest for a few moments and...

I check the time on my phone. It's been four hours since then. It's three in the morning, and there's a strange smell filling the house.

I lift my nose to the air, sniffing intently.

I can't put my finger on it. It's something herbal smelling. Lavender, maybe? And...rosemary? Or perhaps sandalwood?

I sit up in bed, adjusting. It's so strong. I know I'm not imagining it.

As I look around, my eyes land on the front door—and the fact that it's standing completely open.

My heart plummets, my hands shaking as the shock hits me full force. I reach for my phone again, keeping my eyes trained on the phone and then the door as I pull up Tucker's number and place the call.

When he answers, he sounds tired. Distant.

"Help," I whisper, keeping my voice low.

"Maggie?" He's awake now—sounding as panicked as I feel.

"Please." Tears sting my eyes as I ease myself off the mattress. My purse is in the kitchen, with my stun gun in it. I try to decide whether to dart to the kitchen and grab a weapon or to head for the front door and try to make a run for it. Deciding on the kitchen, I grip my phone and tiptoe across the room.

When I step into the kitchen, the floorboard creaks under me, and I jolt, leaping into the air. I grab my purse from the counter, digging into its depths.

Come on.

Come on.

Come on.

Come on.

There.

My fingers connect with the stun gun's case, and I pull it out, turning it on and holding it in the air as I cross back into the living room. I spot a flashlight coming through the window, and for a minute, I'm sure my heart has stopped.

Just as quickly, I realize it's Tucker, running barefoot through his yard and up the porch. When he comes into view, his dark hair is disheveled, his eyes still red with sleep.

"What is it?" he asks before he's made it inside, his voice thick and groggy.

"The door. When I woke up, the door was open," I tell him, still holding my stun gun out.

"Is someone in here?" he whispers, looking around.

"I don't know." I suck in a breath. "In here or out there. And there's that smell. Please tell me you smell it."

He nods. "I smell something. Stay here. I'm going to go check it out. You've got your phone?"

I hold it up. We both know, should I need to call for help, it'll be at least twenty minutes before anyone arrives.

"Maybe we should just call the police," I say. "We could go back to your house and wait for them to arrive."

He rubs one eye. "I'll be okay. Stay here."

With that, he disappears into the kitchen, leaving me alone. I wait in paranoid silence, listening to every creak and groan of the house as he moves through it, opening and closing doors.

My heart races in my chest like it's competing in the Kentucky Derby. I can't breathe. Won't breathe until he's back.

It's been too long.

He should've been back by now.

Something terrible has happened. I know it.

I release a heavy breath when he appears in the doorway all in one piece. "Coast is clear."

The words do very little to calm my nerves. "You're sure?"

"Positive. I checked inside every room, every closet. Behind every box."

"What about the attic?"

"The attic is sealed to keep the heat out. No one could get up there and close themself back in. I checked." He studies the door. "Are you sure you got it latched? Maybe the wind blew it open. It's been storming tonight pretty badly."

Has it? I hardly noticed.

"I...I don't know. I thought it was closed, and I always lock it, but..." But then again, I don't remember falling asleep and hardly heard the storm. Exhaustion is starting to get the best of me. I'm not getting enough sleep.

"It's okay," he tells me. "I'm sure it just blew open with the wind."

I stare at him, not sure he believes what he's saying. Then again, why wouldn't he? I'm the one who seems to be losing my mind to this ridiculous fear.

"If you're worried, you can stay over again if you want. Or I can stay here. I'm sure it was just the wind, but we'll make sure the door is shut and latched."

I want to tell him about the thermostat going too high today, but I don't have it in me. I don't have it in me to hear another theory about what happened or to explain to him why I'm so scared.

Especially when I don't fully know myself.

Every explanation he's given is reasonable.

The house is old. There are drafts. The wiring could be shot.

But none of that explains the scream I heard the other night.

I look back down the hall, suddenly remembering the picture I found in his guest room.

"I need to ask you something," I say, wrapping my arms around myself as I make my way into the kitchen. When I do, I find the golden picture frame where I left it on the counter. "I found this on your dresser."

He stares at it. "Yeah. It's me and my grandpa."

"Who's the other little boy?"

"I'm not sure. Why?"

"Because you're sitting on this porch." I point toward it, just a few feet from where we're standing. "Did your family used to own this house, Tucker?"

"What?" He reaches for the old frame, studying it, then looks up and around. "No. We've never owned this house. Not as far as I know, anyway. But yeah, you're right. It does look like this was over here. I've never really looked at this photo that close. I'm...I'm guessing that's Jason."

My stomach flips. "The little boy who died? The one you used to play with? Are you sure?" I demand again. Staring at his happy smile makes my stomach ache. What secret horrors were hiding behind those eyes?

"No, I'm not sure. I look about three or four there, so the timing would be right. I can't think of any other reason I'd be over on this porch with my grandpa. Or who else the little boy could be. When I used to play with him, sometimes my grandparents would come here to pick me up. I guess they took a picture of us at some point."

I nod. "And that's it?"

"That's it," he confirms. "I would tell you if there was more."

"Alright." I glance at the photo again, no longer sure what I was trying to prove or what I thought I'd found. "If it's okay, I'd like to come back with you."

"It's more than okay."

We walk out of the house. This time I take nothing but my phone and purse with me, and Tucker uses my keys to lock the door, tugging on the handle to make sure it's secure.

Back at his house, I show him where the old, golden frame came from, and he returns it to the empty spot. After that, I head straight for his room, making no effort to sleep alone this time. I just can't. After we've settled in, we lie in silence. I wait until he's almost asleep—until my own heart has found a steady rhythm and the terror I felt moments ago no longer feels so real—to say, "Thank you for always coming to my rescue."

His answer takes a long time to come—so long I worry he might've already fallen asleep.

"You're welcome."

"I'm really proud of you, you know." It's easier to tell him this with my back to him.

"For what?"

"For getting your dream. All those years ago, you told me this was what you wanted. A quiet life in your grandpa's house. To run your own business. You made it happen."

He huffs out a slow breath. "Yeah, I guess so. What about you? Did you get everything you ever hoped for?"

"Working on it," I say softly, a sob catching in my throat. "I, uh, I noticed the painting on your wall."

He's quiet.

I roll over to face him, and he's lying on his back, both hands folded on his chest. "The one I painted. Of the barn. Why didn't you tell me you bought one of my paintings?"

"I didn't think you'd want to know."

Now it's my turn to be silent.

"It's great, Maggie. *You're* great." He glances at me from the corner of his eye.

"Thank you," I say softly.

"It's just the truth." One shoulder lifts in a shrug.

I swallow. "That night was really special."

"Yeah, well, it was a long time ago." One side of his mouth draws in. His tone isn't bitter or angry. It's just honest.

A confession burns the back of my throat, begging to be said. "You know I meant it when I told you I never thought you were guilty back then. That wasn't why I left. I never thought you hurt her."

He turns his head to look at me for the first time. "Can we talk about what happened that night?"

"No," I squeak. The answer should be yes, but I can't. I don't want to talk about it ever again.

"You know you can ask me anything. I'll always be honest with you."

I nod against my pillow, too afraid to speak for fear I might cry. Eventually, I roll back over, too cowardly to face him any longer.

He's quiet for a long while. When he speaks again, his voice is so low I almost miss it. "I didn't hurt her, Maggie. And I damn sure didn't kill her. I'm not a killer."

"I know that." I breathe the words out. "It's why I never told anyone you were together that night."

"I'm sorry," he whispers. "I'm sorry to have put you in that position. You didn't have to protect me. And, more than that —more than anything—I'm sorry I hurt you."

"Why did you do it?" The question seems to seep out of my pores, stale from being locked away all these years.

"Raven told me you and Clayton were getting together. She said she'd seen you hanging out. I didn't want to believe it, not until I heard it from you, but then...well, I did. I just...I lost it. I didn't want her. I wanted you. But..."

"But she was there. And you were lonely."

I hear him nod against his pillow.

There's nothing left to say and nothing left to be said. I let myself drift off to sleep with silent tears.

Like yesterday, when I wake, Tucker is already gone. This time, there's a text on my phone saying I'm welcome to stay at his place all day and asking me if we can get dinner tonight to talk about everything.

I'm too preoccupied to think about that, but with a fresh mind and a decent amount of sleep, I have a new plan.

I open my email account and search for Garrett's name, pulling up the first contract he sent me where I put in an offer to buy the house—an all-cash offer, twenty thousand under asking. I scroll through, searching for the names of the sellers.

When I find them—Cassidy and Derek Allen—I open social media and search for them both.

To my relief, I find them relatively easily. Like Tucker had suggested, they now live in a much larger home a town away with their three adorable kids. They don't look like a family that's been tormented by ghosts, and there are no posts to point me in that direction on either of their pages.

Then again, I feel crazy enough telling my fears to Tucker and Clayton. Would I ever post anything about this online?

I already know the answer to that.

I open Cassidy's profile and click the button to send her a message. I'm not sure if this is against some rule regarding real estate transactions and contact between sellers and buyers, but at this point, I'm desperate for answers.

I send her a quick message introducing myself and asking if she could call me. I leave my number and press send, ninety percent sure I'll never hear from her.

But it's worth a shot.

In the daylight, everything is a little less creepy, so I shower again, fill up a mug of coffee, and then make my way back to my little house of horrors.

Inside, the smell from last night is still there. I walk through the house, but stop in the kitchen when I spot a candle in the center of the small table the movers delivered yesterday. A candle that definitely wasn't there last night.

A candle that I don't remember lighting.

The wax is completely melted, though. The candle is a totally liquid, bright shade of pink, like dancing water beneath the glowing wick. I move near it and lower my nose down. Sure enough, yes. It's the same.

This is what's smelling up my house like lavender.

One mystery solved, but another added to my plate.

Because not only do I not remember lighting this candle or placing it on the table. I've never seen it before in my life.

CHAPTER TWENTY-TWO

THEN

When Clayton calls me the next day, his apology is immediate and thorough.

"I'm sorry. I'm an idiot. I had too much to drink, and Raven and I fought, and she went back to Nashville, and I just... You didn't deserve to be treated like that. Thank you for helping me."

"I'll always help you," I say, although somewhat begrudgingly.

"I know that. But I still want to say thank you."

My mind sticks on something he said earlier. "Raven went back to Nashville?"

"Yeah."

"When is she coming back?"

"I don't know," he says glumly. "I'm not sure if she will."

"It was some big fight, then, huh?"

"I told her about you."

"What about me?"

"That I'm in love with you."

My breathing hitches, my entire body turning to ice. "What?"

"I wanted to tell you this that night at the lake house, but I was scared. I was a chicken, okay? And ever since then, it's all been so messed up. And I know you're with Tucker, and I'm trying to respect that, but I love you, Maggie. Maybe I always have. It just took all of this to make me see it."

"I...I don't know what to say."

"I know. And you don't have to say anything. I just wanted you to know."

"Well, thank you." It's everything I've ever wanted on a silver platter. *But still...* I sigh.

"Do you...maybe want to go do something later? *Just as friends,*" he adds quickly. "I could really use one of your famous pep talks."

I know it's the wrong thing to do. I need to think. I need to talk to Tucker. But Clayton's my weakness. When he needs me, I go. When he asks, I do.

And so, I hear myself saying yes before I've really thought it through.

That night, I agree to go to his new apartment. The place where he's staying while his home in Myers is being built is much bigger than the old one he shared with two roommates.

"Thanks for coming," he says, wrapping me in a hug at the door.

I can't shake the guilt I have over being here, especially because I haven't told Tucker. I know what he'll say, what he'll think, and I can't say I blame him, but he'd be wrong.

Despite how surprisingly dressed up Clayton is, this isn't a date. It's no different than any of the thousands of other nights we've spent watching movies and pigging out on junk food.

"I've got *The Ugly Truth* if you're feeling a comedy or *A Perfect Getaway* for thrillers. And there's rocky road and mint chocolate chip in the freezer. I'll go grab those while you choose a movie."

Of course he got my favorite ice cream.

He returns a few minutes later, after I've put *A Perfect Getaway* into the DVD player, and hands me a bowl of rocky road.

We settle in for the movie, and though I catch him watching me a few times, for the most part, everything feels surprisingly normal. When the movie ends and he stands up to take our bowls, I spot the scratches again.

"I put medicine on them," he says, noticing my stares.

"Can I ask what happened now? I mean, besides the fight. Did she just literally claw you? You still haven't said."

He's hesitant to tell me, but I follow him into the kitchen. He rinses the bowls out and places them in the sink. When he's done, he turns and rests his back against the counter with a sigh.

"Yeah," he says finally. "Like I said, she's always had a temper. But, like I told you at the lake, I feel like I'm only really just now getting to see certain sides of her. That night was the worst I've seen. When I told her about you and said I thought we should end things, she was crying. But then, when I asked her to leave, she just...she snapped. She lunged at me, started clawing me, screaming saying I couldn't do this to her. Calling me...every name in the book." He sighs. "I shouldn't be telling you this. It doesn't matter. She was hurt, and I probably deserved it."

"No. No one deserves that," I say, reaching up to touch the wounds on his neck. "I'm so sorry."

His hand connects with mine on his neck as our eyes meet.

He pulls his bottom lip into his mouth, his gaze falling to my lips.

Then, his head tilts down ever so slightly, waiting to see if I'll object.

I do, before I even realize I'm doing it.

"I'm still with Tucker."

He freezes. "Oh."

"I'm sorry. I don't want to hurt either of you. You're my best friend, and...before you left, I did think, well, I hoped...I wanted to be with you, too."

"But now?"

"Now..." I shake my head. "I'm sorry. I still want to be your friend. Your best friend."

He looks as if I've shot him, his face pale, eyes wide. He nods, but I don't know that he realizes he's doing it. "Oh. Okay. Sure."

"It's late. I should go. But...tonight was fun."

Again, he nods. "Yeah. Um, do you want me to walk you to your car?"

"That's okay."

He leads me to the door and hugs me again, awkwardly, before I leave. On my way to my car, I pull out my phone and send a text to Tucker.

We need to talk.

CHAPTER TWENTY-THREE

NOW

My phone chimes from across the room, and I place the candle down. How did it get in my house?

More than that, who lit it?

Is it possible I overlooked it last night? Or that Tucker did when he was searching the house? We were both so tired...

I grab my phone from where it rests on top of a box and stare at the number that's calling me. I don't recognize it. I swipe my finger across the screen and put it on speakerphone.

"Hello?" I spin around, checking behind me.

"Hi, is this Maggie?" The voice is cheery though apprehensive.

"It is. Who's this?"

"It's Cassidy Allen," she tells me. The name sounds familiar. "You messaged me and asked that I call you."

The last owner.

My blood pressure plummets, and I sink down into one of the kitchen table chairs I haven't managed to get out of the living room.

"Right. Oh. Hi. Thank you for calling me."

"Is everything alright?"

"Um, I'm not sure... Listen, since I've moved into the house, all these weird things have started happening."

"Weird?" Is it my imagination, or does her voice go higher? "Weird, how?"

"Like the thermostat keeps changing randomly, and I'm hearing noises in the house. Did anything like that happen when you were here?"

"Well, the house is old, so there are all sorts of noises," she says with a clipped tone. "You had the inspection done, so I would assume you know of more issues than we did, if there are any. We never had trouble with the thermostat." She's suddenly very defensive, and I understand why, but really, it's me who should be upset.

"Did you know about the history of this house when you sold it?" I ask her, meaning to sound gentle, but I know I don't.

"Excuse me?"

"About what happened here."

She's quiet for a long while. "Look, if you have any issues with the house, you should talk to your realtor or an attorney. We sold it to you fair and square. I called you as a courtesy in case you wanted to know how to work something or where something was, but I think we're done here. Please don't contact me again."

"Wait, I-I didn't mean to—"

It's too late, though. The call ends, the screen going blank in front of me, and I feel the last piece of hope slip between my fingers.

Would she tell me the truth? Maybe I had thought so, but

now, I feel uncertain about everything. Obviously, she knew what I was talking about to get off the phone so abruptly.

I spend the next hour researching haunted houses and reading about ghostly experiences in homes. Most of it feels fake, like something you'd see in a horror film or tell over a campfire, but some of it is oddly reminiscent of what I'm going through.

A few websites offer remedies—everything from burning sage and ringing bells in every corner of the home, to physically cleaning the house as if it's just a case of dust bunnies, and even having an exorcism. One website has a list of psychiatrists who help deal with ghost sightings.

Not surprisingly, nowhere within an hour of Myers has sage bundles, but I do find a store in Chicago that sells them and place an order, which will arrive in a few days.

Turning my attention back to the mysterious candle, I text Tucker.

Did you leave me a candle?

A call from him comes in seconds.

"Hello?"

"Was I supposed to?" There's noise in the background—loud machinery and men talking.

"No. Maybe it was Clayton." With the phone on speaker, I text him the same question. "I found a candle here that had been burning all night. It's what we were smelling. But I don't remember ever seeing it, let alone lighting it."

"Wait…" It sounds like he's moving away from the noise around him. Suddenly, things are very quiet, like he stepped inside somewhere. Maybe his truck. "You think someone came into your house last night, brought a candle, lit the candle, and then left?"

"I...I know how stupid it sounds. How impossible. But what other explanation is there?"

"No. I get it. It's just...strange. Where are you? Are you still at my house?"

"No, I'm home."

"Will you go back to mine until I can get there?"

"I'm fine, Tuck."

"I know you are, but I don't feel good about you being alone. Just...amuse me, please? Go to my house and wait for me."

I look around the room at the boxes that still need to be unpacked, my life that still needs to be put in order, but his request puts me at ease. I don't want to be here alone. Not until I understand what's happening.

I'm strong and independent, but I don't have to put myself through this.

I'm at a war within myself. I never wanted to depend on a man again, yet here I am just a few days after my return, and that's all I'm doing.

"I'm sure it was Clayton. Everything's fine. I'll be here unpacking, and I promise I'll call you or go to the house if anything else weird happens."

He sighs. "Fine. I'll be home in less than half an hour. I just gotta let the crew know."

"No. You don't have to—"

"I know. I want to." He ends the call, and I see a text from Clayton has come in. I'd been so caught up in the conversation I hadn't noticed.

I open it and read his response, which does little to quell my fears.

> Candle?

Half an hour later, there's a knock on my door. "It's me," Tucker calls, before I have time to ask.

"Come in," I respond, elbow deep in a box of books, which I'm carefully organizing on the built-in shelves.

He's dressed for work still, in a pair of khakis, a polo, and a pair of boots.

"You didn't lock the door?" he asks.

"I thought it would make for an easier escape." I'm only half joking, but he doesn't look amused. "Clayton said he didn't leave the candle. Maybe it was something from Garrett, like a closing gift that I forgot about."

"But you still don't remember lighting it?"

I shake my head. "Not really, no. But I've been so tired lately... It's possible I did and forgot about it."

"Text him and ask. If we can at least figure out where it came from, I'll feel better."

"I want to check the attic," I tell him. "It's the one place you didn't check last night."

He glances up toward the ceiling. "And you think someone could be up there? Ghosts?" He's not judging me, I don't think, though we both seem to realize how absurd this conversation is.

"I don't know. But I'm going. With or without you."

He swallows and looks up again. Finally, he nods. "Okay. Fine." He holds out a hand to help me up from the floor and, together, we make our way through the kitchen and into the hall. It's dark here with all the doors closed, but I flip on the light, and to my relief, it stays on.

He grips the string dangling above our heads and pulls it down slowly. The hatch groans, the metal hinges showing their age as he tugs the wooden stairs down and unfolds them.

They don't look like they'll hold either one of us, but Tucker puts a foot on the second step, easing his weight onto it until the stairs are straight.

Above us, I see what Tucker meant when he said the attic was sealed. There's a silver, plastic cover blocking the entire opening that looks sort of like those windshield sun shades people use in their cars to prevent fading.

"Can we even get up there?" I ask.

"It looks like it just zips." He takes another step, then a few more, reaching above his head to grab the zipper tucked in a corner. It's stuck, so it takes a few extra tugs to get it to move, but eventually it does. He unzips the screen all the way around, and a wave of heat crashes down on us.

Tucker looks back at me. "Do you see another light switch anywhere?"

I glance around. "No, I don't think so."

The attic space above us is dark, lit only by the two small windows at either end of the house.

He reaches into his back pocket and retrieves his phone, turning on the flashlight and using it to scan the space.

"Can you see anything?" I call from the ground.

"It's pretty empty. Some old junk, looks like." He climbs the rest of the way into the attic, turning around with the light. "Ah. There."

"What?" He disappears from view, and I hear his cautious footsteps overhead. A few moments later, I hear the metal zip of a chain and a dim light illuminates the space. "Come on." He reappears at the top of the stairs, and I step onto the ladder. "Just watch your step when you get up here."

The space smells of old wood and dust, and when I get to the top, I take in the sight of it. The pictures I saw were somewhat misleading. While a few sections of the wall have unfinished drywall covering them, some parts of the attic's walls are unfinished, with pink insulation sticking out between the studs. Still, other sections look like original walls with paneling. In the back corner, there are a few boxes covered in cobwebs. The floors are mostly plywood, with only a small section of carpet.

What an odd attic. In the middle of the floor, there are studs that look like there may have once been a wall dividing the space. Either that, or someone tried and failed at my initial plan to make this a main bedroom already. I cross the room toward the boxes curiously, but find them mostly empty, with a few old toys and jackets thrown in. Nothing interesting.

Sweat gathers on my back and under my arms as I look around the room again. I fan myself with my shirt. It's not even this hot outside. This is miserable.

I feel dizzy.

"There's nothing up here except spiders," Tucker says, kicking at a piece of plywood that isn't totally nailed down.

I study the space, moving carefully through it. I'd been so sure we'd find something up here, though what I was expecting, I'm not sure.

"What's that?" I ask, pointing toward a spot on a wall that catches my eye. I walk toward it and bend down. In the center of the wall, in the section covered in paneling, is a small door. It's slightly bigger than those mouse holes you see in children's cartoons, with a tiny, golden, oval-shaped knob.

Tucker bends down beside me, rubbing a thumb over it. "It looks like one of those old milk doors, but it makes no sense to have one in the attic. They were for milk deliveries, so they're usually on the main floor."

He twists the knob with his thumb and forefinger, then tugs it open.

The space is small, too small for milk, and dark. Again, he uses his phone to explore.

"There's no floor," he says. "It goes down somewhere."

I nod, seeing it as he's explaining.

"Maybe it's an old laundry chute, but I don't know. It's tiny."

"And why would it be in the attic?" I ask.

"It doesn't make sense. Old houses have quirks. We see them all the time, but yeah, this is weird. I wonder if we could find old blueprints for this house that might make it make sense." He's quiet for a minute, looking around, then sucks in a breath like he's just discovered something. "You know, this might've been an actual second floor at one time." He stands, stretching his hands above his head. "There was room for it, and it makes sense as to why some of it has paneling..." When he trails off, I notice his eyes locked on something across the room.

I follow his gaze.

"What's that?" I ask, but I know. I know as soon as my eyes connect with it.

"Don't," he warns, but it's too late. I'm already going. I cross the attic to the other side of the room, where the walls have been stripped to just insulation, and stop just in front of the spot that caught his eye. Tucker is just behind me.

The dark stain in the plywood beneath our feet is large and faded. It could be mistaken for an oil stain if I didn't know better. But I do. I stare at the splatters, at the proof of what happened here.

Tucker is right. This used to be a second floor. It had to have been. That's why there are studs in the middle of the room. A wall used to exist there.

"This is where it happened," I whisper, a hand to my chest. "This is where he killed them."

He puts a hand on my back. "Someone must've tried to clean it up, started tearing out the walls and flooring, but they changed their mind for whatever reason. They just boarded it up and made it the attic instead. If they didn't have central air here during the nineties, they probably just installed it for the lower floor. Took out the staircase that used to exist and had it replaced with an attic hatch. It's a lot of wasted space, and a fair bit of work, but with the history...it makes sense."

I feel as if I'm going to be sick. My entire body shakes with fear and rage and adrenaline. "How could anyone do this?" It's the same thing I ask when I see the latest tragedy on the news, but now it's so much worse.

"We should go back downstairs. You don't need to see this," he says, nudging me away.

If the first family who bought this house tried to fix this space, restore it, and then ended up sealing it off and leaving it instead, was there a reason? Were they dealing with some of what I'm going through now?

I could swear I hear a baby crying again, and it brings tears to my own eyes. *I hate this, I hate this, I hate this.*

"I'll get the plywood replaced," Tucker says, like that fixes anything.

There was so much blood.

Was there more on the walls?

How could anyone do this? He was their father. Her husband.

We reach the stairs, and he helps me ease down onto the top step, then goes to pull the chain and turn off the light. Once I reach the bottom step, he comes, too, pausing to zip up the seal before he climbs the rest of the way down.

After the attic door is closed, he turns to find me on the floor.

I don't remember sitting down, but here I am. My hands are so cold they burn. He eases himself onto the ground, staring at me with so much concern in his eyes it hurts.

"Are you okay?" I can hardly hear him. It feels like I'm underwater. Everything is blurry, including his voice.

Like I'm swimming.

"Maggie, breathe. Can you hear me?"

I close my eyes, trying to focus on moving my blood to my fingers. I flex them once. Twice.

"Maggie?" His hands are on my shoulders, but I hardly feel them. "Maggie, I'm worried you're going into shock or something. Please. Open your eyes." I'm floating then. He's hoisted me over his shoulder, and we're rushing somewhere.

Anywhere.

Nowhere.

We stop abruptly, as if we've run into a wall.

Perhaps we have.

He spins around. "Maggie..." I'm placed on the ground in the kitchen. "Maggie, did we turn the lights on?"

Looking around, I realize the lights are on everywhere, the light above the sink in the kitchen, the lights in the bedrooms, and in the living room.

How strange...

"The door is open again," he says, his voice even more distant than before.

Then, I'm thrown back over his shoulder. Something is very wrong, but I can't make myself care.

Next thing I know, it all goes black.

How strange...

CHAPTER TWENTY-FOUR

THEN

I'm at Tucker's door an hour later. When he answers, he's still dressed in his clothes from the bar.

"Everything okay?" he asks, his gaze raking over me worriedly.

"I'm fine. I just needed to talk." I walk past him and turn back when he shuts the door.

"Okay, well, before you say anything, there's something I want to talk to you about."

"I went to Clayton's tonight," I blurt out.

He starts to say something but stops, regroups, then says, "Okay. How was that?"

"Do you want to sit?"

He swallows, remains still. "Should I?"

"I, um, he broke up with Raven." My words come fast. "And he said he wants to be with me. Then, he tried to kiss me."

"Tried?" His voice is hoarse, his eyes studying me as if I'm part of a dream. As if none of this is happening.

"I didn't let him."

At his sides, his fists unclench. "Why not?"

"I don't know," I say softly. "It didn't feel right."

His face clouds with uneasiness, and he steps forward. His hand lifts slowly, moving a piece of hair back behind my ear. His thumb comes to rest on my cheek, his fingers on my jaw. "What does feel right?"

His eyes drop to my lips. The prolonged anticipation is unbearable as I wait for him to lean forward. When his eyes find mine, my heart seems to turn over.

Something intense flares in his gaze, and he leans in. His lips brush against mine, leaving my mouth burning with fire as he pulls away.

He raises a brow, waiting for an answer.

"I'm so confused," I admit. "I thought we were...that something was happening at the lake house, but you've been so distant since we got back. I worried you'd changed your mind, and I didn't want to pressure you, but now, now I need to know."

His lips touch mine again, soft like a whisper. "I didn't change my mind."

My stomach spins circles inside me. "No?"

"I don't want to make your choice harder, Maggie. Don't want you to worry about my feelings. But, for the record, I think he's wasting your time. I think he only wants you now because he sees you're wanted by someone else."

"You want me?" I whisper, the only part of that sentence I can focus on.

He looks away, then his eyes come back to me. "How can you even ask me that?" My knees weaken as his mouth descends on mine, pulling me closer as if we can't be close enough.

I drink in the sweetness of him, the ravishing desire pulsing through my body. I can't breathe, can't think. There's only him.

Only us.

He nips and bites, his tongue swiping over mine, exploring.

He scoops me up, gripping underneath both of my thighs as he carries me forward, kicking open the bedroom door. Then, I'm down on the bed, and he's standing above me.

He pulls his shirt over his head, revealing his muscled torso. In an instant, he's back down, and I realize how much my skin has missed the warmth of his. How much I've wanted him.

His lips recapture mine, more demanding this time. "I've wanted you"—he kisses my nose, my mouth, my chin—"from the moment we danced." His lips caress the pulsing hollow at the base of my neck. "From the moment we kissed in that bar." His mouth moves lower. He tugs my shirt over my head quickly, as if he can't stand to be away from me for even a second. "From the moment I tasted you. Felt you. You were mine." He grips my hip, lowering himself farther.

A question passes over his eyes, but my answer is there. Waiting for him.

There is no hesitation, not anymore. No worry about who's on the other side of our wall, about whether or not I'm conflicted. Whether or not this is real.

In this moment, everything has changed.

My entire body is on fire as I wait. His hand eases aside the lacy fabric of my bra as his tongue caresses me gently, then more fiercely. He sucks me into his mouth, and my back curls involuntarily with the movement.

I cry out, which only seems to make him more feral. He sits up, staring down at me. His hands move to cup my hips, my thighs. It's as if he can't touch me in enough places. As if he wants to feel all of me at once.

"You have no idea how long I've wanted this," he says, eyes heavy with desire. "How long I've wanted you. Us."

The way he's looking at my body gives me more confidence than I've ever felt. He presses his pelvis forward, so I can feel his hardness against my heat.

"Me, too," I whisper, allowing the truth to slip out finally.

A tempestuous grin crosses his lips.

"How long?" he asks.

"Since the night in the barn," I say, breaking eye contact as my cheeks flame.

"You wanted me then?" He pulls his bottom lip in between his teeth.

"Things...changed for me then, yes. It stopped feeling fake between us."

He runs a palm over my stomach. "You never said."

"I was scared to get hurt again," I admit, wiggling against him.

"I will never hurt you." He leans forward, running his tongue over the space above my belly button. He places a kiss there, then near my hip, easing himself down. I miss the warmth of him, the hardness, but I'm distracted from that easily as he works the button on my pants, easing them off my hips. For every inch of skin he reveals, he leaves a kiss. As his kisses get closer to the one place I want him, they begin to last longer.

Finally, he stands from the bed, pulling my pants the rest of the way down my legs. Once they're off, he undoes his jeans, staring at me intently as he removes them.

He's straining against his briefs, the outline of him clearly visible, and I feel a new flame of heat rush through my body. He climbs onto the bed, taking my mouth with his, the kisses demanding and passionate.

"Are you sure about this?" he asks, breathless, our foreheads pressed together.

I nod against his lips. "Yes." It's all I can stand to mutter as I feel his hand slip between my legs, his fingers parting me.

I feel his grin against my mouth, though my eyes are still closed.

"You have no idea how bad I want you, Maggie," he whispers, lowering his lips to my neck. My name on his lips is pure sin.

He pulls his hand away from between my legs, easing me up from the bed long enough to unhook my bra. Then, he traces his fingertip across my lips, down over my nipples, teasing me with every move. His grin is delicious. Haunting. Intoxicating.

He kisses me, lapping up my scent left there by his fingertips moments before, then moves to explore my breasts. My body arches toward him again, and the sounds I release are embarrassing and new, yet I can't bring myself to feel shame.

I only feel desire.

I only want him.

His tongue snakes a path down my ribs and to my stomach, and then, just as I feel ready to combust, he's there.

Right where I need him.

His tongue presses against me, his breath hot on my skin. He hooks my legs over his shoulders as my body squirms underneath him. My body is half ice and half flame, half here and half there.

I've never felt so much of everything all at once. Like I could explode.

Fiery sensations pass over my body, and I can't believe this is real. I can't believe it's happening. The world is spinning, careening on its axis, and I'm all too ready to let it go.

To let everything cease to exist except the way he's making me feel.

Pleasure overtakes me without warning, pure and explosive, and I cry out for release. Nothing could've prepared me for this. For him.

He presses soft kisses against my sensitive skin, coaxing new sounds from my throat. As I feel the final waves of lightning pass through my veins, he sits up, obviously proud of himself as he reaches for his nightstand and pulls out a foil package. He tears it open quickly, stepping out of his briefs and rolling the condom over his length.

My body vibrates with liquid fire as I feel him press against the place where his mouth was moments ago. There's a question in his eyes, waiting for the final piece of permission, and I grant it by easing toward him gently, lifting. He grips my thighs, then my hips, pushing himself inside me with one swift motion.

He looks up at the ceiling, cursing under his breath.

"*Fuck.* You're amazing," he whispers, pulling out of me and pushing back inside slowly. It's pure heaven. Everything he does is pure heaven. He's gentle yet reckless, careful yet wild. I'm hypnotized by him, by his touch, his eyes. I never knew anything could feel this way.

I cry out, a glowing image of fire, passion, and desire, as he claims me.

It's a raw act of possession, the way our bodies move together, and I surrender to him completely, passion rising in me like the hottest fire, clouding my brain, silencing all thoughts.

When I feel myself growing close to release again, he leans down so he's over me, pulling us together so we're chest to chest. His hand slips between us, his thumb applying gentle pressure, drawing circles right where I need him.

He kisses my lips once, twice, and then electricity arcs through me, fragmenting me from myself, my thoughts from existence.

Erasing everything except this moment with him.

There is only us.

Me. Him.

It's completely real and totally perfect.

I never want it to end.

CHAPTER TWENTY-FIVE

NOW

When I wake, I'm in an unfamiliar place. I sit up, staring around. My body is drenched in a cool sweat, my hair clinging to my neck.

"You're awake."

I turn to see Tucker sitting in a chair next to the bed. His bed.

"What happened?" I ask, trying to piece together the fuzzy memories in my mind. They come to me as images. The bloody floor. The blurry house. Lights. So many lights.

"You had a panic attack, I think." He gives a sheepish look. "From what I can find online anyway. We went up into the attic, and...it wasn't good."

"The blood..."

"I'm going to fix it. I'll get the boards removed tomorrow. I just didn't want to leave you alone tonight."

I squeeze one eye shut. "And the lights?"

He nods. "When we came down from the attic, they were all on. And the door was open again." His face is serious as he moves to kneel next to my side of the bed. "I don't know what's going on over there, Maggie. I'm not a ghost person. I believe when you die, you die. No afterlife. No haunting. None of that. But I can't explain what's happening in that house."

He presses his lips together. "I know you don't need my help, but I want to help you anyway. I called around and ended up talking to Harry Kline at The Tool Shed. He has a security system in stock. I thought we could go into town later and pick it up, and then I'll install it for you. If someone is doing this, I want to know about it." He pauses. "I'm hoping having cameras that will catch anything strange happening will make you feel safer, but until you do, you're welcome to stay with me."

My head pounds, a dull ache forming in the base of my skull. "Yes. Yeah. Of course. Thank you. A security system is smart. I'll pay you to install it."

"You don't have to do that." He touches my arm. "I've got you."

I sigh. "I promised myself when I moved back, I wouldn't rely on anyone else. I've spent so much of my life waiting on boys and men and trying to make my life fit someone else's mold. I don't want to do that anymore. I don't want you to have to take care of me."

"I get that, but—"

"*But*," I finish for him, "I feel safe with you. I always have. So, thank you. For letting me stay and always being there when I need you." I chew my lip. "I think I'm going to contact Garrett, though, Tuck. I don't think, even with a security system, that I can stay here much longer."

He nods as if he'd been expecting me to say as much. "I can't say I blame you. As much as I'll hate for you to leave, I don't feel safe with you there. Someone was in your house. Someone turned on the lights and opened the door again.

Whether it was ghosts or a person"—he doesn't have to say which he thinks is more likely—"someone was there, and they shouldn't have been. It seems like they're messing with you."

I sigh. The wrinkles around his eyes weren't there thirteen years ago. The texture of his skin. He's changed so much, and yet he's almost exactly the same. "I'm sorry I brought all of this to you. You were living a normal life, the life of your dreams, until I came and ruined it...again."

"You didn't ruin anything," he promises, running a hand over my arm. "When I saw you at the door that day, when I realized you were...*back*. Here. Moving in next door. I couldn't believe it. Maggie, you have no idea how much I've missed you. How badly I've wanted to call."

"I know," I say, taking his hands. "I never thought...I mean, when I bought this house... What are the chances?"

He licks his lips. "I've always kind of liked our odds."

I laugh, staring up at the ceiling. When I see him, it's hard not to think about everything that happened between us. From the moment we met to the moment I walked away.

He clears his throat. "Listen, about what happened that night. I owe you an explanation. An apology. I want you to understand—"

"Please don't. It's been so long, I just...can't. I'm so grateful for all you've done for me, back then and now. You don't owe me anything."

"I know, but I—"

"I just can't, Tucker. Please. If I go down that rabbit hole, I'm afraid I won't make it back."

"Okay. Yeah. Sure. I get it. But, whenever you're ready to talk about it..."

"You'll be the first to know."

He stands and goes to his side of the bed, lying down next

to me. Turning his head to look at me, he says, "Your mom would be really proud of you, you know it?"

Tears sting my eyes instantly. "Thanks."

"It's like that thing you said about how people come into your life for different reasons, and how your mom was your guiding light. Sometimes, I think you were that for me."

I blush, looking down.

"I know things are messed up now, but I want you to know I don't regret what happened between us. You were the first real thing I had in my life, and so much of what I've accomplished since then has been because, I guess in some weird way, I always hoped to run into you again to be able to tell you about a life that felt...worthy of you. Maybe that's a weird way to say it, I don't know."

I want to respond, but something about what he said freezes in my mind. Sticks. Because...

"Wait. How do you know I called my mom my guiding light?"

"You mentioned it the other day..." he whispers, but I can see the confusion on his face. He knows he's messed up.

He could only know that if...

"You were at the funeral."

It's not a question. He doesn't nod.

I adjust in bed, propping myself up on my elbow. "Tucker, did you go to my mom's funeral?"

He turns his head, looking up at the ceiling.

"Tucker."

He puffs out a breath. "I came, but I didn't know if you'd want me there. I just couldn't...*not* show up for you."

"Why didn't you say anything? Find me? I had no idea you were there."

"I didn't want to cause you any drama that day, Maggie.

You looked so broken. And Clayton was with you. I didn't want to be in the way or...have overstepped. I don't know. I just wanted to pay my respects."

He turns his head slightly as a tear falls down my cheek.

"Please don't cry," he whispers.

"You weren't going to tell me?"

"I didn't go so you would know about it. I went in case you needed me. But you didn't."

I puff out a breath, recognizing the part of him I fell in love with all those years ago. "Why are you so good to me?"

"Because I love you, Maggie," he tells me simply. "I..." His eyes dart back and forth between mine, dancing with words unspoken. "God, as much as I've tried to fight it, I've always loved you."

My stomach drops, my pulse racing. He's not asking for anything. Not touching me. Not trying to fix what went wrong. He's just being honest with me. Just protecting me.

But, at the end of the day, he couldn't protect me from heartbreak all those years ago, and that's where the trouble lies.

I don't know if I can trust him—or trust myself—not to go through that again. I'm not sure I'd survive it a second time.

The way he's looking at me right now, I'm not sure I'll survive whatever's happening this time.

"Do you think it could be your ex?" he asks, his voice soft. So soft and unchanged it takes me a second to understand what he's said.

"What do you mean?"

He lifts up on one elbow, like it's just occurred to him. "At your house. The guy who was screaming at you the other morning. Do you think he could be doing all this stuff to mess with you?"

I want to say no, to tell him Nick wouldn't do that, but in

truth, I'm not sure. I don't know who Nick is anymore. He was practically unrecognizable when I last saw him.

"I'm not sure," I admit.

He nods. "It's going to be okay." A promise. A vow. "I'll take care of you."

I snuggle into my pillow a little harder to hide another tear as it falls.

You always have. Until you didn't.

CHAPTER TWENTY-SIX

THEN

When I wake up the next morning, my body is sore. Every move comes with a memory of what happened between us last night. I peek my eyes open and find that he's watching me with sleepy eyes, one arm draped over my waist.

He gives a smile, and I return it.

"Hi."

"Hi."

We're still naked, I realize, and I pull the cover closer to me. Why is everything a bit more awkward in the morning light?

Under the blanket, his hand skates over the skin on my side, up to my shoulders, tracing patterns neither of us can see.

"Sleep well?" I ask, trying not to breathe on him, very aware I likely have a major case of morning breath.

"Like a baby." He snuggles closer to me, pressing his lips to mine, and then pulling away and standing, walking naked and unashamed to the bathroom. I don't shy away from the view.

Heat creeps up my neck at the thought of him last night. Of me. We are so different. *How will this work? What will we be now?*

A phone is vibrating somewhere. I sit up, holding the blanket up to cover my chest as I search the room for the sound. His phone rests on the nightstand, clearly not the source of the noise.

My pants are on the floor, discarded in a moment of passion. I stand from the bed and reach for them, removing my phone from my pocket and checking it just as the phone stops vibrating.

I have three missed calls from Clayton. *Must've been what woke me up.*

Oh well. He can wait.

I'll call him back when I have time.

I drop my phone and grab my clothes, sliding on my under-wear and then pulling my pants up over my hips. I reach for my bra when my phone vibrates again.

I glance over just as Tucker appears in the room.

This time, Clayton has texted me. I lift my phone from the bed as Tucker comes to stand behind me, sliding his arms around my waist, nuzzling his mouth into my neck. He inhales deeply.

> Emergency. I need you. Please. Call me back.

I stare down at the text, my body stiff.

"What's that?" Tucker lifts his head, leaning over my shoulder to see what I'm looking at.

"It's Clayton."

His hands pull away from my waist. "Are you going to call him?"

I don't miss the hurt in his voice. "He said it's an emergency." I reach for my shirt. "I'm sorry. I need to go."

He nods slowly, processing. "Yeah, sure. Okay."

233

I touch his chest, wanting to say so much more, but there's no time. If Clayton says there's an emergency, I have to go. It's what he'd do for me.

"I'm sorry. I'll call you, okay?"

"Yep. Okay."

I hook my bra and pull my shirt over my head, slipping on my shoes as I rush for the door.

When I get to the park where Clayton asked me to meet him, he's sitting on one of the metal benches, his head hung down over his phone.

I touch his back as I move around behind him, and he looks up. When he sees me, he launches forward, wrapping me in a hug. Whatever this is, it's bad.

Very bad.

I've only seen Clayton this upset a few times in my life.

He pulls back, and we sit down next to each other.

"What's going on?" I ask gently, a hand on his arm.

He checks the time on his phone, more out of habit than anything I think, and locks the screen. Then, he looks away.

When he looks back at me, I realize his lip is split.

"Clayton, what happened?" I reach out to touch it.

He winces. "I'm fine."

"You don't look fine."

"Well, I'm not," he admits. "Maggie, I..." His expression is pinched. Pained.

"What is it?"

"She's pregnant."

I stare at him, blank and shaken. The words hit me full force. They're dizzying, making it so nothing else makes sense.

"She told me last night. After you left."

"H-how?" I don't know why I ask it. I don't want to know how. I want to know why. For the past few months, I've been on a path of acceptance, trying to accept that he's with her. That he loves her. And then, last night, I thought it didn't matter to me. Thought I wanted to be with Tucker.

Now she's permanently attached to him.

He's permanently hers.

Forever.

They're going to have a baby.

A child.

They're going to be parents.

Images of them raising a child together flash through my mind—bringing the infant home from the hospital, evenings at the dinner table, board games, teaching them to ride a bike, packing lunches, graduations.

His future is set, and it doesn't include me. Somehow, this makes it all more real.

More final.

I don't know what to say.

"It wasn't planned," he says. "It... I'm not sure what we're going to do. She doesn't know either. Neither of us wanted this, even with the wedding. We had already talked about waiting years before starting a family. We wanted to focus on our careers. A baby ruins all of our plans."

Except, their plans were already ruined if he was telling the truth last night. They're not supposed to be together anymore. "Could she be lying?"

As soon as I ask, I know it's the wrong thing to do.

His eyes go distant, staring hard at nothing at all, as he seems to contemplate the question. "She wouldn't..." His voice is soft. Unsure. "No. She wouldn't do that to me. She was upset, too."

"Of course." I clench my hands together in my lap, thinking. "What are you going to do?"

He looks away, gripping his lips between his forefinger and thumb in a fist. "I don't know what to do. I meant everything I said to you last night, but...this changes things. I'm going to be a dad." His voice cracks and his head falls, chin to chest. "I don't love her, Maggs. I don't. She wants me to move back to Nashville with her, says we'll need help from her family. My parents say I need to go through with the marriage."

"You told them already?"

"*She* did," he corrects. "I wasn't answering her calls, so she called them. Then she came by the apartment."

"She's back in Chicago?"

He nods, rubbing his hands over his thighs. "Yeah, she's back. I don't want to leave. I want to be with you. And I know you said you need more time, and you're still with Tucker, but...I need to know. Is there a chance for us? Because, if there is, I want to fight for you. I want you to know I'm serious about this. About us."

My heart has shattered into a million tiny shards currently floating around inside me, stinging me with every bump. Every slice of my organs. My throat aches with defeat, with sorrow I've never felt before. How could he do this? How could this happen?

"I don't know," I say in a low, tormented voice.

"Please don't cry..." He reaches for my cheek. I hadn't realized I was, but now I feel the cool water brush my skin underneath his thumb.

"I love you, Clayton. I always have, you know that. But our timing has never been right. And now, a *baby*. I don't know how to compete with that." Nor if I even want to. I do want to be with Tucker, I think. But that doesn't make this sting any less.

I'm just so confused.

His brows pinch together. "You don't have to compete. Just say the word, and you win."

"You don't mean that. You can't. Even if you choose me, Raven will always be a part of your life. You'll...you'll have a baby together. A child. An adult, someday. Those sorts of things come with big feelings." I bury my face in my palms. "I'm sorry. I can't do this. You need to talk to her. Work it out, sort through your feelings, and then we can talk. But not now. Not like this."

His face goes soft. "Okay." He looks away, staring straight ahead. "My parents think marrying her is the right thing to do. They say you've just confused me. They think Nashville would be best for us."

I gesture toward his lip, ignoring the sting of their betrayal. His parents have always been like second parents to me. How could they treat me this way? Is that really what they believe? "And did you show them that? Did you tell them she hurt you?"

He doesn't deny it. "She was upset."

"It doesn't matter. Don't make excuses for her. Nothing about putting her hands on you was right."

"She's scared."

"You're scared," I point out.

He nods. "Yeah, I am." He falls onto my shoulder, and I cradle his head. This is just like so many other times. He could be crying over his grandfather passing away or the girl he likes turning him down in front of his friends at school, like he has in the past. I hold him like I always have and promise him that somehow everything's going to be okay.

"Clayton, if she hurts you again, you need to tell someone. Promise me, okay? Someone. Anyone. The police. Your parents. She needs to be stopped. It's not okay."

He nods against my shoulder, and I notice a fresh set of scratches on his neck that weren't there the night before.

"It won't happen again," he promises. "I won't put up with it if it does. She knows that."

I hug him tighter, my heart pounding in my ears at the thought of her hurting him. Scratching him. Bloodying his lip.

"Don't tell anyone, okay? If word gets out... If it got back to the label somehow, or to the press, I'm not sure what would happen."

"I won't. I—"

"*I knew it.*"

We pull apart at the sound of a voice behind us. As I turn to look over my shoulder, my eyes land on Raven. It's the first time I've seen her without makeup. She's still beautiful, but wearier and more washed out, although I suppose staying up all night abusing your ex-fiancé will do that to a person. Her arms are folded as she stares between us.

Clayton stands. "Raven."

"I knew I'd find you here. You were supposed to be going to your parents', but I called your mom, and she didn't know what I was talking about. I saw your car in the parking lot when I drove past." Her eyes cut to me. "Of course you're with her."

"I'm sorry. I needed to talk to Maggie," he says, moving around the bench to stand in front of her.

"You need to talk to *me*," she cries, her eyes welling with tears as she jabs a finger into her chest. "I trusted you. How stupid was I?"

"Raven, it's not what it looks like. Clayton and I were just—"

Her nostrils flare as she whips her head around to look at me. "I wasn't talking to you. Can I have a minute with *my* fiancé? Please?"

I check with Clayton, who nods.

"Call me if you...if you need anything, okay?" I ask, walking toward him. I pat his arm, refusing to look at her.

Everything is so messed up. I bolt back to my car and cry the whole way home.

CHAPTER TWENTY-SEVEN

NOW

After we're dressed and ready for the day, I ride with Tucker to pick up the security system from The Tool Shed, our local hardware store. It's a quick thirty-minute trip, and then we're back at the house. With cameras, alarms, and a keypad in hand, it's everything it will take for me to be entirely safe in my home. At least, in theory.

He sets to work installing alarms on every door and window, with the main keypad next to the front door. He puts cameras in the corner of the living room, above the sink in the kitchen, and at the end of the hallway.

As he works, he explains to me what each thing will do. "So, if you input this code backward, it will send an alert to your monitoring company, who will contact the police. And the same thing will happen if any of the doors or windows are opened and you don't input the code to turn the alarm off in time."

I nod along, mostly listening but still checking over my shoulder at every turn. Every bump. Every groan and creak of the floorboards.

He installs more cameras on both ends of the front porch and near the back door and helps me download an app I can use to monitor them.

But can you see ghosts on cameras? I don't bother voicing that thought aloud.

As I'm sitting on the air mattress, looking over the app while he installs the final window alarm in the living room, Tucker turns to look at me, a strange expression on his face. "Hey, you know, I was thinking—"

We're interrupted by the sound of knocking on the door.

He peeks out the window and looks back at me. "You expecting someone?"

I stand, heart lurching.

From the window, I see Clayton's Jeep parked behind my car. Tucker turns to look at me as I pull open the door and wave at Clayton.

"Hey, stranger," he says, grinning widely at me.

"I didn't know you were coming over."

"Yeah, well, I didn't have anything going on this afternoon, so I thought I'd stop by." He spots Tucker behind me, and his demeanor changes. His eyes take in the drill in his hand. "What's going on?"

I move to the side and let Clayton in the house. "Tucker's installing a security system for me."

He glances around the rest of the room, his eyes bouncing over the few boxes still untouched and the air mattress with sheets strewn about. "Did something else happen?"

I rub my forehead. "It's a long story, but yeah. Someone has been in here messing with stuff, turning on lights, opening doors."

"Like with the thermostat? So, you don't think it's the

wiring now? I've texted you a few times to check in and make sure you're okay, but I haven't heard back."

I do remember seeing a text come in from him, now that he mentions it. Maybe more than one. "I'm sorry. I've had so much going on I haven't been checking my phone."

"It's alright." He nudges my arm. "I just wanted to make sure you're okay."

"She'll be a lot more okay once this is installed. Did you ask your brother why he didn't mention the house's past to her?" Tucker asks pointedly.

"Yeah," Clayton replies, his tone clipped. "He didn't know. The last owners either weren't aware or chose not to disclose anything, and he didn't have a reason to look into it. We knew there were rumors about this house when we were kids, but we both thought that's all they were. Rumors. And I've already told Maggie she can stay with me, and we'll help her sell the house. Garrett said he thinks they could get her money back by selling it again. But if you think there's someone breaking in, that has nothing to do with what happened." He looks between us. "Besides, if you really think someone is breaking in, you should get the police involved. Have you done that?"

Not yet, is the answer. As much as I would love to pass this problem onto someone else, nothing has been stolen, no one has been hurt, and there's very little to actually report at this point. Besides, I don't want to try to explain the story again, and I'm not sure they'd believe me if I did.

I'm not sure I believe this security system will be of much use either, because I don't know that any of this is being done by humans. Nick, as upset as he apparently is, isn't a monster. I haven't heard from him since he left, and he has no reason to come back here and torment me.

But I don't say any of this, or anything else, because I want to seem like a sane individual who knows ghosts aren't real, and houses aren't haunted.

"Right now, we have no proof of anything. We're waiting to see what the cameras catch," Tucker says. "If anything. If it's just someone messing around, we'll catch them on camera and turn them in."

"We found blood in the attic," I tell Clayton.

His worried expression tells me how serious this all is.

"I'm going to take the stained subfloor out," Tucker adds. "It looks like someone pulled up all the flooring and tried to redo the upstairs, but didn't finish."

Clayton nods, pressing his lips together. He takes a step backward, reaching for the wall as he looks up. "Yeah. I, uh, I did some research after we talked, but I didn't know if you wanted to know. From what I read, some of the stuff happened up there."

I swallow.

"We assumed," Tucker tells him, setting back to work. "I'll remove the subfloor, and she'll be good as new. Then, if you want, we can refinish the top floor and build some equity in the house, in case you decide to sell."

"Do you know what happened?" I ask Clayton, hardly listening to Tucker.

"You sure you want to know?" He doesn't look so sure he wants to tell me.

"Stop scaring her," Tucker says. "You don't need to hear this shit, Maggie."

"She's a grown-up. She can decide what she wants to hear for herself," Clayton snaps, not taking his eyes off me.

They're both staring at me, and in a way, they're both

right. I could find the answers for myself, I know, but if I do, I'm afraid of what I might come across.

"I don't need to know the gritty details, but I'd like to know what happened," I say, glancing at Tucker. "I'll be okay."

"You haven't been okay," he argues. "Just that stain was enough to—"

"I promise I'm okay." I put up a hand, halting the argument, though I can see he wants to say more.

Clayton nods, licking his lips. "From what I read, the dude offed the kids, but it was never confirmed whether he took himself out or if the wife got him. Either he thought he'd already killed her, but she wasn't dead and managed to kill him before she died, or she saw what he'd done to the kids and attacked him, so he killed her then. However it went down, by the time the police arrived, everyone was dead."

"*Jesus,*" Tucker mutters under his breath, turning away.

Unfazed, Clayton continues, "The investigation ended inconclusively, as far as I could tell. There used to be a main bedroom and a playroom upstairs. The kids were found downstairs in their beds. No blood or anything there. He just"—he puts his hands around his neck for a second—"but the parents were upstairs in the hall. It's why there's speculation about how it went down." He glances up. "Either way, if I were you, I'd sell the house. I don't think anything good can come from you staying here."

"Maybe not," I admit, wiping away the chills on my skin. "I don't know what I want to do. But I'm not leaving yet. Not until I put in my best effort to stay. Tucker's right, this security system should stop whatever's happening. Whether it's my ex, Nick, or...I don't know, an old owner, or some weirdo true crime creep, I'll be able to find out."

"You're sure you want to be here? You could stay with me for a few days and keep watch on the cameras from there."

"I'm staying," I say firmly. "It's important to me that I try."

"Okay." He points toward the boxes next to him. "Well, put me to work. Where do you want those?"

"Those are more boxes for my bedroom. We can work on unpacking the rest of the stuff in there, if you want." I realize how ridiculous it is to be unpacking while all this chaos is going on, but I'm determined to make this work. I just want all the weird stuff to stop. It's too exhausting to think about leaving, moving all my stuff out, relisting, and going through the selling process, not to mention how humiliating it will be. I need this to work. I need to feel safe. I have to be positive about this. And brave. It's the only way forward.

"Sure." He grins. "Lead the way."

"We'll be down the hall," I tell Tucker, feeling awkward about leaving him but more determined than ever to begin making progress. The longer I let the boxes remain unpacked, the longer I'll have to agonize over the decision.

With the security system installed, I have protection. I have the sage coming, which will hopefully give me peace of mind, if nothing else. Tucker will be removing the floorboards upstairs. I'm doing everything in my power to feel safe.

This is my home, and I'm going to make it work here.

Clayton and I unpack for the next few hours, folding or hanging my clothes and putting them away in the dresser or small closet, while Tucker continues to test the cameras and alarms. When I hear the groan of the door to the attic hatch in the hallway, my body goes numb and ice cold.

"Tucker?" I call, wincing.

"It's me. Everything's just about all set up, so now I'm going up to get those boards out of here. I'll do the alarms on the windows in there when you're all done." His voice is tight as he struggles to lower the stairs to the floor. Seconds later, I hear the thud that says they're in place. "Don't worry."

I stand, moving past the window, and when I do, I notice a breeze. I pause, leaning down. How many times have I walked past this window and failed to notice how cold it is in here?

I lean down and run my fingers along the ledge.

"This window is cracked," I whisper.

Clayton comes over, leaning down to see what I mean. "Broken?"

"Open," I correct him, placing my hands on top of the window to push it up and prove my point. "It was unlocked." I open the window the rest of the way, confirming my suspicion. "Someone left it unlocked."

"What's going on?" Tucker appears in the doorway.

"This window's been unlocked."

He rushes toward us, his expression serious. "I checked in here last night, though. It wasn't open."

"It was just barely. You couldn't see it. I only realized when I felt the breeze." I stare at him. "Maybe this is how whoever's been here has been getting in and out. Not the front door."

He slams it shut, turning the latch and tugging on it to make sure it's secure. "Maybe, but they aren't anymore. As soon as I get the subfloor out, I'll install the alarms in here, and you'll be all set." He touches my shoulder. "Whoever has been bothering you won't anymore. You okay?"

"Shaken a bit," I admit with a sheepish smile. "I can't believe I'd be stupid enough not to lock the window. There are no screens. I should've checked."

"We all should've," Clayton says, looking at Tucker. "It's not just on you."

"He's right," Tucker agrees. "And either way, it's handled

now." He pats my shoulder and returns to the stairs. The sound of his heavy footsteps fills the house as he climbs the ladder, and then they're overhead.

"Do you want to go with him?" Clayton asks. I glance over and realize he's been watching me stare toward the door.

"I think I just need a break from this room," I say, walking past him and moving toward the attic stairs. I have the vague sensation of being watched again. Like someone is staring at me through the window, though I tell myself it's impossible.

Clayton follows behind me and, against my better judgment, I find myself climbing the ladder up to the attic.

"If this used to be a top floor, where's the staircase?" Clayton asks when we reach it.

"Tucker said he thinks someone had it torn down and replaced with the attic hatch when they decided to close it off."

In front of us, Tucker is kneeling down, prying up the stained plywood boards. I try not to look at the bloodstains, turning away and moving to stare out the window.

"This is a good space," Clayton says, filling the room with his positive attitude. Tucker and I glance at him as if he's lost his mind. "I mean, if you decide to redo it. It would add to your value for sure."

"Tucker said he'd help me," I tell him. "I'm not sure I want to. It feels like a big endeavor, but it could help bring some light into the house. Make it feel like it's mine, you know?"

He nods, shoving his hands into his pockets as he examines the space. "Hey, what's that?" His eyes narrow as he moves forward toward the tiny door across the room.

"We think it's a laundry chute," I tell him, moving in that direction, too. "Makes sense if this used to be a bedroom."

"Cool." He drops to his knees and pulls the door open. "Where's it lead?"

I think it over. Now that he's mentioned it, I don't recall finding any place downstairs where a laundry chute would've landed. There's not even a designated laundry room. The washer and dryer hookups are in the kitchen now.

"It probably got closed up at some point," Tucker answers. "Not really a use for it if no one's using this space. Plus, it would've let heat downstairs."

"Fair enough." Clayton leans his head into the dark doorway, trying to get a better view of wherever it leads. "Anyone have a flashlight?" He reaches for his phone before we can answer.

"We tried to look yesterday," I say. "There's nothing down there as far as we can tell."

BANG.

The sound cracks through the air as Tucker pulls the last corner of one of the boards up, causing Clayton to jerk back and knock his head on the doorframe. I don't miss the smirk on Tucker's face, even as he turns away and tries to hide it.

"*Fuck!*" Clayton curses, covering the back of his head. He checks his palm for blood.

"You okay?" I ask.

"Fine." He rubs it again, then returns his attention to the door as Tucker begins to carry the boards toward the stairs. "You know what we should do?"

Tucker stops.

"We should video call each other and tie my phone on a string and lower it down. See what we can see," Clayton proposes.

A shiver runs through me. "What?"

"I'm just saying. There might be treasure or something."

"I doubt there's treasure," Tucker says, his tone caustic.

"I don't know," I say, chewing the inside of my lip. "You could lose your phone."

Plus, the idea of it is terrifying.

"Come on," Clayton eggs me on. "I'm not going to lose my phone. We'll use duct tape. Duct tape never failed nobody." He hops up, dusting his knees and making his way to the stairs. "I want to know what's down there."

CHAPTER TWENTY-EIGHT

THEN

I spend the next week avoiding Tucker and Clayton. I need to clear my head, and I can't do that if they're both always around. Wanting things from me.

Choices. Decisions.

I've never felt so incapable of making decisions.

When I left Clayton's apartment for Tucker's, I thought I'd made up my mind, but this baby changes things in a way I still don't fully understand. It takes away my choice in a way that breaks my heart all over again.

I'm not being fair to either of them, but I know until I make a decision, this is the only honest way to handle it. I can't stand to lie to either of them, and I don't yet know what my truth is.

When Clayton's birthday rolls around, though, I agree to meet him for dinner. Last year was the first year we didn't spend his birthday together in as long as I can remember, and I know he needs me now more than ever.

He's promised Raven won't be there.

When I arrive at the restaurant, he's waiting for me outside.

He looks like hell. His skin is pale and lifeless, his eyes red and puffy. He hasn't been handling any of this well.

Then again, that makes two of us.

"You look great," he says. Er, he *lies*, more like it. I definitely do not look anywhere in the realm of great right now.

"How're you holding up?" I place an arm around him, and we walk into the restaurant together.

"Better now." He tells the waitress his name, and she takes us to a seat near the back.

"You made a reservation?" I'm impressed.

"I wanted tonight to be special." He unfolds the napkin and places it on his lap. "I guess it'll be the last normal birthday I have."

"Normal's relative," I say gently, but I know he's right. Nothing about our lives will ever be the same. That night in the bar a year ago, when he told me he was leaving, a path was set into motion that neither of us can walk back from.

We place our drink orders, and the waitress disappears.

"How're things with Tucker?"

"I haven't seen him this week."

His brows perk up slightly. "No?"

"No. How're things with Raven?"

"I haven't seen her much either. I'm letting her stay in the apartment, and I've been staying in a hotel while we figure everything out."

"How's she feeling?"

"Okay, I guess. She's still pissed at me."

I give him a look that says he deserves it as the waitress returns with our drinks, and we place our orders.

When she's gone, Clayton says, "I know it's the worst timing, and it's not like I won't help her out or do my part with the baby. I just... This isn't what I want. *She's* not what I want.

251

Is it fair to stay with her just because of the baby? Doesn't she deserve someone who actually *wants* to be with her?"

"I guess I just don't understand what changed. When you came back in February, you guys were in love and ready to get married. Now, three months later, you can't see a future with her?" The idea that so much can change in such a short time is both terrifying and heartbreaking.

"I thought she was what I wanted, I really did. But I think I was just caught up in the haze of it all. It was fun, you know? I was living my dream. She was the only person I really got to know in Nashville on a personal level. She'd been doing the music thing there for years and had connections, so I went everywhere with her. Being around her meant I was invited into rooms and to parties I'd never get to attend on my own." He pauses, taking a drink. "I don't mean for it to sound like I used her. I did care about her. I *do*. And I do think I loved her, in a way. It's just that...when we left, that haze went away. Everything that existed there was gone. Including my feelings for her. It just wasn't the same."

"But now she's wanting you to move back. Maybe she felt that, too."

"Yeah, except I don't want to go back. It won't be the same as parents, and even if it was, I'm not the same person. I want different things." He picks up his drink again, swirling the amber liquid in his cup. "Different people."

"People?" I challenge.

"Person," he corrects. "I want one person in particular."

I fold my hands in front of me. "How do I know you don't just want me because I'm suddenly unattainable?"

"Are you unattainable?" he asks.

"I'm with Tucker."

"Still?"

"Yes, still."

"And he makes you happy?"

Warmth fills my chest at the question, the answer undeniable. "Yes, he does. I never thought I could care about anyone the way I care about you. And when you left, and then when you came back with Raven, I thought I'd never feel normal again. But Tucker brought me back. He helped me to not be so broken."

"I'm sorry I hurt you," he says gently.

"I know you are. And I'm sorry I'm hurting you now. I don't want to. It's the last thing I want, but I have to be honest with you."

"I get it," he says with a slight shrug. "I missed my chance."

I don't know what to say to that, so I change the subject. I ask him about his mom, his music, and his brother. I ask about how the new song went over with the label.

We move onto easier conversations, and though I can tell he wants to come back to the topic, he never does.

When dinner is over, he thanks me again for coming, and I give him a hug and tell him I'll call.

Then I head back toward my apartment. I pop earbuds into my ears and turn on some music. I'm in a better place now. I think this conversation is what I needed.

It gave me peace and closure.

I could have Clayton if I wanted to, and even sitting with him, it's still not what I want.

I want Tucker. I know that now, and I'm embarrassed by how long it took me to accept it.

I turn a corner, a smile growing on my lips, and freeze.

Outside the bar where he works, I see him. Except he's not alone. He's in a car with its door open, the overhead light on. A woman sits next to him, a hand on his arm as they talk heatedly.

They're closer than they should be, and a wave of nausea that I recognize as jealousy passes over me.

Because it's not just any woman.

It's the woman who seems determined to take everything from me.

Raven shakes her head, saying something that has him shutting the car door. Within seconds, they're plunged into darkness. Now, I can't see them except for an occasional glimpse of their shapes in the moonlight.

I swallow, trying to make sense of what I'm seeing.

He doesn't notice me. Neither of them is looking at anyone but each other.

Just like that, my entire world implodes.

CHAPTER TWENTY-NINE

NOW

We find duct tape and a roll of ribbon in one of the boxes in the kitchen labeled **Junk Drawer.**

Clayton, who seems way more into this plan than Tucker or I are, wraps the ribbon around his phone several times, then places duct tape over the ribbon to secure it in place.

Minutes later, we're back upstairs, and he places the call to my phone. I answer and see our faces on my screen. Clayton gives a silly grin and sticks out his tongue. He's pleased with himself. To me, this feels like something stupid characters would do in a horror movie.

"Okay," Clayton says, dropping to his knees. "So, we'll lower it down really slowly and see what we can see."

"What if it's too dark to see anything?" I ask.

"That's why you're going to stand over there under the light, so my screen will be as bright as possible." He directs me to stand in the center of the room under the main light fixture as he lies flat on his stomach. "We have to make sure we have just the right lighting and camera angle, or this will never work."

Tucker scratches his head, grumbling, "Easy there, Tarantino."

Clayton either doesn't hear the comment or chooses to ignore it as he lowers the phone down the chute. A lump forms in my throat like dough, thick and unmoving as I watch the darkness on the screen.

"Do you see anything?" he asks eagerly, his voice echoing in the metal shaft.

"Nothing yet. It's all dark."

As he lowers the phone, there are occasional glints of light against the metal casing of the chute, but not much else.

I hold my breath as he continues to unravel the ribbon, lowering the phone down, down, down.

Tucker hovers over my shoulder, staring at the screen intently.

When the camera stops moving, we look up at Clayton.

"Why'd you stop?" I ask.

"I didn't," he says, proving it by lowering more ribbon. "What's wrong?"

"It's pitch black," I tell him. "Before, I could see movement, like light reflecting off the sides of the chute, but now there's nothing. It's like it's landed on the bottom."

"It can't be on the bottom already." He gives a big tug on the ribbon, and the phone flips with a clanging sound. Suddenly, we're staring at a small box of light several feet away. "What's wrong?"

"Hold your hand out over the hole," Tucker tells him.

Clayton does as he's told, extending his hand so it's through the door and over the opening. Moments later, his hand appears on the screen, confirming both of our suspicions. The phone has landed on something and is pointing face up.

"It's like Maggie said. You've landed on something,"

Tucker tells him. "When you tugged on it, it flipped it around. We can see your hand. Must've reached the bottom."

Clayton sticks his head in the door, looking down. "Doesn't go very far, then," he says. "I could almost reach it with my hand." He lays down, stretching out to see if he can. I hold my breath again. We would not be the people to survive a horror movie. His arm would be ripped off, and Tucker and I would scramble and ultimately fail to save him. Eventually, he sits up, arm still intact, and shakes his head. "It's just a few feet down, wherever it goes." He pauses. "Unless it's not the bottom. Let me try something." With an odd look on his face, he sits up, grabbing hold of the ribbon again and giving it a tug.

Our view changes as the light on my screen disappears. He does it again, and this time, for just a brief second, something comes into view. Then it's gone.

"Do that again," I instruct, my body cold.

He does.

Again, the object comes into view for a split second, then it's gone. Tucker's seen it, too. He moves closer to the phone. "The phone's face down now. There's something underneath it."

"No shit?" Clayton stands up, rushing over to get a view of what we're looking at.

"You can only see it when you move the phone. For the short time it's pulled up before it lands," I tell him. "Once it lands, it's just darkness. Pull your phone up just an inch or two and hold it."

He nods. "Got it."

"There." The image becomes clear on the screen. Blue fabric. "It looks like a blanket of some kind." Tucker's voice is barely above a whisper.

"What do we have that would reach down there?" Clayton asks, looking at him. "Surely you have a tool or something."

"We could try some grilling tongs," I offer, trying to think. "I have a pair downstairs."

"Yeah, that might work," Tucker says. "Where? I'll go get them."

I tell him where he can find them—in a drawer I just unpacked in the kitchen—and he disappears down the stairs. While he's gone, Clayton and I keep moving the phone around, trying to get a better idea of what we're looking at, but all we can see is the blue fabric, and if he moves it back farther to give us a better view, we lose it to the darkness entirely.

A few minutes later, Tucker returns, tongs in hand. He quickly clamps them together twice, which I'm convinced is physically impossible not to do when you're holding tongs. Clayton takes them and moves back toward the door. He pulls his phone up quickly, and it bangs and clangs along the chute. Once it's up, we end the call and huddle around him as he lies on his stomach and reaches down. He winces, stretching his arm as far as it will go, before his face changes.

His eyes widen in disbelief. "I think I've got it."

My heart lurches, and I press a hand to my stomach, terrified and intrigued by what we might be about to uncover.

Please don't let it be a body.

Please don't let it be a body.

I won't make it through seeing any more blood, I'm sure of it.

That's why, as he lifts his arm out slowly, I find myself squeezing my eyes shut behind my hands. I peek out between my fingers when I hear Tucker suck in a breath.

With the tongs, Clayton is holding the gathered ends of an

old quilt. I open both eyes and drop my hands. The quilt is wrapped in a ball, obviously concealing something inside.

He lays it on the floor carefully, and I drop to my knees at the same time as Tucker to examine it. Gently, Clayton unfolds each piece of the quilt, which appears handmade and years old. Dust flies in every direction as he moves each piece, dropping it to the ground, and a stale smell fills the air.

"What the..." I'm not sure who whispers the words in my head, too focused on what I'm seeing.

"Clothes," Tucker says, picking up a child-sized shirt. "It's all clothes."

Clayton moves a pair of overalls and tiny shoes as my stomach churns. I feel lightheaded suddenly. *Why would these children's clothes be in my wall? Were they what they were wearing when...*

I don't think so. They can't be. The article didn't mention missing clothing, and these aren't bloody. In fact, besides the dust, they look completely clean and well taken care of. They're old, the tags yellowed and fading, but they've obviously been preserved. Besides, who would've put them in the wall if they were from that day? No one else was here.

When Tucker picks up the next shirt, he tosses it aside. "Oh."

At the bottom of the pile is a folded stack of cash, carefully held together with an old ponytail holder.

"Money." Clayton picks it up, counting it out carefully. "Two hundred and sixty-three dollars."

"Not much," Tucker says, pinching his lips together. He shakes his head. "What if she knew?"

He's thinking the same thing I am.

"The wife?" I confirm.

"What if she knew what he was going to do and was trying to escape?"

Tears fill my eyes at the possibility. "Then she tried. She just wasn't quick enough."

———

When Clayton leaves that afternoon, he reminds me he's going to Nashville for the weekend to do a few co-writes with some other artists. With him gone, the house feels strangely claustrophobic.

When it's time for Tucker to leave, too, he asks if I want to come with him.

I shake my head. "The security system is installed now. I don't have any reason to."

He hesitates, something obviously on his mind. "Are you sure you'll be okay?"

"I have to do this, Tuck. If I'm going to stay here—and I am—I have to get used to staying in my own home. I can't keep coming back to your house like a stray cat."

"You're not a stray cat," he says with a scowl. "You shouldn't have to stay somewhere if you're afraid."

"I have to learn not to be afraid, then." I straighten my shoulders, and even to my own ears, I sound more confident than I feel. "I can't keep hiding out. This is my home now." I put my arms out to my sides, as if embracing the walls around me. "It might seem silly, but I have to do this for myself."

He nods slowly, looking around, then takes a step toward the door. "Just lock up, okay? And make sure the cameras are working and the system is secure like I showed you before you go to bed. If you hear anything strange or get scared, just call me. You're never a bother."

I nod, and as he reaches the door, a pulse of fear shoots through me. I press my lips together, refusing to acknowledge it, but somehow, he senses the shift. As if my terror is suddenly pungent in the air. He turns back, his eyes raking over me, and opens his mouth slowly. "Do you...want me to stay over instead? Just for the first night? That way you're still here, but not alone. Just in case..."

I want to say no, to tell him I'm more than capable of taking care of myself and I'm not afraid to stay here alone, but the lump in my throat prevents it. Instead, I find myself nodding.

He releases a sigh that says he's relieved at the concession.

"Great. I need to run over to the house and get a few things." He rests his hand on the doorknob. "Do you want to go get something for dinner first?"

At the question, I rest a hand on my stomach. "Dinner sounds perfect, actually. I'm starving. Let me clean up a bit, and I'll meet you at the truck."

He pulls the door open. "Sounds good. I'll run to the house to get my things and see you in a bit." There's hesitation in his voice. "You sure you're okay?"

Sometimes I think he's more afraid of the house than I am. "I'll be fine," I lie. When the door closes and I'm alone with my thoughts and the quiet of the house, I make my way to the bathroom, ignoring the patch of cold air that hits me in the hallway. I run a brush through my hair and splash water on my cheeks. In the living room, I change into clean clothes and swipe fresh deodorant under my arms. I'm not exactly ready for a hot date, but it's the best I can do under these circumstances.

I double-check that the front and back doors are locked before I head toward Tucker's truck waiting in his driveway. He's in the front seat, messing with the radio when I slide in.

His eyes land on me, widening slightly, but he clears his throat and looks away just as fast. "What sounds good?" he asks as I buckle in.

"Your choice," I tell him, gazing out the window as we head down the driveway and then out onto the street.

He's quiet for a long while, then says, "Lenny's okay?"

I nod. "Yeah, that's fine."

"Does it...feel weird? Being back?"

I shake my head. "Not really, no. But at the same time, yes. It feels weird being in Myers without my parents here anymore. Everything about this place reminds me of them."

He nods. "I get that."

"Was it hard for you to stay after your grandpa passed?"

"No, but it was different. I never planned to leave, so that made it easier. But...I mean, obviously, I still haven't even redecorated the house."

"Why not?"

"I know he wouldn't care, but it still looks the same as it did when I was a kid. If I change that, I lose it." He wrings his hand against the steering wheel, knuckles white.

"That's nice, actually," I say, staring down at my own hands in my lap. "My parents' things are all in storage. I wish I had a house to go back to that still reminded me of them."

"Once you get settled, maybe you can unpack some of their things, and it'll bring it all back to you."

"I hope so." In truth, I'm not sure how I feel about bringing my parents' things—my childhood things—into this house. Something about it feels odd and out of place. I know he's right, though. Bringing more familiar items into my space will only help me to feel more at home.

We're quiet for a while longer, and I watch as the town I once knew like the back of my hand passes by out the window.

There's the old movie theater where I had my first date, the empty parking lot where my friends and I had snowball fights after a particularly bad winter left mounds of snow piled up for weeks, the gas station where I got into my first car accident—I still swear Clayton distracted me and caused it, though he'll swear he didn't.

Farther down, I see the school where I grew up, where I had my first dance (memorable), my first kiss (terrible), and my first heartbreak (unforgettable). I can practically smell the popcorn from the home games Clayton and I attended and hear the cries from the pep rallies. Next to the high school is the pharmacy where I worked my first job stocking shelves and Nonna's Kitchen, the little Italian restaurant that was always Dad's favorite. In what feels like another life, we walked down this exact sidewalk, carefree and happy, no idea what was coming.

This place is home, and I'm realizing for the first time how much I've missed it.

We pull into the parking lot of Lenny's Burger Shack, and Tucker shuts off the truck before leading me inside. Once we've ordered and received our food at the counter, we sit down and begin to dig in.

After a few bites have satiated my hunger, I realize he's staring at me. I blanch, moving a hand to my lips. "Do I have food on my face?"

He chuckles under his breath. "No."

I glance out the window at an older couple and a young girl walking past. She has a flower headband in her hair as she skips along, her mouth moving with whimsical conversations we can't hear.

"Do you ever think about how many times we might've

walked past each other when we were kids?" I ask, turning my attention back to him.

He leans his head to the side. "Hmm?"

"I mean, we had to have crossed paths at some point, right? You were a year older, sure, and we lived on opposite sides of town and went to different schools, but there are only four restaurants here. A single grocery store. Two gas stations. For all we know, we walked right past each other. Or played together at the playground."

He takes a bite of his burger, chewing slowly.

"You know what I mean?" I prompt.

After he swallows, he nods. "Yeah, I guess that's true."

"Like we used to eat at Lenny's all the time, and when we weren't at Lenny's, we were at Nonna's Kitchen. Dad loved Italian food. Did you come to either place often?"

He shakes his head. "Not really, no."

"Where did you eat, then? What did you do?"

"We didn't eat in restaurants all that often, really. But when we did, my grandpa loved The Porch." He juts a thumb in the direction of the small diner across town. "He was a big fan of their grits."

"They have the best melts, too," I agree. "And ice cream. I used to beg my parents to take me there for the banana pudding ice cream."

He grins. "Peach cobbler was always my favorite." There's something heavy in the pause that sits between us as I muse over the past and wonder if it's possible I walked past him or interacted with him and have no idea it happened.

How could I forget someone like him?

"I would've remembered you," he says softly, as if he's read my mind, before looking down again. "If we'd met, I would've remembered."

I can't help the smile that grows on my face as I look down to hide it. There's not much to say after that.

Back at the house after dinner, we change into our pajamas and take turns brushing our teeth in the small hallway bathroom.

I'm getting used to having him around, and that scares me. I never meant to grow close to anyone again, especially not Tucker or Clayton. Coming home wasn't about that. And yet, here I am.

When I get to the living room, I realize Clayton has texted me to say good night. I send him a quick text and tell him to be careful on his way to Nashville and that I'll see him soon.

Then, I take out my contacts and switch to glasses. Tucker plugs in his phone and sits down on the couch, stretching out.

"You sure you'll be okay there?" I ask. It feels silly. We've slept in the same bed twice now just this week, but the air mattress is smaller than his bed, and I don't trust myself to share it with him.

He nods, hands behind his head against the arm of the couch, as I dig through another box and pull out a spare blanket. I pass it to him and settle onto the air mattress. Once we're both lying down, just the glow from the lone street light pouring through the blinds, I listen to his steady breathing.

The room is too quiet. It's the first time I haven't slept with a lamp or light on since I arrived, but I refuse to admit I need one now.

"Can I ask you something?" His voice is soft and husky in the darkness of the room. I hear him adjusting on the couch.

"Sure."

"Why aren't you with Clayton yet?"

265

The question catches me by surprise. "What do you mean?"

"Oh, come on. You've been home for a week. You're both single. I assumed you'd be all over him by now."

"I'm not that girl anymore, Tucker." I'm surprised by the spite in my tone.

"Meaning?"

"Meaning...whatever feelings I had for Clayton back then, they're gone now. We're just friends."

"Have you told him that?"

"I don't have to. He knows it."

"He doesn't look at you like a friend, Maggie."

"That's ridiculous," I say softly. "We've both grown up. Moved on."

"Could've fooled me," he mutters.

"Where is this coming from?"

"I'd just hate to see you miss out on the opportunity of your dreams again." There's a hint of playfulness to his tone for the first time.

"Clayton is *not* the opportunity of my dreams."

"Since when?"

"Since—" I cut myself off. "A long time ago."

"What changed?"

I pull the covers up to my chest as a chill runs over me. This time, it's not because of the house.

"I don't know," I say noncommittally.

"You loved him back then," he says. "And you had an opportunity to be with him, but instead, you just ran away."

"That's not what happened." I sit up, staring at the outline of his body on the couch in the dim light.

"Then what did?"

266

"I—" I open my mouth, the truth on my tongue, but I swallow it down. "I don't know."

"Maggie," he growls, turning to face me, propped up on his elbow.

"I wasn't going to choose him back then, Tuck."

I can practically hear him processing the words. After a long pause, he asks, "What are you talking about?"

"If you must know..."

"Oh, I must," he teases.

At the same time, I say, "I was going to choose you." My words are a breathless whisper. "That's why I was at your apartment that night." I wait for him to respond.

And wait.

And wait.

The silence in the room is suffocating.

"Did you—"

"I heard you," he answers, the question not even fully leaving my lips.

"You didn't want to respond?"

"I was waiting for you to elaborate." He moves up farther on the couch, resting against the arm. "When did you change your mind?"

"I didn't. I was just... I never made up my mind either way until that night. I was confused."

"It seemed like you'd made up your mind when you texted me."

"I needed time. I told you that. I had a lot going on."

"No, Maggie. Time is one thing. I would've given you all the time you needed, but you never asked. You ran off immediately after we slept together because you said Clayton needed you, and then you stopped coming around, stopped answering my calls and texts. Then, the next time I hear from you, you're with Clayton. I can take a hint, but you laid it out plain as day."

"I wasn't with Clayton. I told you I needed space. I needed to think."

"That's not what you said. And it was right after we'd had sex." The word fills the air with a desperate sort of claustrophobia, memories dancing in the back of my mind. "All I could think about was how I'd finally gotten everything I wanted and, for whatever reason, it wasn't enough for you. That I was just the wild oat you needed to sow to prove to yourself Clayton was the one you wanted. Seeing you out together nearly killed me, but then to know for sure you'd chosen him... I wanted you to be happy, above all else, but it destroyed me. He never deserved you."

"When did you see us out together?" I challenge. "I was avoiding him, too."

"On his birthday. Raven came to see me at the bar that night. Clayton had told her he was sick and didn't want to do anything to celebrate, but she caught him leaving his hotel and followed him to a restaurant. She saw him meeting you. I didn't believe it at first. I trusted you. I thought we were really starting something. But she took me to see for myself."

The night comes back to me in bitter flashes. I'd been so angry with him when I saw him with Raven...but it was all my fault? "That's why you were with her that night?"

He nods. "It was fine. You didn't owe me anything. I always knew what I was signing up for when we started hanging out. I just never planned to fall for you. I didn't know it would hurt so much."

"I never meant to hurt you. During that time, I was realizing that I didn't want to be with Clayton anymore, but those were big feelings to come to grips with. I'd been in love with

Clayton my entire life, and suddenly, I was in love with someone else. I needed time to deal with—"

"In love?" he asks, his voice dry.

"Yeah," I croak. "I was...I was in love with you, Tucker. And it took me a long time to realize it. And once I finally had, my best friend needed me. I had to be there for him, no matter how much I wanted to be with you. I needed to help him deal with everything before I could go all in with our relationship. If that was even something you wanted. I wanted to be able to be with you without the weight of everything going on with Clayton in the background."

"But then everything happened before you could tell me any of that," he says as if he's realizing it for the first time.

"Yeah."

He sits up completely, leaning forward over his knees. The scent of him fills the air. I breathe it in, gulping it down. It hasn't changed a bit over the years.

"All this time, I assumed you'd left because you thought I had something to do with her death. I knew I'd hurt you, but I thought you were still in love with Clayton, so seeing us together couldn't have affected you that much. But I was wrong, wasn't I? You left because of what you saw that night?"

"It wasn't all about that night, no. Not really. Yes, it did hurt, but I'd already seen you with Raven around campus. I assumed you were moving on. And then, when you stopped texting me, it just further confirmed it."

"I never stopped texting you," he says. "Even when you asked me to. Even when I felt like a complete idiot, I still texted you. I tried to call. That didn't stop until I heard you'd left town."

I pause, replaying his words in my head. "When I asked you to? What do you mean?"

"You told me you were choosing Clayton. And to stop texting you. To leave you alone. And, as much as it killed me, I had to respect that. So, I moved on. Tried to, anyway. That's what you saw that night. I was just trying to get over you."

"I have no idea what you're talking about." I shake my head. "When did I tell you that?"

"You...you texted me." His face goes slack, his head cocking to the side. "You texted me and said you were sorry, but you wanted to end things. That you were choosing Clayton, and I should leave you alone."

I can't tell if he's joking or lying. "I did not."

"Yes, Maggie. You did. If you hadn't, I would've never slept with her. No matter what Raven said, I trusted you. I thought, well, I hoped, things would be different. But it was your choice. I always told you that. But...what you saw that night, you have to believe me when I say it meant nothing to me. She meant nothing. I was drunk and hurting and—"

"I never sent you any text like that." I try to think back. I know I didn't send it, so is he trying to make what he did better? Or did someone else send the text? The only person who ever had access to my phone back then was...*Kassara*. But why would she send a message like that to Tucker? She saw firsthand how heartbroken I was over his betrayal. I don't know what to believe, but if what he's saying is true, this changes everything. "I don't understand what happened, but I just wish you would've talked to me instead of running to her."

"I tried. Believe me. I texted you. I called you. Even when you asked me not to. I never got a reply."

I don't remember any texts or phone calls, though those days are a blurry mosaic of heartbreak and confusion. "You knew where I lived."

"I didn't want to be somewhere I wasn't wanted," he says

flatly. "You sent me away that night. I didn't think you'd open the door again."

"I thought none of it mattered to you," I say after a beat. "I didn't leave because you hurt me or because I ever suspected you of being involved in her death. I don't. I didn't. I just...I thought you didn't care, and I cared so much—too much. I couldn't be there anymore, and I couldn't come home to Myers and see your face every day after graduation, so I left."

He dips his head down, staring into his lap. Slowly, his head starts to shake. "It all mattered. I always cared."

"Do you still?" I seem to shock us both with the question. His head pops up, turned toward me. I wonder what he can see of me in the darkness, with the slats of amber lighting poking through the blinds and onto my face.

He slides off the couch and onto the floor, until he's sitting right in front of me. "Do you want me to?"

"I want you to be honest," I manage to choke out.

"I never stopped caring about you." His hand drifts up, brushing my cheek. "I never stopped wanting you."

I suck in a shallow breath, the air in the room shifting. "Me either."

His hand comes to rest on my cheek fully, his fingers in my hair. He hesitates, but only for a moment. Then his lips are on mine. It's warm and familiar, yet different. Stronger. More sure, and yet, more reserved. Like he's still not positive any of this is actually happening. Like I might change my mind.

I fall into our kiss as his tongue grazes mine.

"That." He pulls away breathlessly, resting his forehead against my chin.

I lean back. "What?"

He meets my eyes again, huffing a breath of hot air onto my

lips. "That little noise you just made..." His voice is a growl. "That has kept me up for years."

With that, before I can comprehend what he's said, he's kissing me again, and nothing else matters. Time seems to fade, the room disappearing in my periphery as the universe compresses until it only contains me and him.

I could kiss him forever.

His hand slips down to my waist, gripping my hip and tugging me toward him. I'm on his lap then, my heart pounding so fast in my chest I can hardly breathe.

His lips take mine over and over again in varying degrees of fast and slow, demanding and gentle.

We're lying down then, and I don't know when it happened. He has one hand in my hair and the other sliding up my shirt. His fingers trace the edge of my bra, and I arch toward him.

My body is pure fire.

He sits up, pulling his shirt over his head and then my own.

I unhook my bra just as quickly, and then he's back, and we're skin to skin. I swear I can feel his heart beating through his chest against mine. The heat of his body is comforting, welcoming. It feels right.

He growls against my neck, tracing kisses along my jawbone and back to my ear.

"I have wanted you..." His voice is hot and shaky in my ear, his words taking me back to the first and last time we slept together. They are words I've replayed in my head so many times. It's a promise. A warning. "Every day." He kisses my ear lobe. "Every minute." My jaw. "Every second." My neck. My chest. "Since we met." His hand moves to cup my breast, his thumb rolling over my nipple, and the noise that escapes my throat is practically feral.

I can feel his smug smile against my skin as he moves his mouth to replace his hand. Sparks ignite inside me, sending me writhing. His mouth trails down my body, kissing a path across my chest and down to the waistband of my pajama pants.

He plants teasing kisses there, each one sending a spark of lightning through my body. I reach down, jerking my pants off, and I can see the outline of the smile on his face as he looks down at me.

"Impatient, are we?" he asks gruffly.

He leans down, his lips touching the inside of each of my thighs like a whisper. A torturous whisper that's driving me mad. A hand slides across my belly, rising up to outline the swell of my breast.

I hold my breath as he presses his lips right where I want him. It's brief, over in seconds. I whine. Whimper. Beg.

"Tucker. Please." I can't catch my breath.

My body is half ice and half flame the second his lips meet the space between my legs again. He places another tentative kiss against my sensitive skin, and then—finally—he's right where I want him. His tongue applies just the right pressure, his mouth hot and wet and demanding. I cry out, gasping, my muscles like warm honey under his touch. The pleasure is pure and explosive as he explores me. He hooks my knees over his shoulders and lifts my hips from the bed, giving him a better angle.

"Tucker." My voice doesn't even sound like my own. It's animalistic. Feral. The things he's doing to me, the way he's making me feel is a sweet agony that I never want to end.

It doesn't take long before involuntary tremors course through my body and an electric shock scorches me. I'm a mess of pleasure and ache and wanting this to never end.

My final breath comes in a long, surrendering moan, but I

have no time for questioning or embarrassment. No time to wonder what the hell just happened, because as the final aftershocks pass through me, he eases my hips onto the bed and stands, crossing the room.

I watch as he picks up his jeans from the pile of his clothes, helpless to do anything but catch my breath. I hear the jingling of his belt as he digs into his pocket, then drops the jeans back on the floor once he's found what he was searching for. He tears open the foil packet and steps out of his pajama pants.

Within seconds, he's back to me, lowering himself on the mattress and reclaiming my lips. He moves his mouth over mine, devouring its softness, smothering me with desire. It's urgent and exploratory, and I feel the evidence of his excitement pressed against my thigh. He sits up, hooking my hips again and pulling me to him.

Then, I feel him at my entrance. His hands slide over my thighs, caressing my hip bones. I scoot farther toward him.

"Please, Tuck…"

"Please what?" he asks, gripping himself, running his tip up and down along my seam. I'm coming undone, my body no longer my own.

"Please. I need you."

He gives a wicked grin and pushes inside me, gently at first, then gives in to his own desires, moving quicker than before. He grabs my hips, pushing so deep inside me there's nowhere else to go.

I cry out as he slams our bodies together, over and over again, until I'm an aching mess like I've never been before.

I've missed this feeling, though I've only experienced anything that could compare to it once before. I missed him. As my body begins to vibrate with liquid fire, he holds me tighter, slowing slightly to get a good look at me.

"Let go, baby," he coaxes. "Let go for me."

And so I do. When I cry out, I feel him releasing right along with me. We go over the cliff together, my body clenching around him like we were made for each other.

When it's over, he lies down next to me, and I already miss his warmth inside me. I don't say that, though. I can't. Instead, I hold in a sob as I feel his lips on mine, this time as soft and tender as a summer breeze. Barely there.

I close my eyes, already feeling myself begin to drift off. I feel safe for the first time in so long. Comfortable. Whole.

It's just as I'm nearly asleep, just as the world is beginning to fade and I'm starting to dissolve into the darkness, that I hear it.

Hear *her*.

A woman's panic-stricken scream tears through the house.

CHAPTER THIRTY

THEN

Tucker has texted me twice over the past two days, and both texts have gone unanswered. I'm angry with him for being with Raven. I know I don't deserve to be. I know I have no right to be, but I am. I want to tell him what I saw and demand an explanation, but I can't allow myself to be the girl pining over yet another guy. I can't allow myself to be hurt again.

I want to tell him I've chosen him, to tell him how much our night together meant to me, but what if he's no longer interested? What if he's moved on? Then again, he wouldn't be texting me if that were the case, would he?

My head is such a mess right now. Nothing makes sense, but I can't stop second-guessing every decision I make and every thought I have. It's not fair to him to let silence be the only answer he receives from me, I know, but what would be even less fair would be giving him an answer when I don't truly have one myself.

Everything is so messed up.

I'm confused.

Ever since the weekend at the lake house—maybe even

before that, if I'm being honest—I've felt certain it's Tucker that I truly want. Not Clayton. But if I tell Tucker that, I want to be one hundred percent positive it's the truth. And right now, I'm not one hundred percent positive about anything.

When I hear a knock on the front door, I'm certain it's Tucker, come to demand I give him an answer. I wouldn't blame him if so. He deserves a response, even if it's not a great one.

I cross the room and pull open the door, my jaw dropping when I see Clayton standing there. His hair is disheveled, his eyes bloodshot. He looks worse every time I see him lately.

"Hey…" I say, my voice hesitant.

"Whatcha doing?" he asks, a twinkle in his eye like he's going to prank me.

"Um, watching *Lost* reruns. What's up?"

He leans against the doorframe with a dramatic sigh. "Rough day. Could use some bestie time."

"I'm not really in the mood to hang out, Clay," I say gently.

"Please." His voice cracks as he says the word.

I don't want to hurt him. Don't want to hurt anyone. But I know, deep down, he needs me. I've always been there for him; we've been together through so much. And, if the situation were reversed, I know he'd do the same for me.

So, for now, my own happiness, my own feelings and confusion and whatever else I have going on, will have to wait.

I step back, allowing him inside. "Do you want anything to drink?"

"Soda's fine. Sprite, if you have it."

"Be right back." I head into the kitchen, and when I return a few minutes later, he's on the couch. I place the drinks next to my phone on the end table. "So, what's up?"

When he looks at me, there's a hesitancy there I can't quite understand. I watch as something in him breaks. He stands, coming at me before I realize what's happening, and then his mouth is nearly on mine.

My hands go out to stop him seconds before our lips collide. It feels wrong. Everything about this. I stiffen, pushing him away.

"No. What are you doing?"

"I need you, Maggs," he whines, tears welling in his eyes. "I need to be with you."

"No," I say, indignation rising in my chest. "You don't mean that."

"I do. It's always been you."

"Then why couldn't you admit it when you had the chance? Before you left? When you knew how badly I wanted you. What's changed?"

"I thought I wanted all of this more," he admits angrily. "I thought the fame, the record deal, was my dream come true." He stops, shaking his head with a light breath. "I was wrong. It was you. It was always you." He leans forward again, hands outstretched for my face, but I sidestep away from him.

"Stop it. Now that everything is already messed up, you don't get to come in here and act like we can just be together and figure it out."

"Why can't we?"

"Because..." I huff. "Because she's pregnant, Clayton. Raven is pregnant. And I get that it wasn't intentional, and I understand that it's made you confused, but this isn't what I wanted. I wanted you when it was just you. When things were simple. Now, everything is messed up."

"Raven was a mistake," he says so forcefully I flinch. "You know that."

"Yeah. Because you've decided it this week. Because that's

how you're feeling *today*. But you had months to make up your mind, a year, and you didn't. In fact, you only decided you wanted to be with me when I started falling for someone else."

He opens his mouth, ready to respond, and then it snaps shut, his eyes widening. "You really want him more than me? Honestly?"

"Yeah, I do." I hadn't planned to say the words, the truth, but there it is. For us both to deal with. "And I'm sorry if that hurts you."

"What does that mean for us? I missed my chance?"

"Yeah, maybe. At least for now." I waffle at seeing the hurt on his face. "I don't know, Clayton. I love you. I've always loved you, and I think you know that. But we had our chance, and you chose her. I've... I'm sorry. I've moved on."

Tears fill his eyes, and he turns away from me, moving to sit on the couch again with his face in his hands. "I fucked everything up. All of it. I should've just told you how I felt instead of lying." He looks up at me. "That first night, when you walked into the bar, and I was there with her... As soon as I saw you, I knew I was making a mistake. But I didn't want to hurt her, and then you said you were with someone else, so I...I got scared. I didn't want to mess anything up. I thought I'd just wait it out."

"No offense, Clay, but it didn't really seem like you were waiting anything out. You seemed to be in love with her. Or at least to like her enough to get her pregnant."

"I think she tricked me," he says softly, looking away. "I have no proof, but we always used protection. And she was on the pill. At least, she was supposed to be."

"Okay, well, that's between the two of you." I cross my arms. "You need to deal with everything with her before you come and tell me this. It's not fair to either one of us."

"She means nothing to me, Maggie. Aren't you hearing me? It's you I want." He stands, moving toward me. "*You,* I love. She hurt me." He puts his hand to the place on his neck where she left claw marks not so long ago. "She tricked me. I don't want her."

"I know you're upset, but please stop. You're being cruel. She's carrying your child. Even if you don't want to be together anymore, she's going to be in your life—"

"And because of that, I've lost my chance with you?"

"That, among other things, yes," I concede.

He looks as if I've slapped him—face pale, eyes wide. He shakes his head. "Maggie, I don't know what to say. I'm so sorry I didn't tell you how I felt back then..."

"You don't need to be sorry." For the first time in my life, I think I mean that. "I will always love you, Clayton. You're my best friend. But you've made a choice. You chose Raven, and I understand you're changing your mind now, which is your prerogative, but you have to deal with everything with her regardless. I'll still be here for you however I can, but...I can't be what you're asking me for right now. I'm sorry. I just can't."

His eyes darken. "Because of her? Or him?"

I press a hand to my chest. "Because of me. Because this isn't what I want. I need to do what's right for me. And you need to do what's *right.*"

"I'm not going to marry her," he says flatly.

"That's between the two of you."

"Why are you being like this?" he demands, sneering.

"Being like what?"

"'That's between the two of you,'" he repeats, in a voice that is apparently meant to sound like mine. "You're my best friend—*supposedly*—and yet, you're just dismissing me. If you love Tucker and don't want me, fine, but I've never treated you this way. When I brought Raven home, I still made every effort to include you. We've been through everything together all our lives. How can you just tell me to figure it all out on my own when I need you?"

"That's not at all what I'm telling you. I will be here for you, Clayton. I always, always am. But I can't be your girlfriend. It's too messy. This entire situation. You have to handle this. I can't be part of it. If she decides to keep the baby, and you want my help with...I don't know, diapers or babysitting, I'll be here. But I can't get in the middle of what you've got going on until you've worked it out between the two of you. Whatever that's going to look like."

He nods, still not getting it, as is evident on his face. "Yeah, fine. You've made yourself very clear." He turns to walk away. "I'm going to go."

"What are you talking about? You don't have to leave."

"No, I really do." He stops, looking back. "Just...just promise me you'll stay away from her, okay?"

"Raven?"

"Yeah. She's dangerous, Maggs. I don't trust her with you. I think she's stalking me. And you, probably. She's seriously unhinged."

I nod, suddenly uncomfortable as I think about her with Tucker. As upset and confused as I am with him, I need to warn him about this. Then again, he'll probably just think I'm being jealous and needy. "I'll be fine, but you should take care of yourself, okay? If you don't feel safe around her, please meet her in public and decide what's going to happen. But just decide. You can't keep going on like this."

He nods, his eyes tracing over my face like he's trying to remember it. Finally, he says, "See you around." And then he's gone.

When he leaves, I grab my phone and send a quick text to Tucker. I'll be the bigger person here, even if it stings. I care about him too much not to.

> I just need space right now. I'm sorry.
> Please be careful with Raven, though.
> Can't tell you what to do but Clayton says
> she's dangerous.

With that, I press send.

CHAPTER THIRTY-ONE

NOW

My eyes flick open in a state of shock, a scream ripping from my own lungs to match the one tearing down my hallways... and then, it ends.

Hers and mine. We both fall silent.

It's only Tucker making any noise then, both arms wrapped around me as he searches the room. "What is it?" he cries. "Maggie, what's wrong? What happened?"

He's looking around the room, around the bed, as if he's confused and nervous.

"The woman..." I whisper breathlessly, staring into the darkness of the kitchen as if coming out of a dream. Except I wasn't dreaming. I know I wasn't. I couldn't have been. It's all too real. There are still goosebumps on my arms. I'm still shaking. "You heard that, right? Please tell me you heard that. It was so loud."

"*What* was so loud?"

"She was screaming."

He runs a hand over my back. "I think you were dreaming.

I didn't hear anything, certainly not screaming. Just... Look, just breathe. It's okay. You're safe."

I shake my head, wanting to argue, but he's reaching behind him to grab his pants, so he doesn't hear me. He stands, pulling them up and flipping on the light. He hands me my pajamas, which I put on quickly through my trembling, and while I'm dressing, he paces the room, doing a thorough search, though for what I'm not sure.

"There's no one here." He's apparently been looking for a real woman, not a ghost or...what? I'm not even sure. My mind is a foggy mess of sleep and fear. I don't believe in ghosts. Period. I don't. But I know what I heard. So where does that leave us? "Whatever you heard, it was just a dream. I've done that before. Kind of like when you feel like you're falling and it wakes you up."

"It wasn't like that," I say firmly.

"Okay." He's ever patient, but he doesn't believe me. Fury wells in my chest. "Well, I'm here. I'm right here. Do you want to try to go back to sleep? Or search the house? Or go back to mine? Where's your phone? We can check the app."

That's not a bad idea. I grab my phone from its charger near the mattress and open the security app. Fearing what I may accidentally see on the living room camera—I have no desire to watch our unintentional sex tape—I click on the hallway feed instead. Embarrassed, I make a mental note to delete the living room's history as soon as I get a chance.

I open the live feed and rewind several minutes, then press play. The video is an eerie shade of blue from the night vision effect, but aside from small insects flying in front of the camera occasionally, the hallway is devoid of movement. I wait several seconds, holding my breath for what I know is coming.

And then, I hear it. It's so loud it makes me jump, nearly dropping the phone. The scream tears through the empty hallway, disrupting everything and sending my stomach into a spiral. Tucker puts a hand on my back as I realize he's right.

The scream is only mine.

There is no one else.

What I heard was just a dream. A figment of my worst nightmares.

"Are you okay?" Tucker asks, reaching to touch my arm.

"I...I don't know."

"It was just a dream," he repeats, staring at me warily.

"I heard you the first time," I snap. He doesn't deserve my anger, but I feel it bubbling up in my gut anyway, mixing like a cocktail with humiliation.

"Okay," he says, trying to pull me into his side. I don't budge.

"You should go, Tuck."

His hand drops along with his jaw. "What?"

"I mean it. You should go. I want to be alone."

"Did I do something wrong?"

"I just..." I wave a hand between us. "I can't do this. I can't be this girl anymore."

"What are you talking about?"

"This was a mistake." I stand, moving away from him. Even as I'm saying the words, I know I'll regret them, but I can't stop myself. I'm too angry. Too hurt and embarrassed.

"This? *Us?*" he asks, still not standing.

"Yes." His skin pales, his eyes going dark. I've hurt him, and I hate it, but I can't stop. "I don't want to fall into old patterns. I promised myself this wouldn't be that, but you're very charming. And sometimes you make me forget how much time has passed. I can't do that, though. I can't let myself. When I moved home, it was because I wanted to start over on my own. I wanted to be independent. But, instead, I'm just letting myself need you again—"

"That's okay. I don't mind if you need me," he insists.

"I know you don't, but it's not fair to either of us. I appreciate your help. Truly, I do. But I need to learn to stand on my own two feet. And I can't do that if you're always coming to my rescue. And I certainly can't do that from your bed."

His lips draw in with a dry, defeated look. He shakes his head, brows up. "Yeah. Okay."

"I'm sorry. I just...I've worked hard to build a life that doesn't revolve around the drama with you and Clayton. I walked away from it all and found Nick, and there was still drama. So, now I'm here. Alone. And I need to do this alone."

"Sometimes drama is just the risk you take for being in love, Maggie. For being happy. If you don't want to be with me, say that. I'm a big boy. I can take it. But don't blame it on your imaginary drama. I'm not bringing you any drama. I've done nothing wrong this time. So just be honest."

"I don't want to be with you," I spit out, the words burning me as if each letter is being carved into my skin.

He nods slowly, ducking his head, chin to chest. "Okay. Fine."

"I'm sorry."

"Don't be." Backing away, he reaches for the door. "Good night, Maggie." The word sounds a lot like *goodbye.*

I consider calling out to him, telling him I'm lying, begging him to forgive me and stay, but my pride won't let me. I watch him leave like it isn't killing me. Then, alone in the house, I sit on the couch and fight off the sobs I feel climbing my throat.

After several minutes pass, I find myself drifting off, my head on the arm of the couch. I'm so tired, I can't stay awake, and yet, I'm too afraid to sleep.

I grab my phone against my better judgment and type in the names of the family again.

Chris and Jolene Collins 40 Hemlock Drive

Within seconds, I locate the article again, skimming through it. I don't know what I'm hoping to find, and anything I do find will surely only add to my terror, but I have to do it. The curiosity is too strong.

I read through the article, standing and following the trail it sends me on. The parents were found upstairs, but Jason's body was found in the first bedroom. I push the door open, a lump growing in my throat that's impossible to swallow down.

It happened here. His little body. His cries. His terror. It permeates the room.

I wonder what else this bedroom bore witness to. Were there bedtime stories read? Songs sung? Did he play on the floor with his favorite toys? Or was his short life in this house met with only misery and pain?

When did the man who helped bring him into the world become the monster who took him out?

Tears sting my eyes as scenes of violence play out in my mind, each one worse than the last. The next body, little Shelby's, was in the nursery.

I push the next door open, and a chill runs over me. The house is suddenly twenty degrees cooler. Everything about this room feels wrong, like nothing good or happy could've ever existed within the space.

The small bedroom has a tiny, rusting metal hook still stuck in the ceiling. I imagine it once held a mobile over her crib. Did they choose stars for her? Unicorns? Animals? Did they have dreams for their daughter? Hopes?

I shiver, running a hand over my arm as my eyes dart for the attic. Tucker says these likely used to be stairs until someone closed them off. I try to picture the family spending time upstairs, a husband and wife who, at one point, must've loved each other. When did that change? When did it switch from stolen kisses in the hallway to hiding clothes and cash in the wall with plans to escape?

I know enough about domestic violence to know it never starts that way. Once, they must've been happy. Happy enough to continue having children. At least, I hope that was her decision too.

There's a scream building in my body—terror and rage over their fate—but I can't let it escape. What happened, happened, and dwelling on it will never bring me peace.

Perhaps I can see if they have any family in the area and give them the clothes I found. Or maybe I should turn them over to the police. Or throw them away and let the past remain just that.

I close out of the article and open another. This one has a photo of the Collins family sitting on their front porch. It looks so similar to the one I found in Tucker's room. The photo is fuzzy, like all photos from the nineties, but when I look at it, disgust roils in my stomach.

It's disturbing how happy they look. Chris's arm is around Jolene, and their children sit in front of them. Looking closer, I gasp, trying to make sense of what I'm seeing. There's a little boy on Chris's lap, a baby in Jolene's arms, and another young boy in between them.

Three.

There were three children.

I read the article to be sure I haven't missed something, but no. Only two of the children are mentioned as being killed.

Is it possible?

I study the photo closer. What other explanation could there be?

One of their children survived that night.

CHAPTER THIRTY-TWO

THEN

I'm done waiting.

It's been a week since I sent Clayton away to deal with his mess, and I'm now more certain than ever it's Tucker I want. It's taken everything I have not to text him, and now his texts have stopped coming, too.

On the way to his house, I run through exactly what I want to say to him.

You were there for me when no one else was. Not because you had to be, but because you could be... Because you wanted to be. And now, I want to be with you. I'm sorry I waited so long. I'm sorry I've ignored you. You didn't deserve that. I love you, Tuck. And, if you love me back...

That's the part where I keep getting stuck. *If you love me back, let's make this official?* No, too cheesy. *If you love me back, let's do this.* Again, ick. *If you love me back, I'm ready. I'm finally ready.*

Whatever I decide to say, I hope it sounds better in the moment.

Tucker is the one for me. He's the one who has chosen me.

Been there for me. I don't even care why he was with Raven anymore. I've had time to cool off and realize I trust him, as much as that scares me. I will until he gives me a reason not to. I want to start fresh. Today. I only hope I haven't managed to screw this up beyond repair.

My thoughts trail off as I pull into the parking lot for his apartment.

I ease into a spot next to his truck, my heart thundering in my chest. *Today's the day everything changes.*

CHAPTER THIRTY-THREE

NOW

I haven't slept a wink when the next morning rolls around. I'm deep into the rabbit hole of the Collins family, though I'm finding very little other than what was in the first article. I can't find anything about their extended family or what might've happened to their other son. I can't even find out his name.

Life before social media...

I'm at the sink washing the few dishes piled in there when I hear a car door shut. I freeze.

It must be Tucker leaving for work. Clayton is still in Nashville, and there's no one else I can think of that would be visiting. I turn the water on just as I hear footsteps on the front porch.

Chills line my skin as I turn the water off again and dry my hands.

Then comes the knock on the door.

I cross the kitchen slowly, making my way into the living room and toward the door. I realize several seconds too late that my phone has the new app, and I could've used it to check who's at the door. Instead, I approach the window and peer out through the blinds.

My heart skips a beat at the familiar and unexpected face. "Nick?" I pull the door open and stare at my ex-boyfriend with confusion. "What are you doing here?"

He looks down, and I notice the envelope in his hand. "Hi. Um, this came for you." He holds it out, and I see it's addressed to me from Mom's lawyer.

"What is it?" I ask, taking it slowly.

"Wouldn't know. I didn't open it."

"She must not have changed my address in her system or something. You... You didn't have to come all the way here. You could've just mailed it."

"I know," he says simply. "I had a few days off."

I stare at him, running a finger across the seal of the envelope.

"I'm sorry for the last time I was here," he blurts out like it's been burning his tongue. "I'm embarrassed about the way I acted. I just... I was scared because I knew I'd lost you, and I didn't know how to react. It's no excuse, but you deserved to hear it from me in person."

"Thank you." My voice is soft. Somehow, it's exactly what I needed to hear. "I'm sorry for the way things happened."

He nods with a regretful smile and a puff of air. "Me too. Are you..." He glances behind me. "Are you okay?"

"Yeah, I am," I tell him. Then, more truthfully, I add, "I will be."

He stares at me for a moment longer, and I know he's waiting for me to invite him inside, but I can't. I don't have time or energy for him right now, especially after the way things happened last time. I know he's apologized, but it doesn't change the facts. And I can no longer count on Tucker to come to my rescue should I need him.

"Thanks again." I hold up the envelope. "You really didn't have to bring this, but I appreciate it."

"Of course." He raps a knuckle on the doorframe, swinging a leg back awkwardly. "I'm, uh, staying at a hotel nearby for the weekend. Well, as nearby as I could find. If you need anything or...you know, just want to hang out."

I won't, but I don't say that. Instead, I smile, reaching out to squeeze his arm gently. "Thanks. Be careful going home, okay?"

I don't watch him walk off the porch, which I assume he'll do in slow motion, waiting for me to stop him. Instead, I close the door and stare down at the manila envelope in my hands. Mom's lawyer had mentioned she would be sending me anything that came up, but since I hadn't heard from her, I wasn't expecting to receive mail. I gave her my new address shortly before closing, but it looks like this was sent a while ago. *Was Nick holding it back from me?*

I pull up the two metal prongs, easing a finger along the sealed seam, and peer inside. At the bottom of the envelope, there is a small, handwritten note and a silver key.

I dump the items into my hand, studying the key before reading the letter. The handwriting isn't Mom's, and I realize quickly it must be her lawyer's.

Maggie,

The nursing home found this among your mother's things. It's a spare key to her storage unit, which should match the other key I've previously given you. I believe both will be required to eventually

*get your mother's deposit back. I'm not sure what's
left in the unit, and perhaps you've already emptied
it, but I wanted to pass this along just in case.
Here's the last address I had for it, in the event you
don't have it: 65 North Haverson Street, Unit 13.
As a reminder, your mom had paid it up for six
months, so it will expire in June. If you haven't done
so already, please either make arrangements to
renew it or have everything removed from there by
the end of the month to avoid losing access to her
things.*

> *Call me if you have any questions or issues.*
> *Take care,*
> *Catherine Wilkes, Esq.*

I'm not sure what I should expect to find in the storage unit. I helped Mom rent it when she moved into the nursing home, to store the things she couldn't get rid of and no longer had room for. I remember loading the boxes inside, though the day had been so hectic, I'd hardly spent any time actually looking at what we were packing away. From what I remember, it was mostly Christmas decorations, memorabilia from their wedding, photos, and my old clothes from childhood.

I check the note again. Catherine said her lease would expire at the end of this month. Which means I have less than two weeks to empty it out. As much as I don't have room for anything else in this house, I need to get there and decide what I want to keep and donate before I'm out of time.

And, at this point, I'm just happy for an excuse to get out of here.

When I arrive at the storage unit and begin sorting through things, it seems like I was mostly right about what I remembered. Mom's storage locker smells stale and is filled with boxes of some of her favorite things. The sight of her handwriting on the top of each one stops me in my tracks.

Miss you, Momma.

The first three boxes are filled with the old glass dolls she used to collect, still in their boxes in pristine condition. I can't get rid of those. The next box is Christmas decorations, then another with fall decorations. I choose a few I want to keep and put the rest in a pile to be donated.

In another box, I find her wedding dress in a shadow box frame. I carry it to my car and place it in the back seat carefully, planning to clean it up and hang it on my wall as soon as I'm home.

I spend the next few hours working through boxes of old memories—papers and crafts of mine from elementary school, Mother's and Father's Day cards, photo albums, and more holiday decorations.

After four hours pass and I've made no real progress, I plan to take everything I've decided to keep so far back to my house before it gets too late. I can spend a few hours here every day until I've sorted through everything. With a few trips to the car, I have it loaded down with boxes, and head back to the house.

When I arrive, I begin unloading the boxes one at a time, carrying them up the porch and toward the last bedroom, which is currently still empty, to keep them separated from my own things.

I'm three boxes in when I hear his voice behind me.

"Are you going to bite my head off if I ask if you need help?"

From the porch steps, a box in hand, I turn back to him. He grins up at me, his faded ball cap turned backward like usual. "No. But I don't."

"Could you *use* help?" he rephrases.

I think it over for half a second, the muscles in my arms burning from the weight of the box. "Yes. Thank you."

He points to the car. "Boxes?"

"Yeah, just grab anything from the back seat and help me get them inside."

He does as he's told, stacking two boxes on top of each other and hurrying to catch up with me, barely fazed by their weight. Once we've placed the boxes into the last bedroom, he sighs, dusting his hands off and resting them on his hips. "What's all this?"

"Mom's stuff." I push one of the boxes closer to the wall. "Her lawyer sent a spare storage unit key they found in her room, with a note that her lease was getting ready to expire. I've been going through it all day."

He's quiet for a moment, staring at the boxes. "Look, Maggie—"

"You don't have to say anything."

"No, I want to. I'm sorry for last night. I let things get out of hand. You're in a vulnerable place, and you're scared, and...it wasn't right."

I groan. The old me would've let my pride win, accepted

his apology, and moved on. But I'm trying to be better. Trying to be someone who would make Mom proud. "You didn't take advantage of me, Tucker. I was just upset last night. Not even at you. I was embarrassed and confused, and I lashed out. It was never about you."

"Well, I'm still sorry. Not for what happened—I don't regret it. But I'm sorry it upset you."

"It didn't." I swallow my pride further. "And I don't regret it either, for the record, other than the way I acted after. Last night was something I've dreamed of for a long time."

He can't fight the smile that grows on his lips. "I'm glad to hear it. And, *for the record*"—he repeats my words—"me, too."

I give a small smile and look down. "If it's okay with you, let's just forget the argument happened and chalk it up to me being half asleep and scared."

"Deal." He's quiet for a while, watching me.

"So, um, are you busy right now?"

"What have you got in mind? A hot date?"

I giggle. "The hottest. I was planning to head back to the storage unit and grab a few more boxes that wouldn't fit in my car before it gets dark. You can totally say no."

He gives me a wry grin. "Sure. I can do that."

"Yeah?"

"Don't look so surprised. We'll take the truck so we can fit even more. Let's go."

As we unload the remaining boxes from my car, there's a lightness in my chest that hasn't been there for days.

Later, back at the storage unit, he loads everything I've already sorted through into the bed of his truck while I begin adding new boxes to the pile.

"So, I saw your ex was back this morning," he says, his voice straining as he lifts a box full of books.

"Yeah, he's the one who brought the key." I toss a cook-book into the pile to be donated. "It was delivered to our old place."

He stops in his tracks. "You lived together?"

"For two whole months," I say with a sarcastic laugh. "And then we both realized it was a huge mistake."

He grabs another box without a word.

"Have...you lived with anyone else since I left?"

He looks over his shoulder, something unreadable in his eyes. He doesn't answer as he loads the box into the bed of the truck and then turns to face me, resting his hand against the side. "I've dated a few women since you left, Maggie, yeah. But it was never anything serious. Definitely not serious enough to move in together."

It's the answer I wanted to hear, but didn't expect.

He smiles in response to the blush on my cheeks, walking closer to me as he adjusts his hat. "It was always you, you know that, right?" When I don't answer right away, he goes on, "You haunted me. You left, and I never really got over it. Even before you left. Even when I tried to move on, I knew it was pointless. No one has ever made me feel the way I feel about you. I'll never forgive myself for ruining what we had."

I nod but look away.

"It's the truth. If I could go back—"

"But you can't." I sink down onto the ground, hauling a stack of papers from a box and beginning to sort through them without meeting his eyes. "If there's one thing I've learned over the years, it's that no matter how much we wish we could change things, we can't. There's no point dwelling on it."

He grabs another box, hauling it to the truck.

"Do you ever think about her?" I ask. The question causes him to stop walking. "Sometimes I do," I admit. "Especially when it gets close to the anniversary. The end of May is always so weird."

He gives one nod and continues on his path to the truck. His response is clipped and noncommittal. "She didn't deserve what happened to her."

"Did they ever arrest anyone?" I think I know the answer, but I can never bring myself to look into it. It's too painful.

"Not that I know of, no."

I flip through to the next page of the stack of papers in my lap and freeze. A block of ice slides down my spine, my entire core frozen solid.

"There were a few suspects back then, but nothing could ever be proven and—" He stops talking as he turns to face me, obviously thrown off by my expression. "What is it? What's wrong?"

I stare down in horror at the document in my hands.

It's impossible.

A lie.

A nightmare.

And yet, as I stare at the words, somehow I know it's not.

CHAPTER THIRTY-FOUR

THEN

My heart races in my chest as I approach Tucker's door. I'm practically shaking, I have so much pent-up energy in me right now. I want to be realistic about this, to not get my hopes up, but the truth is, they're so high up I can't even see them anymore.

Because I know this is right. It's always been right. I'm so glad I took the time for clarity, the space to breathe and let this all sink in.

I'm in love with Tucker Ford.

With his gorgeous blue eyes and his ridiculously soft, dark hair, and the stupid sarcasm that drips from his every word.

The way he looks at me. The way he touches me. Kisses me. Holds me. Teases me relentlessly.

He's the one I want, and I'm so sure about it, it makes me sick.

Today is going to be the best day of my life. I know it. I'm refusing to believe anything else. I can't. I'm just too happy.

Is this what love is supposed to feel like? Who knew it could be so easy?

I check my phone, hoping to see a new text come in from him.

> Thinking of you.

> Missing you.

> Hey, if you wanted to come over right now and profess your love for me, that would be cool.

Something.

Anything.

I miss him. I want this moment to be perfect. It's the pressure of a proposal, and I just have to hope he says yes.

When I knock on the door, I can hardly catch my breath. A hint of worry creeps in as I remember the last time I did this. That time, it didn't go so well.

I shove the fear down. Tucker isn't Clayton. He's never treated me the way Clayton does. He's taken care of me, made me feel seen. This isn't that.

Still, I stand there, allowing a few seconds to pass before I lift my hand to knock. But, just as I start to, I remember what he told me before.

You could've just come in. I don't ever lock the door.

Would it be weird to just let myself in?

I picture a grand, sweeping, romantic gesture, where I run into his apartment and find him waiting for me, where I leap into his arms and tell him everything I've been practicing in my head. Where everything goes according to plan, and we finally admit how much we love each other. How silly it's been to be apart all this time.

A girl can dream...

Without allowing myself to second-guess the decision, I put my hand on the knob and turn it quickly. When I push the door open, he's nowhere to be found.

The living room and kitchen are both empty. I step inside and shut the door, preparing to call out for him when I hear it.

Moans.

My entire body goes still.

No.

Please. No.

This cannot be happening.

I move toward the sounds in a trancelike state, pulled by some magnetic force I don't understand. Why am I subjecting myself to this torture? I know, whatever I find, it will destroy me.

It can't be this. It just can't be.

Tucker would never hurt me this way.

I trust him.

I trust him.

I trust him.

When I reach his bedroom door, I almost turn around. I almost go back and pretend this never happened. But I can't. I need to know.

I reach my hand out, taking hold of the doorknob. I suck in a breath, preparing myself, and then push the door open.

The vision comes to me in flashes. I can't take it all in at once.

They're together in his bed, their naked bodies on full display. She's on her knees over him, taking him into her mouth. His head is thrown back, eyes squeezed shut. Her dark hair falls down over her face.

I can't believe this is happening. I never trusted her, but I never believed he'd do this. I thought he was different.

My naïveté is pathetic as I stand here realizing how wrong I've been.

I exhale, breaking the spell. Tucker's eyes rip open; his head turns toward me. "Maggie, I—"

I can't listen to him. Can't hear whatever lie he's going to tell me. This is the worst pain I've ever felt. It's as if I'm literally crumbling into pieces, each break met with searing agony. He pulls himself away from her as she looks up, appearing just as shocked to see me as I am her. He tosses a blanket toward her as he reaches for his clothes.

"Maggie, wait!"

I turn, dashing down the hall as fast as my legs will carry me.

I hate him. I hate myself.

I hate this.

Do I have any right to feel so jealous? Why did I think it would be any different? I'm the one who chose this arrangement. I'm the one who ghosted him. I'm the reason this is happening. Still, I *am* jealous. Furious. Devastated.

"Maggie, please wait," Tucker calls after me, tripping down the hall as he pulls his pants on. I don't look back or respond. I can't. I keep moving, for fear my lungs will explode from lack of oxygen. I can't breathe in this place.

When I reach the door, he catches up with me, grabbing my arm. I shove him away with all my strength. He barely budges.

I hate him.

"Don't touch me!" I shout, anger radiating through me as real as electricity. I pull the door open and dart out, already unlocking my car door as tears blur my vision. *Please don't cry in front of him.* Tucker chases after me with bare feet and no shirt on, but he doesn't stop me as I pull open the door. He doesn't try to touch me again. His hands were on her just seconds ago. He can never touch me again.

The thought comes again, wounding me this time. *I will never be touched by him again.*

"Maggie. Please just listen to me. Will you stop? Please? Please let me explain," he rambles, shaking as he grips on to my car door to keep me from closing it.

I don't care. I slam it shut, his fingers releasing it just moments before it closes, and put the car in reverse. If I talk, I'll lose it, and I can't afford to do that.

There's nothing left to say.

I pull away, knowing I'll never see him again. Knowing I can never allow myself to want to.

CHAPTER THIRTY-FIVE

NOW

"I don't understand." I read over the document in my hands again. "This can't be real."

Tucker hovers over my shoulder, studying the paper with intense scrutiny. "You had no idea?"

I shake my head. It's as if I'm in a dream I can't wake up from. "Why wouldn't they tell me?"

Certificate of Adoption

I study the name listed as my name at birth: **Angela Collins.** And my parents: **Chris Collins** and **Jolene Ray-Collins.** If that wasn't enough proof of my worst fears, my parents' address at the time of my birth is also listed.

40 Hemlock Drive, Myers, Illinois

"My parents adopted me in 1991," I say, reading the adoption decree. I run a finger across the place that holds both my parents' signatures. "Tucker...I found an article that had a photo with the Collins family and their three kids. Only two had been mentioned in the articles I found, but that was because only two died. I thought they'd had a son who lived, but...it was me. I...I used to live in that house."

His nod is soft, eyes haunted. "*Angela.*" He looks away and clears his throat. "That's right. Holy shit, that's right. I...I remember you. That name. Angela. They, *we*, called you Angie. Jason's baby sister." He shakes his head, neck bent, eyes pinched shut. "They...made you cut your hair. *He* made you."

"What?" I place the paper down, looking at him. "You remember me? We knew each other?"

"We tried to hide you. Jason and me. When he found out your dad was going to cut your hair. I can't believe I forgot." When he looks up at me, his eyes are glassy. "You were just his little sister, but yeah, sometimes you'd come out to play, too. *Angie.* When I saw that name, *your* name, it reminded me... I don't have many memories from that time, not even of Jason. We were all so young when you left. But I remember the day you had your hair cut. Jason asked me to help you hide, and we..." He speaks softly, remembering each detail piece by piece. "We hid you in my bedroom. Under the bed. Your dad was furious. I overheard my grandparents talking about it afterward." He pinches the bridge of his nose. "They *really* didn't like him. They said he made you cut your hair because it kept getting tangled." He looks away. "He took you out on the front porch right then and buzzed it off." When he looks at me again, there are full, fat tears in his eyes. I've never seen him cry before. "It was you. All along. I can't believe it, all this time... You were right there."

"You tried to save me? Even back then?" My voice breaks as I search my mind for the memory, but it's not there. It's a photo in an album that I'll never recall.

I think of the photo from the article. The child I mistook for a boy. The little girl with the broken spirit at such a young age. *Why was I the only one who escaped? How did I manage to make it?*

The name Angela doesn't feel familiar. That name will never be mine, just like the memories aren't.

"Tried, but it wasn't enough," Tucker says, swiping a hand over his face. "After that, they always kept your hair short. I can't believe this. How did I not know it was you? How could I have forgotten you?"

I study him. Somehow, it both brings me peace and makes me feel violated to have someone hold memories I can't recall that belong to me. "What else do you remember about me? Or the Collinses?"

He grimaces. "Not a lot. I didn't see a lot of the bad stuff, if that's what you mean. Your dad had a temper, but I never knew..." He trails off. "Jason and I were friends. We kicked each other's butts at hide-and-seek. Sometimes you would play, but not always. You stayed inside a lot, and I was never allowed inside your house." He pauses, his features going serious. "I'm so sorry, Maggie. I'm sorry about what happened and sorry this is how you're finding out."

I place the adoption decree on my lap. "I don't understand why my parents didn't tell me anything. When I was young, maybe it made sense to keep me in the dark, but I must've had questions back then. Did I see what he did? Did I understand? What did they tell me about what happened? About where my family was? If nothing else, when I got old enough, I deserved to know."

He sits down next to me. "I'm sure they just wanted to protect you. If they thought you would never find out the truth, maybe it made sense to keep it a secret. Maybe they thought they were doing the right thing."

"The right thing for them, maybe." I feel sick over the bitterness in my stomach. I don't want to be angry at my parents. Not when they are no longer here to defend their decision.

"Look." He reaches forward, easing the adoption decree away from me slowly. "No matter what this says, your mom will always be your mom. You know that. Nothing you learned today changes that. Your parents are your parents, and they loved you."

I give a small smile. "I know. I do. I just...I don't know what I'm supposed to do with this information. Is this why I've always been so obsessed with that house?" I shake my head. "How can I possibly stay somewhere where I know this terrible history and, to top it off, it was my own family involved? My brother and sister died in that house. My mother."

"You don't have to stay."

Suddenly, something occurs to me. "Oh my god." I glance at him. "*Of course.* Oh my god. That's what has been happening. It has to be."

"What are you talking about?"

I grip his shoulders, staring at him with wild eyes. "It's not ghosts in the house, Tucker. It's *memories. They* are memories. I'm...I'm remembering that night. Her screams. Their cries. The creak of the floorboard when he came looking for me. The scratching sound of her crawling across the floor after he'd..." I can't bring myself to finish the sentence. It's too painful. As if to prove my point, I hear her cries again. Softer this time. I can't picture her face outside of the photos I've seen, but somehow I can hear her.

I look at the next paper in the stack I'd been going through when I found the adoption decree. A letter in an envelope addressed to my parents from someone named Loretta Ray.

I open it with shaking hands.

> *Dear Jude and Alice,*
>
> *You don't know me, but I wanted to write to offer my sincere gratitude for taking in my grand-daughter. By now, you know a lot about her parents' history, perhaps more than even I know, but I do know that my daughter loved her children.*
>
> *When she found out she was pregnant with little Jason, she was just seventeen years old. Her father and I were furious. We didn't have the means to take care of her and a baby and encouraged her to have it aborted. That only pushed her further into marrying the father, Chris. It is my greatest regret. They thought they were in love, but my husband and I could see the truth. We saw Chris for what he was right from the beginning. Bossy and controlling. He had a say in everything our Jolene wore, what she ate, where she went. He stopped letting her see us. We've only met our grandson a handful of times, and I regret to say we were never allowed to meet the younger two, sweet Angie and Shelby.*
>
> *My husband passed away several years ago, and I was barely able to keep the lights on in the studio apartment I moved into. I didn't have room for my daughter and three grandchildren to live with me,*

but I tried. When Jolene finally told me how bad it had gotten, how scared she was for the kids, I told her to come stay with me. We'd figure it out.

She told me she was saving up. She was planning. She mentioned that a kind couple next door was helping her get things in order.

I have no idea how true that is, or if she ever actually planned to leave. Either way, you have a piece of my sweet girl with you now. The last piece that exists. Thank you for loving her as much as I love her, as much as I have to believe her mother did.

I guess I'm just writing this so you know she was loved. That this terrible fate wasn't meant to be hers. That Jolene tried. Please never forget that if you tell her about her mother someday.

Regards,
Loretta Ray

When I finish reading, a tear slips down onto the page, smearing a bit of the ink it was written with. I fold the page, tucking it back into the envelope. To know that Jolene had tried to get us out, that we'd found the proof of that effort in the walls, makes this both better and worse.

I feel guilty for wishing she'd have made it, because it would mean I'd never have had the parents I did. But to be thankful for what happened is so much worse.

Tucker places a gentle hand on my shoulder, and I fall into his chest, allowing silent tears to fall. He rubs my back, whispering softly in my ear.

"Shhhh...I'm here. Whatever you need."

We sit like that for a long time, neither of us saying anything. There is so much to be said, and yet nothing at all that I can put into words to make any of this make sense.

"Are you okay?" he asks gently.

I open my mouth to say yes out of habit, but I stop myself. "I have no idea."

"At least you know the truth now. About everything. It sounds like she really tried. From...from what I remember, your mom was always nice." He gives me a reassuring smile. "She used to make us homemade popsicles with pickle juice. They were always your favorite." His smile swims with nostalgia.

"I wish I could remember that," I say softly.

"I'll bet my grandparents have more pictures of us somewhere," he says. "We can look. Maybe it'll help jog some memories."

"I'm almost scared to do that," I say. He doesn't argue or push. I'm terrified of what it will unearth, what memories will resurface.

He gives me a small, encouraging smile. "You're going to be okay, Maggie. Whatever you decide to do with the house and your future, it'll be okay."

I wipe away tears from my eyes. "I should get back to work."

"No," he says, slowly closing the box in front of me. "That's enough for today. You've just gone through a lot. I'll load up all the boxes in the truck, and we'll take them home to finish going through another day. For now, you need to cry as much as you want and talk and...I don't know, take a nap? A bubble bath? Something other than this."

"I need a drink," I say flatly.

He puts an arm around me, helping me to stand. "Well, funnily enough, I know a thing or two about making a drink. I can probably help with that."

My smile is half hearted at best. "Thanks, Tuck."

His voice is serious when he answers. "Always."

The truth of it resonates with me. Not just now, not just in college. Somehow, this man next to me, once a scared little boy hiding me in his room from monsters he didn't understand, has always been there for me.

I rest my head on his shoulder as he leads me to the truck. "Let's go home."

Back at the house, Tucker helps me onto the couch before unloading the rest of the boxes. I want to help him. I feel so useless watching him do all of the work, but I can't move.

I'm utterly drained. Mentally. Physically. Emotionally.

I don't know how I'm supposed to move on from this. Not only knowing that my parents aren't my biological parents, but knowing the absolute horrors of my early years. Knowing my siblings died here. Knowing the sounds I've been hearing have been their final moments. It's too much.

I'm not strong enough for this.

Tucker brings me a glass of gin and kneels down in front of me. "Is there anything else I can get you?"

I take a sip first, then shake my head.

"Do you want to talk about it?"

"No."

"Okay," he says, brushing a bit of hair back from my face. He crosses the room, picking up the frame that holds Mom's wedding dress, and carries it into the hall. A few moments later, I hear the sounds of hammering and realize he's hanging it up.

When he returns to the room, his eyes are filled with worry. I want to reassure him that I'm fine. I hate feeling like such a burden. But, then again, Tucker has never made me feel that way.

Somewhere in this house, in a box he just unloaded from his truck, is the proof that the home I moved into just days ago is the very first home I ever had. My world has completely imploded, my already crumbling life turning to ash before my eyes.

It wasn't enough that my parents died and my five-year relationship ended and I lost my job, or that I had to come back and rehash every painful moment of my past. No. The universe decided to kick me while I'm down in the form of taking away the memories I have with my parents, tainting them with bitter lies and forever-unanswered questions. It had to let me discover that my past is so much worse than I ever could've imagined. To bog me down with survivor's guilt and guilt over the fact that I can't remember anything about these people except the way they sounded as they died.

I'm wallowing, and I hate myself for it, even as it happens. I don't want to be this person.

"You're strong," Tucker says gently, sitting down on the floor beside me. "Do you hear me? All of this, it doesn't define you. What happened here didn't make you who you are. You've grown, Maggie. Not just from back then, but from college, too. Hell, you've grown in the past week. I've watched it happen. Your parents, the ones who raised you, the ones who matter, they would be damn proud of the woman you are. They had their reasons for not telling you the truth, and maybe you'll never understand them. I think that's okay. But I'm sure they felt guilty over it. I'm sure it's not a decision they took lightly. And I'm sure, whatever happened, however they decided, it was all because of how much they loved you." His eyes soften. "How could they not? How could anyone not?"

Tears cascade down my cheeks as I stare at him. It's as if, without me saying a word, he knew exactly what I needed to hear.

"How do you do that?" I croak.

"Do what?"

"Know what I'm thinking all the time."

"Your face literally screams your every thought, remember?" he teases, echoing what he said to me the night this all began.

I smile through my tears, and he leans forward, brushing them away. "You just rest, okay? I'm not going anywhere."

I wish it was that easy. It's all so heavy. I feel the physical weight of it, as if the news is a barbell on my chest. As if the tension is crushing me from every direction.

Everything about this place is charged with memories and energy I'd never noticed before. It's painful. Terrifying. Like coming into a new space and somewhere I've been a million times. Everything in my head is conflicted. I need to rest, but I can't.

I can't do anything but cry.

For a while, that's all I do. I allow silent tears to fall from my eyes, as if each one is a small weight off my chest. A small piece of dust I've managed to chisel away from my heartache.

When I open my eyes again, Tucker's forehead is glistening with sweat.

I reach out, rubbing my thumb across it as if he's Simba, and I'm Rafiki. He lifts his hand, drying his brow.

"It's hot in here," he explains. When he says it, it's as if a

315

spell has broken. Suddenly, I realize I, too, am drenched in sweat. I pull my shirt away from my body, fanning myself.

"The thermostat," I whisper, sitting up.

"Is it still doing that?" Tucker asks, his face serious.

"It hasn't in a while. I was kind of hoping it had stopped."

"I'm going to go check on it." He rests a hand on my leg. "Are you okay if I leave you for a second?"

"I'm fine."

He disappears into the kitchen, and I stand up, fanning myself again. A few moments later, he reappears. "You know, I never thought about it, but did you reset the system when you moved in? These are those smart thermostats. I wonder if the old owners are accidentally adjusting it."

I follow him into the kitchen. "Smart thermostats? Really? In this old house?"

At the thermostat again, he works through the settings. "Yeah. The last owners probably had them installed. It all looks fairly new." He speaks slowly, distracted by his work. "I haven't worked with this brand before, but there should be an option to disconnect it from any apps from here. I don't see anything that says it's connected to one, but it'll be a good precaution anyway. I'll look up how to do it and we'll see if that fixes anything." He lowers the temperature another notch, down to sixty-eight, and I hear the heat kick off finally before, moments later, the air kicks on. He reaches for his phone to search for instructions, but we're interrupted by a knock on the door.

He looks up at me, brows drawn down. "Expecting someone?"

I shake my head. With Clayton in Nashville and Tucker here, it could only be Nick. I do not feel like dealing with this, but I won't dare ask Tucker. He's done enough.

However, when I pull the door open, I see a face I haven't

seen in years. Her dark hair is shoulder-length, her bright eyes as happy as I remember.

"Hi, Abby," I say, catching sight of Clayton jogging up the stairs behind her. I pin a smile on my lips, hoping they don't see the exhaustion or tears in my eyes. "What are you guys doing here?"

"She's staying with me for spring break. We just got back into town. Thought I'd bring her by so you could see how much she's grown."

"Dad, stop!" Abby groans, ever the teenager.

"Yeah, what's it been since I saw you last? Six, seven years? You're all grown up. And you look just like your mother." She's practically her spitting image.

"Everyone says that," Abby agrees, flicking hair off her shoulder with a bashful smile. She's blissfully unaware of how sore the subject still is.

Then, my eyes connect with Clayton's. "How is Raven, anyway?"

CHAPTER THIRTY-SIX

THEN

Tucker is at my door an hour after I arrive home. He's breathless and still only dressed in his jeans—no shirt or shoes. I'm almost positive he ran here.

"What do you want?" I ask, not bothering to move so he can come inside. He can't. Not ever again. "Shouldn't you be back home? You'll keep Professor Eden waiting."

He grimaces. "Maggie, what the hell? I've been texting you for over a week. You're apparently with Clayton now. What's going on? Why did you come tonight?"

"Better question: *did you?*" I ask dryly.

"It was a mistake." He looks as if he's going to be sick. I catch a hint of alcohol on his breath.

"Sure didn't look like it."

"I was mad. Hurt. I knew I'd lost you, so I didn't see the harm in..."

"In sleeping with a professor?"

"In trying to get over you," he says. "Why were you there?"

"It doesn't matter anymore. You hadn't lost me, for the record, but you made sure to fix that, didn't you?" I study his face, disgusted with myself for never considering that he might hurt me. I thought he was different. That *we* were different. My nostrils flare as bitter tears sting my eyes. "I trusted you."

He rubs a hand across his mouth. "I'm sorry, Maggie. I truly am. If I'd known I still had a chance... But what was I supposed to think? How was I supposed to know you'd change your mind? I hate myself for the way you're looking at me right now. I never meant to hurt you."

I fold my arms across my chest. "Well, you did anyway."

"You've been with Clayton. How is that any different?"

"I was with Clayton as a friend." I jab a finger toward the ground. "Trying to help him navigate the whole Raven-pregnancy thing. I needed to do that for my *friend*."

"That's not how you made it seem. Why couldn't you talk to me because of it? What was I supposed to think? You were pretty clear about where we stood. We slept together, you disappeared, and then suddenly you're with Clayton. You broke my heart, Maggie."

I wave both hands next to my ears. "Do you even hear yourself right now? *I* broke *your* heart? A week was enough for you to completely forget about me and jump into bed with someone else, but *I* hurt *you*?"

"It was over a week, practically two, and I'd never forget about you. Don't you dare say that." His voice cracks. "I thought you were walking away from me."

"No. I wasn't. I had a lot going on. I'm not saying it's okay. I'm sure I could've handled it better, but it's been a crazy few days."

"I'm not mad at you, I just—"

"Well, it doesn't matter anymore, Tucker. Because I'm mad at you. I can't forgive you for this."

"I don't expect you to forgive me right away, but—"

"Not ever." I step backward.

His eyes drop. "It was a mistake, Maggie. Can't you understand that?"

"No. I'm sorry. I can't. Because I wouldn't even let Clayton kiss me, and you were in bed with someone else."

His jaw drops with despair, tears glimmering in his crystal-blue eyes. He looks away, drying them. "I was trying to get over you. I was devastated."

"That's no excuse. If you cared about me, you would've given me more time. You would've tried harder."

He doesn't answer. "Maggie, I thought you were with Clayton. I wanted you to be happy, but it killed me."

"I told you the night we slept together that I wasn't going to be with him."

"*Exactly*," he cries, exasperated. "What changed?"

"I told you, nothing changed. My head has been a mess. I was confused. I needed time to deal with everything. I didn't want to be with you halfway. I wanted it to be real."

"It *is* real." He reaches for my hand, but I jerk it away.

"No, it's not. Whatever this was, it's over."

He looks as if he's been slapped. "You don't mean that."

"I very much do," I say firmly, gripping the door. I wave a hand in his direction, shooing him. "Run along, Tucker. You'll be late for extra credit. Please just...don't ever contact me again." With that, I slam the door and run to my room as bitter, heartbroken tears cascade down my face.

CHAPTER THIRTY-SEVEN

NOW

Abby and Clayton come inside the house, where Tucker is still waiting in the doorway between the living room and the kitchen.

"Abby, this is my friend Tucker." I gesture toward him. "Tucker, Clayton's daughter, Abby."

"Hi," she says, her cheeks turning pink.

"Hey." He nods.

"What are you guys up to?" Clayton asks, wrapping an arm around his daughter's shoulders, his voice too cheery.

I want to tell him everything, but I can't get into it now, and certainly not in front of Abby. It's all still too raw. I force myself to push through it. "Nothing, really. Tucker's been helping me go through some of Mom's stuff from storage."

Tucker's eyes cut to me, but I look away. I can't do whatever he thinks I should do right now. I don't have the strength to send Clayton away. Even if I tried, it would take a conversation I'm not strong enough for yet.

"Well, I hope you don't mind the break. I just thought we'd stop by and visit for a few minutes. This is the first time Abby's come to stay with me in a couple years. You guys need to catch up. Maybe at some point this week we can take her to some of our old favorite places." He looks at Tucker and adds, as an obvious afterthought, "Sorry, we aren't interrupting anything, are we?"

"Nah, that's okay." Tucker puts up a hand, his voice dry. "I, uh, I guess I should get home anyway." He looks at me as he moves past, stopping to check in. A silent conversation passes between us. He wants me to tell Clayton the truth, that I'm not ready, not in the mood for this tonight. Not at all capable of hosting Abby or entertaining. But I can't. I just...can't. I can't explain the power Clayton has over me, not even to myself. I just refuse to let him down. "Unless you need me to stay?"

"I'm okay," I tell him, regret in my voice for only him to hear. "Thank you for today. For everything. You don't have to leave, though. Stay and hang out with us. I want you to."

"It's okay," he says. "I should let you catch up. Just...call if you need anything. I'm around."

I hate myself for being relieved he's not staying. I don't have any extra bandwidth to deal with their egos and tension right now. I'm barely holding it together as is. "I know. Thank you, Tuck. I'll call you later tonight." I lean in, placing an awkward kiss on his cheek before he slinks away.

"See you around," Clayton calls after him. Something about his tone annoys me, like he thinks he's won, but I brush it off. Maybe it will be easier with Clayton and Abby tonight. They don't know what's going on, so there's no added pressure. I can pretend to be totally fine, and there will be no one around to call my bluff. "So, since he's gone, do you want to have dinner? Just the three of us?" We haven't all eaten a meal together since Abby was in kindergarten. She's so rarely here.

"Um, sure. What did you have in mind?"

He clicks his tongue, thinking. "Why don't you come to the house? I could cook dinner."

"Yeah, okay."

"Yeah? That was easy. I was prepared to beg." He winks. "Well, cool. Are you ready now, then, or...?"

"Sure, let's go." I grab my phone from the coffee table and tuck it into my back pocket.

"Cool. I'm going to use the bathroom really quick. I'll meet you guys out there."

"Sounds good." I pass him the house key. "Lock up when you're done, will you?"

He tucks it into his pocket. "You've got it."

Abby and I head for the Jeep, and I try to fill the awkward silence with questions. "So, Abby, how's school going?"

"It's fine."

"Do you want to ride up front with your dad? I don't mind the back."

"It's cool," she says, climbing up into the back seat before I can object.

"So, what are you into lately?" I'm terrible at this. "Your dad said he got you a guitar."

"Yeah."

Great. With nothing else to talk about, I drum my fingers on the armrest, anxiously waiting for our Clayton-shaped buffer to arrive.

When he finally does, he tosses the key back to me. I don't miss the way he keeps grinning from the driver's seat on the way home, watching me out of the corner of his eye. I know, in his mind, this is how it was meant to be. This is a chance for us to start over, but it will never be that. Not anymore.

When we get to the house, Abby hurries inside, texting on her phone and leaving Clayton and me to carry her bags.

"So, how is Raven? You never really answered."

"She's good. She's actually planning to go on a small tour soon. Mostly local places, but a few here and there. She's really leaning into that side of her career now."

I detect a hint of jealousy there but decide not to pry. "Oh yeah? And what will that mean for you?"

"Abby goes with her most of the time, but I told her she can stay here with me if she wants. It's hard on her, I think. Being on the road so much. Her tutor is great, but you know, what kind of life is that for a kid?"

"I don't know. It doesn't sound so bad. Are you and Raven...in touch often?" Neither of them ever married anyone. I can't help wondering if unresolved feelings are to blame for that.

"No. Not really. We co-parent well. We're on the same page, a united front. But if it doesn't involve Abby or music, we rarely talk."

"That must be tough."

"Not really," he admits. "Raven and I never worked, you know? Abby's the best part of our relationship."

I elbow him playfully. "I'm proud of you. Have I mentioned that? You've done well with her. Your mom is always telling me what a good dad you are."

He rolls his eyes. "Yeah, well, Mom is president of the fan club. I do my best."

"You've done great." I stop talking and take in the property. I'll never get used to how grand it is. While Clayton's career hasn't panned out in terms of touring and releasing albums, his true love has always been songwriting, and being able to do that from home has given him a nice life. His home is on the seven acres he bought when he was engaged to Raven, and he had it built exactly how he wanted it. It's stunning.

He grins, seeing my appreciation. "I've had the brick painted white since you were here for the funeral. What do you think?"

"It's beautiful, although I'm surprised your mom hasn't killed you over painting brick in general."

He laughs. "She wasn't happy, but she likes the final product." He stops and holds open the door for me to pass through. "So, what should I make us for dinner?"

CHAPTER THIRTY-EIGHT

THEN

Clayton laughs from where he sits across from me at the restaurant. He takes hold of a fry, tossing it at me playfully. This is the happiest he's seemed in a long time. Why, then, do I feel the worst?

"It's an interesting thought, though, I guess," he says, mulling over what I've just told him. "Completely ridiculous."

"Why is it ridiculous?"

"Because that's just...not what happens."

"And you would know because of your extensive experience with dying?" I challenge. "No one knows what happens when we die. Why can't it be possible?"

Sometimes I like to think the people who die go on living without really knowing they've died. Isn't that a peaceful thought? That those we've lost are just out there, living and loving, happy and at peace. That they don't know anything happened to them. That they exist in a reality that is exactly what they hoped for. That someday, we'll each fade off, die, and have no idea it's even happened. I guess I've been thinking about death a lot since my dad's diagnosis in the fall.

"I don't know," Clayton says. "You mean you think there are alternate versions of us living in other people's heavens?"

"Not heaven, just an afterlife. Like a simulation. We only exist in their minds. Sure, why not?"

He shakes his head, smirking. "Okay, whatever you say. Anyway, I was thinking we could go see a movie tonight."

"Sure."

"And...maybe you could stay over?"

Before, I wouldn't have thought twice about staying over. It's something we've done since we were kids. But now, it carries weight and implications it didn't always have. Now, if I stay over, he'll expect more.

With Tucker permanently out of the picture, I've brought down my walls for Clayton, allowed us both to think there's a possibility this might happen, but I can't go that far. Not yet. It's too much. Neither of us are ready.

"I don't know. I have an early class."

"I'll drive you. Wake you up. Bring you coffee."

"If I ever see you awake before ten a.m., I might die of shock."

He laughs. "Fair enough. Movie, though?"

I nod. "Yeah."

"Cool." He clears his throat. "I'm...I'm having a really good time with you, Maggie. I know things are still weird, but...I guess, just, thank you. For giving us a chance."

The genuine smile he gives me is piercing. I want to return it, to feel an ounce of the happiness he's experiencing, but I can't.

I'm so numb, I can't feel a thing.

My mouth stretches into a smile that doesn't reach my eyes.

He doesn't seem to notice.

Just then, a group of people move past us, whispering excitedly. One of the girls places a flier on the table in front of me. "We're having a memorial service for Professor Eden later today, if you guys want to come."

Her name sends a shockwave through me. My mouth is suddenly like cotton. "A memorial service?" The girl and her group of friends are already gone as I stare down at the photo of the woman who ruined everything.

"No..." My voice is a low whisper. "No. No. No. No. No." My world has been kicked off its axis.

"What?" he asks, putting the straw of his milkshake in his mouth.

"Nevermind." I stand. "I have to go." My legs wobble underneath me as I make my way to the door. *How did she die?* She was perfectly healthy, young... This doesn't make sense. Tucker wouldn't have done this. I know he wouldn't. It could be anyone else, but when I look at the date she died listed on this flier, I can't help realizing it's the same day I caught them together. The day I told him I'd never forgive him. The last day we spoke.

What happened after he left my apartment?

CHAPTER THIRTY-NINE

NOW

We're in the middle of the movie Abby has chosen for us to watch, bellies full and curled up on the couch, when my phone vibrates twice from where I've left it across the room. Both notifications are quick, probably text messages or emails, so I ignore it.

Clayton looks over at me, a question in his eyes, but he turns his attention back to the screen when a car chase starts. Abby squeals and covers her mouth as the car flies down an alleyway.

Clayton removes his hand from my knee, standing with a stretch. He grabs his empty wineglass. "I need a refill. Do you want anything while I'm up?"

"I'm okay." I point to the glass next to me, still mostly full. "Thanks, though."

When my phone buzzes for a third and fourth time, I sit up, untucking my feet from under me and crossing the room to check it.

My throat goes tight as I process what I'm looking at. I have several notifications from my home security system. Two from the front porch cameras, one from the camera in the living room, one from the kitchen, and one from the hall.

Someone is in my house.

I stand, moving away from Abby to check the camera feed. When it appears, the first thing I notice is that one of the bedroom doors is standing open.

Then, I see the man.

Tucker.

What are you doing there?

Tucker is in my house. I study the grainy image of him moving through the rooms. What's going on? How did he get inside? Why is he there? What is he doing?

In a hurry, I head for the kitchen, prepared to ask Clayton for a ride home, but I stop when I see his phone on the edge of the end table. Its screen is lit up, and the icon there catches my eye.

It's one I had never seen before until earlier today.

Clayton appears in the doorway, his smile fading. "What's wrong?"

"Why do you have the Control Hub app on your phone?"

The smile completely wipes from his face. "What? Do I? I'm...I'm not sure." He hurries forward, but I grab his phone before he can. I don't care that I'm breaking half a dozen societal norms, because suddenly, everything makes sense.

"Have you been the one messing with my thermostat?" I demand. Tucker was supposed to disconnect it earlier, but we were interrupted by Clayton's arrival. I'd nearly forgotten about that conversation until now.

"*What?*" he asks in the most unconvincing voice I've ever heard. "No. What are you talking about?"

"This app." I point to it on his screen. "It's the one used to control my thermostat. Yours is different." I glance at the thermostat on the wall behind him, clearly sporting a different logo than mine does.

"What's going on?" Abby asks, pausing the movie.

"Nothing," we say at the same time. Clayton grabs my arm, tugging me into the kitchen.

"You need to start talking. Right now."

He looks ready to argue, but eventually, his shoulders drop. "I'm sorry. It was stupid."

I can't believe this. "Why would you do it? I don't understand. What was the point?"

"I just..." He reaches for his phone, but I keep it in my grip. "I wanted to convince you to sell. I thought if you thought there was an issue with the wiring, and that it would be too expensive to fix, you'd decide to leave. And then, after you mentioned strange things happening, I remembered all the old rumors and thought I could make you want to get out of there even more." He smiles sheepishly. As if this is all just a harmless prank. "I realize how bad that sounds. I shouldn't have done it."

"Then why did you? You wanted to scare me?"

He sighs, rubbing a hand in his hair. "Garrett was an idiot for ever letting you buy that house."

He knows about my connection to the house? How? "What do you mean?"

"You can't live next to Tucker, Maggs. You just can't. I just got you back. I can't lose you again. And, as long as you live next to him, I'm not blind enough to think I stand a chance."

"Not pulling stuff like this, you don't." I wag the phone at him. "I can't believe you did this. This is low, Clayton. Like, the worst thing you've ever done."

"I know. I just...I can't control myself when it comes to you. Call it crazy, but I'll do whatever it takes to be with you.

To prove I'm finally enough for you. I love you. I'm *in love* with you. Don't you see that?"

"This isn't love. It's control. Don't *you* see that?" I cry, doing my best to keep my voice low.

"It's more love than he's ever shown you," he whisper-shouts, his lips tight and wrinkled.

"How would you even know that? You don't know anything about him."

"I know that he hurt you. I know he's the reason you left. The reason you couldn't be with me back then."

"That's not true," I say. A partial lie. "I would've been with you if I'd wanted to. I didn't. I left for myself."

"Yeah, okay." His tone drips with sarcasm.

"What's that supposed to mean?"

"You're just so blind when it comes to him. He can do no wrong. I saw it back then, just like I see it now. I just thought you would've learned your lesson when he slept with Professor Eden. But instead—"

"How do you know that?" I demand. I never told him. Never told anyone. No one knows about that night except me.

His jaw goes slack, devoid of any answer he can give me. In my hand, his phone buzzes again, and I look down. Another thermostat notification. I type in his password, wondering what prank temperature he's got it set on right now, and my heart plummets.

High Temperature Warning

"What the hell?" I switch phones, opening my security app again and selecting the hallway's camera feed.

Immediately, the screen is filled with bright white flames. *Fire.*

My house has caught on fire, and it's only then I realize what Tucker's doing there. Standing in the middle of the hall, he cups both hands around his mouth, shouting. I enable the audio.

"*Maggie?* For God's sake, where are you?" he cries, hands on either side of his head as the flames grow around him.

He went there to find me.

He must've seen the fire.

And Clayton's Jeep is gone, but my car is still in the driveway.

Tucker has no idea I'm not home.

CHAPTER FORTY

I drive Clayton's Jeep like a mad woman through the streets of Myers, sure a cop is going to catch me at any moment.

Let them try.

I can't get there fast enough. I've called Tucker's number seventeen times since I left Clayton's house, but I'm getting no answer. He either left his phone at home, or something terrible has happened. I can't allow myself to consider it. I'll never make it if I do.

I can see the smoke in the already dark sky long before I ever arrive on our street. The smell of it, even with my windows rolled up, permeates the air. Each smoky breath I struggle to take bites at my throat.

My thoughts come in fragments: worry, fear, panic, anger. A blurry mosaic of terror.

I can't believe Clayton. I grip the steering wheel tighter as I remember that. I'm so angry with him, but that's not my biggest concern. It can't be. I have to know that Tucker's okay.

When I pull into the driveway, all thought seems to dissipate. We're far enough out that no one seems to have noticed the fire yet. No one is here trying to help. I called for a fire truck on the way, but it will be another fifteen minutes at least before they arrive. Ten, if we're lucky.

I should've called sooner. I was too busy panicking to realize someone had to call, and that someone could only be me.

I basically fall out of the Jeep, leaving the door open in a rush to get to the door. The entire top floor has been engulfed in flames, which have begun to creep down the sides, burning the house from the back forward. Embers fly through the sky, and the heat reaches me where I am.

"*Tucker!*" I shout, cupping my hands around my mouth to help the sound carry. It does no good. My voice is masked by the roar of the fire, by the creaks and groans of the old house as it burns before my eyes. "Tucker!" I rush forward to the porch and unlock the front door as quickly as my suddenly uncooperative fingers will allow. I shove it open.

The window is broken, and I realize that must've been how he made it inside. If I'd have thought to arm the security system before we left, maybe help would already be here. "Tucker! Where are you?"

The air is so hot it feels like I've stepped into an oven. The heat sears my skin. Everywhere I look, flames lap at the things I love, melting and destroying everything in its wake.

I'm too late.

No. I can't give up.

He's counting on me.

I hurry into the hallway, the last place I saw him, and my knees nearly buckle. *There he is.*

It's hard to make out his shape in the bright white and orange of the flames surrounding him, but I know it's him. Just like I know I can't get to him.

There's no way I can make it through the fire. It's too much. It's everywhere.

"Tucker!" I shout, willing him to move or acknowledge me. But he doesn't. He's on the floor, his body slack. Has he passed out, or...

Smoke burns my lungs, and I cough, covering my mouth with my shirt as I try to get a better look at him. His arm is dripping with blood, an injury that must've come from the window.

CRASH.

In front of me, through the doorway of the back bedroom, I see a wall collapse, sending soot, smoke, and flames in every direction. It sucks the air from my lungs. I bend down, my knees weak, as I break into a coughing fit. My head aches, vision blurring.

I don't have time to think. I can't be in this smoke much longer, and neither can he. Standing on my feet again, I rush into the kitchen and grab the table, turning it over on its head and dragging it across the floor. In the hallway, I spin it around so it's in front of me and shove it forward to clear a path through the fire. It won't last long. The cheap wood begins smoldering in an instant, but it's long enough for me to reach him. I grab hold of his shoulder, turning him onto his back. "Tucker! Tuck, can you hear me?" I place a hand on his chest, tears welling in my eyes when I feel his heartbeat. He's alive. His chest constricts, and he coughs, but he doesn't open his eyes.

What do I do? What do I do?

I have to be quick. There's no time for indecision or second-guessing. I grab hold of his shoulders, trying to ease him into a sitting position, but I can't carry him or drag him.

I look around, feeling hopeless.

Come on.

Come on.

Come on.

Think.

There has to be a way.

Suddenly, a light bulb clicks on in my head. A plan. I have a plan. The bedroom to my left, the room I'm sure was Jason's, isn't yet on fire.

Okay. Here we go.

With every ounce of strength, I hook my arms under his and pull. I groan, digging my heels into the linoleum floor, pulling, pulling, pulling. He moves slowly, but it's happening. I'm making progress.

The carpet in the bedroom slows us down as I hear another wall crash somewhere in the house. I drop him, my head throbbing as I break into another fit of coughs. I feel dizzy.

Holding my breath, I try to ignore the smoke stinging my eyes. I hadn't realized I was coughing again. It's clear I'm choking and suffocating from the smoke. I'm going to die if I don't get fresh air soon.

Tucker is already dying.

No. I can't focus on that.

Keep moving.

I reach the window and undo the latch, gripping the wooden sash and shoving it up with all my might. The old wooden windows are hard to move. It barely budges an inch against my strength at first, but eventually, it gives way, lifting open with a groan. Smoke swirls past me on the way out, and my head spins again. I feel as if I might puke.

I stick my head out the window, gulping in clean air until

my eyes no longer burn so badly I can't see. I cough and hack, my throat burning from the smoke.

With one last gulp of air, I pull myself back in the room and slip my arms under his again.

This drop is going to hurt so badly I'm not sure he'll make it, but it's our only chance. I have no idea how much time has passed, but as I hear the walls groan around me, I'm more sure than ever we don't have time to wait for fire rescue. I have to do something, or we'll both die.

"I'm sorry," I tell him, lifting him to his feet. He doesn't move, and I try not to dwell on that as I hang him out the window and, with a giant shove, push him to freedom. He lands facedown with a thud, and I can't see whether his eyes have opened. Whether he realizes what's happening.

I'm about to jump myself when I remember Mom's dress hanging on the wall just outside this room. I'm so thankful Tucker hung it up for me. It's the only reason I'll be able to reach it in time. If it was in the back bedroom with everything else from storage, it would be gone. I'm going to lose all of my things, all of my parents' things, which is hard enough to swallow right now, but at least I can save that.

I rush out into the hall. The table is now engulfed in flames, licking at the air with a vengeance. I grab the dress in its frame and hurry back to the window, pushing it out first. The glass in the frame shatters as it lands. I feel sick. My head spins, dizziness overwhelming me. With all my strength, I launch myself forward and out the window.

I land with a thud, my head smacking the ground, and I break into another round of coughs. My head pounds, my chest burning. I can't focus on anything anymore.

For a moment, it's like that second where you're drifting off to sleep, and it feels like you're actually falling.

Tucker said that to me once.
His voice replays in my head.
"Tuck..."
Then, there's nothing.

CHAPTER FORTY-ONE

"Maggie, can you hear me?"

I open my eyes to an unfamiliar voice, but nothing about what I'm seeing makes sense. Blurs of multiple shades of white. Lights. Something is beeping.

Ouch.

When I move, everything hurts. White-hot pain shoots through me.

Someone places a hand on my head, pulling open my eye. More lights. More pain.

"Maggie?"

I blink as my eyes finally begin to find focus. An older woman with a kind smile is looking at me. Like the room, she's all in white.

An angel.

No, a doctor.

She places her small light in her pocket, taking hold of her stethoscope.

Hospital.

I'm in the hospital.

It clicks for me finally.

"There you are." She places the stethoscope against my chest, and I jolt, sending a wave of pain across my body. The metal of the stethoscope is icy against my warm skin. "Do you remember what happened?"

I shake my head as the answer comes to me. "Fire," I mumble, my throat tender and incredibly dry. It feels like I've been sunburned from the inside out. My eyes widen. "Tucker. Where's Tucker?"

She puts up a hand to stop me from moving. "It's okay. He's okay. He's still sedated, but he's going to make it. You both are." She drapes the stethoscope around her neck. "You sustained some damage to your lungs from smoke inhalation, a few minor burns to your arms and legs, and a bump on the head, but other than that, you're okay."

"And the house?"

She gives a sad smile. "I'm sorry. I...think the police will be in to talk to you soon, but you should prepare yourself."

She means it's gone. That the fire destroyed everything. I'm not sure I expected anything else. "When can I see Tucker?"

"As soon as you're cleared. Let's get your oxygen levels up a bit more, and then I'm happy to release you." She glances out the door. "You do have a visitor right now." Clayton. I can't believe he'd show up here. The nerve of— "Would you like me to let her in?"

"Her?"

She nods.

"Who?"

"I didn't get her name. She has dark hair."

I nod wordlessly. Abby. How will I ever explain this to her? What has Clayton told her about what happened?

When the doctor leaves, I'm surprised to see someone else

appear in the doorway. The last person I ever expected to see again.

"Raven?"

Two men stand just outside the door as it swings shut, and I realize she must require security now. *How different things are...* Though, aside from the fame, she hasn't changed too much since I saw her last. Her hair is longer, neater. She's dressed in a red jumpsuit, her face makeup free.

Her expression says she doesn't know how this is going to go.

"Hi, Maggie," she says gently.

I continue to stare at her. "What are you doing here?"

"Abby called me. She said you and Clayton got into a fight. She wanted me to come pick her up. Like usual."

"I'm sorry," I tell her. "I didn't mean to fight in front of her."

She waves me off. "I'm not here about that. I just...I know we aren't friends, but I also know you might not have anyone right now. Clayton went to his parents'. When I got to the house, Abby was there alone. I wanted to make sure you were okay."

Her kindness shocks me. "Honestly, I don't know."

She takes a hesitant step forward. "Look, I know we didn't get off on the right foot back then, but as someone who has seen Clayton for who he is, I wanted to say...I get it. He can be charming, and I know you know him better than I do, but you also only know him in one way. I've seen the other side. The side that thinks the world revolves around him. That doesn't consider anyone else in any of his decisions. The hot-and-cold side that flips like a switch. The side that will do whatever it takes to get what he wants. Right now, he wants you, Maggie. And, if you don't want him back, you need to be careful."

Chills line my skin at her ominous words. "What are you talking about?"

"Abby said you were arguing about some app on his phone. I'm assuming he's stalking you."

"Stalking? Oh. No, not exactly."

She purses her lips like she doesn't believe me. "I've seen Clayton at his worst. All those years ago, when I broke it off, he lost it."

Her words remind me of his wounds back then. The scratches on his neck. The busted lip. I can't help thinking of how she treated him. "I'd say you both did."

She looks at me strangely. "What do you mean?"

"It doesn't matter. It's in the past. We're all grown-ups. We need to move on."

She bows her head. "I'm sorry if I overstepped. I just... If something happened to you, and I didn't speak up, I'd never forgive myself."

"Something like what? You don't think he'd actually hurt me."

"I know he would," she says, no room for negotiation in her tone. "Clayton doesn't like being told no. He doesn't like not having his way. You saw a piece of that tonight, I'm guessing. And you've probably seen other pieces..."

I think about what he admitted to me. He'd tried to scare me into selling my home. He's been torturing me lately and seemed to have very little remorse for it.

She sees something in my expression that encourages her. "I don't want Clayton, for the record. I'm happy. I just want you to be safe."

"Whatever happened between you guys back then, I know you hurt him, too."

Her eyes widen. "Excuse me?"

343

"The claw marks on his neck? The bloody lip? He told me you hurt him. I know we were all just kids, but you can't judge him for whatever he did. You're no better."

She gives a firm shake of her head. "I never hurt him, Maggie. He did that to himself when we fought."

I eye her, but there's something in her voice that makes me want to believe what she's saying.

"He hurt himself, probably to get your sympathy. I assumed you knew. He's... There's no other way to say this. He's a master manipulator. He wants to control everyone in his life, and he'll stop at nothing to do that."

I start to argue, to defend him, but I can't. She's right. Tucker saw it, too. *Why have I been the only one blind to that part of his personality?* The manipulator. It's exactly what he was doing with the house. He didn't want me there, and he was doing everything he could to prevent me from staying.

A new, painful thought hits me...

The last person who was in the house tonight was Clayton, when he'd claimed he needed to use the bathroom. Just seconds after he'd seen me kiss Tucker on the cheek.

"What is it?" she asks softly, like she's afraid to know.

"You don't think he would've started the fire tonight, do you?" I hate the question as soon as it leaves my lips. I don't know why I trust her, but I do.

Her expression goes dreadfully serious. "Maggie, I think there isn't anything he wouldn't do if it meant getting you."

There's a knock on the door, and the doctor pops her head in again. "Maggie, when you're finished here, the police want to speak with you."

"I should go," Raven says. "But if you need anything, even just to talk, I'm always around." She hands me a card with a phone number written on it, patting my hand gently before she disappears through the door.

After a few moments, through the tiny glass window, I see the police headed my way.

CHAPTER FORTY-TWO

My entire world has already been turned upside down, and I feel like this is just the beginning. The investigating officers stand at the end of my bed, their expressions stoic.

"I'm Officer Miller. This is Officer Carter," the first officer tells me. She's blonde with a sleek ponytail and freckles. "How are you feeling?"

"I'm okay," I say softly.

"Can you tell us what happened tonight?"

"Yeah, um...I was out with a friend when I got a notification that someone was in my living room. When I checked the cameras, I saw my neighbor had broken into my house. That was when I realized there was a fire, and he was trying to save me."

"I see." She pulls out a notepad, jotting down notes. "Do you know about what time that was?"

"Around eight, I think. I'm not totally sure."

"And did you try to call him? The neighbor?"

"I tried to call him over and over, but he wasn't answering, so I drove there as fast as I could. I called for the fire department, but I wasn't sure how quickly they could make it to us. I beat them there."

"So then what happened?"

"I tried to find Tucker."

"Tucker Ford?"

I nod. "Yeah. My neighbor."

"And did you have any communication with Mr. Ford tonight?"

"He was at my house earlier today. I hadn't talked to him since he left my house around six."

"So, you didn't text him?"

I shake my head, but there's something in her voice that makes me pause. "Why?"

The officers exchange a glance. "Miss Ellis, Mr. Ford told us you texted him and asked that he come over. That's why he was at your house tonight."

"But...I didn't." Why would he lie? I look to the side table, reaching for my phone. I open my texts, holding it out to show them. "See, there's no message."

"It could've been deleted," she points out.

"Why would I do that?"

"I certainly would if I'd invited someone into my home while it was on fire."

My brows knit together. "I wasn't even home. I have no reason to want to hurt Tucker."

"Has anyone else had access to your phone tonight?" the second officer suggests.

I start to say no, but I cut myself off because that would be a lie. I think about my phone waiting on the table all night at Clayton's house. How many times did I walk away from it to go to the bathroom or get a refill?

Now there's no doubt in my mind Clayton was the one who started the fire. And he tried to kill Tucker.

"How did the fire start?" I ask.

"We're still investigating," she says. "But, to be perfectly frank, our theory right now is arson. It looks like someone started the fire in the attic."

"My friend, Clayton," I whisper, feeling the betrayal deep in my bones. "He had access to my phone and to the attic just before we left."

They take his full name and contact information, seeming intrigued, and leave a business card with me in case I think of anything else.

"Did you say you talked to Tucker?" I ask before they can leave.

"We did."

"So he's awake?"

"Very recently, yes."

I nod, clasping my hands together in my lap as they disappear from the room. Seconds later, I press the button to call the nurse.

I don't even allow her to get fully into the room before I ask, "Can I see him?"

As the nurse wheels me into his room, I do my best not to break down. His arms are bandaged from burns, the skin around his hairline and ears still dark with soot. When he sees me, his eyes widen with relief, and tears instantly fill them.

His voice cracks as he says, "You're okay."

Once she leaves the room, I lock my wheels, standing from the wheelchair carefully. My legs ache and tremble as if I've just run a marathon. I approach his bed slowly, tears choking my words. "You tried to save me."

"Tried and failed," he mutters, puffing out a breath.

"You almost died, Tucker." I don't have time for his sarcasm.

His face wrinkles as he looks at me, his eyes dancing between mine. "Of course I tried to save you, Maggie. I just got you back. No way in hell was I going to lose you again."

It's as if I can feel my heart cracking. *I came so close to almost losing him.* How silly does all the rest of it seem now? Why did I waste so much time? "I'm so sorry."

"What are you sorry for?" He holds out a hand for mine, taking my fingers in his.

Where do I even begin? "Clayton did this. He started the fire. He was the one messing with my thermostat. He's the one who texted you and told you to come over. He tried to kill you. It's all my fault. You almost died because of me." I try to hold it together, failing miserably.

"It's not your fault." If he's shocked, he doesn't show it. "You don't control him. The doctor said you saved me, which means I *didn't* die because of you."

"It is my fault, though. I'm the reason he was around you, the reason he targeted you. All because you were helping me, all because he was jealous, and now...look what happened." My voice cracks, and he pulls me closer to him.

"Hey, look at me." His thumb strokes the back of my hand. "I'm going to be fine. Do you hear me? It's going to take more than a fire to take me out. I'm here, Maggie. We're here. We're fine. We always will be." Slowly, he lifts my hand, kissing my knuckles despite the obvious pain it causes him. Tears blur my vision, and I brush them away, choking back a sob. "I meant what I said. I'm not going to lose you again, even if it takes thirteen more years to convince you you're mine."

"But you were right all along. You warned me. You saw the truth, and I wouldn't listen. You said he'd do anything to get me here, and you were right. Except, once he realized you lived next door, he was trying to get me out of the house by scaring me. He wanted me to think it was haunted so I would leave. Sell and move in with him. He kept offering... Why didn't I see it?" I stare at nothing at all, furious with myself.

"All that matters is that you see it now. And that you're safe."

I rest a hand on his chest, and he tries to hide his wince. I wish so badly I could trade places with him. "I need to ask you something."

"Anything."

"When the detectives told me you said I'd texted you and asked you to come over, it reminded me of something. When we talked the other night, you mentioned that I'd texted you once and told you I was choosing Clayton."

"Right." He squints his eyes, thinking. "During that week, we didn't talk. You sent me a text that said you wanted to end things. That you were choosing Clayton, and I should leave you alone."

"When you told me, I thought it might've been my room-mate, Kassara, who sent the text. She was with me during all of it, and while I didn't understand why she would do it, she was the only one who could've, as far as I knew."

He watches me carefully.

"Do you remember when you got that text?"

He doesn't have to think. "Yeah. It was the same day you texted me to stay away from Raven. You texted about the breakup first, then a few minutes later, the text came in warning me to stay away from her. I tried to call you. I texted. But...I never heard back. I'll never forgive myself for giving up on you. I'll never forgive myself for hurting you."

"It's not your fault," I tell him, rubbing his hand. My voice is as weak as my knees feel, because he's just confirmed what I feared most. "None of this is your fault."

And it wasn't Kassara's either.

CHAPTER FORTY-THREE

"We need to talk."

I step down into the finished basement of Clayton's parents' house, where he's resting on the sectional, a video game controller in hand. At the sound of my voice, he sits up, pausing the game.

He grabs the bag of chips next to him and places it on the table. "I didn't know you were here."

"Your mom let me in." I keep my distance, standing at the far side of the room with my arms crossed.

"I'm so glad you're okay," he says in a breath.

"You started the fire, didn't you?" I don't give him a chance for niceties. Tucker is still in the hospital, and my house is a smoldering pile of ash, along with all my things and everything I just took out of my mom's storage unit. And it's all Clayton's fault.

He looks down. "The police were already here asking about that."

"And you told them what, exactly?"

"Why would I want to hurt you, Maggie?"

My smile is bitter and taunting. "Oh, that's what's so brilliant. You didn't want to hurt me." I bounce a fist in my palm. "You made sure I was going to be out of the house. I was with you, not supposed to be home for hours. And then you texted Tucker to get him out of the way permanently."

He runs his hands over his legs. "That's ridiculous."

"I agree. It's also true, isn't it?"

He scratches his eyebrow. "Maggie—"

"Please don't lie to me, Clayton. I'm done with the lies and the manipulation. Just like when you lied to me about Raven hurting you all those years ago. It wasn't actually her who scratched you, was it? You did it to yourself."

His cheeks flame. "I don't know why I told you that. I was just embarrassed, okay? I was such a mess back then. The pressure of everything...it just piled up."

"And what's your excuse now?"

"Look, I get it. I'm a fuck-up. I'm a terrible person. A worthless excuse for a human being. You shouldn't want anything to do with me. I wouldn't blame you if—"

"Don't do that!" I shout, putting an end to his pity party. "Don't make this about you."

"I'm not trying to."

"You are. Because that's what you always do. You twist and turn everything, manipulate me so all I can focus on is you. So all that matters is you. Not my feelings or my problems. You never cared about any of that." I stare at him as if I'm seeing him for the first time. That's how it feels. "I never mattered to you, did I? Not really. You kept me around because I was good for your ego. Because you could use me and hurt me, and I just kept coming back. It's what I've done my whole life—a pattern I'm breaking right now. We're going to focus on me, and you're going to answer every question I have."

"Why would I do that?"

"Because, if you don't, I'm going to go to the press with every one of my theories. And Raven will back me up. Even if I don't have proof, it's enough to get your album canceled. How would that look?"

He stares at me, his expression hardening. "What do you want to know?"

"I know you were controlling the thermostat in my house, but that doesn't explain the other things. The doors opening, the lights flickering, and the candle I don't remember lighting. All of it was you, wasn't it?"

His jaw goes tight. "I've already told you I wanted you to leave. To sell."

"So, you broke into my house and tried to make me think it was haunted?"

"The lights are controlled through the same app as the thermostat. I made them flicker a few times, yeah. But I didn't break into your house." He pauses, looking down. "Garrett had a key he asked me to bring you. I was going to give it to you eventually."

The breath is swept from my lungs. "Like that's any better."

"I didn't hurt anything. I lit a candle, so what?" He scowls.

"And left my door standing open. God knows what could've happened."

He scoffs. "*Please.* This is Myers we're talking about. We both know you were totally safe."

I cover my face with my hands, inhaling deeply. "What about the other time the door was left open? And all the lights were turned on? That was you, too?"

"I came over that day. I was coming to visit you, but you were up in the attic with *him*." The word is venom on his tongue. "So, I did all of that and left. I know how insane it sounds, okay? But you have to know I was doing it for you. I just wanted you to be somewhere better. You didn't belong in that shit hole of a house, Maggie. You belong somewhere better. Safer."

"Like with you?" I demand with a scoff.

He doesn't nod, but he doesn't have to.

I'm struck by how odd it is. Like hemlock, the plant, sometimes things aren't what they appear. Sometimes, something that looks so safe, so beautiful even, can be what puts you in the most danger.

"And when you realized your plan was backfiring and I was actually spending more time with Tucker because I was so scared, that's when you decided to kill him?"

"No," he insists. "No. I never planned that. Last night, when I was at your house and you kissed him, something in me snapped. I wasn't in my right mind. It just happened."

I swallow, doing everything in my power to keep my face emotionless. This is just further proof I caused this. I kissed Tucker. I left with Clayton. A single different choice could've changed everything.

"And what about the rotten smell that night we ate Nonna's? What was that?"

"I really had nothing to do with that. It must've been a mouse or something." He looks pleased to finally have a good answer.

"And the open window in the bedroom? Was that you?"

His expression falls again. "I snuck out of it the night I put the candle on the table. You woke up while I was in the house, and I couldn't leave through the front door."

"Why the candle?"

He swallows, rubbing a hand over his forehead. "I thought it would start a fire."

It's as if the floor has shifted under me. "I was still inside that night."

"You had smoke alarms," he insists, eyes wide. "I checked first."

I shake my head. How did I miss this side of him? How is it possible everyone else could see it, yet I was totally oblivious to it all?

"I never meant to hurt you, Maggie. I just wanted to be with you. I'm so in love with you, it makes me do crazy things."

I press my lips together, drawing in a long inhale. "What else don't I know, Clayton?"

"Nothing, I swear. That's it."

I stare at him, wondering when the last time he told me the truth was. How long have I been believing the lies? Why has it taken me so long to see him for who he really is? "Back in college, on a day you visited me and had access to my phone, someone texted Tucker and told him I was breaking up with him. That I was choosing you and he should never contact me again. We both know that text didn't come from me." I stop, letting him fill in the blanks.

He winces. "I *may* have had something to do with that."

"You texted him?"

He rubs the back of his neck. "It was wishful thinking, Maggs. Come on. I had to get rid of the competition."

"That was not your decision to make." I can't believe how cavalier he's being about all of this. As if it was a simple prank, not a completely selfish, life-shattering act.

"Did you block his number, too? He said he called and texted me after that, but I never got anything."

His expression says it all without a word.

I release a ragged breath, feeling nauseous. "*That's* why I never heard from him. Why I never saw his calls." Not because he didn't care. He always cared. "You had no right to do that." The only reason I've been able to reach him now has to be because I switched cell phone carriers a few years ago.

In front of me, Clayton isn't bothering to defend his actions.

At this point, I can't even be shocked anymore. "Why, Clayton? Why did you think that was okay? Were you okay winning me that way? Through manipulation and lies?"

"It wasn't like that. It wasn't a plan. You were getting us drinks, and I saw a text come in from him saying he missed you. It was just an impulse, and you were back before I had a chance to think it through. I couldn't undo it at that point, even if I wanted to."

"You're a monster, Clayton. You realize that, right? None of this is normal."

He's up on his feet then. "You deserve someone who goes to these lengths for you. Someone who knows what you're worth. Don't you get that?"

"I don't *want* someone who would do this. It isn't special. It's terrifying. It's terrible."

He steps toward me. "You don't see it now, but if he loved you, he'd do the same thing. He doesn't, Maggs. Not like me. No one will ever love you like I do."

"Clayton..." I step back, shaking my head. "You need to get help. You need to talk to someone."

"I only need you," he argues, raising his voice.

"Yeah? Well, too bad, because you've lost me. For good this time. I'm done." I put my hands up, walking away. He launches forward, grabbing my shoulders.

"You're hurting me!" I shout.

"You have no idea what I've done for you, Maggie. No idea. You can't just walk away from me. I won't lose you again."

His words repeat in my head. The honesty in them.

You have no idea what I've done for you, Maggie.

When I speak, my voice is powerless. His grip on my shoulders is painful. "What did you do?"

He blinks as if coming out of a trance and releases me. He staggers backward.

"Clayton. What did you do?"

He shakes his head. "Nothing. It was just an exaggeration."

A heavy tension fills the room, the weight of his lies. Then, all at once, it hits me. "How did you know Tucker slept with Professor Eden?"

He blanches, his eyes darting away. "I didn't."

"You slipped up before, back at your house, when you mentioned it. You would have no way of knowing about that unless..." I shake my head, not wanting to believe it. "Unless you really were doing everything you could to get me all those years ago."

He looks as if he's going to argue, has his defenses ready, but then his shoulders drop. "It's not like it was hard."

I blink. "What are you talking about?"

"Eve slept with half the students on campus. Nearly all my friends. She just needed to sleep with Tucker. I knew if she did, if she could just send me a photo or a video as proof to give you, it would be over. I would've won. It didn't take much convincing on my part, trust me."

"You asked her to do it? To sleep with him?" I can't breathe. It feels like a car is crushing my chest.

"*Asked* is one way to put it." His grin makes me sick.

"What did you do?" I spit out.

"I told her if she didn't do it, I'd show the board a particularly inappropriate photo she'd sent to my friend. She'd gotten away with a lot, but with my connections in the media, I didn't think she wanted to chance making me angry. I get what I want, and she knew that."

I hardly recognize this man. The person standing in front of me, recounting such horrors, is a stranger.

"Well, congratulations, you did. You got what you wanted, I guess. Your plan worked." A tear cascades down my cheek. "I can't believe you would do this to me."

"*For* you," he corrects. "Everything I've ever done has been for you."

"Well, do me a favor"—I throw my hands in the air—"and don't ever do anything *for* me again. Just...stay away from me."

"You don't mean that." His mouth twists into a smile as if this is a game.

"I really, really do. Do you understand what you cost me, Clayton? The fire you started destroyed everything I had left of my parents. Everything I had left, period. All our memories that I literally moved out of storage yesterday. My past is gone, thanks to you. My paintings. Any photos I had of my childhood, of my parents' wedding. Of *us*. Surely you care about that, at least. You stole everything from me, and I hate you. Do you hear me? I never want to see you again."

I step back, heading for the door again, and something crashes across the room. Explodes.

When I turn back, I realize he's punched a hole through the sliding glass door behind him. Shards of glass are scattered across the floor, a field of white, as pristine as snow until red droplets begin to coat it.

Drip.

Drip.

Drip.

His entire fist is bloody, red liquid oozing and trickling down his forearm and onto the ground. He holds it up in front of his face, studying it as if it's a science experiment and not his own appendage. He doesn't even seem like he feels the pain.

I resist the urge to run to him, to care for him like I always have. I'm not that person anymore. He is not the boy I loved. Whoever he has become, I have to walk away from him. This man is a monster.

His mouth warps into a wicked smile. "Don't you get it, Maggs? You aren't like them. You aren't trash. Tucker, Eve... they deserve each other. No, *we* deserve each other. They deserved to die."

A wave of nausea passes over me as I finally understand what he's saying. The final piece of the puzzle clicks into place. "You were going to kill Tucker..." I nod, trying to catch my breath. "Just like you killed Eve."

His eyes darken. "It was an accident. We fought because she hadn't done what I told her to do. I shoved her." He wiggles his bloody fingers, all but the pointer, which he seems incapable of moving anymore. "It was over quickly."

It's as if he doesn't feel or comprehend the words he's saying. As if he's gone numb to it all.

I take another step back, but this time, I don't stop. Not when he calls my name, not when his parents try to head me off in the kitchen to make sure everything's all right.

I don't stop until I'm in my car, and even then, it's only a brief pause to process everything I've learned.

It was only as I told Clayton how everything burned up that I realized it myself. My adoption papers. The letter from Loretta. Crafts I made as a child with my mother. Every single photo from my life and my parents' lives—there were never any photos from my infancy or earliest years, which my parents always blamed on a flood in our basement. Now, I guess I know the truth. Still, every photo from the years after is gone. School pictures, family portraits... All ash. Every Christmas, birthday, summer vacation. If I'd gone to the storage unit a day later, if Nick had brought me the key next week instead, they'd all still exist. Clayton took that from me. The man I trusted more than anyone else. The man I thought cared about me more than anyone else.

He caused the fire, and Tucker ran into it and risked his life to save me. He killed a woman, and Tucker has carried the burden of that guilt—thinking I believed he was to blame—all these years. He got away with it. Got away with everything. Lying about Raven, killing Eve, lying to Tucker, destroying my life. None of it affected him because he believes he's above reproach. Untouchable. I've seen firsthand how his parents instill that belief in him. How many times has his mother told me what an amazing father he is to Abby, when I've known he rarely sees her? How have I been so fooled by him for so long?

Clayton hurts me, and Tucker protects me. Over and over and over.

If it wasn't for Clayton, if he hadn't blackmailed Eve back then and texted Tucker to break up with him without my knowledge or consent, none of this would've happened.

I would've been with Tucker; I know that somewhere deep inside of me. We would've ended up together. I would've gotten my happily ever after instead of having my heart shattered. I would've moved back to Myers and spent my parents' last years with them instead of living hours away, only returning home on rare occasions. I would've gotten closer to them. Been here to help. Maybe they would've told me the truth eventually.

I wanted to see the best in him, and he used that against me.

Because of Clayton, I've lost so much. It's the single thought running through my mind as I put the car in drive and head to the police station, where I plan to tell them everything.

CHAPTER FORTY-FOUR

ONE YEAR LATER

Tucker shields my eyes with both hands, guiding me forward. "Just a bit farther."

"If I trip on something, I'm go—"

"You're not going to trip," he says, his voice close to my ears. He pulls his hands away slowly. "Okay, open."

My eyes were already open, though, seconds before he gave me permission, taking in the view he's surprising me with. I scan the room in utter shock, then turn to face him. "What is this?"

He runs a foot over the drop cloth we're standing on. "I thought you could paint our living room. I'm just not feeling the white. The woman who's going to be opening up her own gallery soon needs a magical living room."

I grin, turning to look at the wall again, a perfectly blank canvas. "You mean it?"

"Yeah, duh." He swats my butt. "Paint it however you want."

"You're serious? However I want?"

"Of course I'm serious, Maggie. This is a big deal. This is

our house. Ours. I never thought I'd be able to say that." He kisses me, and I soak up the truth of his statement. This future, this happily ever after, almost didn't exist. I never want to take it for granted again. "So, let's make it your own. Paint the walls however you want. Hell, paint the ceilings and the floors if that will make you happy. If this place isn't as magical and whimsical as you are, I'm going to be disappointed. And you'd better get started, so you can finish before the movers get here with all of our stuff Wednesday." He points to the cans of paint scattered across the floor. "I didn't know what you'd want, so I got every color they had. The saleswoman loved me."

I laugh. "This is perfect."

"I want you to feel at home here," he tells me, his eyes locking with mine.

It's strange being here, in a new city. Wilmington is somewhere fresh for the both of us, somewhere without tainted memories. Somewhere where we won't be the people who helped the police convict our town's golden boy of arson. Somewhere where history won't haunt us. I suppose it should feel scary, but it's the strangest thing. I'm not scared of anything anymore. Not when I have him. Not after all we've been through.

"I'm home wherever you are," I say, kissing his lips. "Thank you for this. Seriously. It's exactly what I needed." I bend down and grab a paintbrush, sorting through the colors until I find the one that I want.

"Downpour Blue," he reads the name. "Good choice."

I point at his eyes. "Someone once told me I have a type."

A grin tugs at one corner of his mouth. I stir up the can of paint before picking up the brush again and setting to work covering a patch of the wall with the deep-blue paint.

"I think I'll do this color everywhere, and then maybe use some of the lighter colors to paint trees as an accent wall."

"Sounds perfect."

"Are you sure? I want you to like it." I glance over my shoulder.

"Whatever you do, I guarantee I'll love it," he says, slipping his hands around my waist.

"Are you sure you're happy here?"

He nuzzles into my neck, and I run my hands over his arms, feeling the bumps and raised edges of his skin—scars left over from the fire. Proof of how hard we fought to get here. Evidence of all we've been through together. "I told you, I'm the happiest I've ever been. You don't have to keep asking. The answer won't change."

"I know, but you always planned to grow old in your grandparents' house. I just worry that—"

"And now I plan to grow old with you." He kisses my cheek. "A house is a house. You're my home."

At his sweet words, I spin around in his arms until we're face to face. "You, my friend, are one extraordinarily *amazing* individual."

"Try again," he says simply, a glimmer in his eyes.

"Hmm?"

"Say it again, but this time..." He sucks in a breath, his shoulders rising and falling. "This time, repeat after me."

I giggle, drawing out the word. "Okay..."

"You."

"You," I repeat.

"My husband."

"My hu..." I stop, chills lining my skin. "What?"

"It has a nice ring to it, doesn't it?"

Tears blur my vision. "Are you serious?"

He pulls me in tighter, taking the paintbrush from my hand and placing it down. "Maggie, I have lived in three cities in my entire life, and I have loved you in every single one of them. You are the most real thing in my life. You are the first person I think of when I wake up and my last thought before I fall asleep. You're the person I want to build a life with. A home with. Because you are my home." He grins. "I know I already said that, but it's true. I don't care where we end up, what dreams we chase, what our future looks like. As long as you're with me, it will be a dream come true." He stares at me, waiting, his blue eyes piercing me in a way only he can.

"I think there's supposed to be a question after that," I tease.

He reaches into his pocket, producing a velvet ring box. Reluctantly, he releases me, opening it to reveal the most perfect ring I've ever seen in my life. "Will you dance with me, Maggie? At our wedding? Where you become my wife."

I'm so caught off guard by the question I laugh out loud. "Is this you finally asking me to dance after all these years?"

"Is this you saying yes after all these years?" he whispers, already sliding the ring on my finger. He doesn't need me to answer. There was never any doubt.

"I will dance with you for the rest of our lives, Tucker Ford." With the ring firmly on my finger, I place my hand on his shoulder, snuggling my head onto his chest, and then, just like when it all started, we begin to dance.

Perfectly content, I glance over at the mantel, where a single photo sits in an old, golden frame. It's one of the only things we brought with us instead of packing it for the movers —that and the barn painting, the only piece of my art left from before the fire.

This photo is much too special. Something I can never

afford to lose. It feels like a lifetime ago when I found the picture in the frame on the dresser at Tucker's house and demanded answers.

Now, I finally have them. A tear cascades down my cheek as I stare at the photo of Tucker, his grandfather, and a child I don't remember. The kids grin at each other in the photo, pure happiness radiating off of them. Tucker kisses my cheek, reading my mind as he always does.

Recently, when we took the photo out of the frame to clean the glass, we discovered handwriting on the back that doesn't belong to either of Tucker's grandparents. We've decided it could only be Jolene who wrote the words.

On it, in neat penmanship, she'd inscribed:

Cliff, Tucker, and Angie
1990

WOULD YOU RECOMMEND HEMLOCK?

If you enjoyed this story, please consider leaving me a quick review. It doesn't have to be long—just a few words will do. Who knows? Your review might be the thing that encourages a future reader to take a chance on my work!
To leave a review, please visit:
https://www.kierstenmodglinauthor.com/hemlock

Let everyone know how much you loved
Hemlock on Goodreads:
https://bit.ly/KMhemlock

STAY UP TO DATE ON EVERYTHING KMOD!

Thank you so much for reading this story. I'd love to invite you to sign up for my mailing list and text alerts so we can be sure you don't miss my next release.

Sign up for my mailing list here:
kierstenmodglinauthor.com/nlsignup

Sign up for my text alerts here:
kierstenmodglinauthor.com/textalerts

ACKNOWLEDGMENTS

As always, I need to start by thanking my amazing husband and sweet little girl—thank you being in my corner through every step of this journey. Thank you for being my cheerleaders, my sounding boards, and my safe space. I'm so lucky to get to spend this beautiful life with you both and make it ours. I love you so very much.

To my wonderful editor, Sarah West—thank you for seeing the story through the chaos and helping me bring it to life.

To the awesome proofreading team at My Brother's Editor —thank you for being my final set of eyes.

To my loyal readers (AKA the #KMod Squad)—thank you for everything you've done for me. Thank you for cheering on every story, for loving my characters and worlds as much as I do, for every email, social media shoutout, review, recommendation to friends and family, and purchase. You guys are my dream come true.

To my book club/gang/besties—Sara, both Erins, June, Heather, and Dee—thank you for coming into my life and bringing all the laughs and love. I don't know how I survived before you and I hope there's never an after. Love you all.

To my bestie, Emerald O'Brien—thank you for being my loudest supporter in every room, the one who celebrates and vents with me with equal enthusiasm, and the person I'm most excited to tell my latest story ideas to. Thank you for making my world brighter, better, and more whole. Same moon, my friend.

To Becca and Lexy—thank you for keeping me above water, for supporting me through it all, and for always being there when I need a friend.

Last but certainly not least, to you, dear reader—thank you for purchasing this book and supporting my art. When I sit down to write each story, you are the first person on my mind. I want to entertain you, make you laugh, make you cry, make you angry. I want to know which parts will have you breathless and which will make your jaw drop. In every sentence, every scene, every chapter, you are all I see. Years ago, a little girl wished for all of this—I wished for you. Thank you for making those wishes come true. Whether this is your first Kiersten Modglin book or your 40th, I hope it was everything you hoped for and nothing like you expected.

ABOUT THE AUTHOR

KIERSTEN MODGLIN is an Amazon Top 10 bestselling author of psychological thrillers. Her books have sold over a million copies and been translated into multiple languages. Kiersten is a member of International Thriller Writers, Novelists, Inc., and the Alliance of Independent Authors. She is a KDP Select All-Star and a recipient of *ThrillerFix*'s Best Psychological Thriller Award, *Suspense Magazine*'s Best Book of 2021 Award, a 2022 Silver Falchion for Best Suspense, and a 2022 Silver Falchion for Best Overall Book of 2021. Kiersten grew up in rural western Kentucky and later relocated to Nashville, Tennessee, where she now lives with her family. Kiersten's readers across the world lovingly refer to her as "KMod." A binge-watching expert, psychology fanatic, and *indoor* enthusiast, Kiersten enjoys rainy days spent with her favorite people and evenings with her nose in a book.

Sign up for Kiersten's newsletter here:
kierstenmodglinauthor.com/nlsignup

Sign up for text alerts from Kiersten here:
kierstenmodglinauthor.com/textalerts

kierstenmodglinauthor.com
www.facebook.com/kierstenmodglinauthor
www.facebook.com/groups/kmodsquad
www.twitter.com/kmodglinauthor
www.instagram.com/kierstenmodglinauthor
www.tiktok.com/@kierstenmodglinauthor
www.goodreads.com/kierstenmodglinauthor
www.bookbub.com/authors/kiersten-modglin

ALSO BY KIERSTEN MODGLIN

The Reunion

Tell Me the Truth

The Dinner Guests

If You're Reading This...

A Quiet Retreat

The Family Secret

Don't Go Down There

Wait for Dark

You Can Trust Me

Hemlock

ARRANGEMENT TRILOGY

The Arrangement (Book 1)

The Amendment (Book 2)

The Atonement (Book 3)

THE MESSES SERIES

The Cleaner (Book 1)

The Healer (Book 2)

The Liar (Book 3)

The Prisoner (Book 4)

NOVELLAS

The Long Route: A Lover's Landing Novella

The Stranger in the Woods: A Crimson Falls Novella

Printed in Great Britain
by Amazon